Outstanding praise for the novels of V. S. Alexander

The Sculptress

"The novel is thoroughly researched, drawing readers fully into the saga with descriptive, often graphic details and strong characterizations. For fans of World War I historical fiction."
—*Library Journal*

The Irishman's Daughter

"Skillfully blends family ties with the horrors of a starving country and the hopefulness of young love."—*Booklist*

The Taster

"An absorbing, well-researched story that brings to life an extraordinary period in history, told from within the inner circle of one of the twentieth-century's most notorious characters."
—Gill Paul, *USA Today* bestselling author of *The Secret Wife*

"Alexander's intimate writing style gives readers openings to wonder about what tough decisions they would have made in Magda's situation. The 'taster's' story adds to a body of nuanced World War II fiction such as Elizabeth Wein's *Code Name Verity*, Anthony Doerr's *All the Light We Cannot See,* and Tatiana de Rosnay's *Sarah's Key*. Book clubs and historical fiction fans will love discussing this and will eagerly await more from Alexander."
—*Library Journal*

The Magdalen Girls

"A haunting novel that takes the reader into the cruel world of Ireland's Magdalene laundries, *The Magdalen Girls* shines a light on yet another notorious institution that somehow survived into the late twentieth century. A real page-turner!"
—Ellen Marie Wiseman, author of *The Orphan Collector*

"Alexander has clearly done his homework. Chilling in its realism, his work depicts the improprieties long condoned by the Catholic Church and only recently acknowledged. Fans of the book and film *Philomena* will want to read this."
—*Library Journal*

Books by V. S. Alexander

THE MAGDALEN GIRLS

THE TASTER

THE IRISHMAN'S DAUGHTER

THE TRAITOR

THE SCULPTRESS

THE WAR GIRLS

Published by Kensington Publishing Corp.

The
WAR
GIRLS

V.S. ALEXANDER

KENSINGTON
PUBLISHING CORP.

www.kensingtonbooks.com

KENSINGTON BOOKS are published by

Kensington Publishing Corp.
119 West 40th Street
New York, NY 10018

ISBN: 978-1-4967-3480-8 (ebook)

ISBN: 978-1-4967-3479-2

First Kensington Trade Paperback Printing: August 2022

10 9 8 7 6 5 4 3 2 1

Printed in the United States of America

To Emanuel Ringelblum—who fought with words

PROLOGUE TO WAR

In their blackest dreams, none of them could have foreseen what the future held. August 1939 was like other summers, with heat that rose from the streets, late summer roses, and smoky pink and red sunsets that faded into night—except for conversations filled with dread and the rumors of war.

Stefa and Janka had passed on Krochmalna Street in Warsaw countless times, but had never spoken. Stefa was a Jew and Janka a Catholic—the two did not mix readily. They knew each other by sight, as neighbors, with little in common. They were aware but oblivious, as distant as residents of the city and farmers in the Polish countryside.

Stefa had been told little about what was happening in Nazi Germany because her father didn't want to upset her or the rest of the family, especially her mother. Most news about the war came from her impetuous younger brother.

Janka's husband was nearly as silent, although she could tell that some part of him would welcome an impending war. "The Nazis will do what they have to do," he cautioned, telling her to be ready for a "great invasion." They would be ready, he said, to take advantage of the war—the winner taking the spoils.

Stefa's older sister, Hanna, had left Warsaw in January to live in London. Unable to bear the constraints of her traditional family, she had deserted them to live with her mother's sister and her husband. England was on edge, but Hanna tried to shun the forces that were moving in destructive patterns far beyond her control. She was happy to be free and living a life outside Warsaw.

None of them could have known what was about to happen. Only Hitler knew.

None of them could have known they would become "the War Girls."

Upper Silesia, after 8 p.m. August 31st, 1939

"Shoot him."

The SS officer nodded and looked at "the Pole," Franciszek Honiok, who lay sprawled near the entrance to the radio station at Gleiwitz. Tall transmitting towers thrust into the sky on either side of the modest stone building like pillars embellishing the entrance to a temple.

One shot to the back of the head and "Franz," as they had come to call him, would be dispatched to the netherworld of God's choosing. In his drugged state, "the Pole" wouldn't know the difference. In the hours after Franz's arrest the day before, the SS men had grown to like him, banter with him, kid him about his Polish sympathies despite being a German national. What a pity that Franz would end up on the wrong side in the war. With one quick action of the trigger, it would all be over, and the world would learn how the "Polish Nationalists" had attacked a German radio station and beaten the employees in order to spread their message of anti-German hate. This event would lead to the justifiable death of Franz at the hands of the German protectors.

Before he fired his pistol, the officer had time to reflect upon the tactical blunders committed under Operation Himmler, the National Socialist excuse to annihilate Poland. "If there's the slightest provocation, I shall shatter Poland without warning into so many pieces that there will be nothing left to pick up," the Führer had said earlier in the month.

But the operation had not gone smoothly. The station was

only a transmitter relay post, not a radio station. The SS agitators couldn't find a microphone, and only an emergency channel was available for transmission of their short anti-German message. How many people would be listening? Not the hundreds of thousands the Führer had expected. Gleiwitz, a sleepy German town on a flat plain dotted with trees in the first blush of fall, would record perhaps the first death of the upcoming war.

"Shoot him!" The command echoed in the SS man's head.

Franz, still sedated, moaned, shifted his leg, and lifted his groggy head. His eyes fluttered and then closed again.

The Nazi "protector" pulled the trigger. Franz's body jerked as the bullet entered his brain, blood pooling around the wound then flowing down his face.

The local police took photos of the body, but Berlin wasn't satisfied. One death wasn't good enough for propaganda purposes. Even a second body and more photographs failed to convince the Gestapo that enough had been done to persuade the German public that Poland must fall to the Nazi war machine.

Wieluń, Poland, 5:40 a.m. September 1st, 1939

Annoyed by the buzzing overhead, Tomasz pulled the wool blanket over him, turned, and snuggled into the warm cocoon of his bed. The room was dark, the solitary light bulb hanging from the ceiling switched off for the night. Sometime after midnight, he'd wet his fingers with spit and extinguished the wick of the small candle that he often lit to keep him company while he drifted off to sleep. The talk of war exchanged by his parents at supper had jangled his nerves and kept him awake. They whispered of a German battleship near Danzig; Nazi troops and tanks amassed at the Polish border.

Now, deep into the night, his parents slept in the room next to his on the second floor.

When he was lonely—for at eleven years of age he had no brothers or sisters—he would stare at the picture of the Virgin that his mother had hung on the wall across from his bed, as a reminder to be a good boy full of devotion, piety, and dutiful works. Sin was for the wicked. Evil men and women would spend eternity in Hell; however, God would look after and protect the devout. His mother had repeated this so often he could parrot her words as if they were inscribed in one of his schoolbooks.

The Virgin's eyes always seemed to follow him no matter where he was in his room, especially if he was thinking of girls and their curious figures, so different from his.

He often wondered if Mary's wounded heart, pierced by a sword and wrapped in white roses, pained her. Mostly, she looked serene swathed in her blue robes, the golden halo behind her head lighting her angelic face.

The buzzing grew louder, filling his ears. He threw off the blanket and sat up, straining to see the Virgin on the dark green wall. A brilliant flash of yellow light lit her image, followed by a thunderous *boom* that shook the house. Plaster and billows of dust fell from the ceiling onto his head and bedclothes.

His mother and father called out from their bedroom. What he heard wasn't normal—their voices were high-pitched and frantic, laced with fear. His father, a craftsman, was never scared. Tomasz's father had never expressed such a feeling, not even when he'd chopped off the end of a finger with a hatchet. "It's only blood and a little meat," his father said, wrapping the bleeding stub with a handkerchief.

He shoved off the blanket and planted his feet on the braided rug. More shock waves pounded the house, and, somewhere, from a distance not too far, came the sound of rapid gunfire and screams. Wondering if what he was hearing and seeing was a nightmare, he imagined he would wake up in a sweat and be safe in bed, as he had many times before when he'd eaten too much chocolate torte for his own good.

He sensed something bearing down upon him, the weight, the pressure, slicing through the atmosphere in a monstrous wave. It zoomed over his head and exploded with a deafening roar, and the house seemed to lift from its foundation and fall back to earth with a thud. Everything in the room bounced into the air and then fell, including the picture of the Virgin, whose protective glass and wood frame shattered on the floor. Tomasz found himself facedown on the rug, covered in chunks of plaster and stone. Blood trickled down his right arm and leg, but he stretched, moving them. That was a good sign.

"*Mama . . . Tata . . .*" They couldn't hear his voice over the planes and explosions.

He pushed himself up from the floor and then realized that the room was tilted at a crazy angle. Only his bed had kept him from rolling toward the window that looked out upon the roof. He crawled up the angled floor to the bedroom door, opened it, and screamed. The rest of the house had been blown apart: the stairs lay in a jumbled mass four meters below, orange flames leaped up from what had been the kitchen, from his mother's now-buried stove. He looked left, around the door to his parents' bedroom and saw only empty space. The sky, barely visible through the smoke and haze, lay black with a meager dusting of stars.

He lurched toward his bed, fumbling over the splintered wood and stone, sliding over the mattress, which had come to rest against the wall near the window. Wrestling with the latch, he opened the frame, taking care not to cut his hand on the broken glass, and climbed out on the sloping roof. The drop from the eave to the village road winding below in the semidarkness was a few meters.

As he descended, he spotted the silvery-black outlines of planes circling the town. To his right, the hospital burned and bodies lay jumbled in the street, patients' gowns spattered with dark patches upon white cloth. Low on the horizon, but approaching fast, a needlelike shape spat fire from its wings. Tomasz covered his head and flattened himself against the stone tiles. The plane roared over him and he heard the *thunk, thunk, thunk* of bullets whizzing past him, penetrating wherever they landed.

He had never seen such a weapon of the air before. He and

his father had watched one day as a Polish biplane cut through a nearly cloudless sky, but he never imagined that creations so fast and fierce could slice through the heavens.

It was unwise to be on the roof. Tomasz slid down, his pajama top catching on one of the jagged tiles. Ripping the fabric free, grasping at anything to break his fall, he tumbled into the branches of a tree that had been shredded in half by the bomb and gingerly lowered himself to the ground.

The first haze of yellow crept up from the horizon, but the emerging light offered nothing to his eyes. He could see clearly from the fires burning around him.

His home had been dissected from the force of the blast. The roof had collapsed on his parents' crumpled bedroom. The sudden shock of seeing the jumbled timbers and debris sent a wave of fear through his body. He called out again for his mother and father, but they didn't answer.

"Tomasz, Tomasz, come inside, get out of the open," a neighbor yelled through a broken window across the street.

Another explosion rocked his body so hard he thought his bones would slice like knives through his skin. The plane streaked over him, pulled up, and disappeared into a sky now growing lighter with the dawn.

He ran in his bloody pajamas away from the town center, away from the bombs and the planes that strafed anyone in the streets, taking shelter in a grove of trees until night fell. Then, he walked back to his home to find more destruction and the men and women of Wieluń mourning the dead.

His neighbor told him that two hundred townspeople had been killed by Nazi bombs during the day, and his parents were among them.

He looked up at the stars and wept.

PART 1

CHAPTER 1

September 1st, 1939

When the bombs fell near Krochmalna Street in Warsaw, Izreal Majewski called for his family to take shelter under the heavy dining room table. He worried that his wife, Perla, who often succumbed to nerves, the news of war having already preyed upon her mind, might cry out and run into the street—not a safe place to be as far as he was concerned. Aaron, his son, would do just the opposite and fly to the window to watch the bombers.

"Quickly, under the table," Izreal ordered, as the air-raid sirens droned their rise-and-fall song.

"It won't protect us from Nazi bombs," Aaron said. As Izreal suspected, his son, small for his twelve years, thin and lanky, his trousers cinched at the waist, his white shirt blossoming around him, bounded for the window.

"Oh, God, why is this happening to us," Perla said, shuffling around the table, massaging her temples, her fingers extending toward the kerchief that covered her black hair. "Where is Stefa? Where is that girl? And on Shabbos, they come to bomb us."

"She's gone for a walk," Izreal said, beckoning Aaron to step away from the window.

Grinning, Aaron looked over his shoulder. "She's gone to see her boyfriend."

Perla stopped and pointed at him. "Never dishonor your sister by saying such things. Stefa holds a place in this family as an observant girl. She obeys the laws."

Izreal bent to his own curiosity, a trait he had instilled in his son, and stood in front of the window. The clouds hung low and gray over Warsaw, with occasional patches of blue sky that succumbed to the overcast as quickly as they appeared. The normally busy street had come to a standstill: Pedestrians stopped with their eyes to the sky; coachmens' heads tilted upwards; automobile drivers had pulled over, doors open, their faces peering out the side window. Neighbors from the many tenement buildings that stretched down Krochmalna stood on their balconies or took refuge behind the fragile protection of glass.

Aaron bolted toward the small balcony that jutted out from their apartment on the top floor of their building. Izreal caught him by the arm and pushed him toward the table.

"Go," Izreal said. "I will see what's happening."

"Not fair," Aaron said, as his mother pulled him under the table with her.

"Life is filled with injustice," Izreal shouted back while opening the double doors to the balcony. He stepped outside and put his hands on the wrought-iron railing that rose up to his waist. Above him, the stone-carved head of a smiling man looked down from the decorative turret of the fifty-year-old structure. A warm breeze struck him, ruffling the buttoned edges of his shirt and nearly lifting his yarmulke from his head.

He could hardly believe what he was seeing and hearing. Bombs were falling on the city. The explosions seemed far away, almost dreamlike, and the faint whir of the bombers sounded more like bees buzzing over spring flowers, but even he—an untrained civilian—could tell that the cloudy conditions had inhibited a prolonged bombing. Poland should get down on its knees and beseech God for rain—days and days of water turning roads to mud, halting the tanks, the artillery, and Hitler's Wehrmacht—shielding the city from the bombers.

The Nazis were well aware of their military limitations on this day, he thought. If September was clear and warm, and the

Polish Army was ineffective at repulsing a German advance, the month ahead would be hellish. Hitler had made it clear that he intended to crush Poland. Rain or no rain, the family had better be prepared. He hated to think about such an unimaginable situation: an educated, analytical mind torn from its focus on family and tradition.

Across the Vistula River, to the east, a blast vibrated through the air, followed by a rising column of grayish white smoke. He'd not seen the black speck of a falling bomb. The unannounced, invisible, utterly random hand of Death scared him and shook his confidence. However, he knew he needed to be strong for the sake of his son and wife.

He left the balcony and returned to the table to find Perla, her face flushed and her eyes red with tears, sitting beneath it across from Aaron, both huddled against its heavy oak legs. Their faces were barely visible through the airy handiwork of the lace tablecloth. Izreal got down on his knees and slid between them.

"I'm worried about Stefa," Perla said, blowing her nose into a white handkerchief.

"She'll be fine and home soon, I'm sure." Izreal said. "The bombing is erratic—not much of a threat."

"Daniel will protect her." Aaron smiled and leaned back against the leg that supported his back.

"You know this Daniel better than we do, child that you are," Perla said. "I must talk to Stefa. She's much too interested in this man—more than she should be. Her husband should come from our arrangement or not at all." She winced, apparently thinking of her daughter who had left Warsaw for the same reason.

Another bomb fell closer to Krochmalna and a shudder rippled through the building.

"Who can think of marriage at a time like this?" she asked. "I'm glad, at least, that Hanna is safe in London, despite how it ripped my heart out to see her go. Now I worry that she'll have nothing to come home to."

Izreal pretended not to hear his wife, wanting to scold her

for even imagining the worst, but Perla had always been sensitive. He knew that from the moment he met her, when she had dared not even steal a look at him. She was prettier than he'd expected when they gathered at her family's farm outside Warsaw, with her skin reddened by work outside, her body lean and taut. Her shy face caught the shadows from the ash trees circling the house, along with a play of sunlight flashing on her body. Despite Perla's display of modesty in this arranged marriage, he knew that she and her family were proud of him—a mashgiach—an educated man who supervised the kashrus of a Warsaw restaurant, a man who gave blessings to the kosher slaughter of animals.

His profession and his wife's homemaking skills had allowed them to build a family with only a few tragedies along the way: the stillbirth of a girl between Stefa and Aaron, and the departure of his eldest daughter, Hanna, who had left nine months ago to stay with relatives in London and never returned. But he didn't want to concern himself with Hanna as the bombs were falling in Warsaw, other than to think that she was safe as war began. His eldest daughter had ripped out his heart as well, and she had not done it as neatly as he would have done when he was a younger man, a shochet—a butcher—at the slaughterhouse.

"This is silly," Aaron said. "If a bomb hits, it will go through the roof and blow up the building. We might as well get out from under this table."

"Hush," Perla said, shaking her head. "The young have no fear of death."

Aaron sighed.

Izreal lowered his head and twisted his legs under his torso. Sitting with his neck arched against the bottom of the table was uncomfortable, but at least it offered some protection should the ceiling crack. After ten minutes of agony, he was about to agree with his son's suggestion to leave their shelter when the apartment door opened. Stefa had returned, her sturdy legs showing beneath her calf-length gray dress, her feet in the low-heeled black shoes that Perla had purchased for her.

Aaron held a finger to his lips.

Stefa called out for her parents, her voice rising in panic with each cry.

When she stepped too close to the table, Aaron reached from under the lace and grabbed his sister's ankle.

Stefa screamed, hopping away in terror.

Laughing, Aaron slid from the under the table, across the polished oak floor, as his sister sank into a chair.

"Got you!"

Izreal and Perla poked their heads out from under the table.

"You little brat!" Stefa fanned her red cheeks with her hands, a sprig of light brown hair protruding from her kerchief fluttering in the breeze. "I'll kill you someday." She stopped, placing her hands over her mouth, thinking better of her words as the bombs continued to fall.

Izreal, his body cramping, crawled out from under the table. He stood up and checked for dust on his trousers and jacket, but found nothing, a testament to his wife's immaculate housekeeping.

Perla followed her husband, apprehensively inspecting the ceiling, before chastising Stefa. "At last you're home. I was worried sick."

"I feel safer outside than I do in here," Stefa said. "On the street, I can run away."

"You could never run as fast as Hanna." Aaron rested his head on his intertwined hands, his body stretched across the floor. "How was Daniel?"

Stefa sniffed. "I took a walk—and even if I did see him, it would be no business of yours."

"We must talk about this man," Perla said.

Stefa held up her hand. "I know what you're going to say, Mother, about arrangements and marriage rites, and what a woman must do for her husband." She looked down into her lap. "But I'm not ready for marriage . . . and now the war seems to have begun."

"Your mother and I will make the arrangements," Izreal

said, judging his daughter's discomfort. Stefa's words led to his own uneasiness because they reminded him of Hanna and her self-imposed break from the family. Two daughters of like mind would bring him no comfort.

She stared at him, her hazel eyes flashing. "I *did* see Daniel today from across the street—me on one side, he on the other. He thinks I'm beautiful, and I think he's handsome, and we like each other. Doesn't that count for something?"

Izreal turned and looked across the tops of the buildings that lined Krochmalna, and the gray sky above. The family should remain firm and strong. Did it matter anymore? The war was real now—he could feel it in his bones, in his soul, and there was nothing anyone could do to stop it. He had little confidence that the Polish Army could match the German soldiers. Hitler had stopped his lies about amassing a Nazi war machine: the bombers, fighter planes, the millions of troops and armaments that he had ordered, as the world offered him appeasement gifts but still prayed that Germany would come to its senses.

Such thinking had been swiftly destroyed in one day—on the eve of Shabbos.

He had looked forward to eating the Sabbath meal, had always looked forward to Friday sunset and Perla's lighting of the candles on the sideboard. He could smell the meal that she had already prepared: the baked chicken, the potatoes, the summer squash that would be served this evening, the cholent that would simmer overnight to be eaten at lunch on Saturday after synagogue.

Izreal looked back at his daughter, still sitting in the chair. She, sixteen years old, was the second child after Hanna, more pliable than her older sister, but used to getting what she wanted. She had a temper and could be stubborn, but she also had used her fair skin and modesty to charm as well, a mystery to him at times, as if she had been born of another mother and father. Stefa had Perla's softer, rounder, face, while Hanna favored his longer facial structure and angular lines.

In a few hours, it would be sunset and time for blessing,

prayers, and songs. The drone of the bombers seemed to have drifted away, thwarted by the cloudy weather.

He wondered what Stefa saw, perhaps loved, in this man, Daniel. He wouldn't say anything to Perla yet, but the Nazis had changed everything, including love. Would happiness last in the years ahead? Would the fighting be over quickly? Arranged marriages might be a thing of the past—like peace—in a future too terrible to behold. Maybe the time had come to be flexible—in the face of disaster.

"Get up," he told Aaron, who was still sprawled at his sister's feet. "Let's look out on Warsaw. See what we can see before the world . . ."

He took in the faces of his wife and children and silently prayed for God to save them from a world consumed by war, wondering if his prayer would work.

The bombs faded and the afternoon grew long, darkening the clouds and her spirit.

Perla had a few moments alone in the bedroom before sunset, and she used the time to soothe her nerves and still her shaking hands. She sat on her bed and grasped them firmly in her lap, aware that the flesh had become more fragile, the first faint, brown spots showing irregularly between her wrist and fingers, knowing that at thirty-eight years of age these minor distractions would only get worse. The only luxury she afforded herself was a tin of petroleum jelly, which she applied lightly twice a week to keep her hands smooth. Stefa and Hanna, when they were younger, were fascinated by this routine. Her younger daughter had taken after her, secretly buying a jar of *krem kosmetyczny*, face cream. Perla had found the white porcelain container stashed at the back of a drawer. She hadn't told Izreal and wouldn't unless Stefa became too wasteful with its usage. That was unlikely to happen.

As she looked out the window at the failing gray light, she patted the bed's coverlet and thought how wonderful it would be to fall into a deep sleep and awaken anytime before this day.

The sun would shine brighter, the spring sun would be warmer, the winter snow would land lightly on her shoulders and melt on her coat before a fireplace. She tried to banish the memories of the afternoon: the sirens, the bombs, the neighbors screaming and yelling in the halls as destruction rained from the sky. How could life change so fast? Yet, what had happened was real. She hoped the Polish troops would rally—they would give their lives to save their homeland—but would it be enough?

She ran her finger along the intricate pattern of the spread, a wedding gift from her Hungarian grandmother. Flowers of yellow, red, and blue burst forth in blossom from intertwining green vines. Izreal allowed this ornamental display, the bright spot in the house, because it made her feel happy. She was not as good with the needle as her mother and grandmother, although she had crocheted the lace tablecloth that graced the Sabbath table.

She and her husband had pulled together what they could to decorate their home. Two landscapes from the Holy Land hung in the living room. The mizrach in praise of God took its place of honor on the east wall between the windows. Displayed on the sideboard and small cupboard positioned against the wall in the dining area were the precious objects of their religious life: the Shabbos candlesticks, the Seder plate, a wooden spice box, and the silver kiddush cup, all as necessary and meaningful to her as any limb of her body. And, when not in use, tucked away in the top drawer of the sideboard were Izreal's knives, the steel gleaming, and the blades free from nicks, pits, or other obstructions that would go against the laws of slaughter. In their way, those instruments were the most precious of all because his use of them, first as a butcher, had allowed the family to thrive.

Her hands shook again at the thought of their future in Warsaw . . . their lives threatened, perhaps disappearing. Horror had been thrust upon them by a madman from Germany. If only European leaders hadn't capitulated, if only Britain and lagging America had stood up to Hitler's bullying, Poland might continue to enjoy pleasant summers and warm falls. Now, everything was in question. Even the radio reports had given them some hope, never once mentioning the threat of an invasion or the start of a war. The broadcasts were always about Hitler, the ravings of a man obsessed with Germany's power.

She rose and ran a finger over the plain gray blanket covering her husband's bed. The cotton pillowcase and the sheet that extended beyond the blanket were pressed and as white as a blinding desert sun. Everything was in its place.

It's growing late. I must attend to my duties.

She walked, head bowed, from the bedroom to the table.

Inner peace and the spirit of joy. Holiness. My family. We are here at the table.

Izreal smiled, hoping to lift his family's spirits. The Sabbath was supposed to be joyous, but this evening, the first of September, was different. Sabbath was a time for putting aside problems, communing with God, and contemplating the blessings given from above.

Perla kept her head bowed and eyes closed, as if tears would pour out if she looked up at her husband. Stefa looked sullen and out of sorts, bearing the world's weight on her shoulders, probably concerned about Daniel's well-being. Only Aaron, in the naivety and freshness of his youth, looked bright-eyed and ready for the Sabbath meal. Izreal wondered if his son might have *enjoyed* the first day of the war, likening it to a game played by adults instead of children.

Izreal put his hands on Aaron's bowed head, resting his fingers on his son's black yarmulke. "May God make you like unto Ephraim and Manasseh." He walked to the other side of the table and placed his hands on Stefa's head. "May God make you like unto Sarah, Rebekah, Rachel, and Leah."

He returned to the head of the table and stood for a moment, looking out upon them, his children on either side, Perla across from him. What might he offer as a personal prayer, something that might lift the evening, hopeful words devoid of woe and despair?

"I thank God for the many blessings that He has given us," he began, clasping his hands together. "Even upon this day which the world will mark in future generations as a dark stain upon humanity . . . but let us not think of that now. Let us rejoice and enjoy our time together as a family, the time that God has given us. We must be strong and know that God will protect us from our enemies as He has always done in the past. That is all we can do—have faith and praise Him for our many blessings. Let us remember the light as we have through the generations."

Kerchief in place, Perla rose from her chair, and stood in front of the candles on the table. She struck a match, lit one of them, then, circling her hands three times and drawing the light toward her, she closed her eyes and recited the blessing: "Blessed art thou, O Lord our God, King of the Universe, who has commanded us to light the Sabbath candles." Through the years, she and her husband had worked as two separate religious individuals, instilling the holy traditions in their children. Still shielding her eyes, Perla lit the second taper. Izreal recited, "Observe the Sabbath day."

Izreal said the blessing over the wine and the bread before starting the meal. The usual chatter at the joyous table was limited to Izreal and his son. Perla and Stefa ate slowly, Perla often gazing toward the window to see if Warsaw would suffer again from the Nazi bombers.

With eyes alight, Aaron said, "I wish I had seen—"

Perla glared at him, her look vicious enough to cut off his words. "Don't speak of war tonight. I *know* what you wish you had seen." She rested her fork on her plate. "People died today—I'm sure of it . . . no one around us, but what of our relatives in the country, our cousins in Kraków, or those living on the Polish border? Were their bodies ripped apart? No one should wish they had seen the bombs explode."

The excitement in Aaron's eyes died and he looked down at his chicken and potatoes. "I'm sorry, Mother. I will pray for our relatives."

Perla nodded. "And for your sister, Hanna, as well. She deserves our prayers—she is still a member of this family." She lifted her fork and positioned it in her hand so the tines pointed toward Izreal.

Hanna had driven a furious wedge between Izreal and his wife in January, the most troublesome and argumentative time of their married lives, when Hanna went to live in London with one of Perla's five sisters, a woman who had renounced Judaism and converted to her husband's Episcopalianism. Her other sisters were scattered throughout Poland.

Hanna had left Warsaw the day after she turned eighteen on January eighth. The "plot," as Izreal called it, had been clandestine and deliberate, even down to the travel schedule arranged by Perla's sister Lucy—her Christian name. There had been one day and one terrible night to consider the consequences of Hanna's actions.

"You will no longer be my daughter," Izreal had said while hardening his heart to her.

"I don't love the man you've chosen for me. I will love my family always, but *he* won't be my husband. I will not raise his children, wash his clothes, cook and clean for him. So much of life is forced on us. The world is changing." Hanna beseeched her mother. "Look at your sister! Happy and carefree in London! I pleaded with her to let me come, and, after many tears, she relented. It was the most difficult decision of her life. She didn't want to hurt either of you, after having gone through the same trouble herself when she left the family." Hanna looked at Izreal. "My aunt hoped you would eventually forgive me."

Stefa and Aaron had sat silent during the argument before they were told to go to their rooms. Hanna's argument failed to melt the icy shield that protected Izreal. Perla's subdued sympathy for Hanna added to his irritation.

"You are going?" was all Perla could ask. "Truly going to my sister's?"

"Yes, Mama. Aunt Lucy has worked with the Immigration

Service and will be my sponsor—I can work in England as long as I don't take a job from a citizen who needs it." Hanna looked down at her dark blue dress. "Look at us. Could we be any more drab?"

The question set Izreal off, as if he had been personally insulted. "Drab! You are a beautiful Jewish woman who we've raised to honor the laws and traditions set forth in the Torah. Yet, you spit in our faces."

Hanna straightened, her tall figure matching his. "Papa, I would never spit in your face. You know I love you more than life itself, but if I stay here I will die, and what good would that do either of us? That I know as sure as I'm standing here." She threaded her fingers through her long black hair.

Perla gasped and Izreal looked away.

Suppressing his anger, he'd remained silent. The words tried to rise from his lungs, but they caught in his throat, a maddening combination of fury and disbelief, stopping him from speaking and forcing him to fling open the balcony doors and thrust his fists into the freezing January air. Sleet peppered his coat, but after a time, he didn't feel the cold at all, only a quaking rage that shook his body until it finally subsided like a spent earthquake.

When he returned to the living room, all three bedroom doors were closed. Hanna had gone into the one she shared with her sister, to spend her last night in the apartment. He softly pushed the door open to his room.

Perla lay in her bed, her back turned toward him, legs curled close to her body, hands covering her face. A beam of silver light from a streetlamp fell like a knife across the blankets.

Izreal touched her shoulder.

She flinched and choked on tears. "She won't come back," she sputtered. "We'll never see her again. I'll die and I'll never see my daughter again . . . but I must obey my husband."

He took off his coat, placing it over a chair, sat on the edge of his bed, and sighed. "She will come back." He said nothing for a time, but then chuckled. "She's a strong girl . . . I've always known it. She used her brain as well as her body—who ran and swam behind our backs because I would not allow it for modesty's sake. The child who could do things neither of us could do. A sharp mind can get you into trouble."

Perla, balling a handkerchief in her hand, turned toward him, her eyes dim in the blackness.

"I thought she had tamed herself—come to know her religion and herself—as only a woman can, but I was wrong," he said. As his eyes adjusted to the dark, he lay back on the bed and stared at the white speckled ceiling. "The spark was always there, but I thought she had controlled it. The *arrangement*— Josef must have been the feather that broke her back."

"Marriage is no feather," Perla said.

"It is an eternal union sanctified by God."

"Izreal . . . you don't need to lecture me. I know the law nearly as well as you do. I'm not happy, but I want my children to be happy. If that means they must go their own way, so be it—I won't stand in their way, no matter how painful. Eventually, they will leave us for their husbands and wives no matter what we do . . . or say. You don't need to give her your blessing, but you need to *understand*."

"I don't know if I can, for what I am is all I know."

Perla turned toward the window as he undressed. He slid into bed, the cold sheets sending gooseflesh skittering over his skin. He stared at the ceiling for an hour and then at the blade of light falling across Perla's body, watching her chest rise and fall beneath the blankets, before he fell asleep.

Izreal was up early and off to work, the house still and silent as he closed the apartment door.

He saw Hanna in his mind as he walked the dark, empty, streets: from her birth on that cold January day in 1921, through her schooling, her teachers telling him what a gifted young girl she was, how fortunate it was that she picked up languages so easily—she could speak Polish, Yiddish, and German, with ease, as well as some English—and what a lovely daughter and woman she had become . . . until yesterday.

All the time, the fuse was burning and he didn't know it.

When he returned home that day, Hanna was gone.

Bombs fell on Warsaw, morning, afternoon, evening, and night the month of September. Stefa stood in bread lines near Daniel's home in the Praga District across the Vistula, while Aaron remained closer to home. Both siblings felt somewhat guilty about taking two helpings of bread for the family. They weren't starving; however, the leftovers from the restaurant where Izreal worked had become their main source of meals as food staples disappeared during the siege. "We should have thought ahead," Perla lamented one day, despondent about not being prepared for the war. Shaking his head and muttering that he feared the war would grow worse, Izreal told her that women harvesting potatoes in fields around Warsaw had been strafed and killed by Nazi planes. "We are lucky we have food. Those women took a chance rather than starve to death. In the end, the Nazis made sure it didn't matter."

The Germans bombed the city on the eighth, and the fifteenth, on the eve of the Sabbath, but living in Warsaw had become a matter of survival, not of observing the holy days. Izreal tried to keep the family together as hope for an early peace faded. The Sabbath prayers, the lighting of the candles, the blessings, the songs, seemed hollow, professed to a God who didn't care whether they lived or died.

Stefa called out to Daniel as they helped the men and women of Warsaw dig fortified barricades around the city center. "Dig harder, *drogi.*"

Daniel smiled at the Polish word of affection, pushed the low-slung wool cap back from his head, and wiped his brow with a handkerchief. "Dig harder?—I'd rather be in the army." He stabbed his shovel into a ditch and watched the line of volunteers, conscripted men who had come back from losing battles, move the earth. "My father says *we* are of the Jewish Nation, not Poles. I told him I was a Polish Jew, and I'd be happy to go to war." He grabbed the shovel's shaft, pulled the blade from the dirt, and held it like a lance in front of him. A Polish army man, attired in his brown uniform jacket and brimmed field cap, rifle slung over his shoulder, shot Daniel a look of disgust.

He dug into the earth again, looking away from the man's eyes.

Stefa knew her parents would be angry if they found them together on this Sunday, the seventeenth of September. Her father was at work. Her mother had stretched out on the bed after suffering a headache while trying to figure out how to make the most of their remaining supplies. Stefa had excused herself to take a walk, mentioning a bread line even though most of them were closed on Sunday. She thought Daniel's parents would be angry, too, if they knew they were together. She had met them briefly once. They were courteous, but distant, making it clear to Stefa that she was not on the list of his intendeds.

"Wouldn't it be nice, if . . ." Her voice trailed off.

"What?" Daniel asked, digging deeper, tossing the brown dirt with ferocity to the top of the ditch.

"I was just thinking it would be nice if we could go for a walk by ourselves and be happy." Down the street, the blackened shell of a bombed building stared back at her. Hardly a block had been spared from the destruction. Industrious Poles had moved the rubble into piles, clearing the debris wherever possible, but now railroad tracks were being torn from the earth and positioned at forty-five degree angles near the trenches to stop the anticipated advance of Nazi tanks.

The Warsaw of her childhood had been delightful—lovely tall buildings constructed of pale stone with red striations gracing their façades, stately apartment buildings with carved cornices and lacy wrought-iron balconies, domed government buildings and churches, verdant parks with an abundance of summer begonias and roses of all colors, a lively Jewish quarter with so many people she couldn't count them, and a magnificent synagogue.

But so much had changed since the first day of September. Smoke from incendiary bombs had become commonplace, the hateful clouds filling the skies over Warsaw night and day. White, gray, and black ash fell like rain at all hours and added to the feeling that the world was on fire. Her father told her of another development in German warfare—one that hadn't been used before—a heavy bomb that tore through buildings without detonating until its timer set off a delayed explosion. Hundreds had been killed by this new atrocity.

Now, the Germans were on Warsaw's doorstep, and it appeared that nothing could stop them.

Daniel stopped for a moment and looked at her. The wild spark in his eyes scared her; his mood had gone from fiery resistance to one of abject horror. She knew from her own experience that despair would be next—falling through a hole in the earth with no bottom in sight, flailing in the darkness until you were swallowed, like being underwater and struggling to breathe.

"My father saw something terrible yesterday," Daniel said. "A Catholic hospital near us was bombed last Friday, on Erev Shabbos. Mothers and their babies were being cared for in that hospital. Some of the children were injured before the doctors and nurses had time to lead them to safety in the basement." He rested for a moment against his shovel. "On Shabbos, my father got a look inside—he offered to help—he put aside his differences. As far as I'm concerned, it makes no difference whether we are Catholic or Jew—we need each other. Some of the babies were only four days old . . . what a time to be born. No one expected it would come to this. Who would have believed it?"

His eyes glazed over, as if he had traveled somewhere far away from Warsaw. A shadow, a darkness of mood often covered Daniel, and Stefa loved him for it. She saw this characteristic as a strength rather than a weakness. At first, his capacity for gloom had scared her, but as she grew to know him, in the odd times they could piece together, she realized that he drew courage from these somber moods. A state of melancholy challenged him. Overcoming adversity would be an asset in the trying times ahead. Of course, it wasn't just his temperament that drew her to him. She found his features handsome, a man at seventeen, slightly taller than she. He wore a beard, blacker than her father's, that complemented the dark arch of his eyebrows. The dusky skin beneath his eyes faded to pale white, with a dash of pink on the cheeks above the beard line. He wore wire-rimmed glasses when he read that gave him an intellectual, sophisticated look she loved.

"He helped them clear some of the rubble at the hospital, move a few undamaged beds, and they were grateful," he continued, unaware of her thoughts. "Windows had been blown out, the cracked ceiling was ready to collapse, broken glass and rubble covered everything, but there were a few surprises, too. An ornamental potted palm survived, as did the crucifix on the wall. It hung above a shattered window."

Stefa grabbed a spare shovel and dug into the earth, forcing the blade in with her foot, lifting the load, and pitching it to the top of the trench. Bits of rock and dirt rolled back toward her, but she didn't mind. She was here with Daniel, doing something good for their city.

The noise sounded like an angry insect at first, the buzz rapidly intensifying. Several men threw down their shovels and spades and looked to the sky behind them. One pointed to a black speck that grew larger by the second, the machine-like roar soon pounding in her ears.

Daniel tossed his shovel, grabbed her by the waist, and threw her down on the side of the trench facing the oncoming plane. Spreading his coat over their heads, he landed on top of her, his body shielding hers.

His warm, frantic breath brushed against her cheek as she gripped his clenched fists. She prayed that they would not die on the bank of this slope, that they might have life instead of an early death. Strangely, she wondered what her parents would think—beyond their grief—if their bodies were discovered together. Would they allow themselves to mourn two dead children who had no business being together, or would their anger at such "foolishness" temper their grief?

After the initial uproar, the line of people gathered in the trench quieted in fear. Nothing could be heard above the hiss of the fast-moving fighters and the *twang* of bullets driving themselves into whatever lay in their path. And, far off at first and then growing closer, explosions rumbled throughout the city, shaking the ground beneath them.

Daniel tightened his body as the shock waves grew closer. Clods and pieces of stone rained down upon them.

Stefa thought she heard the muffled cry of someone in pain. The sound was soon obliterated by the Nazi death machines roaring overhead.

In a few minutes the worst appeared to be over, as the fighters advanced to other parts of the city.

Daniel rolled off her, his face coming close to hers. "Are you all right?"

She nodded and lifted herself from the earth.

"The Stukas may come around for more," he said, searching the skies.

About three meters from their spot, a man lay sprawled across the top of the trench. Blood seeped from two holes in the back of his brown coat. Stefa believed the man had panicked, tried to escape, but took two machine gun cartridges in the back instead. Several people bent over him, but it was clear that he was dead.

Daniel crawled to the other side of the trench and peered over the edge. "Look!"

Stefa joined him.

Many blocks away, the dome of Warsaw's Royal Castle blazed, yellow and orange flames bursting forth from its onion-shaped spire, the tower's clock having stopped at the moment of the attack. A group of men, powerless to stop the flames, gathered in the street until a fire brigade could come; even then, little could be done to save the structure. Every German sortie had ruptured water lines, causing outages across the city. Water had become a scarce commodity.

Daniel stood up, surveyed the damage, and shook his head. "Nazi bastards."

Stefa had never heard him swear.

She brushed away tears as Warsaw burned.

CHAPTER 2

———•◆•———

"Hanna?"

Aunt Lucy's confident knock boomed against her door. "Time for breakfast."

"Be there in a jiffy." She stretched her arms over her head, turned, and looked at the radiant dial of the alarm clock on her nightstand. It was shortly before 8 a.m. on Sunday, September 17th. Hanna only had to run a comb through her hair, slip into a dress, put on her slippers, and pad down the stairs to the breakfast room off the kitchen. Life was so much more pleasant in London than in Warsaw.

Pleasant.

Even that word had taken on a different meaning since Britain had declared war on Germany two days after the Nazi invasion. The London papers were full of nothing but war stories now: How correspondents on the front line in Poland, barely escaping with their lives, had smuggled their newsreels out of war zones so they could be shown between films in cinemas; tales of the brave Polish Army being driven back by the relentless Nazi forces; stories of bombing and horror in Poland and *Warsaw.* She sat up, trying to ignore the mixture of fear and guilt that roiled her stomach when she thought about the war.

In the months since her arrival in Croydon, about fifteen kilometers south of central London, she'd done her best to become a Londoner, improving her English, even inserting the vernacular into her speech. It was a "lie-in" instead of a nap, a "film at the cinema," never a "movie."

She tied back the blackout curtains, walked to the walnut dresser, sat on the makeup stool in front of the blue-hued mirror, and picked up the pearl-handled hairbrush. Her hair was the right color now—the dark tresses that she had grown up with had been lightened with peroxide with Lucy's help, turning her hair a golden brown like ripened wheat. Several times before leaving Warsaw, Hanna had dreamed of eradicating all traces of her Jewish heritage, but she could do nothing about her brown eyes or, more importantly, the religious traditions she carried in her memory despite leaving them behind. In this foreign land, rejecting her heritage was more difficult than she'd imagined. The past lingered.

The brush slid smoothly through the wave over her forehead and the hair curling from the crown down to her neck. She daubed a bit of rouge on her cheeks, then found an ivy-green dress she thought would be perfect for the morning, and, finally, put on her slippers. She dreaded only one thing as she prepared to go downstairs: the Sunday morning newspapers that Lucy's husband, Lawrence, would be reading at the breakfast table. More war news, more terrible reports from Poland, more threats from Hitler. Lucy, of course, would try to soothe her while Richard would report the headlines matter-of-factly with traditional English aplomb. How lucky she was that Lawrence and Lucy worked with his connections and the Immigration Service to sponsor her. Otherwise, she might have ended up in an internment camp on the Isle of Man like some Jews who fled to England.

Lucy, Lawrence, and Charlie, the Cavalier King Charles spaniel, were already dining when she arrived. The weather was warm enough that her aunt had opened the French doors to the patio. A fresh breeze wafted through the room on its way to the windows on the front of the house.

"Good morning." Hanna pulled out the chair nearest the doors, sitting between her aunt and uncle.

"Did you sleep well, dear?" Her aunt's tone on the last word reminded her of the Polish word *drogi*, meaning "dear one."

"Yes, thank you."

Hanna remembered little about Lucy from childhood because, among Hanna's grandparents' children, Lucy had been the one who had left the house never to return, the one whose name was never spoken. Her mother rarely talked about what happened to Lucy, and then only in brief, whispered remembrances.

Her aunt had discarded her Hebrew name of Liora, the Polish Lucyna, and settled on the Anglicized version, Lucy, which mirrored her husband's name of Lawrence. Hanna knew that a bond of sisterly love existed between her mother and aunt, and that they had even exchanged letters.

Lucy had thickened a bit from the vague picture Perla had painted of her. Her aunt had adapted well to English life, marrying a middle-class assistant bank manager whom she had met in Poland by chance and had fallen madly in love with, much to the dismay of her teeth-gnashing father. The ironic knife to the heart came from the fact that Lucy's father had arranged the meeting to help finance his farming operations outside Warsaw, and a London bank had been called in as part of the negotiations. Lucy described their meeting as true case of "love at first sight."

The family rift soon became an unspoken, festering wound, never to be touched or tended, best ignored. For her part, Lucy had embraced Anglican life, adopting hairstyles and fashion, using makeup, making full English breakfasts, doting over her husband, cooking, managing the house and keeping it spotless while her husband commuted to London. They had no children, however. Apparently, this was a mutual agreement between husband and wife because Lucy had never mentioned wanting any heirs to the Richardsons' small fortune.

Lucy poured tea for her husband while he slipped a slice of sausage to Charlie under the table. The good-natured, white-and-tan dog licked his chops at the expected treat.

"Tea?" Lucy asked.

"Yes, thank you," Hanna replied, always striving for an English formality when in the presence of Lawrence Richardson. Since arriving in Croydon, she'd found herself, at first, trying to replicate the closeness of her traditional family, but soon discarded the idea. Her relationship with her aunt was more formal than she'd anticipated. They weren't like sisters, or girlfriends, more like mother and daughter; in fact, she often wondered if Lucy kept some distance because of guilt—thinking of herself as even more of a traitor to the family now that she had agreed to help Hanna. That subject had yet to be broached.

Her aunt poured the tea, placed the pot on a porcelain trivet, and covered it with a cozy.

Lawrence turned his newspaper pages between bites of sausage and eggs. Hanna and Lucy sat quietly waiting to speak, not wanting to disturb his concentration. He considered Sunday sacrosanct, his day of rest, valuing peace and quiet above anything else during those precious hours, and God help the person who ruffled his Sunday pages.

She saw her uncle-in-law's angular face between the flick of newsprint, the compressed blue eyes set on either side of an aquiline nose, the straightness of the back against the chair splat, the thinning blondish hair, slick with pomade, that swept back from his forehead, the gray jacket and red tie that he wore for a "relaxing" weekend. Lucy and Lawrence had been so young when they married and Hanna wondered if ever, even at eighteen, she would find the right man to marry.

Hitler's Forces Near Warsaw. The headline stopped her cold—she stopped mid-bite and put her fork on the plate.

Lucy reached a warm hand toward her. Lawrence noticed his wife's action and folded the paper neatly, placing it by his plate.

"It's a lovely morning," he said, somewhat apologetically. "I may go for a walk after breakfast if anyone cares to join me."

Beyond the doors, a flock of sparrows chattered and hopped on the irregular pieces of slate inset into the garden grounds. The birds were nothing new to the Richardson household.

Hanna had seen her aunt throw breadcrumbs to them on many occasions. A small willow tree grew inside the brick fence that surrounded the property; otherwise, the lawn was filled with flowers and perennials that thrived in the mostly shady yard.

"I'm sorry about the news," Lawrence said. "It's very distressing."

Lucy nodded, her eyes glistening with unshed tears.

"If I'd known the war was going to break out, I wouldn't have come," Hanna said. "But now you have me—like it or not." She chuckled nervously, knowing that she was living in her relatives' home thanks to their good graces.

"I worry." Lucy clutched her knife. "My parents, my sisters and brothers, my cousins—our family—they're all there and God knows how they're suffering."

"Hush, Lucy," her husband said, in the manner of a mild reprimand. "Our boys will take care of Hitler when the time comes. All we can do now is wait and watch as the war proceeds."

"Your family is less than one hundred kilometers away, safe in England. Hanna and I worry every day about our relatives."

Her aunt rarely used Yiddish, but when she did, something or someone had struck at her heart. When Hanna heard the news about the Nazi invasion and the start of the war, Lucy's prayers had gone out to the entire mishpacha, her extended family; but, instead of relief from the invocations, darkness shrouded Hanna. She'd made her choice and nothing could be done about it. Hindsight was tragically late. She had left Warsaw for many reasons, but none of them seemed good enough once the war started. They all seemed so petty, selfish, and self-serving on that terrible day, so she could only look at the newspaper headlines or listen to the radio in horror and think that her move to London had been an untimely mistake.

Charlie, his ears flopping in time with his bounding legs, leapt past the doors to the garden grounds, scattering the sparrows in a noisy array.

"We'll give the family a nod—do as much as we can," Lawrence said. "I wish we could do more." He scratched his forehead. "Perhaps Hanna should write more letters to her parents so we won't be kept in the dark."

Hanna had written to her mother several times since January, but there had been no answer to either her or Lucy. Most likely, her father had stopped Perla from writing. She didn't know that for sure, but the reason—the abrupt break from the family—seemed like one Izreal would support. Perhaps it pained her mother too much to write; she was, after all, the more sentimental, the more sensitive parent. If tears fell, it may have been hard for Perla to pick up the pen.

Lawrence finished his breakfast with gusto and wiped his mouth with his napkin. "Where is Charlie . . . if he's digging near the willow . . . ." Stepping outside, he withdrew a pipe from his pocket and lit it as he looked for the dog. "Ah, there he is . . . muddy paws and all. I'll leash him and take him with me. Good to get fresh air. No need to bother you two."

Hanna ate the last of her sausage and then helped her aunt clear the table. They put the dishes in the sink and watched Lawrence, gray smoke circling around his head, leash Charlie. The midmorning sun shone upon the row houses across the street, the light sparkling on the windows. Her aunt was lucky to have a home on the corner with a bit of private space, unlike the cramped units across the busy street.

Her uncle headed for the gate, but stopped short and returned to the breakfast room doors, Charlie in tow.

"I'm thinking of purchasing an Anderson shelter." He puffed on his pipe, a few red embers flying into the air before he removed it from his mouth.

Hanna had no idea what he was talking about. Lucy looked equally puzzled.

"Not to be an alarmist, but I think Hitler's intention is to put an end to Britain." He pointed to the sky, holding the pipe stem out from his fist. "Bombs may fall and I want to be prepared. The shelter will cost us seven pounds, but well worth it for our peace of mind . . . Besides, that willow needs to come out to make room for it. Damned if I know how that tree got here. We can plant a vegetable garden on top of the shelter . . ." He smiled at Lucy. "Like you used to do on the farm outside Warsaw . . . minus the Anderson." He returned the pipe to his mouth, turned, and walked away.

Lucy placed a bowl in the sink and turned on the hot water. Bubbles circled around the soap. Her aunt lifted the glassware first and dipped them into the water.

"He's a good man, a real mensch," she said, running a washcloth around the glass rims. "He'll take care of us . . . but he doesn't truly understand what we've gone through . . . what we've sacrificed to live our lives. How could he?"

Hanna nodded as she placed a glass on the wooden drying rack and watched the sparrows, pecking at grass seed, return to the garden.

Hanna made her bed, sat at her dresser, and looked through her window at the houses across the street. Feeling at odds with herself, particularly after Lawrence's stated need for an Anderson shelter, she opened one of the drawers and took out the newspaper clippings from the first day of September.

Her new family had given her the bedroom on the front of the house. It faced the street, which from Monday through early Sunday morning bustled with people and thrummed with automobiles. Her aunt and uncle-in-law slept in quieter quarters on the back of the house. The noise didn't bother her particularly, having grown up on Krochmalna, a busy street in its own right, but she hadn't expected the melancholy she experienced in Croydon once the shock of the new had lessened. Although September generally had been warmer and drier than usual for England, the damper weather and the different weather patterns took getting used to.

Clouds hung lower over London than they did in Warsaw. They had a billowing luminosity in summer she wasn't prepared for, unlike the sharper, bolder thunderstorms that struck her home city. In the spring, fog covered Croydon, reducing its buildings to smoky gray blobs, hard-to-define shapes. A newcomer could get lost in the murk. The rain, when it came down, poured in relentless sheets, or pattered for days on end, soaking everything, rendering a brolly useless, the only saving grace from the chill being a sturdy waterproof mac.

The day promised to be a fine one, but she had no company for the morning. Her girlfriends were at the Episcopal church where she had attended a few services with her aunt and Lawrence. She found the atmosphere within its vaulted ceiling, stone arches, and wooden pews somber, strange, and not to her liking. Her aunt probably held the same view, judging from her less than lively response. Therefore, Sundays were mostly spent in the home rather than in church.

The few English boys she'd dated—all recommendations from girlfriends—were the opposite of solemn: boisterous, loud, smoking creatures with slick hair, who drank cheap whiskey and wore the most expensive suits they could afford in an effort to impress their dates. Most seemed ready to act in service to England upon the outbreak of war. That attitude added to their proclivity to "live it up" while they could.

A few months into her English sojourn, the thought struck her that living near London was the opposite of living in Warsaw. At home, the Sabbath was a joyful occasion marked by thanking God for His blessings, filled with prayers and songs; yet, the men in her religion maintained a modest, thoughtful, and often somber attitude. Here, Sundays were sober, and, after church, the men returned immediately to their libertine ways. Life was so different in Croydon—but that was what she had wanted.

She counted the reasons for her decision as she sat at the dresser and picked through the headlines she'd clipped: *Nazis Invade Poland, Germany at War, Europe in Flames*. The words seized her, making her feel slightly nauseous from her breakfast. For years, everything had screamed at her to get away from her family: an arranged marriage with a man she couldn't possibly love, raising children, washing, cooking, continually honoring traditions that had been drilled into her since childhood—even having the temerity to eat a pork sausage for breakfast. She'd known she was different from an early age, but it took years to act upon those feelings. Knowing that she wanted a different life, dishonoring her family, upsetting the expectations of her future, kept her emotions in a state of flux—until she had reached out to her aunt—the *oysvorf* of the family, the outcast.

She had picked through the few letters Lucy had sent to her mother and found the Croydon address. Her hand shook while writing the first letters at sixteen years of age. Every word had to be kept a secret, Hanna begging her aunt not to answer her directly, but to relay her sentiments in coded sentences in letters to her mother. She was thrilled when her aunt wrote back in successive letters, giving best wishes to Stefa and Aaron, but adding these words to Hanna.

Tell your eldest I miss seeing her grow to womanhood. I'm sure she has a fine future awaiting her no matter what she does. I hope she is able to travel to England someday—it would be a happy reunion.

Hanna's heart had leapt as her mother read the words and she felt as if stones had been removed from her weighted body. Eventually, she saved enough from her meager spending money for calls to Lucy to firm up plans.

She put the headlines back in the drawer, frustrated by her inability to cry, frozen by the anxiety that gripped her. The sun had traveled higher and a warm breeze filtered through her window. She wanted to go outside and see her friends after church, but worry about her family in Poland forced her to stare at the houses across the street and wonder if Croydon would be bombed someday.

They don't care who they kill.
The bombs over Warsaw fell like October leaves, explod-

ing to the east and west of the Vistula, artillery shells shrieking overhead as well, the blasts never-ending. The walls of Janka Danek's apartment shook, the windows bent inward from the shockwaves, on the verge of fracturing. After an especially pernicious detonation close by, Janka grasped a doorframe and held on to keep from being flung to the floor.

Her husband, Karol, would be safe at the copper processing plant where he worked—an industry where the precious metal was transformed into brass for cartridge casings. The managers had constructed shelters in anticipation of German attacks and stored provisions in case workers couldn't make it home. Overtime might be needed for ammunition production—that is, if the plant withstood the latest Nazi bombings. The attacks began at eight in the morning. Karol reported for work at seven and ended his shift at three. She didn't see him several nights after work until late because he stopped at a nearby bar. Depending on his mood, the actions of his employers, and the Nazi air force and artillery units, Karol might show up drunk after eleven or not at all.

Damn them, damn them to hell!

During a brief break in the siege, she ran to the window, opened it, and peered out. Columns of smoke coiled in ribbons over the city. To her left, flames broke through the windows and roofs of several buildings on Krochmalna. Rubble from bombed structures had spilled into the street like stone waterfalls. Frightened residents, those who had escaped with their lives, stood frozen in the street, unsure where to go and what to do. Men clutched their wives. Many, covered in dust and ash, kneeled on the street, their hands covering their faces. Others extended their arms to the heavens in pleas to a merciful God. To her right, on the other side of the river, the view was much the same—smoke, fire, and, certainly as an accompaniment to both, death.

Janka swore at the sky and clasped her hands so tightly her knuckles turned white. Every second in the apartment felt like

hours as the bombs pounded the city. A small voice told her—
*better to be in the middle of the street than have the building
collapse on you.*

Concerned that the apartment might explode at any second,
she grabbed her coat and headed down the stairs, leaving the
door open. There was nothing of value to steal anyway.

Each succeeding day in Warsaw had become more hellish as
the Nazis advanced. Army men, already veterans of this new
and terrible war, had limped home, joining civilians in digging
trenches, fortifying Warsaw's vulnerable sectors in feeble efforts
to stave off attacks. But little could be done against the constant waves of German bombers and the Wehrmacht's superior
weaponry. Medical supplies were limited. Hospitals had been
destroyed and doctors and nurses were overwhelmed with patients, many with critical injuries.

Water had become scarce because pipes had been blown up,
or shut off completely to stop flooding, leading to long lines at
the few available sources. Some had even taken water from the
Vistula, boiling the liquid over crude fires from the dwindling
supplies of available wood. The water shortage only aided the
fires started by incendiary bombs.

Hunger had begun to gnaw at the city as well. Dead horses,
most from the carriage trade, some killed while serving in the
Polish cavalry, were carved up for meat by a starving populace.
It turned Janka's stomach to see the men sawing away at the
beautiful animals' hindquarters, but she understood how her
fellow citizens could be driven to such measures. Starvation was
a powerful motivator.

At the bottom of the stairs, she pushed the door open, brushing past a few neighbors who also had decided to seek safety in
the middle of the wide cobblestoned street.

"Look," a woman who lived on the floor above her shouted.

Janka lifted her head toward a sky turned gray with swirling
smoke. At intervals, the sun broke through the thick haze. A
flight of bombers swarmed overhead and she gasped at the sight
of the bombs falling from their mechanical underbellies. The

ash and smoke again obscured her vision, while the sharp, acrid odor of burning wood filled her nostrils.

She tilted her head to the left and spotted a boy, not quite old enough to be a man, on a fourth-floor balcony down the street. He was bent at the waist, leaning over the railing so far Janka was afraid he might tumble to his death. His youthful curiosity had gotten the better of him in his quest to see what was happening to his city. His mother, Janka presumed, appeared behind him like a shot. She was a nervous woman who waved her arms wildly and pulled at her son's shoulders before he relented and followed her back inside.

Before closing the balcony doors, the young man, attired in long breeches and a white shirt, took one last look down to the street. Their eyes met. Something about his face cheered her, as if the boy knew that he would live through the war, that what was going on around him was something to be viewed with wonder, like a game to be enjoyed. Only life mattered and he had it to give. He smiled despite the war going on around him, and Janka waved in a desperate greeting, not caring if he was Jewish or Catholic, feeling cheered by his confident display.

The doors closed and he was gone. His disappearance saddened her, but she fixed the apartment location in her mind.

She had little time to think upon anything else, when a hand grabbed her roughly by the shoulder.

"Are you an idiot?" She turned to find her husband staring at her with bloodshot eyes already clouded by drink.

"So early in the morning?"

"Yes. Nothing wrong with that. The boss let us go. My friend shared some of his flask. Good thing. Don't know if we'll go back at all. Damn Nazis. You might have to go to work so I can afford to drink." He slurred his words, each short sentence coming with a blast of liquored breath.

Karol grabbed her arm and pulled her from the street to the door. "Get inside."

She knew better than to contradict him, especially after he had been drinking.

Farther west on Krochmalna, a series of blasts sent walls tumbling into the street and a wave of smoke and dust hurtling toward them.

"Quick," Karol ordered, and shoved her inside. He held onto the door behind them as the neighbors tried to get in.

The choking billows swirled past them, coating those still outside with grit and ash.

"Fools," Karol said. "Let them suffer. Look out for yourself."

A volley of curses followed them up the stairs when the door finally opened. The stragglers hacked and coughed behind them.

"Shut up, idiots," he shouted at the ghostly figures on the steps. "This is a war—not a circus."

He slammed the apartment door.

Dejected and unhappy that her husband was drunk so early in the day, Janka dropped to the sofa and stared at him. The work shirt and pants she had washed in the sink on Sunday and pressed with an iron warmed on the stove were covered with mud and ash and smelled of smoke. They would have to be cleaned again by morning for Karol to return to work.

He sat in his favorite chair near the window and lit a cigarette. "Why the hell were you in the street?"

"I was afraid the building would collapse."

"You can be so stupid." He puffed on the cigarette and then exhaled a white spiral of smoke.

"I'm afraid of the bombs." She didn't know whether to look upon him with pity or hate. When they'd met, Janka had thought Karol the most handsome man in the world. His jaw was strong, almost sculpted, his hair full, black, and wavy, his eyes a devilish blue. She considered herself lucky to find such a good-looking man who would even look her way. Even her parents had told her how fortunate she was to find a good Catholic with a decent job, who would support her in marriage.

"You won't do any better," her mother had told her.

When Janka looked in the mirror every morning, her brief courtship with Karol came rushing back to her. Lately, she always looked as if she had just gotten up. Her hair was an unruly mess because she couldn't afford to have it done even by the most inexpensive of shops; she hated her white complexion, too pale from lack of sun and her wifely confinement in their three-room apartment. Under Karol's strict control of the household finances, there was no money for niceties like makeup or new dresses. Early in their marriage, he had told her that children were out of the question—Catholicism be damned. "We can't afford any brats," he said. "We're poor enough as it is."

He had used contraception at first, despite her objections. Then the sex had dried up. She often wondered if he took comfort from other women now, particularly those who loitered around the bar where he drank.

Why had he even looked at her in the first place? As the years went on, one answer always rushed into her mind. Karol viewed her as property, something to be possessed and manipulated— perhaps he'd thought that her parents had more money than they did. She was vulnerable and intimidated by men. He dominated her with ease, with a look, with the harsh words that came from his mouth. As hard as she tried, she couldn't break free. There was no place to go; no one, not even her parents, would take her back, because they believed a wife's place was at her husband's side. Now the war had broken out. She shuddered to think that perhaps he needed her—even a little bit.

"Get me a drink," Karol ordered.

She rose obediently, knowing that to resist was useless. He would only beat her down with words. He had never struck her, although he had come close with his right fist poised above her head. She didn't know what she would do if he did.

She walked to the cabinet over the stove, opened it, and withdrew a bottle of vodka. Even liquor was becoming scarce since the Nazis had invaded. That thought caused a smile to break out on her face—with her back turned to him. She got a glass and tipped the bottle in a healthy pour.

"The vodka's almost gone," she said, and returned the liquor to the cupboard.

"That's a crime," he said, stubbing out his cigarette. "Hell with the Nazis. I wish they'd get it over with. We can't win. Conquer and divide the spoils. Maybe I'll get some liquor that way."

"You'll be on your knees in front of them." She handed him the glass.

He swigged the vodka. "Maybe . . . survival . . . only survival."

Janka took her place on the couch and sighed. "They'll starve us to death, too."

"You worry too much. We'll get along. They like Catholics."

"How do you know? They hate Poles."

"They'll kill some—the ones that resist—the ones that don't come around to the Nazi way of doing things. The government should have known. No need to go to war. They'll overrun us like they did Austria and the Sudetenland." He clutched his glass and raised it toward the ceiling. "All hail the conquering heroes."

Janka leaned back against the now scarred and rickety sofa her parents had given them as a wedding present. "I'll look for a job when they *conquer* us."

They stared at each other with nothing more to say. The apartment walls rumbled as the bombs continued to fall.

Less than a week later, Poland surrendered and the Wehrmacht marched into Warsaw at dusk.

Janka watched the procession of troops and artillery from her window. The Nazis had spared the copper plant, because they knew it would be useful later. Karol was in his usual seat at the bar, so she viewed the city's fall alone.

She found it hard to believe that the parade below was happening at all; the view of Krochmalna struck her like a horrific nightmare—only it wasn't in her sleep, it was real. A neighbor had told her that what was going on in front of her was nothing compared to other events in the city. Streams of the defeated Polish Army had flooded into Warsaw, along with Polish and Jewish refugees from the surrounding towns and countryside.

She pulled back the lace curtains she'd made for the apartment and stood safely back from the glass, preferring not to be as obvious as the boy across the street had been six days earlier during the bombings.

A German tank rumbled down Krochmalna, followed by a small unit of goose-stepping Wehrmacht soldiers, rifles poised hand to shoulder, their gray-green uniforms and steel helmets blending with the dying light. A few men attired in slightly darker uniforms and long leather coats patrolled the street as well, swiveling their heads in time to their steps. These men looked particularly dangerous—something about them screamed "evil"—as if their eyes could pierce the walls of the buildings they hadn't destroyed.

Behind them, an open-bed truck rolled over the cobblestones, carrying even more soldiers in its back, their rifles pointing to the sky.

Her gut churned as she contemplated a future under German rule. Karol had told her of the rumors—how Hitler might treat the Jews. In fact, some neighbors had voiced their opinions on the subject vehemently. The country would be better off without them, they said, noting that it would be a good thing to get rid of them. They were like lice, parasites feeding on the lifeblood of others, taking jobs away from deserving Poles and Catholics, stealing the hard-earned money of other workers to enrich their own pockets. Her husband had nodded his head upon hearing this, making his feelings clear. She had turned away, not willing to show her disgust to him or the others.

Now, as she turned her head from side to side, Warsaw's downfall struck her in the face and she wondered what in the world it was all for. Hitler's ambitious war had destroyed a beautiful capital city, killed thousands of innocent civilians, and forced the surrender of the government—but for what? Janka had heard of no grand plan for Poland and its citizens. And what was to be done with the Jews—or the Catholics and the Poles that Hitler had no use for? She had no answer to those questions, but her stomach clenched as she considered the frightening possibilities. He was a madman who saw no obstacles to his power. With the people of Germany behind him, he felt invincible—of this she was certain.

She turned a few degrees from the window, horrified by what she saw, hoping she could overcome her anxiety enough to eat a bit of supper; instead, a blur in the corner of her eye captured her attention. She swung around. A young man raced west on Krochmalna and she immediately sensed who it was. She knew this boy, his lean, compact form, the black pants and white shirt confirming his identity. He shouldn't be out—it was too dangerous.

Without hesitating, she grabbed her coat and raced down the stairs.

Open the door slowly. Walk out on the street—don't let them notice you.

She waited until a truck filled with soldiers had passed before stepping out in the evening air. The smoke from still-smoldering fires, combined with the exhaust from the military machinery, swept into her nose and she fought the urge to sneeze. The soldiers had passed her by, and none were approaching from the other end of Krochmalna.

Down the block, near the house where the boy lived, someone struggled in the shadows. One of the long-coated officers held the child in his grasp, shaking him so violently she thought the young man, who was clutching his chest tightly, might be ripped apart. She ran toward them.

"Karol! Karol!" She could think of no other name from her racing mind.

The officer released his grip and drew a pistol from a holster underneath his coat.

"Halten Sie!"

Janka knew enough German to know that the officer had ordered her to stop. She could also tell by the frantic tone of his voice that he meant what he said. He turned to look at her and the light from a window crossed his face. He was a handsome man with a square jaw and firm mouth, but his eyes fired into her like bullets.

"Karol, my son, I told you not to go out this evening. You had no business disturbing this polite German officer." She spoke in Polish, hoping the man would understand some of it.

As if rehearsed, he replied in Polish. "Soon, you will learn German."

"I know a little and would be happy to learn more."

He grabbed the youth's arm, and asked in broken Polish, "Is this your son?"

She nodded. "I sent him out on an errand. He's so fascinated by the war and everything National Socialist. He's been watching your advance with pleasure every day."

The officer turned to the boy. "You shouldn't be out now. Where do you live?"

Janka and the boy pointed to the same house. "A few doors from here," the boy said.

"All right, go on, but be careful. Your world will change very soon—for the better." He re-holstered his pistol and strode off to catch up with his companions.

Janka put her arm around the young man, turning him toward the house and forcing him to walk quickly.

"I saw you on your balcony last Monday—I'm sure of it."

"My name is Aaron." He clutched something under his shirt and then withdrew a white package. "I was getting chicken from the restaurant where my father works. He buys it and my mother cooks it."

They reached his home. Aaron stood for a moment before speaking. "Would you like to come up and meet my mother?"

"Not now—it's too dangerous. You need to be more careful."

"We didn't know the Germans were marching in today."

"You must be prepared at all times now that we've been conquered." She put her hand on his shoulder. "I'll meet your mother soon. You live on the fourth floor?"

Aaron studied her, taking her in from head to toe with his eyes. "Are you Polish Catholic?"

"Yes."

"We are Polish Jews. Our name is Majewski."

Janka thought of what her neighbors had said about the Jews and thrust her hands into her pockets. "Aaron Majewski. I like your name. It reminds me of the Old Testament. Wasn't Aaron—"

"—the brother of Moses."

Aaron withdrew a yarmulke from his pocket, touched the mezuzah on the right side of the door, held his fingers to his lips and kissed them.

"I am Janka Danek. Watch out for the Nazis." She pointed to the disappearing column of soldiers, then turned and hurried home. Heart pounding, she stopped at the top of the stairs and wondered why she had come to the boy's rescue. It was unlike her to be so impulsive, to put herself in danger, but the feeling that she had done *something*, a small, brief exchange with a German soldier that might have saved a boy, exhilarated her. She was tired of being nothing—a servant to a husband who loved the bottle more than he loved her.

God didn't want man to kill, she thought. God wanted man to help and love others. That's why she had run to Aaron's aid. It was the right thing to do, and she had done it willingly in her own small way.

CHAPTER 3

Stefa thought her parents tried their best to observe the September holidays despite the bombings and the rumors of the pending surrender of the Polish Army.

Perla lit the candles at sunset on Rosh Hashanah Eve and recited the blessing and shehecheyanu benediction, barely holding herself together as she intoned the holy words. Because of the bombings, Izreal decided that it was too dangerous to go to synagogue for the evening service and instead exchanged the holiday greetings at home with the family.

The eve of Yom Kippur had a similar melancholy feel. Perla was distressed most of the day because the family was again unable to attend synagogue. Instead, she lit candles in memory of the dead as Izreal recited prayers and solemn offerings. Normally, he would have performed kaporos before sunset and slaughtered a chicken according to ritual. The fowl would be cooked and eaten for dinner. Stefa knew the meaning of the ancient ceremony and how the life of the bird was to be a substitute for the death and sins of the bearer.

"I wish we had a chicken," Stefa said. *If ever a bird can be substituted for a human life, now is the time.*

The Day of Atonement passed in prayer and fasting. However, Aaron was able to break the fast because he was under thirteen years of age. Stefa concluded after the meditation upon atonement that forgiving the Nazis was ridiculous. Despite such a day, enemies weren't going to become friends. And for the first time since the war started, Stefa thought about Hanna and what she might be doing in London. She could forgive her sister's defiance, her differences with her parents, and also the spats she got into with her brother, but how could she forgive Hitler for his indiscriminate killing? For that matter, how could she forgive the German people, or Nazi sympathizers no matter where they resided, for supporting such a cruel madman? She had no idea what her parents thought about these matters and she didn't dare bring up such questions on a holy day; instead, she sought to control her emotions as the silent hours enveloped her.

Before Yom Kippur, Izreal blessed Stefa and Aaron, in preparation for the Kol Nidre declaration. Again, Stefa thought of her sister and also Daniel, a man she had grown to love. In past years, they would have been at the Kol Nidre service, but this year Izreal felt it his duty to speak the words at home.

As her father declared that vows and obligations not carried out are forgiven, null, and void, Stefa pondered the true meaning of the declaration. If a Jew was forced or compelled to do something contrary to Jewish religion, Kol Nidre voided that obligation. When Jews were subjugated as Christians, many, in order to save their own lives, continued to secretly practice their religion. Hanna wasn't forgiven because of these words—she had left of her own accord—but Jews, under normal circumstances, according to Jewish law, respected the declaration's tradition. But what if she and Daniel resisted the Nazi occupation? Wouldn't the Kol Nidre declaration apply to them? What if she or Daniel had to kill a man, or even a woman?

She shuddered in her chair for a moment as the dark sensation of killing filled her. Her father had killed nearly every day of his life when he was a butcher, but those deaths were animals destined to find a place on the table. She looked at Izreal, his prayer shawl draped over his shoulders, his head rocking as he silently mouthed a blessing. Could he kill a man—and forgive himself?

Now they were in the time of Sukkos, the Feast of the Tabernacles, a holiday for rejoicing. Now that the Nazis were in

Warsaw, building outdoor sukka booths would be risky, if not forbidden.

Late afternoon on the last day of Sukkos, Stefa noticed German officers standing outside the building. Her father was at work and Aaron had not arrived home from yeshiva.

"Mama, look." She peered over the balcony and motioned for her mother to come to her side.

"Who are they?" Perla asked, the pinched concern in her voice coming through.

"I don't know, but they look important . . . and dangerous. They're not soldiers."

Three men, two attired in gray uniforms, the other in a brown suit, studied the names listed on the apartment directory. One of the men took a knife from the side of his coat and pried the wooden mezuzah from its place on the doorframe. He threw it on the ground and crushed it with his boot, while the man in the brown suit scribbled in a notebook.

She pulled her mother inside, not wishing to take the chance of being spotted. She closed the glass-paned doors, and stood looking, holding her breath for a moment, listening for footsteps coming up the stairs. Instead, she saw her brother approaching from the east on Krochmalna.

"Wait inside," she told her mother, opening the doors as quietly as possible, hoping that her brother would look toward the balcony.

Aaron, attired in his school clothes and wearing his yarmulke, lifted his head briefly after spotting the men, and then dropped his gaze. In those precious seconds, Stefa waved her hands to the right, urging her brother to keep walking past their apartment.

To her relief, he did so. She crept inside and watched from a window as her brother disappeared behind a pile of debris that had yet to be cleared from the sidewalk.

"Who was that?" her mother asked. "Aaron?" Perla grasped a strand of hair that had fallen from her kerchief and pushed it back in place. "Did you see him?"

Stefa nodded. "He walked past. He saw the Germans at the door." She studied her mother's face as Perla drifted toward the sofa that had been placed years ago against an inside wall so the tufted green fabric wouldn't fade in the sun. The weak afternoon light showcased how far her mother had diminished since the war began. Perla had always been slight, always thinner than her daughters, but the bones had begun to show under the flesh of her arms. Her face had taken on a chalky appearance; the woes of the world etched and colored in the creases that spider-webbed her skin, along with the dark circles underneath her eyes, her hair now streaked with wisps of gray.

Stefa sat beside her mother, both of them listening for any movement on the stairs. Perla grasped her daughter's hands, her mother's fingers feeling cold and bony against her own.

They waited, listening as the wall clock ticked in their ears and the minutes dragged by. Finally, they heard shouting and pounding on doors, some creaking open. The doors then closed, usually with a thud.

Even without hearing the steps, she knew the men were in the hall—the crackle of the clothes, the swish of the coat against the air heralded their presence. Stefa wondered if they were noting the mezuzahs on all the doors. She could sense one of them balling his fist, heaving it toward the door with force, nearly breaking it down from the blow. A booted foot was next, splintering the knob and the lock, the men gaining entrance, pouring inside.

A severe knock brought her back to her senses. They were at the front door across the hall—that of her neighbor Mrs. Rosewicz. She was a widow, more than eighty years old, in ill health for several months, and had lived on Krochmalna for more than forty years.

One of the men shouted in Polish. "Open up!"

Perla drew in a sharp breath and Stefa held a finger to her lips. She thought of Daniel and what he would do in this situation. He would charge the men, maybe even fight them, forcing them back down the stairs. Ridiculous! A naïve fantasy at best. Daniel was unarmed and no match for three Nazis.

The pounding continued until the neighbor's door opened and the small voice of Mrs. Rosewicz filtered into the hall. Stefa whispered to her mother to remain seated. She walked on cat feet to her own door, placing her ear firmly against the wood.

Mrs. Rosewicz spoke first, asking the men what they wanted.

"Who are *you*?" one of them gruffly responded.

The neighbor responded in a soft voice.

"Do you live alone?"

"Yes. My husband is dead. My two sons live in Kraków."

"They are Jews . . . like you." The man stated this as a fact, not as a question.

Mrs. Rosewicz didn't answer.

"Step aside," the man ordered.

A small commotion ensued as the woman muttered a feeble objection. Stefa heard muted voices, furniture moving about, scraping against the wooden floor. The neighbor and the men continued talking, but Stefa couldn't make out what they were saying.

She walked back to the couch to join her mother as the door closed.

Their door rattled under an onslaught of heavy knocks.

Stefa started to answer, but Perla, terror gleaming in her eyes, clutched her arm.

"Mother, we must," Stefa whispered.

Perla shook her head, her face gripped with panic.

The door knob rattled—then the noise stopped. A terrible silence enveloped them. Stefa prayed that her brother had kept away from the building, that he had noticed the men had gone inside.

They held their breaths as the quiet dragged on.

"We'll come back later," one of the men said in Polish. Finally, they descended the stairs, air whooshing through the hall as they left.

After a few minutes, Stefa rose from the couch, walked to the balcony and looked out upon the street. The three men marched in near unison to the east, the direction Aaron had come from.

"They're gone," Stefa said. "I'll check on Mrs. Rosewicz."

Perla muttered, "Be careful, daughter," knotted her fists, and stared through the window.

The hall was empty and quiet—with no indication that the men had ever been there. They had disappeared like the demons of a bad dream, only they were real. She had seen them and heard their voices, the memory burned into her mind.

Stefa tapped on her neighbor's door, asking in a whisper, "Mrs. Rosewicz?"

After a few moments, the woman responded with questions of her own. "Stefa? Is it you?"

"Yes."

The door creaked open and the woman's sagging face appeared around the edge.

"Are you all right?" Stefa touched the mezuzah, and then kissed her fingers.

"Yes . . . come in. See what they did."

Nothing had been damaged in the apartment, but everything looked askew, off-kilter, from the usual spotless rooms that Mrs. Rosewicz kept. The couch had been moved from the wall, the closet doors were flung open. The men had rifled through the pantry.

"They thought someone might be hiding here," she said, shaking her head. "Can you imagine me—an old lady—trying to hide someone from the Germans?"

Stefa tensed. If the Nazis occupied the city for any length of time, she feared that question would become routine. Could the German war machine be in Poland for years to come? She cast the thought from her mind and offered to help the woman put back the furniture. "Let me take care of it," she told the grateful Mrs. Rosewicz.

Fifteen minutes later everything in the apartment was where it was before: The couch now rested again against the wall, the closet and pantry doors were secured, the mussed bed made up, and the rugs straightened. Displaying nothing but intimidation, the Nazis had made a mess.

After saying good-bye, Stefa stepped into the hall and nearly collided with Aaron as he sprinted up the stairs.

"Did you see them?" he asked in a giddy voice breaking toward manhood.

She ushered her brother into the apartment. Perla rose from the couch and rushed to hug her son.

"Yes, but we kept quiet," Stefa answered. "We didn't let them in."

"Good," Aaron said. "They would have torn up our apartment."

Stefa patted her brother's shoulder. "Yes, but they will come back. We must be prepared."

Perla sat in a chair and covered her face with her hands. "How? How can we stop them?"

"They are Nazis, Mother," Stefa said.

Perla shook her head. "I don't want to speak or hear the name—no misfortune shall come to this house. Why summon the devil?"

"Mother, we may have to challenge them—as best we can." Stefa smiled to encourage her mother and spoke with a lighter tone. "Don't worry. Father will know what to do. We have two men to protect us." Even as she spoke, she doubted her words, but her mother's well-being was more important than telling a white lie.

Aaron smiled at his sister. "I turn thirteen in March."

"Yes, you're a man as far as I'm concerned."

Perla scowled. "He's a boy, until he's declared a man."

Stefa retreated to her room, her mind racing with the thought of a German occupation. The Majewskis needed a plan.

Daniel would know what to do, if only she could see him. She sat on her bed and imagined Hanna enjoying life in London. Had Hanna forsworn the Jewish faith? Maybe her sister smoked, drank, dated men, and perhaps had even changed her hair color. She didn't know whether these things were true. Communication between them had been sparse. Her mother had received a few letters, and the only words spoken by Perla upon opening them were, "She sends her good wishes."

She leaned back, placing her head on the pillow, as Hanna floated like an angel over her. All these thoughts she held without malice or jealousy toward her sister. Hanna had chosen the life she wanted and Lucy and Lawrence had chosen to make life comfortable for their niece. Her mother and father couldn't change that.

Did Hanna think of them often? Stefa's eyes closed.

Not far away on Krochmalna, Janka walked home in the dying light after a day of window-shopping. She thrust the apartment key into the lock, and already knew what she would find. Karol, still attired in his dirty work uniform, was stretched across the couch, one arm slung lazily across his eyes, his snoring rumbling through the room.

She didn't dare wake him—with one sniff she could tell he had been drinking. The biting odor of cheap vodka permeated the room. Disturbing his late-afternoon drunk would incite rage and name-calling—something she didn't want to hear today.

Her morning had been discouraging enough without additional stress from her husband. Had she capitulated to the sights and sounds of Warsaw, it would have been easy to lose composure. Her travels took her past destroyed buildings she once admired, and her nostrils filled with the acrid smells of oil and smoke, the lingering odor of explosives still clinging to the air, the gut-wrenching stench of dead horses in the gutters and bodies not yet lifted from the rubble. Only the opportunity to be out of the apartment, to dress up a little and use a bit of makeup, to take a walk despite the destruction, to see others who had survived the bombings, kept her sadness in check. Of course, she was also struck by the increasing Nazi presence—one on every street corner, if not one in the middle of a block as well. The tanks, trucks, and troops continued to pour in.

The worst part had been her failure to find a job. Many shops were still closed and those that weren't had no need of her limited skills. Only one—a Jewish clothier who sought a "qualified seamstress"—seemed a possibility, but she had turned away from the hand-lettered poster pasted on the window, head down, clutching her purse, feeling that many more women, particularly Jews, were much more capable of sewing than she.

She resisted the urge to fall into despair while trudging home, knowing that Karol had probably stopped off at the bar after work. The routine of her life was maddening, even as she reluctantly counted her blessings of a husband and an apartment, however miserable they might be.

Karol was at home when she returned. Janka crept past him in her usual manner, although he rarely woke up from his liquor-induced stupors, and if he did he usually snorted, turned on his side, and fell asleep once more. He demanded, however, that his supper always be ready when he awoke, almost predictably at eight in the evening. Then he would eat, undress, sometimes take a bath—even less likely now because of the water shortage—and then crawl into bed without so much as a kiss.

In the bedroom, she took off her coat, placing it softly over a hanger in the closet, and then changed into another dress and pair of shoes. The bedroom clock's hands were poised at seven and the trials of an unfinished supper called.

Creeping to the cupboard, she found a few tins of soup and some canned milk. Supplies were diminishing as the Nazi foothold increased, and there were rumors of rationing, even bans on the sale of meat. Today, she hadn't had the time to go to the market and stand in the long line. Karol would be angry when he discovered he had no chicken or meat for dinner. It couldn't be helped. The vegetable bin contained a few scrawny carrots and several medium-sized potatoes, one of which had begun to sprout greenish-white tendrils. Her husband would have to settle for a fried potato and beef broth, not exactly a meal to set before a king.

After lifting a frying pan quietly from the cupboard, dipping her fingers into a half-finished can of lard, and spreading the grease on the bottom of the cast-iron skillet, she struck a match, lit the stove, and wiped her hand on a towel.

She had collected two jugs of water which had to last as long as possible. Janka didn't bother to wash the potato because water was precious; instead, she wiped it off with a damp cloth and began quietly slicing it on the kitchen counter already perforated by the knife's sharp edge.

The grease sizzled, but not enough to wake her husband. She was about to drop the potato slices into the hot oil when a loud knock sent her heart thumping in her chest.

Snorting, Karol awoke. "What the hell is going on?" His voice rose from a sleepy growl to irritation.

The door thumped again. Karol, still half-asleep, struggled to lift himself from his slumbers. "Well, God damn it, answer it! If it's the shitty neighbors, they'll think twice before knocking on this door again."

Janka put down the knife, turned off the stove, and then smoothed her dress as she walked to the door.

Three men stood in front of her. Two were attired in the gray uniforms of German officers, the other wore a coat, which partially covered a brown suit.

"Frau Danek?" the man in the brown suit asked in German.

She nodded as the others focused on her husband rising from the couch. The men in black looked at him casually, but with interest, much as a train conductor might view a passenger searching for a ticket.

"May we come in?" the brown-suited man asked in perfect Polish.

Janka turned to her husband, who with a nod of his head gave the men permission to enter his home—she suspected that "no" would have been an unacceptable answer.

"What can I do for you gentlemen?" her smiling husband asked while emphasizing the obsequious manner of his question. Karol planted his hands firmly against the couch and got up, pretending to be sober. Janka had seen this behavior before.

The three men stepped inside and she closed the door behind them.

"A few questions," the man in the brown suit continued. "As the founders of a new government for the Polish people, we are conducting a census. This will take a short time, while the officers accompanying me take a brief look around. The National Socialist Party wants to make sure you are comfortable. I'm sure you have no objection."

Karol nodded and pointed to the couch. "Care to sit?"

The man eyed the somewhat soiled green fabric and wrinkled his nose. "No. I'd prefer to stand." The officers set off to search the apartment.

"There's not much to see," her husband told them as they passed.

"Let's start with your names."

Karol shot Janka a look—*keep your mouth shut while I talk.* "Karol and Janka Danek."

"Where are you employed?"

"At the copper processing plant not far away, west on Krochmalna."

"I know exactly where it is. Good . . . an essential worker. And your wife?"

The man scribbled in his notebook, ignoring Janka. She didn't dare answer him or interrupt the questioning.

"She is a housewife."

"Taking care of her husband—all good women should. In Germany, women bear children and offer undying loyalty to the Reich . . . and their husbands. Some may work, but only if the Reich needs them to leave their husband's side."

A grin broke out on Karol's face and he sat again on the couch. The wardrobe door slammed in the bedroom.

"That's the way it should be," her husband replied. "My Janka is a good wife and forever loyal—even to our new masters. We will do whatever you ask . . . I may even be of service to you."

The man stared at Karol with piercing, raptor-like eyes. "You get ahead of yourself, Herr Danek. I'm cautious of men who fall over themselves when they don't even know what we expect or want. Still . . . I will make a note in my book. An announcement will be made shortly that all Polish men and women of working age must be employed. Your wife will have to find a job."

The two officers returned from their search of the small apartment and stood by the questioner. He looked at them, his face already signaling what he wanted to know.

"Nothing," one of the men said.

"A few more questions. Are you Jews?"

Karol laughed and pointed to the bedroom. "Did you see the crucifix hanging over our bed? Jews? No, I hate the dirty scum. They're scoundrels, taking our money and jobs. The whole lot of them should be shot as far as I'm concerned." He looked at one of the other men.

While not so much as lifting an eyebrow, the man penned additional notes. "You are Catholic?"

Karol nodded.

"It seems odd that you have no children. Catholics, like the Jews, reproduce."

Her husband's face flushed and for the first time he appeared as if he had no response to the man's questions.

Janka broke in. "I'm barren."

The three Germans turned to her with looks that ranged from pity to disgust. The man in the brown suit seemed the most sympathetic.

"I see."

"We want to have children, but we can't," Janka said, continuing the lie. Karol was the one who had always been opposed to children: they were messy, took up too much time, and devoured the family's money. The real reason for his distaste was his drinking, and its required freedom from familial responsibility; he didn't want to spend precious resources on anything but liquor.

"Hush, Janka," Karol said. "The man doesn't want to know that."

"No, it's useful information," he replied. "One last question. Have you ever befriended Jews or given them comfort?"

"That would never happen in this house," Karol said quickly, his eyes widening as if shocked by the implication. His gaze shifted to Janka. "My wife wouldn't either—you can be sure of that. We are Poles—Catholic Poles who understand what you're trying to do in Warsaw."

The man closed his book. "And what is that?"

"I don't know, but I support it," Karol said.

"See that it remains that way." He turned toward the door with the others, but before opening it, he looked back and said, "It would be helpful for you to learn German, especially you, Herr Danek. Most helpful."

In a moment they were gone, banging on a neighbor's door.

Karol rose from the couch, charging toward her. "Are you mad? Why did you say you were barren, you fool?" His red face matched his bloodshot eyes. He raised his hand, as he sometimes did when he was angry, and kept it poised above her face.

She turned, not backing down. "Did you want them to know the real reason? The Nazis will make *anything* their business, including why we don't have children. I told a lie to protect *you*. It was obvious you couldn't think of anything to say."

Karol's face softened and he lowered his hand. "I didn't think of it that way."

"No, you didn't, and it could have gotten us in trouble."

Rubbing his forehead, he skulked back to the couch and sank into it. "What's for supper?"

"Broth and a fried potato." She struck a match and lit the stove again under the cold grease.

"Broth and a potato. I should have stayed at the bar."

"Then you would have missed a visit from our saviors," she said with her back to him.

He snickered. "Don't go near a Jew. Do you hear me?"

She nodded, knowing that she had already made a potentially deadly mistake.

CHAPTER 4

The weather turned colder at the end of October in Croydon, the trees had lost most of their leaves. Even the small willow in the sheltered side garden displayed a sickly yellow color on its drooping branches. It remained, still rooted, because Lawrence had not yet received the parts of the Anderson shelter he had yet to build.

Hanna had written three letters to her mother since the German invasion, but had not received a reply. The news from Poland continued to shock her, while most of her English girlfriends took it in stride and told her not to worry—Hitler wouldn't get far and an all-out war with the Nazis would be over as soon as Britain was able to ramp up its fighting forces.

Through her uncle, she was able to find an afternoon shift four days a week in an antiquarian bookstore, mostly Tuesday through Friday, with some weekend work as required. The old gentleman who owned the shop, Mr. Cheever, was a pensioner who rarely stepped inside the store he had founded before the Great War. He kept it running for the benefit of his long-standing customers. His family was well funded in other endeavors and didn't want, or didn't need, a musty old curiosity shop.

Hanna loved the fragile, papery smell of the books, the crackle of the pages when turned, the insights and the drama that unfolded inside them. The most valuable of them were kept locked in a glass cupboard at the back of the store with Mr.

Cheever holding the single key. Only a few select clients ever viewed these books—by appointment only with the owner. The most prized possession in the shop was a second edition copy of *The Monk*, by Matthew Lewis, published in 1796. In her two weeks on the job, no customer had requested to see any rare item.

She also loved browsing through the store when no customers were present, touching the red, blue, green, and black bindings, leafing through them with reverence, feeling the rough or slick texture of the pages between her fingers. The books, mostly used, in good condition, at a modest price, had been lovingly catalogued on the worn oak shelves according to subject matter.

There were spaces for fiction, history, medicine, art, business, languages, and many more categories. The languages section held special interest for her, particularly the books written in German and the few in Hebrew. Her mother had encouraged her innate ability somewhat, recognizing her proclivity for speech. Polish and Yiddish had come naturally to her through the family. The leap to German, because of its similarity to Yiddish, was undertaken without much difficulty. In her youth, of her own accord, she had chosen to study some of the great nineteenth-century texts of German writers. She found herself lost in their words, aided by a German dictionary, during the long winter nights in Warsaw.

While she was working, her girlfriends, whom she got to know through Lucy's friendships with their mothers, would drop in at different times depending on their own school or work schedules. The sisters, Margaret and Ruth Thompson, often visited together. Margaret, a vivacious, long-haired redhead of the flashing smile and devil-may-care attitude, reminded her of a movie starlet. She worked as a clerk for a Croydon barrister, although she'd told Hanna many times that the job didn't suit her. Most of the time, she missed the "grand excitement" of the court cases, her duties relegated to reception, stenography, and filing. She was a young woman with greater expectations on her mind, although she wasn't quite clear what those expectations were. Hanna suspected they included marrying well.

Margaret's sister, Ruth, was somewhat like her elder sibling, but much more no-nonsense, with her feet planted solidly on the ground. Ruth, not quite as tall as her sister, had auburn hair, more reddish than brown, and a pleasing oval face. She worked in ladies' wear at a local department store. Of Ruth's dreams, Hanna had no idea. Her friend seemed more than happy with her job and position in life. Hanna also suspected that Ruth wanted to marry as well, but was biding her time for the right man, moneyed or not.

The final young woman of the quartet was Betty Martin, who, despite her petite stature, championed the war effort and wanted more than anything to volunteer for any kind of military service available to women. When they saw each other, Betty gave Hanna the most up-to-date information about the war and had already started a knitting club comprised of local women. The club made socks and scarves and other items they felt the uniformed men could use, in addition to mending their own clothes as a conservation measure. Although Betty had asked her, Hanna wasn't a member of the club. Stefa was much better with a needle and hook than she, and, frankly, she found it boring to sit for hours stitching, mending, and gossiping about the war and men.

Betty adopted a kind of military style in her dress—trousers and a jacket—and carried a large handbag in case family belongings needed to be stuffed into it during the anticipated Nazi air raids. She kept her mascara in place, her cheeks rouged, and her long black hair netted, as she scanned the skies for German bombers.

Hanna was at the store late one Friday afternoon when she spotted Betty through the large glass window. Her friend stubbed out the cigarette she was smoking and inserted a piece of gum in her mouth instead, dropping the glittery foil wrapping in her jacket pocket. As Betty opened the door, the shop bell tinkled overhead.

Her friend's mouth curled into an odd smile, as if Betty knew something, or anticipated something, which Hanna was soon to be privy to.

"How's business?" Betty asked, sidling up to the counter.

"Quiet today. How are you?"

"Couldn't be better, but I'll be much better tonight at the pub."

Her evening plans intrigued Hanna and she leaned over the counter toward her friend. "Really? Do you have an engagement?"

"A date with a bloke?" Betty asked demurely.

"Yes."

"No." She smacked her gum. "I wish . . . but you should come along. I'd like you to meet someone."

Suspecting that Betty was trying to arrange a date for her, Hanna shook her head. "Not tonight. I'd rather be at home."

"Too many of those and you'll turn into a mouse—we'll only be able to get you out of your hole with cheese." She smiled, her white teeth circled by an oval of red lipstick. "And it's not a bloke . . . if that's what you thought. It's a woman. I've told her about you."

Hanna sat in the chair behind the counter, fascinated by what sounded like a mystery plot. "Go on."

Betty plopped her oversized bag on the counter, opened it, and withdrew a piece of paper from her bag. "I won't go into it now. You close up at five?"

"Yes."

"Meet me at the Stag's Horn at seven sharp. The phone number and address are on the slip, in case you can't make it." She handed Hanna the folded paper. "Don't be mousy. We'll expect you. It's important that you come." Betty blew her a kiss, picked up her bag, and walked out the door.

Hanna opened the note. Everything she needed to know was written in Betty's neat hand. In fact, Hanna knew exactly where the pub was located in central Croydon. What she didn't understand was why meeting this mystery woman was so important, as Betty put it. She had planned to spend the evening after supper with her aunt and uncle, but this engagement seemed too interesting to pass up.

The Stag's Horn had been constructed centuries ago near the crossing of two major roads in Croydon. Its slate roof, old bricks, comfy booths, and long wooden tables had heard and preserved the laughter, tears, and secrets of locals for generations. It wasn't the only pub in the city, but, as the oldest, it remained a popular gathering spot for those who loved Croydon and celebrated its history.

Hanna made her excuses to her aunt and uncle and struck off for the pub after a change of clothes and a refresh of the makeup she had worn to work. After nearly ten months in London, she was still uncertain that her choices in dress and cosmetics were correct—although no one had said anything against her. Her aunt had guided her with a gentle hand, but that was to be expected from someone in the family. No disparaging remarks had been made by her girlfriends. She considered herself somewhat in the middle of taste—not as glamorous as Margaret on one end, or as severe as Betty on the other. Her emotional state was the problem.

It took courage to leave Warsaw, but had she really left it behind? The traditions, the teachings of Judaism, a life with her mother, father, sister, and brother couldn't be erased in ten short months. Yet, she had tried her best to lose the trappings of her old life, even sneaking a cigarette now and then, trying beer and shots of liquor instead of a glass of wine, experimenting with hair color, trying various shades of lipstick, powder, and rouge, all in the interest of making herself beautiful and different from her old self. Hanna had attempted to banish modesty and all that it implied.

Yet, as she walked to the pub, doubts remained. Her father appeared before her at times with gentle eyes; at other times, glowering with an almost demonic intensity. That strictness of religion, that dogged suffocation with no letup, had fired her thoughts of separation in the first place. What was wrong with making a new life? Answering that question was harder than anyone could ever know.

She stopped for a moment outside the Stag's Horn and looked through a crack in the blackout curtains into the warm yellow light that seeped through the window. Laughter. Smiling faces. A haze of cigarette smoke. Pints of ale, sipped or swigged. All that awaited her when she stepped inside. The pub was as far removed on this Friday night from her family's Sabbath eve as Warsaw was from London. The thought froze her and tamped down any joy she attempted to feel.

Her hands chilled by the late October wind, she clutched her coat collar and peered into the sliver of light, looking for Betty and the unidentified woman. She spotted them in a corner booth near a crackling fireplace. Her friend had added a surprise— a handsome army man with a thin mustache, probably in his midtwenties, who sat across from the two women.

The thought of turning back crossed her mind, but she gathered her courage and grabbed the brass door handle. The pub's warmth enveloped her, eliminating the chill from her hands and face. She took off her coat, hung it on a hook near the door, and walked toward them, clutching her handbag at her side.

Betty spotted her and with a vigorous wave of her arm, called her over.

Hanna stepped up to the booth. The only available seat was to the right of the soldier. Standing, he extricated himself from the cramped confines and offered her the place next to him. She scooted across the polished oak plank and found herself cozy and warm, but feeling a bit cornered.

"Have a pint?" Betty asked.

"Why not?" Hanna said, bowing to convention. A tall glass of the dark brew, as warm as the temperature inside the pub, sat in front of everyone at the table.

Betty raised her hand and a waitress drifted over, a slight girl with dark hair and eyes who looked as if she had worked too many hours. Everyone ordered another round.

After an awkward pause, Betty tapped her glass using the underside of the ring on her right hand. "Hanna Majewski—or should I say Richardson—I'd like you to meet Rita Wright and Phillip Kelley."

"Hello. Nice to meet you." Hanna found herself at odds, crushing her hands against her purse, unsure what to say next.

"A pleasure to meet you," the soldier replied with a smile.

She smiled back, having no idea what he did or what his rank was in the armed services.

Rita Wright, on the other hand, studied her with a stare so determined that Hanna shifted her eyes toward Betty.

"It's somewhat bitter this evening," Hanna said, attempting to start an innocuous conversation that would draw attention away from her.

"Not really," Rita stated bluntly.

Hanna blushed and lowered her gaze to the table. After another awkward moment, she thought of what her father used to tell her when she was teased as a girl in Warsaw for being too tall and gangly: "No one is better than you. We are proud Jews. Always remember that."

She lifted her head. "In my opinion, it's cold."

"You don't know what cold is," the woman replied.

"I beg your pardon. I do. I grew up in Warsaw." Irritation crawled up from her chest into her throat, the itch inside her growing as the tension between them thickened, the air overheating.

"It's warm enough in here," Betty said, fanning herself with a napkin.

Rita pulled a gold case and lighter from her handbag and lit an expensive French cigarette. She screwed up her mouth into a narrow slit and exhaled the smoke in a carefully crafted curl into the hazy pub air. A rather sarcastic smile appeared on her lips but disappeared as quickly as it formed.

Hanna studied the stony face of Rita Wright. The woman was pretty in an upper-class, regal way. Her black hair fell to her shoulders from a wave atop her forehead and formed a circular coiffure around her aristocratic face. Hanna noticed that the eyebrow pencil, the mascara, the burnt-red lipstick were all perfectly applied, as if she had spent hours in front of the mirror, or someone with great skill had worked with meticulous care to her advantage. The skin was powdered, but remained almost white, accenting all her features. Rita's face, from the neck up, resembled the ancient bust of a wealthy Greek woman that one might find in a museum.

Betty's eyebrows shifted downward, and she gave Hanna a sly wink before sliding an ashtray across the table to Rita.

"Tell me about yourself," the woman said to Hanna, in a flat voice that betrayed no hidden meaning.

"Would someone mind telling me what's going on?" Hanna asked. "Am I being interviewed? I already have a job."

The tired waitress brought Hanna's pint and the second round of drinks for the others. She lifted her glass and took a sip, but wasn't fond of the warm, bitter taste of the dark ale.

"I wish we could," Phillip said, reaching for his second pint. "Let's just say that you interest us."

"Me? Interest you?"

Rita smiled and Hanna thought her face might crack underneath the powder. "If you have nothing for us, it will be apparent. We can go our separate ways with no harm to anyone."

"I'll answer your questions, if you answer mine."

"I'm sorry, it doesn't work that way," Rita said, after puffing on her cigarette. "Betty was kind enough to set this up because she believes you might be an asset to the war effort, particularly against the Nazis in Poland."

"My family is in Warsaw. I haven't heard from them since the war began." Her hands trembled a bit as she clutched her glass.

"We know," Rita said, delicately balancing the cigarette between the second and third fingers of her right hand.

"I'm at a disadvantage." Hanna leaned against the paneled back behind her.

Rita drove on with her questions. "How many languages do you speak?"

Hanna sighed. "I don't know why you're asking me this, but I speak Polish, my native language, and Yiddish. My German and English are fair—I get by."

"Your German piques our interest," Phillip said. "A talent for those languages could be most helpful."

Rita touched the lacquered hair on the side of her head and then placed the cigarette in the ashtray. "Did you participate in sports when young?"

"I swam, I ran, but for my own enjoyment. I enjoyed being outside when I could . . ." She paused, remembering the times when she couldn't do the things she loved because they were forbidden—prohibited for women regardless of the Sabbath or Holy Days. The rare times she could get away she hid those activities from her parents.

"You seem in good shape," Rita said. "Any medical issues?"

Hanna shook her head.

Rita studied her again before speaking. Hanna returned the stare.

"We'll be in touch through Betty," the woman said.

Hanna started to speak, but Rita held up her hand. "You're bursting inside with questions that I wish, with all my heart, I could answer, but the government is dealing with a delicate situation at the moment. I *can* tell you this is just the beginning. The war is real. I've just returned from Warsaw, and the devastation is horrific. We need people on the ground."

"Are you suggesting . . . ?"

"I'm not suggesting anything, but if we ask for your help at a later date and you decide to give it, the government would be most grateful in ways you might not expect."

The soldier turned to her and placed his hand lightly on her arm. "Consider what we're asking. Think about it, so when the question comes you'll be ready."

"That's enough for one night," Rita said, showing a row of fine white teeth through the curve of her red lips. "Shall we turn our attention to the gods of ale?"

Betty quickly steered the conversation to her knitting club

and how it was aiding the "boys at home," although nothing was really going on in Britain—as Rita pointed out. After a few jokes and more banter about the preparations for war, they finished their pints. Rita paid the bill and they got up from the booth.

Phillip helped Hanna on with her coat at the door. "It was a sincere pleasure to meet you. I do hope we meet again."

Rita and Phillip turned in a different direction upon leaving. Betty and Hanna pressed against an adjoining brick wall that sheltered them from the wind.

"Blimey," Hanna said, parroting a word that Lawrence often used. "What was that about? My head is on fire."

Betty arched her neck, breathing in deep drafts of the chilly air. "He was handsome, don't you think?"

"You're not answering my question."

"Neither are you."

"All right. I suppose. His eyes were a pleasing pale blue, almost translucent, wavy black hair, a good figure, a cheerful smile—and he didn't smoke—nice for a change." If she hadn't been so absorbed in the mystery of the evening, she might have paid more attention to the man to her left. He did seem friendly and interested in her . . . but for what purpose?

"You shouldn't cast stones, having a smoke yourself now and then."

"Purely an experiment." She turned toward her friend. "Who are these people?"

"I can't say any more than they did."

"It all sounds so secretive, so cloak-and-dagger. How high up does this go?"

Betty took gloves from her handbag and pulled them over her fingers. "To the top."

Hanna gave her a puzzled look.

"To Chamberlain and a man you may not have heard that much about—Winston Churchill."

"So, it's serious business. This evening wasn't a charade. How do you know them?"

"Deadly serious." Betty wrapped her scarf around her neck. "I have contacts."

"It's quite amazing, really."

They parted with a kiss on the cheek. Hanna walked toward home under the fast-moving gray clouds in the blackout darkness, aware that the conversation she had had with Rita Wright was real and consequential. The secrecy made her uneasy, and she picked up her step, looking back over her shoulder and to the skies, as if German bombers might appear at any second. Rita Wright's white face dominated her thoughts. She wondered if this mysterious woman might change her life. She shook off the possibility, more concerned about Poland and her family than her own future.

The thin metal bands cut into Perla's hands as she struggled to keep the water from sloshing out of the buckets. The liquid was too precious to waste, especially in preparation for the upcoming Sabbath. Water was needed for cooking and cleaning, and each day the stifling Nazi presence made it more dangerous to venture out.

Even the ritual bath, the mikveh, faced an uncertain future. Rumors swirled that the Nazis knew of its significance to the Jews. The rabbinic laws regarding family purity, both physical and spiritual, were loathed by the Germans who, for the time being, only harassed and mocked those women who dared venture there. The baths tested the true believer. The waters, in addition to being scarce and potentially polluted, were cold as heat sources disappeared.

Perla stopped for a moment and rested by the side of a building, leaning her tired body against the brick, her hands shaking from the weight. She had stood for nearly two hours in the early afternoon to get water from a spigot—one of the few operating in Warsaw. No one from the family was able to help her. Izreal was at work, Aaron at yeshiva, and Stefa was in search of bread. Perla imagined she might meet her on the street. How sweet it would be if Stefa could help her with the heavy buckets.

Krochmalna remained a jumble of blasted buildings interspersed with those spared by the bombs. No one could make their way down the street without skirting piles of rubble. Today, Perla noticed something different as she returned from gathering the water.

Wehrmacht soldiers, with rifles pointed at their surprised victims, forced anyone to abandon what they were doing, the only exceptions being the few Polish children who happened to be out. The soldiers thrust shovels into the hands of the conscripted workers and shouted orders in German. "Get to work! Clear the streets! Work as if your life depended on it!"

A group of Poles and Jews had been unceremoniously rounded up a few houses from her apartment on Krochmalna. Three soldiers stood guard while the workers lifted fractured rock and bricks from the street with their hands and threw the refuse into the crater of the destroyed building. Others dug into the debris with their shovels, lifting it, and carrying it to the growing mound of rubble.

Perla adjusted her kerchief, lowered her head, picked up the buckets, and headed across the street, hoping to escape the soldiers' attention. She looked up briefly for a moment and spotted one other person not under Nazi control—a young Jewish man who stood across from her building. He had his back turned toward the workers, calmly looking at the nameplates on another apartment building.

She strode past him, head down, until she heard a harsh voice call out in German, "Jews! Come here! Your friends need help."

Her first urge was to go on, to pretend she hadn't heard the command, but she knew that such "ignorance" would be foolhardy and perhaps deadly. She stopped and looked back at the young man who stood near her.

The solider was enraged by her reluctance. "Both of you! Come here! Bring your buckets!"

"Do what they say," the young man whispered.

"My water," Perla replied. "If I don't have my water, I can't honor the Sabbath."

"The Sabbath will wait," the young man replied. "There will be no Sabbath to honor if you're dead."

They walked slowly across the street, approaching the officer who pointed his rifle directly at them. He was a tall man whose body was clothed in a gray field coat, whose epaulets, buttons, and helmet flashed in the sun. His two German companions watched with a muted chuckle as their eyes shifted back and forth between Perla and the workers. The soldier smiled, blond hair shining from beneath his helmet, metal-hard blue eyes sparkling. A streak of cruelty crossed his face, his mouth wrenched shut for a moment after the smile disappeared.

"What do you have there, mother? he asked, lowering his rifle.

Perla rested the buckets near her feet.

The soldier poked at the handles with the rifle's barrel and banged one of the pails with his booted foot. "Water?"

Perla nodded. "I need—"

The young man grabbed her arm, silencing her.

"You need?" the soldier objected, his voice rising. "You don't need anything." He drew back his leg and kicked the pail, splashing the water across Perla's dress and shoes. Black rivulets of the precious liquid drained into the street.

As his companions watched, the soldier picked up the other bucket, and tossed the water over the workers. The men and women yelped and shivered from the cold shock.

The guards laughed and called them "weak Jews."

"They need refreshment after all their hard work," the soldier who had called them over said after the laughter had died. "Now it's your turn. Get busy. Use your hands."

Perla stared in disbelief at the man, who turned his back on them, daring them to strike in revenge from behind.

"Come," her young companion whispered. "I'll help you."

He led her to the other side of the rubble as far away from the guards as possible. Still, they were within the eyesight and earshot of the Germans.

"Pick up something light and carry it to the pile," the man said. "Make sure they see you." Cupping his arms together, he bent over and gathered a clump of bricks. "Pigs."

Perla did as he ordered and followed him to the crater's rim. "I knew several people who lived here—an old man and a young family. I wonder if they are still alive?"

The young man gathered strength in his arms and swung the bricks into the air. They fell in a jumbled dance, striking the pile, raising a gray cloud of dust. Several of them rolled end-over-end to the bottom. "Those friends can do nothing for us now," he responded. "What is your name?"

"Perla Majewski."

She caught sight of his widening eyes, the flush that spread across his cheeks. He was handsome, Perla thought, with his dark hair and soulful eyes; his expression strong, but not in a vengeful or dominating way like the Germans. He was a man who knew himself, who exuded strength through his self-confidence. From his callused hands and powerful arms, she could tell he was used to hard work. She was happy to have him by her side.

They walked back to the scattered rubble together. "What is your name?" she asked.

He hesitated, as if he was giving something away—perhaps he didn't want to tell her. The sun caught his face and he blinked. "Daniel . . . Daniel Krakauer . . . Krakowski, Mrs. Majewski."

Perla understood the distinction between the Yiddish and Polish surnames, but what was more important was the young man's first name. Her intuition told her that this was the man Stefa had been seeing. Suddenly, it made sense that he had been waiting across from their apartment building. Apparently, a secret meeting had been interrupted by the Nazis.

"You are . . ." She bent down to pick up more rocks, a slight strain in her back tugging at her.

"Yes. I'm seeing your daughter." He continued with the work, cradling more debris between his arms. A thick coating of dust now covered the lower half of his jacket. "I'm sorry we had to meet this way. Stefa wanted me to meet you and your husband, but the war got in the way."

The guards shouted more orders, exhorting the men and women to "work faster." The one who had called them over threatened to strike an old man with his rifle butt.

They walked back to the crater and threw the debris into the pit. "I can't say out loud what I'm thinking," Daniel said on his way back. "We should be good Jews and forgive them, but I can't find it in my heart. This war's just begun and I already hate them. I can't stand to see their arrogant, sneering faces, their swaggers down our streets, Nazis taking over our buildings and commerce. They will lie to us and then they will kill us."

Perla quivered at the thought, shaking her head and dropping the rocks she had lifted in her hands. "Now you're making matters worse than they are. We must not think that way. Surely, God will look after us."

He stopped mid-stoop, turned his head, and looked at Perla with sad eyes. "I'm sorry. I shouldn't have spoken those awful words to you; but, as Stefa knows, sometimes I can't help myself. No good can come from this. Who knows what the Nazis will do next? I put nothing past them. They've already demonstrated that they have no regard for life—human or animal." He pointed to the rotting carcass of a horse down the street that had been picked clean to white bones by scavengers.

"No talking!" A soldier fired a shot above their heads. The bullet slammed into the wall of an adjacent building, raising a cloud of powdery dust.

Daniel rose, faced the soldier, and stood like he was at attention. "Yes, sir!"

Perla grasped his arm and pulled him down beside her. "Don't antagonize them."

"I could shoot you dead . . . dirty Jew." He patted his rifle. "Get back to work."

Having been warned, they continued working without words until the rubble had diminished and the sun had begun to set.

A truck pulled up in the middle of Krochmalna. The guards collected the spades and shovels, threw them in the truck, and set off in the open back, lighting their cigarettes and laughing at the "poor Jews." They disappeared down Krochmalna, as if the people they had subjugated were never there.

The tired and stunned workers, Poles and Jews, drifted away in the eerie calm.

Perla straightened and rubbed her back. "I'm not used to lifting rocks." The strength that she had carried throughout the afternoon faded and a sudden exhaustion swept over her. "I've done nothing for the Sabbath, and now I have no water."

"I'll go for it and bring back full pails, Mrs. Majewski."

The silvery buckets sat empty in the dusk, the disc of the nearly full moon jutting over the buildings to the east. Perla wiped her brow with a handkerchief. "That's generous of you, but I couldn't ask it."

"Mama!" The voice rose from a whisper to a cry. "I've been so worried." Stefa rushed down the sidewalk into her arms. "I saw the guards when I was coming home. I went out of my way to avoid them and, luckily, I found Aaron so he wouldn't fall into their hands. We've been sitting at home—waiting."

"Daniel!" Stefa stepped back, surprised by the man at her mother's side.

"Yes, we've met. I've been with your mother all afternoon."

"Mr. Krakowski has offered to get water for us, but it's too dangerous."

Stefa nodded. "Yes . . . you shouldn't be out after dark. They're looking for Jews, anyone who steps out of line." She took her mother's hands in hers. "We'll get by without the water. Father will know what to do."

"Yes, yes," Perla said weakly. "Your father. I'm tired, let's go home."

"May I see your daughter on Sunday, Mrs. Majewski?"

Perla tilted her head, taking in the dark eyes so full of life that locked onto hers. "I will talk to my husband. We haven't considered yet what Stefa should do, what the arrangement will be . . . but I don't think it would do any harm to call on her—as long as you know in your heart that nothing is certain."

"Mama," Stefa said. "Let's go. You're tired."

"Thank you," Daniel said. "I will see you Sunday, Stefa. Good Sabbath."

"Good Sabbath," Perla and Stefa responded in unison.

Daniel turned east, as they gathered the pails and walked toward home.

As they neared the door, Perla said, "I like him. He's a good man. I can tell."

Stefa leaned her head on her mother's shoulder. "I like him, too, Mama."

CHAPTER 5

The Catholic church that Janka and Karol attended, when Karol could force himself out of bed after a Saturday night of drinking, lay some distance from their home. The church had been spared from the worst of the bombings, but had suffered some damage when nearby explosions had sent debris crashing through the roof of the north transept.

Janka had missed Mass on the third of December 1939, so she found her way to the church midafternoon the following day, Monday, to find the narthex doors open and the nave nearly empty. Despite her rather rigorous and strict Catholic upbringing, she didn't like to attend Mass by herself, for it made her feel like a widow—or, worse yet, a future divorcée. She was acquainted with the women who attended regularly with their husbands and found them somewhat sanctimonious in their beliefs—a club that didn't accept her. If she considered it closely, she wanted little to do with them anyway. In her natural shyness, she had nothing to say.

She said a prayer for peace, and lit votives in memory of deceased relatives, and watched as workmen climbed like spiders up the interior scaffolding to work on the roof. The priest, dressed in his black cassock, silver hair flowing like a mane, looked on from below, occasionally shouting orders to the men.

She pressed her back against the stiff pew and tried not to think—instead eliciting the opposite effect, her mind racing.

The weight bearing down upon her wasn't from church attendance or what others in the parish thought—it was primal. She wondered, through a building fear, how she and her husband were going to survive. She hadn't been able to find a job since the order of October twenty-sixth that all Poles between fourteen and sixty must work. Jobs were scarce and she was hardly qualified to do anything.

Everything was disappearing: water, food, good tempers, even civility among neighbors. Instead of *watching out* for each other, neighbors were *watching* each other. Everyone had become an enemy of the Reich, at the very least a person not to be trusted. The cause of this shift was easy to ascertain. It had started on September first with the invasion and had continued since that day.

Karol admitted to her that he didn't trust the Germans, while trying as hard as he could to ingratiate himself into their deadly club. Things were going badly at work, with increased hours and new production schedules instituted under Nazi management. "Of course, they tell us that our plant manager is changing the rules," he told her. "We know better. Those black uniforms swarming the plant are Nazis, not Poles. *We're* Poles. They hate us as much as they hate the Jews. But don't worry. I'll have them eating out of my hand like a starving dog before long."

She hadn't asked how he planned to achieve this far-fetched objective.

Supper was her immediate concern, however. She gathered her handbag, kneeled to make the sign of the cross, and headed for home.

The day was brisk, somewhat cold, but not unpleasant. The sun's slanted rays shot through white clouds moved by the wind, warming her shoulders but not her spirits.

She saw the thin figure across the street as she neared her apartment—the young man—Aaron was his name, if she remembered correctly. He must be coming home from school, she thought. He demonstrated a natural bounce in his step from the freshness of youth, walking in strides large enough for a man. He was on the cusp anyway, and his energy and enthusiasm for life seemed undeterred by the war.

Janka called to him and he stopped, shielding his eyes from the sun with his hand.

"Karol," she called again, not wishing to brand him as a Jew if Germans lurked in the buildings' recesses; however, she spotted the white armband with the blue star of David on the right arm of his coat.

He crossed the street, and they stood together near a bakery that had nothing to display in the window but bare shelves. Before the invasion, the store would have been sold out by late afternoon, but that wasn't the case now. Flour and baking soda were in short supply. The baker probably kept everything for his family. She didn't blame him.

"Hello, Mrs. Danek," he said, remembering her. "I'm happy to see you."

She looked at his boyish body. "I'm impressed. I have trouble remembering names. I meet someone and a minute later I have no idea what their name is. It's embarrassing—my husband says it's because I'm . . ." She grimaced and then gazed at the sidewalk for a moment before lifting her head. "It's Aaron, isn't it? How are you and your family? Are you coming home from school?"

He lifted the large notebook he was carrying, almost as wide as his chest. "Yes, at the yeshiva, but I'm supposed to help my father this evening at the restaurant." He looked away, his cheeks coloring.

"Stretching the truth?" she asked. "You can tell me. I'm not your mother."

He turned his head, gazing at her, the color fading from his cheeks. "I know what's going on—my family needs help. I look for things that might be useful for us. My mother doesn't like it when I'm late—but she doesn't tell my father. I'm always home before he is."

Janka looked both ways on Krochmalna, making sure no Germans or nosy neighbors had spotted them. Several pedestrians passed by, a few smirking because Aaron wore the mark of a Jew. "What are you looking for?"

"Money. Knives. Guns. We're at war. My father avoids the truth—to keep us happy. He thinks he's protecting us, but he knows the Germans will make things worse. We're far from starving, but how long can we go on? The ration cards will come soon."

She wanted to take his thin body into her arms and smother him with a hug. A young man—a boy—like Aaron shouldn't have to live with death hanging over his head. No one should. Yet, the Nazis courted death, kept it close to their hearts. One only had to look at the death's head, the skull and crossbones on some of the officers' caps. *Death.* The image draped her mind with blackness, and she shook her head to rid herself of the cursed picture. She was shocked that the young man would be hunting for zlotys and weapons. Did he really understand the danger of his actions?

"It's not safe to be out."

"I'm small. I can disappear. I find things and then hide them behind the building."

She spotted two fast-approaching Germans striding in their direction. If they spotted her talking to a Jew there would be trouble.

"Quick, my apartment. There's no time."

"I shouldn't, Mrs. Danek," Aaron said, trying to shield his armband with the notebook.

"My husband isn't home. You can hide until they pass. Get behind me."

She stepped beside him, blocking him from the soldiers' view, leading him down the street, praying that no one from her building was on the steps or in the hall. She couldn't see through the frosted glass, so she listened for a few seconds before pushing the door open. No one was there. "Step quietly."

Soon they were inside.

Aaron stood, as if frozen, clearly uncomfortable about entering a stranger's apartment.

"Take off your coat, if you wish . . ." She walked to the window, keeping some distance from it, and stared at the street, her head moving from side to side. Krochmalna's buildings had blocked the sun, and a black spear of darkness spread down it. A few yellow lights burned in other apartments since there was no longer a need for a blackout. The two Germans continued their spirited steps away from them—that much she could see.

"Maybe you should keep it on," she said, suppressing a shiver, without turning toward him. "It's cold in here."

"I can't stay long. I'll go when they're gone. You're right, it's too dangerous to be out."

The Germans finally disappeared. Janka left the window and turned on a floor lamp near the couch. From the light that seeped through the stained cloth shade, she could see the boy. He had opened a few buttons on his coat. The garment swamped him. He was thin, having the characteristics of a beggar child: trousers that swallowed slim legs, lean wrists and thin fingers that clutched at his notebook, a flat chest that had not yet developed into manhood, dark eyes that bulged from the whiteness of his face.

"I wanted to thank you for saving me from the Nazis the last time," he said. "Now, you've done it again. You should meet my mother." He looked around the room, taking in whatever might interest his eye. "You have a Victrola!"

He had spotted the rectangular oak cabinet that stood near the window. "My mother gave it to me . . . us . . . my husband and me. When we were first married, we used to listen to recordings every night." She swiped a finger across the lid; a gray pillow of dust collected on its tip. She rolled it between her fingers and watched it float to the floor.

"Things have gotten worse, haven't they—for the Jews?"

Aaron nodded. "My father told us that all Jewish businesses have to display the star of David on doors and windows, even his restaurant, because they serve mostly Jews. The Nazis have started going there, too, because the food is good. That's why we have enough to eat. The Nazis make sure that their food gets delivered." He pointed to his armband. "Any Jew older than twelve has to wear this. I'll be thirteen in March. My father said I should wear it to be safe."

"That's the irony—it doesn't make you safe. It makes you a target."

"I know, Mrs. Danek. I'm not scared. I'm proud to be a Jew." He clutched the notebook tighter to his chest. "How are you . . . I mean the Poles?"

"Life could be better. I'm having trouble finding food . . . everyone is. Winter is making things worse. I light the stove now and then for heat. The coal to heat the building is hard to get. My husband and I wrap ourselves in blankets to keep warm . . . most of the time he doesn't need them. . . ." She left the thought unfinished. Aaron wouldn't understand that Karol often passed out and sweated the night away.

"I want you to meet my family. My father might get you leftover food from the restaurant . . . a thank-you for being so kind to me."

"That's nice of you—" The downstairs door opened and a cough echoed from the bottom of the stairs. "He mustn't see you," she whispered, rushing to turn off the lamp. "Do as I say." She grabbed his arm and led him to the cedar wardrobe in the bedroom. "Stay in there and don't say a word." She closed the mirrored double-doors and the aromatic scent of the wood spread into the room.

Seconds later, Karol, hacking from the cold, was at the door, pushing it open. Janka threw off her coat and sat on the couch. He slouched in, stiff and unkempt, but not drunk.

"You're home early—didn't you stop at the pub?"

"No, too many damn Nazis. Suddenly, they have a taste for Polish vodka. I'm in no mood." He took off his coat and tossed it on top of hers.

"I just got home," she said. "We'll be eating canned beans again."

"Shit. I have to take a piss." He sauntered off to their small bathroom, adjacent to the bedroom, and shut the door.

"I'll hang up our coats," she said, calling after him. She picked up both and strode to the bedroom. She tossed his atop the bed and opened the wardrobe's doors. Putting a finger to her lips, she covered Aaron with her coat, pulled him from the wardrobe, and walked him quickly to the apartment entrance. Moving in silence, she let him out, and hurried back to the bedroom.

Soon after, the bathroom door creaked open and a scowling Karol appeared, like a shadow in the dim light. "Not enough water to flush the toilet. Nazi scum."

"I'll make supper," she said, peering around the bedroom door.

"Why are we living in the dark?" He stifled a yawn and scratched his chest.

"Saving on the electric bill." She hung up his coat.

"Beans, again. I don't worry about the electrics. I worry about food. *You've* got to do something about that."

"I'm trying my best. Can't your friends at the plant share what they have?"

He snorted. "Remember who's running this country. My friends have nothing to share."

She breezed past him into the living room, turning on the lamp again. "I may be able to get some better cuts of beef and chicken, despite rationing."

He turned, eyeing her suspiciously. "How will you manage that?"

"Does it make a difference? We're at war."

He yawned. "I suppose not—as long as my stomach is satisfied."

Before going to the kitchen, she walked to the front window and looked out upon the purple hues outlining the street. Looking west, she could just make out the small figure of Aaron, standing on his apartment balcony, looking down upon the same tired, mad world they both lived in.

* * *

Stefa had seen Daniel on the previous Sunday, but he'd made no mention of what was bothering him. She could tell, however, that he wasn't himself; it was apparent in his slow, hunched walk, somber mood, and the darkness that filled his brown eyes. This Tuesday, the day before Hanukkah, he had begged her to get away for a half hour so they could be alone.

She hadn't used an excuse—some might call it a lie—as she had in the past to get out of the house. Now that her mother had met Daniel and tacitly approved of him, she didn't feel the need to stretch the truth. Stefa had assured her mother that she would be back long before sundown to help with the cooking and the other chores.

Perla had reluctantly agreed, even though she was preoccupied and distressed that the household was missing a Hanukkah candle. "We'll make do—your father can find one in time," her mother told her. "He hates to be bothered at the restaurant."

A cold wind and the ever-present December clouds choked the city. This would be a Hanukkah like no other. The world had shifted after the Nazi invasion. The irony of the festival was not lost on Stefa—the commemoration of the siege that ended with the recapture of the Temple in Jerusalem, the fight for religious freedom led by Judas Maccabeus. Now, as jackbooted soldiers wound their way through Warsaw streets, shouting orders, taking away freedoms that Jews had enjoyed for years in the city, what Jew could embrace a festive mood? Instead, Poland suffered as a divided nation, the Nazis in the west, the Red Army in the east. Would this Hanukkah be their last as a family? Such thoughts were harmful and did no good. She pulled on her coat, making sure the star of David was visible on her right arm.

She kissed her mother on the cheek. "I promise I won't be long. Daniel has news."

Her mother said nothing, forcing a polishing cloth over the sideboard.

As Stefa descended the steps, it occurred to her that Daniel's news might be bad. What if he had decided to break off their relationship? What if his parents had voiced an objection to her? She stopped at the door, tightening her kerchief, steeling herself for whatever news he might bring.

He stood across the street near the baker's window, a hand thrust into his long coat, the flaps on his felt cap pulled down over his ears. He lifted the other in a meek wave, mildly, as if not to draw attention to himself.

Stefa crossed the street and stood next to him.

"Let's walk to Saski Park," he said. "We can be alone there."

"We'll have to sneak in," she replied. "Forbidden for Jews."

"If we don't make it inside, we'll go someplace else," he said stoically.

Even an innocent stroll could be dangerous with Nazis on every street corner, but Stefa was willing to take the risk. The large and inviting park, with its grand central fountain, ornate sculptures and stone walkways, was little more than a kilometer away. The fountain was also a meeting place for young couples.

They walked east on Krochmalna—in the gutter, as required by the Nazis.

"We're not a couple," Daniel said. "We're brother and sister if we're stopped. If I spot danger, I want you to turn away . . . leave me behind."

She bristled at his words, gooseflesh rippling across her body despite the warmth of her coat. "Leave you? I would never do that."

"Walk with a sure step and don't make eye contact. I don't want them to notice us."

She picked up her pace to keep up with him. Tenement buildings, businesses showing the star of David on their doors, sped by. Mirowski Square, the home of once bustling markets, now subdued, holding the bombed-out remains of a few classical-style buildings, flowed past before they arrived at the park.

Once there, Daniel seemed to relax. No one was in sight. He led her down a walk, deep into a line of trees that launched bare branches into the cold, gray air. Already, some had fallen, chopped down for firewood. Despite that, the park remained much as it had been before the war. Stefa wondered how long the statues, the magnificent fountain, and the naked trees would survive under Nazi rule. The park's probable destruction depressed her.

He found shelter within a cluster of tree trunks and pulled her close. "Take off your armband—let's enjoy a moment of freedom." He removed his own and stuffed it into his pocket.

The penalty for not wearing the star of David included arrest and prison, even death, but she removed hers and reveled in the wave of defiance that washed over her. She wanted him to kiss her, but it wouldn't have been right.

"I have two things to tell you," he said.

"Good news, I hope." She stepped away as a Polish couple skirted past them on the nearest path.

He motioned for her to come back. "Here we can enjoy each other."

"How?" she asked. Daniel continued to surprise her. "As friends . . . or something more?"

He smiled, the first time she had seen him do so in more than a week. "I'm trying to tell you that I love you . . . I want us to be together."

Her heart quickened at his words, but the brief leap of joy ended precipitously, as if she had been drawn to the edge of a cliff. She drew away, sadness touching her.

"Aren't you happy?" he asked. "Don't you love me?"

She had admitted to herself many times that she believed she was in love with Daniel—at least that was what her heart told her—but she'd never felt certain enough to admit it to anyone else, especially her parents. So much needed to be worked out. And now, with the war, their future seemed even more precarious.

"I'm happy," she said, watching the dry leaves shiver in bunches around her shoes. "My parents . . . your parents. The war."

He put his arm over her shoulders, urging her to walk deeper into the grove. "Our parents—what they think only matters to them, not to us. We must have the final say."

The thought terrified her. How could she go against her father and mother like Hanna had done? It would kill them. She had seen the outcome—the guilt, the recrimination, the silence from her father, the toll upon Perla, who had never been the same since her eldest daughter left.

She snapped a dead branch from a bush and brushed it through the fallen leaves at her feet. "It's not that easy, Daniel. You know how hard it is to go against them. Hanna made her decision and it hurt them. I've told you about her—my mother and father were determined to arrange a marriage she didn't want. That's what drove her away . . . well, one of the things. After she left us all in tears, I swore I'd never do that to my family. I'll honor that promise."

A biting wind chilled her face, filling her lungs with bracing air, stimulating her already speeding heart. Like a caged animal clawing to escape, she coveted the power and determination to break free that her sister had used, and, for an instant, she claimed it. But then her mood soured again. She couldn't do what Hanna had done, particularly in this uncertain time. Her relationship with Daniel would have to play out cautiously, if at all. She wouldn't force him on her parents.

"I've never admitted to anyone that I love you," she said, "but we'll have to work at it . . . we'll make my parents see that it's what we both want, and that *our* decision is for the best. We have to take our time."

"My parents are fine with me marrying the daughter of a mashgiach; in fact, they'd consider it an honor to have such a learned and respected man as a relative." He took the branch from her hands, tossed it to the ground, and pulled her toward him once again.

They stood together in the pale light, underneath the bare branches, the only colors in their eyes being the withered brown leaves and the gray tree trunks.

Daniel cupped his hands around her face and kissed her, meekly at first, and then a second time with more passion.

Despite the forbidden nature of their embrace, she let herself travel to a heaven of light and color, a world of love and bliss, far away from Saski Park and Warsaw. When she opened her eyes, she was pressed against him, her cheek touching his.

"I should tell you my other news," he said somewhat breathlessly. "It's important, too."

Whatever he had to tell her, it couldn't be more important than what he'd already said.

"You know of Adam Czerniaków?" he asked.

Stefa had heard her father mention the name, in rather ambiguous terms, in relationship to the man's standing on the Jewish Council. She had seen the round-faced Czerniaków, with balding head and pince-nez glasses, from a distance, and had been struck by his authoritative demeanor and stately gait. Other than that, she knew little about him.

"I've heard of him," she replied, without relaying her father's implied distaste.

"He's been named head of the Judenrat," Daniel said. "The Jewish Council is recruiting members for a Jewish Police Force. I've applied."

She gazed at him quizzically, unsure how she felt about this latest surprise. "Isn't the Judenrat controlled by the Nazis?" She removed the armband from her pocket and positioned it over her coat sleeve. "I should go home."

"Hell, the Nazis control everything," he said, retrieving his own armband from his pocket. "My position is far from certain—they want men who've served in the armed forces, which I haven't, but I do have the education they require."

Spotting no one on the cold day, they emerged from the grove and walked down the path that led to the park entrance and Krochmalna.

"Is it dangerous?"

"Policing your own people? I suppose it's as dangerous as any job enforcing the law."

"Father's talked to Mother about the Judenrat. He used to call it the kehilla, the community council. My parents don't talk much about politics because my father feels it's not a woman's place to hear such things, but he said Czerniaków is a puppet, put in place by the Nazis to keep the Jews under German thumbs—the animals won't mind the cage if they have a benevolent master. Now he calls it the German . . . Judenrat . . . because he knows." She walked faster after leaving the park. "It's getting dark, and I told my mother I'd only be back before sundown. She'll be frantic."

Daniel hurried to catch up with her and caught her by the arm. "The Germans won't give us guns; I doubt we'll even have uniforms, but think what it'll mean if I'm accepted. It'll be easier to get food—they have to feed the police force—I can make decisions that . . ." He released her arm and fell behind.

She looked over her shoulder. "What? What kind of decisions can you make? Life and death? *You'll* decide whether someone lives or dies?"

He muttered a curse under his breath, which Stefa ignored.

"All right . . . so I want you and our families to live . . . *us* to live."

She stopped and faced him. "This is so unlike you, Daniel. I could understand if you picked up a gun against the Nazis, but to fall in with them, under their control?"

"That's not what I want, or what I'm thinking about." He brought his clasped hands up to his chest. "I'll never surrender to them . . . the only thing that matters is getting out of this alive."

"At what cost? Who will die to save us?" She strode away, looking up at the murky sky, now deepening to indigo as the sun sank.

"What I'm doing is right for us," he yelled after her, and then in a strangled voice, like a whisper on the verge of a cry, "Look out."

Two Nazi officers, laughing and smoking cigarettes, approached from the opposite direction. She slowed as Daniel crept up beside her, both of them shifting to the gutter to make room for the men to pass. As the officers got closer, Stefa and Daniel stopped and bowed before them—as they had been instructed to do. Otherwise, they might be beaten.

"Good Jews," one of the men said. "They will go far." The men swept by in their long coats, barely glancing their way, continuing a story in German that kept them amused.

Stefa and Daniel walked on in silence, a gulf growing between them that Stefa hated, particularly on the eve of Hanukkah; yet, her anger festered. She whirled when the two Germans had receded in the distance and blew him a kiss, despite her irritation. They had come to the point where they needed to go their separate ways.

"Happy Hanukkah," she said. "I'll see you soon."

"Happy Hanukkah," he replied. "Think about what I've said."

"I will." A confused mixture of anger and love muddled her mind. She turned and hurried toward home, where she knew her mother would be looking anxiously over the balcony awaiting her return.

"Well, what do you think?" Lawrence asked. He leaned against the shovel and wiped his brow with a handkerchief despite the cool, foggy December day.

A soggy pit about a meter and a half deep lay in front of Hanna and Lucy as they peered from the breakfast room steps into the garden.

"It's quite the mess, isn't it?" Lucy said. Turning to Hanna, she whispered, "That poor willow—I'd hoped he would save it. I rather liked it." The willow lay in pieces on the green turf near the rear brick wall, a victim of the Anderson shelter's location near the front garden gate. Charlie, the spaniel, sniffed at the pit and lapped at the brown water inside it before deciding that he didn't like the muddy taste.

"How's that supposed to protect us?" Hanna asked Lucy, looking at the inverted U of corrugated steel panels that her uncle-in-law had placed in a temporary position next to the pit.

Lawrence overheard the question. "The steel takes the brunt of the ground shock and protects you from the blast, much better than concrete in this case, except for a direct hit. In that case, we're dead." He chuckled at his morbid prognostication.

"Larry!" Lucy's eyes widened, horrified at the thought.

"That won't happen. The Jerries don't have the Richardsons in their bomb sights, I guarantee it. After it's set in the ground— too damn wet now—I'll line the sides with sandbags and then cover the top with soil. Lucy, you can plant something pretty— even vegetables—on top. Then it's ready for use—should we need it."

Hanna traversed the garden path and peered inside the curved structure. "It'll be a tight fit."

"Panels on both ends seal it up. One is the entrance, of course . . . the three of us will fit comfortably inside." Lawrence spotted Charlie, who was relieving himself on the downed willow. "And the dog, naturally."

"Cozy," Hanna scoffed, and immediately regretted her tone. Her uncle-in-law was doing his best to protect the family. She had no right to think otherwise, particularly since her own family was now under Nazi rule and she could do nothing to help them. During the past week, Hanukkah had crossed her mind, but she was ashamed to admit that she hadn't even remembered the exact dates until she'd seen a story about it in one of the London papers.

"The point is to save our lives," he said, retrieving his jacket from a garden chair and withdrawing his pipe. He lit it and the woody, aromatic smoke drifted through the air. "That's enough for today—too murky to muck about. Need something to take the chill off. Perhaps a cup of tea?"

Charlie's long ears lifted in sudden awareness and he sprinted toward the kitchen door.

"Grab him, Hanna," Lucy said. "His paws are wet. Someone's out front."

Hanna collared the dog just as he was about to leap onto the tile floor. He wriggled in her arms, struggling to break free.

"Charlie's a good watchdog," Lawrence said. "Who'd be calling on a Sunday afternoon?" He gathered a towel from the kitchen, taking his time to wipe down the dog's paws as Hanna held the animal. "No sense in tracking dirt through the house. Lucy doesn't like it either."

Her aunt reappeared with an astonished look on her face. "Someone here to see you, Hanna . . . a woman . . . a very put-together woman by the name of Rita Wright."

"Rita is here?" Usually if she had company on a Sunday afternoon it would be Betty, or the sisters, Margaret and Ruth. She handed Charlie to Lawrence.

"Who is she?" her aunt asked.

"Betty Martin introduced me. I'll tell you about her later." Hanna stopped at the door to the living room. "Would you mind waiting in the kitchen? Otherwise, I'll have to take her upstairs so we can talk privately. I'm sure that's what she would want. Can she use one of your ashtrays, Uncle Lawrence?"

Their brows bunched together, both looking strangely at her.

Lawrence nodded and sat at the kitchen table. "We'll have tea," he said.

Hanna closed the glass-paned door between the kitchen and living room, catching her reflection before she met Rita. She certainly didn't look her best. Her dress was cut from pleated turquoise, with pockets, free from pattern; she hadn't put makeup on because no one had ventured out, not even to church; her hair was pulled back in a loose ponytail.

On the other hand, Rita, sitting in front of her, looked as if she had arrived from an elegant Saturday night party that had carried over into Sunday afternoon. The uninvited guest, attired in a full navy-blue skirt with a white bodice and bolero jacket, smiled at her as she entered the room. Rita had already made herself at home, sitting stiffly in one of Lawrence's favorite wing chairs, cigarette lit, the glass ashtray on the walnut side table at her disposal.

Hanna was at a loss for words as she took a seat across from her. The room was rather dim in the afternoon light. Only Rita's white complexion and red lips seemed to illuminate the space.

"*Guten Tag.*" Rita's German salutation was formal and precise.

Hanna replied in a more familiar form, hoping that her Yiddish accent wouldn't get in the way. Rita was testing her.

"*Ich hoffe, Sie haben Zeit gehabt über unser letztes Gespräch nachzudenken,*" Rita said.

Hanna replied in German. *Yes, I did have time to think about our last conversation, but I wasn't sure what to make of it.*

"Good . . . excellent." Rita switched to English, bringing the cigarette to her lips in a slow, restrained gesture. "Have you written your parents lately?"

"Yes, but there's been no reply. I'm worried about them."

"Worried enough to do something about it?" She cradled the cigarette in the ashtray and rested her hands on top of her puffy skirt. "Your aunt and uncle are out of earshot?" she asked, tilting her head toward the kitchen door.

"Yes. They're having tea."

"Good. What I'm about to say is confidential—for no ears other than your own—not even Betty's. It would be best all-around if you kept this to yourself, with the possible exception of Sir Phillip Kelley."

"*Sir* Phillip?"

Rita smiled. "Yes. He prefers that his title remain private, with the exception of a few confidants. If you decide to cooperate with us . . . help us, if you will . . . then you would be one in whom he confides. He liked you well enough after our initial meeting that he believes you might be right for our work."

Hanna straightened against the hard back of the Chippendale chair.

"We need a woman like you," Rita continued. "We need someone familiar with Warsaw, with Poland, who can speak German and Yiddish comfortably. We need a woman willing to take risks, possibly even give her life, to act as a courier between our own agents, the resistance, and the government here." She frowned and a few lines showed beneath the white powder. "I won't paint a rosy picture. The war is getting worse. A firm timeline for action hasn't been set. However, you'd be paid for your work and trained as well. You would join an elite corps of patriots doing the best possible work for England; in fact, for the world. For if the Nazis win their battle against humanity . . ." She picked up her cigarette, took a puff, and exhaled into the room. "Well, the consequences are too horrid to imagine."

Hanna thought of her parents. Where were they now? How were her brother and sister? A sense of doom, like cold arms, encircled her. She thought for a moment. "Can I help my family?"

"An obvious question . . . and one I must answer in an official capacity." She paused, studying Hanna again, as if judging her character. "The answer is no . . . your primary job will be to relay information when and where it's needed, to spy upon the Nazis, to aid resistance efforts whenever possible—for there will be resistance within the population at some point. Your parents and your siblings are separate from your duties."

"I see," Hanna said with a sigh.

Rita cocked her head, apparently aware of Hanna's misgivings. "Once you get to Warsaw, you're on your own for the most part. Contact between you and our headquarters will be limited. What transpires there, outside of your official role, will be up to you—but caution is urged. You could jeopardize our entire operation if you are captured or . . ."

Rita left the thought unfinished, but Hanna knew the logical extension. She lowered her gaze and thought of her aunt and uncle in the next room, beyond the glass panes that blocked their voices. Lucy had taken so many risks to marry the man she loved, effectively cutting herself off from the family. Hanna had done the same, knowing the step, once taken, would break ties, possibly beyond repair. She had been in England nearly a year, had barely gotten a taste of the country, and now the British government wanted her as a spy?

"I have to think about it," Hanna said. "There's so much to consider."

"I understand," Rita said, rising from her chair. She opened her purse, withdrew a business card, and handed it to Hanna. It listed an address in London, along with a phone number. "I didn't expect you to make a decision today. As I said, there's a long road ahead before any action is taken."

Rita put on her coat and stopped at the door. "Please retain secrecy . . . remain discreet. We wanted to plant the seed in your mind in the hope that it might grow. Have a good afternoon." She turned without a look back, opened the door, and got into the back seat of a black sedan. It pulled away from the curb, the exhaust pipes puffing in the damp air.

Hanna looked at Rita's cigarette burned to ash, with its smudges of red lipstick coating the yellowed paper. The ash triggered thoughts of Warsaw and the destruction it had suffered. Rita Wright was asking her to be a hero, to take on something she was totally unprepared for. She had made her choice to come to London, and today she was paying for it in ways she couldn't have imagined when she left.

Now, she had to face her aunt and uncle and come up with an excuse for the strange woman's visit.

The year 1940 was approaching.

No December had been more solemn than this one, as Stefa remembered. Izreal had procured a Hanukkah candle to replace the missing one. Even the silver menorah seemed muted on the dining room table as her father lit the shamash candle, then lit the candle for the first night, reciting a prayer. Stefa looked at her young brother when the words were spoken: "Almighty Father, Thy spirit protected our ancestors and led them safely through all dangers . . ." Her mind stopped, her body rigid in fear, tears building behind her eyes. What of Daniel, her father, and Aaron? The men would suffer most, she thought. The world had become an ugly place, and the God who had protected them for five thousand years had deserted them, leaving them to the inhuman wolves known as Nazis.

Izreal and Perla gave the Hanukkah gelt they had managed to procure, considering the world was at war. On past occasions, like birthdays, they gave presents. Aaron and Stefa might get new scarves for the winter, Aaron's in a deep blue and hers in black. Her father once received a new coat that had cost her mother dearly. Recently, Stefa and Aaron had looked for new shoes for Perla's birthday but, with the shortages, they couldn't find a pair that fit. Instead, they'd presented her with kosher salt, a hard-to-find commodity slowly disappearing from her kitchen. The idea of shoes seemed so plain and dull. Their mother should have received a piece of jewelry, or perhaps a new dress. Now every celebration seemed off, and Stefa's separation from Daniel only added to her melancholy.

Now, in late December, before Asarah b'Tebet, the fast day commemorating the siege of Jerusalem, and the approach of the new year, she stood for a moment at night on the balcony, overlooking the quiet that now pervaded Krochmalna.

She buttoned her coat and checked the pins that held her kerchief in place, her eyes and ears stinging from the bitter wind. Few ventured out after dark now. Down the street, Nazi sentries flickered in and out of light and shadow like a film reel flapping in the incandescent beam of a movie house.

She hoped to see Daniel soon, but her hopes were interrupted by shouts from German soldiers somewhere in the distance. Those human calls were followed by three gunshots, a scream, and the bellow of a crying woman. Another shot . . . and the crying stopped.

Her mind filled in the disturbing pictures. She wheeled from the balcony and stepped inside to be greeted by the worried looks of her family.

"We heard it," Aaron said.

Her father and mother nodded and, after that, not a word was spoken.

PART 2

CHAPTER 6

April 1940

The worst of the long winter was over.

Janka opened the windows on the few sunny days of early spring, the noise from Krochmalna filtering into the apartment: chattering pedestrians, the ring of trolley bells from distant streets, the occasional clop of hooves as a horse cart pushed through the human traffic.

But something else was happening during the new season that welcomes life—a wall was encircling nearby streets. She had noticed the construction on Pawia to the north, Sienna to the south, even on Krochmalna. The wall skirted the popular markets of Mirowski Square and the entrance to Saski Park. A workforce of Jews had been conscripted for the job. They had begun the first of the month and labored each day regardless of whether rain fell, fog choked the city, or the spring sun heated them to sweaty exhaustion. Most of her Polish neighbors ignored the implication, concerned with their own well-being and not the Jews', but Janka understood what was going on. This part of Warsaw, predominately Jewish, was being sealed off from the rest of the city. Only a feeble mind would have mistaken the wall's objective as the bricks rose day by day, until the ugly barrier was higher than the workers.

When she'd mentioned the wall to Karol, he'd responded,

"Let them stew in their own juices," a statement that left her with a bitter taste as she considered its inhumanity. "And, worse yet . . . the Nazis are rounding up Jews outside Warsaw and shipping them here," he continued. "We've already got more than we can handle. They're bringing them in from the country villages. We Poles will have to relocate. That's the rumor. It's not fair that we have to leave our home and go somewhere else." He pounded his fist on the arm of the couch. "By God, not our house! I'll make sure of that."

Janka wasn't certain how her husband would solve that problem. However, she had no desire to move either.

A tentative knock interrupted her thoughts.

Janka opened the door to find a sturdy young woman with a pleasing smile and bright hazel eyes standing in the hall. "Mrs. Danek?" Wisps of light brown hair framed the visitor's face.

"Yes?"

"Stefa Majewskianka."

Janka recognized the name—at least part of it. Stefa had referred to herself in the manner of an unmarried woman. "You're Aaron's sister?"

"Yes. Aaron Majewski. I'm sorry, I didn't mean to confuse you."

"You didn't." Janka thought how wonderful, yet sad, to be Jewish in Warsaw, to be so young with so much of life ahead, yet in such uncertain times. Stefa wore a coat without a star of David on the right sleeve.

The young woman caught her looking at her arm. "I took it off to cross the street." She pulled it from her pocket.

"That's dangerous—you could be arrested."

"Or worse." Stefa looked down the stairs toward the frosted glass door. "I can't stay long, Mrs. Danek. I came as a favor to my mother—do you have time to meet her? Aaron told us how you came to his rescue twice. She would like to thank you."

Janka turned and involuntarily looked into the apartment, seeking her husband's approval. He was working and wouldn't be home for hours, but the guilt of doing something so blatantly defiant briefly gnawed at her. Karol had forbidden her to interact with Jews, yet she had done it twice. She could sit at home or go shopping in markets that were nearly empty thanks to rationing. *Oh, why not.* "Let me get my coat."

Stefa stood outside while she hurried to the wardrobe. She put on her coat, gathered her purse, and rejoined her visitor.

"I'm going without the armband and kerchief," Stefa said. "We can walk together that way. You should break away if there's any trouble."

Janka marveled at the young woman's bravery, defying the Nazis, realizing that simple actions like crossing the street without an armband were acts of resistance.

Soon, they were headed toward the Majewskis' apartment, a short distance away.

"My brother is at school and my father's at work," Stefa said as they weaved through the crowd.

If there were Germans or Gestapo members on Krochmalna they had been absorbed in the crush of pedestrians. The sun broke through the overcast now and then, spreading a flickering light across the street. Following closely behind her visitor, Janka thought that the young woman could pass for a Pole with her lighter hair and hazel eyes. Such characteristics might serve her well in the future.

They arrived at the apartment in a few minutes. Stefa studied the throngs of people, as Janka had done as well, before they stepped inside. No Germans were to be seen, at least none in uniform.

Stefa ignored the mezuzah at the building entrance, and ushered Janka in. The hallway was dim, but the smell of freshly baked bread filled the air. "We put up another mezuzah—the Nazis destroyed the one that was there. I didn't kiss it—well, no need to explain. They take them down, we put them up."

"Another act of defiance," Janka said.

Stefa nodded in a way that said, *We know the chance we're taking.* "My mother's name is Perla. She's waiting." The young woman stopped outside the apartment, touched the mezuzah, and brought her fingers to her lips. Such an odd custom, Janka thought, but no stranger than genuflecting before the cross.

Stefa knocked softly and opened the door.

The room was airier and lighter than Janka expected. A wide expanse of windows opened toward the south; to the left, the filigreed wrought-iron balcony stood over the bustling street. The furnishings were sparse, but spoke of a lineage of prosperity in their understated elegance. Janka could only dream of having such fine furniture in her apartment. She envied the windows, too, that so captured the light, no matter the weather, and ushered it inside for warmth and comfort. How it would bring her such joy! Instead, she lived in the soulless darkness of her apartment.

A frail woman with folded hands sat on the couch, looking out the windows into the dance of sun and shadow covering Warsaw. She turned her head slightly as they entered the room.

"Mama, this is Mrs. Danek," Stefa said quietly, as if to calm her mother's mind.

The woman's smile was melancholy; perhaps a permanent fixture, judging from the creases that ringed her mouth. "Hello, Mrs. Danek. Please sit."

"Please, call me Janka."

Perla failed at another smile. "All right, I will—only if you will accept my invitation to call me Perla."

Janka nodded.

"I'll leave you alone," Stefa said. "Can you make your way home . . . Mrs. Danek?"

"I'll be fine. I have shopping to do."

Stefa nodded, walked to her room, and closed the door.

Janka sat in a chair opposite the couch and looked at the pale woman with no makeup on her face. The thin strands of Perla's black hair, streaked with gray, extended from her temples into the recesses of her white kerchief.

Having nothing to talk about but the weather, Janka kept silent for a time, until Perla spoke.

"I understand you have rescued my son twice from the Germans," Perla said, her hands still folded in her lap.

"That's true, but I take no credit for something anyone would have done."

Perla shook her head. "No . . . not anyone . . . only someone of valor and goodness." She unclasped her hands and placed them over her heart. "I wanted to thank you for what you have done. You've been a friend that even those close to us might not be, considering the world we live in. You see, my son, small though he is, is an adventurous young man. I fear his spirit will get him into trouble and there will be no one to rescue him. My husband works and Stefa and I can't follow him around like dogs."

"He is a fine young man," Janka said and then looked to her right toward the sideboard where the silver menorah gleamed in the light. She thought for a moment, not wishing to take more credit for Aaron's rescue. "You have a lovely home."

Perla sighed, an unexpected burst of sadness issuing forth again. "Yes, I love it here. We've been in this apartment for most of our children's lives. Aaron turned thirteen in March."

Janka knew Perla was concerned about losing her home, if the rumors that Karol reported were true. She kept the conversation focused on Aaron. "Did you have a . . . celebration?" Janka wasn't sure what to call it.

"A bar mitzvah." Perla brought her hands to rest on either side of her body, as if to prop herself up. "Yes, it wasn't much . . . a quiet celebration of prayer and thanksgiving, a few gifts . . . my son called up to the Torah. Everything is so different now from the way it used to be." Perla's eyes teared as she talked of Aaron and the way life had become.

"We had it in the basement of the restaurant where my husband works," Perla continued, lowering her gaze. "It was safer there than at the synagogue—we invited a few friends and neighbors—ones we could trust. We couldn't even walk in groups; it was too dangerous." She withdrew a handkerchief from her dress pocket and wiped her eyes, still staring into her lap. "And when it was over, Stefa and I walked together, while Aaron and Izreal followed—all of us in the gutter in case *they* were about." She blew her nose, replaced the handkerchief in her pocket, and looked at Janka directly. "My son is now considered a 'committed Jew' for the rest of his life."

"I'm not familiar with your ways," Janka said. "I'm Catholic, but we all fear what is happening."

Looking up, Perla sank against the couch. "We don't talk about it much. My husband and daughter try to protect me, but it's my son who brings the war to our door with his enthusiasm for life. I worry so much about him. That's why I wanted to thank you. I beg of you, if you see him on the street, or see him acting in a way that might bring him harm or shame, watch over him . . . if we can't."

"Of course." The words came from her mouth naturally, but she wondered what she could really do under the Nazis' bootheels. She didn't feel strong or courageous, but here was a family who needed her. She'd experienced nothing like it in her life—not even with her parents, who had always ruled with a strict religious hand rather than with expressions of love. Perhaps she could be of help to the Majewskis. It would be her way of resisting the horrors taking place in Warsaw. But as the thought streamed through her head, she wondered how she could ever do anything of value for anyone, especially with Karol and the German forces staring at her with cold eyes and keeping track of every move.

"I must tell you one thing," Perla said. "We have a saying—if you save one life, it is as if you have saved the whole world."

Janka drew in a breath. Had Perla read her mind?

"You are married to a man who doesn't like Jews." Perla's lips pursed, as if she found the words distasteful. "Aaron told us you hid him from your husband."

Janka had no desire to hide the truth. "My husband drinks too much and says things he shouldn't, but that's my burden . . . not yours." It was her turn to feel as if the world had turned against her. "What I've said should stay between us—like friends who keep secrets."

"Our words will never leave this room," Perla said, her voice softening. "I'm sorry that we didn't meet sooner, but I've not been well."

Janka leaned forward as Perla's voice dropped. Clearly, the woman had suffered as mirrored by her thin arms, the chalky face, the dark half-moons of skin under her eyes. "I haven't seen Aaron in weeks—I was beginning to worry."

"The Nazis have banned communal prayers. We can't even gather at the synagogue. Everything must be done in secret."

Janka hadn't heard of such a prohibition. "I'm sorry."

"God will see us through. He always has." Perla's voice brightened somewhat, but her words were tinged with worry. "I have something for you." She pushed herself off the couch, hands flat against the cushions, like an old woman struggling to get up.

Janka wondered how old she really was. Was Perla in her sixties, as one might have assumed from looking at her? Her daughter and son were too young. Life had not been kind if she was in her forties.

"Come to the kitchen."

Janka followed Perla into an immaculate space filled with light. On a counter lay a loaf of freshly baked bread covered in white butcher's paper and a flat package wrapped equally as well.

"A loaf of bread and kosher chicken for you," Perla said.

Janka gazed at the two gifts, amazed that she could be so lucky. Food was scarce whether you were a Jew or a Pole, and cuts of beef or chicken were delicacies few could afford. "I can't take this from your mouths. How will I explain these treasures to my husband?"

Perla almost laughed. "You can tell him that the Jews down the street gave you a present—a kosher present. Eat while you can."

She picked up the two packages. "Thank you, Perla. You've made my life easier tonight."

"Perhaps you will make our lives easier one day, Janka."

Not knowing whether she should hug the woman, offer her hand, or go to the door, Janka decided on the latter.

They said good-bye and she walked down the stairs, amazed at her good fortune, her mind racing with all the possible lies she would have to tell Karol about how she managed to find such a beautiful loaf of bread and perfect pieces of chicken.

Aaron walked in front of his sister, hoping to keep out of sight of the German soldiers and the Polish Police, blending in with the crowds on Żelazna, brushing past the military and police presence that seemed to be everywhere.

"He's working on the wall near Sienna," Stefa whispered to her brother. She had gotten a note earlier in the day. Meeting Aaron after yeshiva, now conducted in secrecy, they had struck off together—Aaron in his excitement to see what was happening in Warsaw, Stefa in her quest to see Daniel.

As they turned onto the street, Aaron was struck by how much work had already been done on the wall, some sections now higher than the workmen's heads. It was going up, brick by brick, a pillar here and there used as supports for doors. The Jewish laborers fashioned the bricks, their chisels and hammers clanging with dull thuds, the trowels rasping against the layered stone as the cement was smoothed on top like cake icing. The wall seemed to stretch on forever to the east, along with the men working on it.

Stefa cupped her hands around her eyes, searching for Daniel among the many workers who scurried like ants in their jobs.

"There," she said, pointing to her boyfriend when they had walked about halfway down the street. Fortunately, no German guards were in sight. A few of the Polish Blue Police were across from the wall, smoking cigarettes and chatting.

She rushed to him, Aaron following behind because he'd only heard about, never met, the man his sister so admired.

Daniel turned, leaving the workers at the wall, and stood in front of her. "You can't stay long," he said. "They'll become suspicious and then there'll be trouble."

Aaron was thrilled by his words—the sense of danger filling the air. Here was a real man, like his father, but one who was more concerned about real life rather than going to a job. His father's work provided wages and food, but what good could come from isolating in a restaurant when the Nazis were in control?

"I wanted to see you," Stefa said.

"And I want to see you." He paused and looked down at his hands, which were red and cracked from working without gloves. "They hurt like hell, but everyone has the same problem."

Stefa wanted to grasp them, squeeze her fingers around his, massaging away the pain. "Any word about a police position?"

"Not yet. The Judenrat put me on this work detail in order to test me. They made me a quarter-block supervisor. I'm responsible for seeing that this portion of the wall gets done and done right. If I do a good job, I might get a post as a policeman in the fall."

"You know what they're doing, don't you?" Aaron asked, looking at the star of David armband wrapped on Daniel's shirtsleeve rather than his coat.

"They're walling us in," Aaron continued.

Daniel nodded. "Yes . . . walling us in. When more Jews arrive, it's easier to control us . . . easier to . . ."

"Stop," Stefa said. "I don't want to think about it right now. Can we go one minute without thinking the worst? The Germans say it's because there's an epidemic."

"You're just like Father," Aaron said. "Mother knows how bad it is, too, but she keeps her feelings inside."

"You should go," Daniel said. "I can't stand here doing nothing—I'll be reported and I won't get the police job."

"I'll help you," Aaron said.

"No, you come home with me," Stefa said, tugging on Aaron's arm.

"I'll stay here—I'm a man. I can help Daniel. How long do you work?"

"Until sunset," Daniel said.

Stefa let go of his arm. "Mother will be angry."

"Don't tell her I'm here. She's used to me being late."

"I'll walk him home," Daniel offered. "Now that he's a man, he can make his own decisions."

Stefa shook her head in dismay. "All right—I can't fight both of you—but be careful." She smiled at Daniel and started for home.

Aaron waved as his sister disappeared among the throng of laborers.

Daniel extended his hand. "I'm happy to meet you—you're not as small as your sister said."

Aaron scowled.

"Would you like to work or supervise?" Daniel asked.

"Work."

"All right—put your coat over there with mine, but be sure to put your armband on your shirt." Daniel pointed to a patch of green grass. "No trouble here. The Nazis show up every half hour to keep us on our toes. The Blue Police don't pay any attention." Daniel walked to a pile of bricks and picked up two. "Grab as many as you can. We have to make sure they fit firmly against each other."

Aaron folded his left arm and put a brick in the crook created by his elbow. He piled another on top of that and pressed his arm against his chest. He carried a third in his right hand. The weight caused him to tip backward slightly, but he was grateful to be doing something useful, despite the intended outcome.

Daniel stopped at the wall and piled his bricks on the ground.

Aaron did the same. They stood next to a middle-aged Jewish man on a ladder, still wearing his coat and felt cap in the sun, who slathered cement on the bricks that had been laid down upon the wall with careful precision.

"Make sure the edges are smooth so they go against each other," Daniel said to Aaron. "Take this pick and knock off any protrusions, no matter how small." He handed him the instrument.

Aaron studied the brick on both sides and found some uneven areas. He began his work, striking the stone with the metal point. Salmon-colored chips flew into the air. After he'd done three, he went back to pick up more.

Daniel followed the mason, positioning the bricks firmly in place, wiping off the excess cement with a trowel, and then scooping it off the metal blade with his finger before dropping it back into the mixer.

After about an hour of work, sweat broke out on Aaron's brow. They had laid two rows of bricks in the area Daniel supervised. Aaron couldn't reach the top of the wall, so he handed the bricks to Daniel, who stood on a ladder and placed them into position.

They walked back to the pile for more.

"Are there holes?" Aaron asked, his voice barely above a whisper.

"Holes?" Daniel looked at him as if Aaron had gone mad. "Not under my supervision." That look turned to one of narrow gaze and furrowed brows. "Ah . . . I see what you're getting at." He lifted four bricks with his sturdy arms. "Your sister is right—you're itching for trouble."

Aaron picked up three and followed him back to the wall. "It's a fair question. Holes—places where the wall isn't as sturdily built as here—they might come in handy if the Nazis do intend to lock us up like zoo animals."

"Look . . . Aaron . . . I don't want to tell you what to do or talk down to you because you're younger than I am, but you have to be careful. I know what you're thinking . . . or planning. If they do wall us in, what do you think would happen to those who escape?"

"They'd be arrested—or, more likely, shot."

Daniel climbed the ladder and positioned three bricks on the fresh cement and then stepped down. "Come close."

Aaron stepped next to him, so close he could smell the earthy grit on Daniel's body.

"Pretend we're working." Daniel tugged on his beard, turned over one of the bricks, and struck it lightly with a chisel. "Why do you think I've applied for a police position? Let me tell you why—so I can protect our families. That way I'll have some say over who lives and dies." He lifted his head and gazed at the other workers to make sure they weren't listening. "I haven't mentioned that to anyone except Stefa, and, frankly, she wasn't too happy about it."

"I think it's brave."

Daniel smiled. "I'm glad you think so, but I'm not sure my rabbi, or any rabbi, would agree. It's self-centered, and it's not the way we Jews should think."

"What do you mean?"

"God wants us to help others, but He doesn't want us to make judgments about who should live or die—to kill or let live—to play God."

"What about self-defense? I'd do anything for my family, and I don't care who knows it. That's why I asked about the holes." Aaron picked up a brick and studied one end of it. The cement mason had moved several meters beyond them to the east.

"We've got to catch up," Daniel said, looking squarely at Aaron. "Please don't play the hero—for your sake and the good of the family. These are dangerous times and you're much more appreciated and helpful alive. I'm being honest. Leave the protection to me. At some point, you may have to be the young man to lead us out of the wilderness."

Aaron nodded. "The Nazis are coming."

Daniel jerked his head toward the west. Two Wehrmacht soldiers were approaching; one swinging a baton, the other with his rifle drawn and pointed at the workers.

"No more talking," Daniel said. "Back to work. No holes here."

In slightly more than an hour, the sinking afternoon sun had thrown the wall into deep shadows and slowed work for the day. Daniel did a quick inspection of his section and then, true to his word, escorted Aaron back to Krochmalna.

Along the way, Aaron stopped several times to examine parts of the wall that had been constructed already.

"I know what you're doing," Daniel said. "Come on. Your mother will be worried."

Aaron rushed back to him, not wishing to draw attention to his inspections. "Looking for holes."

Daniel put his arm around Aaron's shoulders and pulled him close. "No more today."

Aaron was fine with that, and even as he arrived at home, he burned into his mind the location of several "holes" he'd found in the wall near Krochmalna, where the cement was thin and cracks could be seen around the bricks. Those spots might serve him well in the future. He was happy with the day—excited that he had worked like a man, and buoyed that Daniel would be there to guard his family in the future. He had begun to think of him as a big brother, and that made him smile.

The Wicekról Hotel, the Viceroy, had been constructed in the 1870s on Jasna Street in the grand architectural manner of the time. Izreal Majewski walked through its massive entrance every working day, pushing open its three-meter-high oak doors, marveling at the side panels of stained glass depicting lush pine forests and smooth-furred noble stags, as well as the half-circle fan light above that allowed sun to flow into the lobby.

The Viceroy exuded old-world charm despite the art deco neon sign above the entrance that announced the hotel's location in pale blue every night. Two similarly designed vertical side sconces, in the same style, hung on either side of the doors.

But to Izreal's thinking, the most amazing thing about the Viceroy was its consistent ability to maintain its solid, stately presence—the heavy stone construction and the arched windows that lined its front added to its solidarity—no matter the weather or time of year. In the winter, a cheerful marble fireplace welcomed guests to the lobby as well as those on their way to the Palais, the hotel restaurant housed in a secluded courtyard at the back of the building. There, a spiderweb of iron latticework held up a glass ceiling that allowed ornamental palms and other exotic trees and flowers to capture the sun and grow year-round.

In the summer, a pronounced coolness permeated the Viceroy, perhaps because its façade was white stone. It had the humid feel of an enclosed courtyard where the smell of food and palms mixed.

As the mashgiach, Izreal supervised every process that made the Palais kosher. Wealthy Jews, the first customers, and the Poles who came later, found the restaurant as stable as its foundation, offering fine food and wines for every taste. In his job, he made sure that the dishes served maintained a strict high standard. He had started his working life as a shochet, a ritual slaughterer, and had worked his way up to his current position. For years, the hotel and restaurant had been owned by a Jew. That particular man had the uncanny ability to understand his public and gauge the future. As Hitler rose to power, he had sold it to a new Polish owner who wanted to continue the successful business. Izreal's job was secure, thanks to the new owner and the well-off clientele, but he wondered how long his position would last now that the Nazis had taken over.

The hotel had suffered little during the invasion, other than a few cracks in the stones, which were repaired quickly. Even the glass ceiling over the restaurant had survived, its only sacrifice to the conflict being a thick coating of dust and ash that covered it. The detritus had been washed clean after Poland capitulated.

Now, Nazis dined under brilliant daylight and in the dim recesses of evening. They came in all sizes and shapes, mostly highly decorated Wehrmacht officers who enjoyed good port and cigars; tables of field-gray-uniformed men that Izreal knew only as the SS or SD, who stared at and whispered about the other diners with disdain; and, finally, the brown-suited men of the Gestapo, with smirks on their faces, who laughed at their own good fortune, eating fine food while others starved, joking about "rooting out the traitors." Occasionally, the restaurant received a visit from men in the Einsatzgruppe, a designated corps that no Jew or Pole wished to cross. These diners couldn't care less about whether the food was kosher—only that it was "excellent," and Izreal had contributed to that excellence. Because the Germans ate at the Palais, food unavailable to anyone else in Warsaw flowed into the hotel.

No matter the hour, day or evening, as long as the restaurant was open for business, the tables were dotted, like the alternating squares of a chess board, with swastika-wearing Nazis, dining among the wealthy Poles and the few Jews with money who managed to evade Nazi scrutiny.

On one of the wondrous days of late May when the air was clear and filled with the promise of spring, Izreal was interrupted by the chef, a large Polish man who appreciated the efforts of his mashgiach and the customers he served.

Izreal, wearing his dark jacket, white cotton shirt, black pants, and felt hat, had finished checking the eggs for blood spots and now stood at the vegetable counter, looking over the lettuce to make sure it was free from disease and insects. The hours could be long after the restaurant closed, with the koshering process extending into the early hours of the next morning. Sometimes he didn't arrive home until two or three, long after Perla had gone to bed.

The chef placed a fleshy hand on his shoulder. "The boss says there's a man who wants to see you."

"Who?" Izreal asked, amazed that someone would seek him at two in the afternoon. The lunch rush was over. He had come to work at ten and was already tired. "Tell the boss that I'm busy. If this man wants to see me later when I'm done for the day, he's welcome."

"You might know him." They walked to the glass portals encased in the kitchen doors that looked out to the dining room. "There . . . next to the palm in the corner . . . do you know him?"

"I don't think so," Izreal said. The man had a kind, oval face, with deeply set eyes below dark brows, and thin lips that seemed born to smile. Clad in a dark suit and stick-pinned tie, he was the kind of man who looked comfortable in the Palais, a person of intelligence who might be a teacher. He looked vaguely familiar—Izreal might have seen him in the restaurant, or in the synagogue. Whether he was Jewish or Polish, he couldn't say, but he had the feeling that the man might be someone important.

He walked to a sink and washed his hands. "I'll be back in a few minutes. I should see what he wants."

The chef nodded and returned to a row of pots and pans.

What if he's a Nazi—or an informer? What if someone's in trouble? These questions occupied him as he pushed through the swinging doors and strode into the dining room, where a few people still lingered over lunch. Around him, white-jacketed waiters moved through the space unobtrusively and with an efficiency that always impressed—whether they were taking an order, delivering or picking up plates, or serving coffee and dessert.

Izreal straightened his jacket and then clasped his hands in front of him as he approached the table.

The man looked up without smiling. "Mr. Izreal Majewski?"

He nodded.

The man rose from the table still cluttered with lunch dishes. "Emanuel Ringelblum. I would shake your hand . . . but I understand your work." He sat down again. "The food at the Palais is always excellent, as is the service . . . and always kosher." His smile widened. "I've only been here a few times because I really can't afford it . . . and you have a new class of diners that I don't much care for. However, they seem to appreciate good food."

"I don't mean to be rude, but I'm busy. What do you want?"

"Can you sit for a few minutes? I have something I wish to say only to you."

Izreal surveyed the dining room, thankfully free of German officers except for one table near the door. The few remaining diners were scattered far from this corner table, nestled between a palm and the wall.

"I'd prefer to stand. I only have a few minutes. I have much work to do."

Emanuel settled in his chair, pushing it underneath the fronds that swayed over his head. "I know you by reputation, and I know you are a good man, but you must know something about me first." He tapped on his water glass and one of the white-coated waiters appeared with a pitcher.

"Like gold," he continued after the waiter had replenished the glass and left. "I wish every Jew could afford to come here." He took a drink and put the crystal glass back on the white tablecloth. "I'm a historian. I graduated from Warsaw University in 1927 with a doctoral thesis on the history of the Warsaw Jews in the Middle Ages. My family and I recently were *relocated* back to the city by the Nazis, after having left it." His eyes turned a shade grayer. "You see, history is important to me. We need a record—to tell the truth about what's happening to the Jews in Poland."

Izreal shuffled his feet, feeling that he should return to the kitchen. What the man was saying made no sense. "I don't understand. How can I help you?"

Emanuel leaned toward him. "You have a unique advantage," he said, lowering his voice. "You observe people in this restaurant that most don't see. You can watch them, noting the Germans, Poles, maybe a Jew now and then, and record how they and the city change as the war goes on. Someone must record our history so it won't be forgotten. If no one does, no one will understand the truth, and we will be no more significant than the dust we're made from."

His words sent a shiver up Izreal's back. "Are you asking me to record—to write—what I see? You make it sound as if we'll all die—that there will be nothing left of us."

Emanuel nodded. "This is what we, as Jews, have to look forward to. You're not the only one I've asked to participate in this project. We must record our history for future generations. No one will believe what has happened unless we tell the story."

Izreal shook his head. "I'm not a writer. I could never do what you ask. Besides, I'm too busy. I work long hours with little rest."

He grasped Izreal's sleeve. "Think about what we've been through. Do I need to list what has happened, or do you know? The Nazis won't allow us to publish obituaries. There's even talk of a death tax on Jewish burials. Who can afford that?"

Izreal nodded.

"We were forced to burn our books for heat this winter. Conditions will get worse. We can't visit public libraries . . . but those are the small things." His grip on Izreal's forearm tightened. "Not only have we been humiliated, forced to submit to slave labor, forced to abandon our religion; our people are now being slaughtered."

He drew away from Emanuel, the words stinging his ears.

"I understand your reticence, Mr. Majewski," Emanuel continued, "but we must face the truth. Last November, the Jews of Ostrów Mazowiecka were slaughtered, forced to sit on the edge of pits that the East Prussian police had dug. The SS ordered them to be shot and the policemen killed them all. They fell into the pits and were buried, some still alive. More than two hundred were arrested here in Warsaw in January—taken to the Palmiry Forest and shot. The Nazis threw a Jewish woman from a moving streetcar in February. You might not have known these things because we're kept in the dark in our little world that keeps getting smaller every day. They're going to *imprison* us behind a wall." Emanuel's voice rose from a whisper to a half cry—a plea for help.

Izreal had heard rumors, but they floated around the city like clouds. No one ever knew if what was happening was real—except for the wall. Izreal looked at the German officers near the door. They huddled around the table, talking quietly, lifting dessert forks from their cake to their mouths. "I don't speak of these things . . . I can't speak of the atrocities. It would kill my wife."

"You have a family—two daughters and a son, in addition to your wife?"

"No—one son and a daughter."

Emanuel sipped his water. "I see. Hanna left for England, but Stefa is a young woman coming into her own, as is your son, Aaron, who just became a man." He paused. "Before you ask me how I know so much about you, let me mention the name of Daniel Krakowski. His father supports this project. You can do the same."

Izreal recognized Daniel's name immediately, even though he had not met him. "What you ask—it's not possible."

Emanuel stood. "I'm sorry if I've upset you." His eyes shifted toward the table near the door. "This project goes against everything they stand for. This record will let us live long past our years on earth. At least think about it, Mr. Majewski. Stefa could write what you tell her." He blinked. "Or maybe she could write it herself. She might recognize the importance of this task."

He stood with his head down, gazing at the tiled floor. "My daughter is strong, one who honors tradition . . . unlike her sister. I still speak for her, and I will consider it."

Emanuel withdrew a piece of paper from his pocket and handed it to him. "You can reach me at this address or phone number. Either way, burn it once you've made your decision. You must not tell anyone what we've talked about. If you do,

Jews will die." He relished another sip of water. "I'm done with my meal, and I'm weary of hiding from them. After I pay the check, I'm going outside where the air is free."

Izreal returned to the kitchen, his head swimming with thoughts about this insane project. The chef asked him who the man was, but Izreal brushed off the question. "He was an old friend I haven't seen in many years. I didn't recognize him."

He walked to the meat counter, where a set of knives sat boxed in their clean corner. He opened it, staring at the instruments, so carefully packed in their sheaths, which served the cooks so well. *No one will know the truth, and we will be no more significant than the dust we're made from.* Emanuel's words troubled him as he returned to his work.

CHAPTER 7

The summer of 1940 had not been a good one for Britain, as Lawrence Richardson, quoting from the London newspapers, pointed out daily to Hanna and Lucy.

Hanna cried when she learned that Paris had fallen in June. The Wehrmacht had entered the city without resistance. Disturbing news came from Poland as well. Reporters had risked their lives to get information back to England, where their stories made front-page news. There were reports of "camps" set up in the Polish countryside to detain political prisoners. The exact purpose of those camps was unknown. Were they built to put detainees to "work"? In September, "Jews Only" trams displaying a yellow star of David traversed Warsaw streets. In October, the same Jews were forbidden to leave their homes at night. The only legal hours to work or shop were from eight in the morning until seven in the evening. Hanna wondered whether her father's job at the restaurant had ended.

More immediate and threatening to the town of Croydon was the end of the "phony war" that had lasted for a year. The first Nazi bombing raids on London and the surrounding area signaled the start of the real war on the isle. German bomber sightings—real or imagined—had prompted Lawrence to finish the garden Anderson shelter in early August, tightly fitting its parts together, sandbagging the sides, piling sod on its curved top, and fashioning makeshift bunks inside in case the family needed to hunker down for the night. Lucy had even planted violet phlox on its top in order to "pretty it up."

In mid-August, Hitler showed he meant business when a dozen or so Messerschmitt bombers destroyed the Croydon aerodrome. Lawrence had spotted the planes from the garden during a summer evening. Before he'd had time to gather Hanna, Lucy, and Charlie into the shelter, the planes had dropped their deadly payload and passed by. Then, too late, the air raid warning sounded its monotonous, wavering shriek, which Lawrence called "Moaning Minnie."

Even more destruction rained from the skies a few weeks later, on September seventh, when three hundred German planes attacked in the late afternoon. Incendiary bombs targeted the Royal Docks and the Surrey Commercial Docks, starting infernos that German pilots used as landmarks for targets. The fire brigade did what it could, but the conflagration spread out of control.

Everyone was at home that Saturday, and the attack drove them to the shelter. During a lull in the bombing Hanna stepped from the Anderson, awed by the greasy black smoke that hung in the sky to the north. In another two hours, everyone was driven back into the shelter, holding on to its sides as high explosive bombs, guided by the fires, fell. The great explosions, many kilometers distant, even shook the earth in Croydon. The raid continued until dawn, ravaging not only the docks but the East End, Woolwich, Deptford, West Ham, and Whitechapel, killing more than four hundred people, including seventeen firemen. The "Blitz" had officially begun.

Londoners seemed to withdraw from social life, as if walking a tightrope, a tedious suffocation taking over as they prepared for the next air attack. Even the buoyant, glamorous Margaret used less makeup, conserved her stockings, and told Hanna how grateful she was to have her position as a clerk in the law office despite her earlier statements to the contrary. Ruth and Betty were infrequent visitors now that the raids had begun.

But in early October, the bombs fell closer to Croydon. Lucy and Lawrence attempted to keep their spirits up, but the strain showed on their lined faces, along with an unhealthy pallor from insufficient sleep.

A few weeks later, just after dark, with the blackout still in force, the air raid sirens wailed again. Lawrence, sitting in the living room and smoking his pipe, sighed and put down his book. "Can't we have a quiet evening?" he asked, while Charlie shivered at his feet from the noise. "Get some fresh blankets—in case we have to spend the night," he instructed his wife.

Lucy headed up the stairs to the linen closet as Hanna lifted Charlie from the floor and held the shaking dog in her arms.

"Take him to the garden so he can do his business before we shelter," Lawrence said.

Hanna did so, and released Charlie in the garden, where he reluctantly sniffed near the back wall. A strange stillness hung in the air. The day's breeze had dropped and the sky was shifting from brilliant blue to the inky hue of dusk. The first evening stars revealed themselves with twinkling light. Hannah cocked her head, listening for any sound in the silence, now that the sirens had faded. Gooseflesh raced over her bare arms to her shoulders. She thought of getting a jumper, but decided the blanket would suffice in the shelter. Her uncle-in-law hadn't installed a heater yet, fearing it might be too dangerous in the close quarters. Yet, winter was coming.

Her aunt and uncle appeared at the garden door, Lucy clutching three blankets in her arms. Lawrence had emptied the bowl of his pipe, still holding the stem between his clenched teeth, but no embers glowed, no smoke rose from the blackened receptacle. Charlie ran to him and shivered against his leg.

"Come now, Charlie," he said. "Inside."

"I hate this," Lucy said, as she brushed by Hanna. Charlie rushed to the door and was the first in the shelter, followed by her aunt, and then Lawrence, who had to stoop to enter.

Hanna, coveting a breath of air before committing herself to the stale atmosphere and the sticky heat of the refuge, walked to the white gate and peered to the east. The sky blossomed in purple, except for a few streaks of fading sun that tinged the high clouds with pink.

A row of black dots appeared on the eastern horizon—and, as the seconds ticked by, more came into view, waves of bombers spreading across the sky like the wings of giant locusts. The planes couldn't be counted. Their number was more than she had ever seen, more than she could have imagined.

As the crest of the wave moved ever closer, flashes of light struck the horizon followed by the low rumble of rolling thunder. Yellow and orange flames flared and then receded as the bombers now covered a quarter of the sky. Rising from London, to the north, streaks of anti-aircraft fire raced into the darkness leaving blazing trails of white behind them. The distant rumblings swept over her like an advancing tank.

Hanna retreated to the shelter, stepping down into the earthen pit. The corrugated metal overhead, about two meters high, brushed against her scalp.

Lucy sat on a blanket at the back of the Anderson, cradling Charlie in her arms. Lawrence had reclined on one of the bunks, his long legs stretching to the earthen floor. A candle standing upright in a sand-filled jar threw flickering light against the walls of their silver prison.

Lawrence leaned toward her, his face bathed in the amber glow. "How many bombers?"

Hanna took a blanket from Lucy and sat near the shelter door. "Not that many," she lied, not wishing to worry her aunt. Soon enough, the explosions from the raid would fill their ears and Lucy would know the truth.

They said nothing as the bombings increased in intensity. Hanna covered her body and head with the blanket, and pushed the wool into her ears as their cramped space shook with the vibrations. The fabric muffled the sounds outside, but she could picture clearly what was happening.

Incendiary bombs shrieked from the heavens, landing on roofs, sometimes bursting through them, igniting anything they touched. Even if they landed harmlessly in the street, not detonating until a minute or so after impact as designed, nearby objects would explode in incandescent white flames. Trees, vehicles, anything wooden, would be sprayed with the flammable chemicals.

Homes and buildings crackled as they burned. Masonry split and windows shattered from the heat, cars' petrol tanks exploded in great fireballs. Whole blocks would be destroyed, square kilometers if the flames weren't brought under control.

Heavy explosive bombs usually followed the incendiaries, knocking out water lines that served firefighters. Hanna feared them most. The noise was deafening and the destruction catastrophic. The bombs left nothing but craters, shattered bricks and stone, and splintered wood. A direct hit meant death. One couldn't escape their powerful devastation in a home, an Anderson shelter, or in an underground Tube stop.

The air sizzled around them and Hanna looked at Charlie, hoping the sight of the dog might calm her nerves. Instead, she looked into the animal's terrified face, his brown eyes wide with dread. He seemed to recognize that this raid was different.

She choked back the fear that threatened to swamp her. One could die from heat and asphyxiation in the shelter if a fire surrounded them. The thought of her aunt's home going up in flames caused her heart to thump madly. Everything the family had worked for would be destroyed. Lawrence had put much of his money into the property, as well as its refurbishing. He had provided the salary, but her aunt had fashioned the house into a home.

They listened as the incendiaries bounced in the street in a series of metallic clangs, followed by the explosive hiss—the sign that the white-hot thermite had exploded from the magnesium casing.

"I should go out," Lawrence said, getting up from the bunk. "I can put the fires out with dirt before they burn the house down."

Lucy grabbed his arm. "You'll do no such thing. It's too dangerous."

Lawrence shook his head and sighed, resigned that he was powerless against the bombs.

They sat for a few minutes as a momentary stillness filled the shelter. Even Charlie dropped his guard for a time, his eyes softening in the candlelight.

"Maybe they're—" Hanna's words were cut short by a blast so severe that she felt as if her insides had been twisted—that her body was floating in the air. Dirt and blackness rose before her eyes as everyone in the shelter disappeared behind a thick veil.

How long she was unconscious she didn't know. Emerging from the darkness, she spotted the blurry outline of flames somewhere to her right. She moaned and tried to move her legs, but they were covered by something large and heavy.

She cried out, but no one answered. Hanna felt herself slipping, and before long the sick feeling in her stomach advanced toward her lungs, then to her throat, and, finally, into her head.

She gagged and the world slipped away.

A pall of dense clouds covered Warsaw after they'd shared a sparse lunch. Stefa had helped her mother in the kitchen with the dishes, and was sitting in her room when her father came in.

"I want to talk to you before I leave for work," he said. "I won't be home until late."

Stefa nodded, acknowledging the long hours her father now worked for his Polish boss.

Frowning, her father stepped into the room and closed the door, as if what he wanted to say was a private matter. "Weeks ago I had a talk with a man. His words bothered me at the time, but they bother me more now. I didn't say anything because I've been thinking about what he said."

"Who, Father?"

"Emanuel Ringelblum."

Stefa shook her head. "Who is he? I don't know him."

"Daniel's father is a friend of his."

Stefa stared at him, surprised that her father would mention her boyfriend's name.

"Daniel is a policeman now?" Izreal asked.

"Yes."

Pulling at his trimmed beard, he sat at the end of Stefa's bed and gazed through the small window that overlooked Krochmalna.

"The street can be quiet or noisy now," she said. "It used to be busy all the time. I don't know how Hanna and—" She paused, aware that she had mentioned her sister's name in front of her father. Although he hadn't forbidden the family to talk about her sister, everyone avoided the subject. "—I slept through it. I guess we get used to things."

"I want to meet this man—Daniel."

"Of course, Father. I'm glad. He wants to meet you." She wanted to tell him that her mother had already met him, but felt it was better to keep that meeting a secret, as well as her mother's introduction to Janka. As in any family, there were things that were better left unsaid.

"Is he doing well . . . as a policeman?"

She lowered her gaze, somewhat embarrassed by the question, a degree of intimacy about Daniel that she hadn't expected from her father. "Yes. He has a uniform now. It makes me nervous, but he wants . . . to make things easier for us."

"I understand and admire him," Izreal said, keeping his gaze fixated on the window before finally turning to her. "I understand you better than any of my children. Aaron is his own man—I can instruct and guide, but will he listen?" His eyes glistened as he talked. "I have no doubt that you will become an *eishes chayil*, a woman of valor, as is your mother. But your mother and I are getting older. She is more fragile than she used to be. This war has not been kind to her."

"It hasn't been kind to anyone, Father." She wondered if he thought of Hanna at all these days, or if he had somehow managed to divide the past from the present.

"Yes. That's what Emanuel Ringelblum wanted to tell me." He placed his hands on the end of the bed, as if it gave him some kind of comfort. "He wants me to record what I see—to record our Jewish life for future generations. At first, I thought he was out of his mind, a crackpot of some kind who was exaggerating what he feared, but since we talked months ago, the Nazis have taken over more of Europe. A wall has gone up near us. We are forbidden to leave our homes at night. Things have gotten worse for everyone."

"But what has this to do with me?"

"I'm not a writer. You would be much better recording our history. You could write down what I have to tell, and include it with your own story—even Daniel's if you want."

She didn't know what to say, never having heard of such an idea.

"He's named it Oyneg Shabbos—this 'enjoyment of the Sabbath' is his project. It will record what we Warsaw Jews have lived through."

An unsettling thought flashed in her mind and, by the flick of her father's head, she knew he was aware of what she was thinking.

"This is the hard part," he said. "He wants to record our history . . . in case . . ."

"In case we should die."

". . . *all* of us should die."

A knot, like cold steel, settled into her stomach. "Do you believe we will die?"

He grasped her hands. "I've seen brutality that I would never have imagined. Jews taunted, their beards shaved and trimmed by Nazis. Old women shoved to the ground. Men and women forced to work like slaves. I've been spared so far because the Nazis love the Palais—and the owner keeps me on through his good will. If that ends . . . I'm not sure what will happen. If they herd us into this walled camp, things will grow worse. I'm certain of that." He patted her hands. "Think about it. I want to give him an answer. I can say no."

She kissed his hands. "I will think about it, Father."

"Don't say anything to Daniel about Ringelblum yet, even though his father is involved. The man wants to keep his project a secret. If the Nazis find out, the consequences could be deadly."

She nodded.

Izreal left the room, leaving her to think about what he'd said. She'd seen Daniel dressed for work as a policeman. The sight had shocked her at first—she wasn't sure how she felt about him as an enforcer. After this conversation, she wondered if Daniel was right. Perhaps he would be a way out for all of them, a protector of the family. Had she been called upon to do something as well?

Hanna's rescue played out like a nightmare each time she relived it.

Hands grasping her, like claws digging into her arms. Screaming. Cold water from fire hoses soaking her head and back, lights barely seen through the mud and grime that clouded her eyes, sirens unheard through ears that seemed plugged with cotton. Yet, the fire brigade trucks were only six meters away in the rubble-filled street, water hoses snaking over the piles of stone and slate.

One face looked familiar to her as it bent over hers, yet different in the garish light from flames that spread against the dark. Was it her friend Betty? The woman's lips were red, but the face shone white, as if lit by a searchlight. Betty's black hair, usually netted for wartime readiness, fell loose around her neck and face. Her friend was screaming at her, telling her to hold on, to be strong, that they were going to remove the rubble from her legs and pull her free.

How long this crew of friends, neighbors, and Auxiliary Fire Service men had worked on her she couldn't remember. Time grew meaningless as she slipped in and out of consciousness. At one point, she screamed and a pair of hands held her head, stroking her hair and cheeks, as if calming a frightened animal.

She clenched her teeth and cried out even more. What of her aunt and uncle . . . and Charlie? Were they alive . . . or dead?

She twisted her head backwards but she could only see the sweaty heads and flailing arms of the men who dug at the excruciating load covering her legs. The stone, the bricks, the timber that they flung off her legs seemed to make no difference in the weight. Could she even feel them? Were they there?

She retched in the mud, the bile flowing from her mouth. The fear that she would never walk again consumed her.

"Take a deep breath," someone said. "We'll get you out of here."

Darkness overtook her again and she awoke to find herself on a gurney near the curb; Betty on one side, holding her hand, and a nurse on the other, positioning an intravenous bag.

"My aunt and uncle . . ." She forced the words from her throat, the phrase catching in her throat like smoke.

Betty mouthed something she didn't understand. Hanna grasped her friend's hand, begging her to bend close so she could understand.

"We haven't found them yet," her friend yelled. "The Anderson's been destroyed. You were thrown clear."

She had no tears, for her head seemed as dry as a desert.

As they pulled the gurney away, Hanna turned her head to the side and her mouth opened in horror and sadness.

Lit by the orange firelight, she saw the shattered home. All that was left were the fractured shells of walls and the vertical thrust of timbers that poked up from the debris like burned matchsticks. The bomb had struck the back half of the residence almost squarely, pushing the exploding debris forward like a gigantic earthmover until a huge lump of mud, timber, and rock had covered everything in the garden, including the shelter. And to make matters worse, a water main had shattered in back of the house, flooding the garden and turning the debris into muck.

That was all she remembered until she woke up one afternoon in the hospital. She attempted to talk to a nurse in a starched white uniform, silky hose, and circle cap, but the woman lifted a finger to her lips and instructed her to go back to sleep. "Rest is what you need. Your friends have visited—but you've been asleep."

"My aunt and uncle . . . my legs?"

The nurse scrunched her mouth, choosing her words. "The good doctors saved your legs. It was touch and go. You'll have to learn to walk again . . . but I know nothing about your relatives. They haven't inquired after you. Maybe your friends can tell you more." The nurse left.

Hanna's bed was situated in a large room filled with patients whose own beds were surrounded by white curtains. Hers was near a window on the second story of the building. She was able to look out across a green lawn and past trees that still held the brown leaves of fall.

A blur of days and nights crawled by. Was it days . . . weeks?

One late afternoon, as the sun was setting behind slate-colored clouds, a visitor appeared. At first she didn't recognize the stylish woman, clad in a black coat that hugged her body from her neck to her calves, who carried a matching purse with a brass handle. The woman smiled, unbuttoned her coat, and sat in a metal chair near the bed. "They told me I shouldn't smoke. So I won't be long." She took her gold cigarette case from the purse and tapped it with her red fingernails, as if mere contact with the container gave her some connection to its precious contents.

Hanna's hearing had cleared somewhat, but many conversations still sounded as if they were being conducted underwater. She motioned for the woman to move closer.

"You do remember me?" the woman asked, rising and scooting the chair forward with an elegant push from her arm.

"Yes, but I'm finding it hard to remember your name."

"Rita . . . Rita Wright." She sat again.

"Of course." The two previous meetings with Rita popped into her mind, the last being at her aunt's house.

"How are you?"

Hanna attempted to sit up, but the effort was too great and she fell back, laid low by strain on her back.

"Don't force anything. You must get well."

"I've been in a daze. What day is it?"

Rita lifted the gold case, looked at it, and said nothing.

"You have bad news, don't you?" Hanna had expected the worst, but she had never expected the messenger of death, grandly dressed and manicured, to sit across from her.

Rita crossed her legs and rested the case in the folds of her dress. "Yes. I've been in touch with Betty—she didn't want to tell you. It's been an emotional time for everyone. Even Phillip has been here. I think he cares for you more than he should—not something to be encouraged."

Hanna wasn't concerned about visitors. "They're dead, aren't they—my aunt and uncle and Charlie?"

Rita nodded. "Your aunt and uncle had no chance of making it out alive."

The tears built in Hanna's eyes.

Rita sighed. "You can think of it this way . . . they were merciful deaths . . . as merciful as the Nazis can deal out. Your aunt and uncle didn't suffer. You were thrown clear—the shock wave blew out the door. The back half of the Anderson, where Lucy and Lawrence were sitting, was buried. They had been crushed by the blast when the water covered them."

"Oh, my God," she whispered, turning away from Rita, seeing her own pale reflection in the now-dark windowpanes. Rage consumed her, and she wanted to curse the Nazis and then God for allowing such a tragedy to occur. "And Charlie?"

"He died in your aunt's arms."

Hanna rose on her elbows and winced in pain. "I have to take care of the bodies . . . get out of here."

Rita leaned forward, her eyes softening; still her face conveyed the stern look of someone in charge. "It's too late for that. They've been taken care of, buried with the other Croydon victims. There was no time for services or grief. The bombs continue to fall." She paused. "I'm terribly sorry."

Hanna struggled to move her legs, but with every twitch, no matter how slight, the pain raced into her chest. How could she do anything after this? She wasn't even sure she could walk. "Please tell me what day it is." A tear slipped down her cheek.

Rita looked at her watch. "I want you to think about what has happened. The *Nazis* did this to you and your family. Conditions in Warsaw are growing worse by the hour. I'm telling you this not to destroy your spirit. My advice is to channel your anger into something that will make the world better for everyone. You can be a War Girl like the rest of us—someone who stands against the Nazis and fights for freedom. Mark this day—the day you found out what really happened to your family—as a badge of honor—for God and country." She rose from the chair, opened her purse, withdrew her calling card, and placed it in Hanna's hand. "Fighting them—standing up for what is right—is the best way to honor your aunt and uncle, and the rest of your family."

Rita turned to leave, but stopped at the curtains concealing Hanna from the other patients. "You asked what day it is. It's been ten days since the bombing. The muscles and tendons in your lower legs were crushed and bruised. You have a fracture in your left leg. These injuries need time to heal. The hospital will take good care of you, but don't forget what I've said. I'll be waiting for your answer."

Rita drew the curtains and Hanna was left alone. Over the past few days, her legs had buzzed with electricity like needles were being pushed into her skin. One doctor had told her that was a good sign, even though she had to take a sleeping potion at night to allay the annoying pain.

She looked at the card. It was identical to the one Rita had given her before, the impeccable printing in scrolled script detailing her address and phone number.

She choked back sobs, unsure whether she should tear the card into little pieces or clutch it to her breast. Now she had no family in London, only a few friends, no place to live, and no way to contact her parents except through letters that probably would go unanswered. It was easy to blame her mother and father for her predicament—their demands and restrictions had caused her to flee Warsaw—and easy to blame an absent God, who could have saved them all from tragedy if only He had reached down his almighty hand. But Rita was right—the Nazis were to blame.

A sudden tiredness overtook her as she placed the card underneath the pillow and weighed Rita's words. *You can be a War Girl, like the rest of us—someone who stands against the Nazis and fights for freedom.* As she closed her eyes, hoping to dream of revenge, of taking an eye for an eye, a tooth for a tooth, she wondered what she should do after she could walk again.

CHAPTER 8

Shortly after the Hebrew month of Cheshvan, November 1940, footsteps thudded in the Krochmalna apartment hall, along with violent shouts and cries for mercy. The wailing caused Perla to cover her ears and sink in dismay on the couch.

Stefa had dreamed of what was coming, heard the rumors from Daniel, and seen the sad change in her father's face. Even Aaron seemed distracted and perplexed by what was happening, his enthusiasm for the war changing to one of trepidation and fear.

She rushed to quiet her mother, patting her hand and stroking her pale cheek. "I'll see what's happening. Stay here."

Perla held out her hands, her face sagging with terror, silently pleading for Stefa to stay with her, but the time had come to face the evil that lay in wait outside. She and her mother had seen the desperate line of stragglers on Krochmalna, the march of Jews driven from the countryside and the Warsaw suburbs, into the "resettlement area," now known as the ghetto. Stefa had no idea of the number of people they had seen: men pulling carts loaded with bedding, pots, pans, and clothing; women pulling children along, many holding babies to their breasts; old men with beards and long coats clutching at their wives; horses, donkeys, and dogs jostling with the crowd. The exodus seemed endless, and that didn't include the refugees who had entered the ghetto from other streets. How were all the Jews going to exist in this tiny area walled in by the Nazis?

Stefa wanted to force her father to talk about what was troubling him, what he was keeping inside. They had heard the loudspeaker announcement on October twelfth that all Jews must relocate to the ghetto at the end of the month. Her father had told her not to worry, that it didn't apply to their building on Krochmalna, he had everything "in hand." Everything would turn out for the best because of his position at the Palais. The Germans who dined there loved him, complimented him when the chef told them with what loving care Izreal Majewski approached the food. Her father accompanied the owner and chef now and then when they would offer a bottle of wine to the high-ranking Nazis. One of the entitled officers remarked that they were "the good Jews," even though the other two men were Catholic.

Even Aaron had attacked his father's apparent diffidence at supper a few times, only to be rebuffed with a cold stare and the words "Do not think upon it." Her father had given her a few thoughts to write in the "diary" for Emanuel Ringelblum, but she found herself more often than not recording her own words on the page. It was easy to see what was happening outside her window, and to write the stories told by Daniel and her brother.

The rumblings grew louder in the hall.

"Stay with me, Stefa," her mother said, wringing her hands.

Loud bangs on the door jolted them both.

"I'll go," Stefa said, her heart pounding in her neck, a dry scratchiness filling her mouth. She took a deep breath and rushed toward the door.

Someone kicked at the wood, nearly splintering it.

Stefa yanked it open. A uniformed SS officer stood outside, surrounded by five Wehrmacht men. The officer held a clipboard, while the army men pointed their rifles at her.

"This is the home of Izreal Majewski?" the SS officer asked in German.

Stefa nodded.

He switched to Polish, removed a piece of paper from his clipboard, and shoved it into her hands. "You have twenty-four hours to relocate to a new address on Krochmalna."

She looked at the address and then at the men. "Twenty-four hours? That won't be enough time."

The SS officer thrust his face close to hers, his right hand lowering to the pistol at his side. "Listen, Jew. *You* are lucky. You've had more than enough time. You have another apartment to go to. Others will join you." He paused. "Twenty-four hours." He looked at his watch. "By noon tomorrow. Is that a radio?" He pointed to the machine resting on the sideboard.

Stefa nodded.

"You were supposed to turn it in to the proper authorities." He signaled for one of his men to retrieve the radio. When that was accomplished, the officer raised his hand stiffly in a salute to the Führer, and then turned his attention to Mrs. Rosewicz's door.

He pounded on it, and the old lady appeared a few moments later, her face tearstained, hair disheveled. Stefa listened as the officer repeated the same instructions to Mrs. Rosewicz, but offered no piece of paper. The SS officer turned and the army men followed, flowing down the stairs like water over river stones.

Mrs. Rosewicz, stunned by what had happened, stood in her door, her eyes wide and red. She placed her hands on her sunken cheeks. "I have no place to go. What shall I do?"

Stefa crossed the hall and held the quivering woman in her arms. She was like a translucent shell ready to break, all skin and bones, with little warmth to her body. She tried to reassure her neighbor that all would be well, but she wasn't sure—not after what she had just heard. "We will find you a place—maybe with us. If not, someplace else safe and warm."

". . . but a day to pack my things. Everything I own is here. I have a lifetime in this apartment. All my memories."

Perla appeared at the door, just as fragile, arms and legs quaking, struggling to stand as she clutched the doorframe.

"What will we do?" her mother asked. "Your father will have the answer."

Her mother always relied on her father, but this time was different. This wasn't a question of what to make for dinner, what relative to visit, whether it was necessary to go to synagogue—this was a question of life and death, the obliteration of a home. A strange voice came into her head. *This is more than the obliteration of a home—they want to kill us. They want to wipe us from the face of the earth so that no one will remember who we were. Ringelblum is right. We must go on . . . if only in the world's memory.*

She wanted to dismiss everything that had occurred since the invasion, but she was under no illusion that the Nazis were a nightmare created by a troubled mind. Her eyes had seen what the Germans could do, and unlike a bad dream that was over in the morning, the piece of paper that she held in her hand was real. Every day held a new horror.

Stefa clutched Mrs. Rosewicz's hands and told her to pack what she could. "I will talk to my father."

When she turned back, Perla had disappeared. Stefa returned to the apartment and shut the door. Her mother was bent over the sideboard, her hands clutching the menorah, then shifting to the silver cutlery so carefully placed inside the drawers.

"So the radio is gone. What to take . . . what to take . . ." Perla brought her hand up to her throat, looking as if she might collapse.

Stefa clutched her mother's arm. "Let's wait for Father. He will help lead us from this desert."

Perla's brows crinkled in concern, her gray eyes filled with tears. She collapsed against Stefa and cried.

God protect us . . . God lead us out of this desert. The words bounced feebly in her head, and she wondered whether He would answer her with kindness, or the prayer would disappear into the void alongside a million others.

*   *   *

Janka Danek also had seen the procession of Jews winding their way through the streets to the ghetto. She had witnessed this cruel act from her window overlooking Krochmalna. These shuffling lines of humanity were subjected to blows from armed guards, to insults hurled by the Poles, even abuse from the Blue Police. Shouts filtered through the window, but she could see how people were being treated as well as hear their cries. If they moved too slowly they were bludgeoned, if they moved too fast and something fell from a wagon or their arms, they were whipped if they stopped to pick it up.

"Move faster, Jews," the guards snapped, with snarls on their faces. It seemed like a game for the Nazis, but "game" wasn't a fair assessment. What was happening in Warsaw was much more than perverse sport; it was an infection that had spread through the German troops, to the Poles, to anyone who felt the Jews should be ridiculed, spat upon, or obliterated.

These resettlements took place during the day, when Janka was at home or out shopping. Everyone who wasn't involved could see what was going on. She had never seen a procession at night—it was illegal for Jews to be on the streets after seven, unless they were being escorted by a guard—an equally bad situation for a Jew. Those caught after dark would be arrested and punished. Even Karol had laughed at their plight and made fun of those nabbed by the Nazis after dark. He was rarely home during the day to witness the worst of it.

One evening, a few minutes before seven, as she waited for her husband to wander home from the bar, she took a break from cooking to go to the window. The evening meal consisted of three link sausages and some beans she had purchased secretly from a Polish butcher. From her vantage point, she saw two shadowy figures emerge from the blackness into a patch of light they couldn't avoid. One she recognized as Aaron. She wasn't sure if they saw the German who was headed down the street toward them.

She turned off the stove, leaving the sizzling meat to stew in its juices, and darted down the stairs.

The two figures crouched behind the rubble of a bombed building.

"Officer . . . officer . . ." she shouted, uncertain how to address the approaching soldier.

Clutching the rifle slung over his shoulder, he crossed the street in long steps. Wary, he unbuttoned his coat, withdrew a pistol, and pointed it at her. Despite that, she was not afraid. He was nothing but a boy with ruddy cheeks holding a day's growth of beard that needed the benefit of a razor.

"Do you speak Polish?" she asked in German.

"*Ein bisschen*," he replied. *A little.*

She pointed down the street, east, away from the figures that had taken refuge behind the rubble. "*Jude!*" she repeated several times in an urgent voice. "*Z mojego okna.*" From my window.

The young soldier lowered his gun and pointed a thin finger in the same direction as Janka.

"*Ja*," she said.

"*Danke.*" He sprinted down the street, pistol pointed, looking left and right for the errant Jew.

As soon as the soldier had disappeared, she walked across the street to the pile of stones. Peering behind it, she found Aaron and a man, flattened against the rubble. "It's all right. He's gone."

The youth lifted himself from the rocks—the older man had a harder time of it. Aaron helped him up.

"Mrs. Danek," Aaron said. "We were on the way home when we saw the soldier . . ." He paused, as if embarrassed by what he wanted to say. "This is my father . . . you haven't met."

Aaron was right—she hadn't met him. She strained to see the man in the dim light, his dark coat blending in with the stone and shadows. He had a trimmed salt-and-pepper beard that covered most of his face, which was visible between the brim of his hat and the scarf that covered his throat.

"Go inside now," Izreal commanded his son. "Help your mother. I'll be there soon."

Seeing that no German was near, Aaron vaulted over the stones and disappeared from sight.

Izreal brushed the dust from his coat. "Who are you?" He sounded suspicious, as if no one in their right mind would help a Jew at night.

"Janka Danek . . . my husband and I live on the other side of the street." She pointed to the roof of her apartment building, which jutted above the debris. "I've met your son before and . . ." She stopped, unsure whether she should mention that she knew Perla and Stefa.

"Ah . . . you're the one." He put a finger to his temple. "I wouldn't have found out, but chicken and meat went missing. My wife isn't good at telling lies—my son is much better—but I forced it out of her after the food disappeared."

"I'm grateful. Everything's so hard to get these days." She shivered and rubbed her arms, for she wasn't wearing a coat. "My husband thinks I bought it . . . that I was able to make a devil's deal with the butcher."

"Thank you for getting rid of the soldier, Mrs. Danek," he said. "I probably would have been fine with the man, since I work at the Palais . . . but my son. I can't stay long. We have to be out of our apartment by noon tomorrow."

Janka's breath caught.

"My son came to get me. Since the Nazis arrived, the hotel phones can't be trusted."

Janka knew the restaurant, but had never set foot inside because it was much too expensive for her and Karol.

"They're forcing you to move—like the other Jews?"

Izreal nodded. "Yes, like all the rest—even some Poles. I'm surprised you haven't been forced to leave." He stared at her with an unsettling look of indifference.

She shifted on her feet. "My husband, Karol, works at the copper plant. He told me that's why we still have our apartment. He's considered essential now that the Nazis manage it. They've overlooked me—I don't have a job."

He lifted his hat, brushed his hand through his thinning hair, and put it back on. "We Jews are dirt to the Nazis." His gaze shifted toward the street. "I must go. Thank you again, Mrs. Danek. You'll get no more food from us now." He turned toward Krochmalna as a few Poles passed by.

"Mr. Majewski," she said, stopping him as he prepared to step out. "Thank you. If you need something, remember my name—Janka Danek on Krochmalna. I hope all goes well for your family. I wish I could do more."

He looked back at her before he disappeared, saying, "I will remember . . . Janka Danek."

She had scrambled from behind the debris, crossed the street, and grasped the outside doorknob when a boozy voice called her name.

"What the hell are you doing?" Karol asked, stumbling near her as he flung open the door. "Did I see you with a man?"

"No . . . you must be mistaken."

Karol butted against her, and shoved her inside. She landed roughly against the staircase railing.

"Why were you out . . . in the night?" The acidic astringency of his vodka-laced breath stung her face.

"I . . . I . . ." Karol had caught her off guard and she could think of no good excuse. Anything she could say or make up would sound like a lie.

He raised his hand, palm open, as if to strike her, while she cowered on the stairs. "Don't lie. I saw him—a dirty Jew—with that beard. Why?" His cheeks flushed red under the single bulb that burned in the entrance.

She lowered her head, crumpling under his brutal gaze. Karol had never struck her before but she feared that he might in his drunken anger, perhaps in a lesson learned from the Nazi occupiers.

The only way out was the truth, with a bit of embellishment. She steadied herself against the steps, and, gathering her courage, faced him. "Did you ever wonder where we got the meat that has kept us alive? It wasn't from the Polish butcher. It was from the kind Jews who thanked me for helping their son."

He teetered against the door, dumbstruck by her words, the color in his cheeks fading from red to white. "You helped a Jew?"

"Yes, and I would do it again, so we . . . *you* . . . could have something to eat . . . something to put on our table besides a few measly potatoes and carrots."

Karol caressed the stubble on his face. "We've been living the high life thanks to a Jew?"

She nodded. "And you should count yourself lucky to have such gifts."

He bent over as if to laugh, but muttered instead, "What are we eating tonight?"

"Three link sausages from a Polish butcher, who told me I was lucky to get them." Her body felt heavy and lifeless, each foot like a weight as she trudged toward the apartment. "They're getting cold in their own juices."

He followed her up the stairs. "What did you do to earn such favor from a Jew?"

She lowered her voice so the neighbors wouldn't hear. "Just after the war started, I protected him from a German soldier by calling him my son . . ."

Karol spit on the landing. "Your son?" The disgust in his voice was palpable. "What is their name?"

She stopped at the door and stared at him. The flush of alcohol had returned to his cheeks, his lips curled into a sardonic half-smile. A shiver rushed over her. She knew what he was thinking—some dangerous notion hatched by her husband. If there was a way he could make a profit or protect himself from the Nazis, Karol would do it. He would turn knowing a Jewish family to his advantage.

"I don't know their names," she said.

"You're lying."

"No. We felt it would be safer for everyone." She opened the door and the smell of grease wafted over them. "It doesn't matter anyway . . . they're being sent to the walled area. There will be no more food from them."

Karol took off his coat, settled on the couch, and put his feet up on the coffee table. "Too bad." He rested his head on the green fabric. "They're probably as good as dead."

She turned on the stove and stared at the brown sausage, now cold and covered in a thin layer of gray oil. Sticking a fork into one of the links, she shifted her gaze to her husband.

With closed eyes and crossed arms, he seemed on the verge of sleep; however, the smile lingered on his lips and Janka knew he was thinking about the Majewskis. It didn't matter if he knew their name—somehow, he would work that knowledge to his advantage.

Stefa, stunned from the realization that time in her childhood home was ending, had watched with a mixture of disbelief and numb resignation as the family tried to make sense of the strange new life that awaited them the next day.

Her father, often a man of few words, offered only a brief explanation, addressing them as they gathered around him in the living room after supper. "The time has come to leave our home. We have no choice. The General Government and the Judenrat have made it clear. We have been lucky so far. Take only what you need. Sentiment should be left behind. I will make the final decision on what goes or stays."

Perla had spent most of the evening in tears, opening drawers, looking at every manner of object, whether it was in the kitchen, the dining room, or the living room. Izreal had indulged his wife, admonishing her to "take only what will serve us in our new home," while extending a comforting hug when he could. Time was slipping away quickly; and noon, the appointed hour the next day, weighed heavily upon them.

Aaron, perhaps, had it easiest of all, Stefa thought. She had looked in upon him in his bedroom—watched while he put clothes and a few books in a suitcase and slammed the lid shut.

He didn't have much to take, he told her. However, he may have lost the most of all of them—his youth ripped away and his future thrown into an uncertain manhood.

She had attempted, with discerning eyes, to keep only what was necessary: warm clothing, scarves, gloves, three pairs of shoes. Although she wanted to take the few nice dresses that she had, she wondered how practical they would be in the ghetto. How many dinners, special religious ceremonies, or festive occasions would she be attending? Part of her burned with desire for a better life, an unfettered optimism that the world would get better. Thoughts, with no evidence behind them, flitted through her head like butterflies: the British would invade and save them; enslaved nations would revolt and rise up against their Nazi captors; her family would somehow escape the ghetto; however, none of that was based in fact. The little she knew about world events confirmed that everything in life was getting worse. Hitler and his forces had swept through Western Europe, overcoming a failed resistance. No liberating army was coming to save the fallen nations—or, least of all, the Jews of Warsaw.

They were exhausted when they crawled into bed near midnight, with little hope for the future despite encouragement from Izreal. During the long night, memories flooded her, a lifetime's accumulation of her seventeen years, while mourning the possessions she would leave behind. The bedrooms were silent; in fact, the apartment was strangely quiet. Finally, near four, she fell into a fitful sleep.

It was still dark at six in the morning, when the family gathered in the kitchen. They had switched on the apartment lights, but nothing happened. Izreal concluded that the building's electricity had been cut off. There was no water in the bathroom. Aaron tried the tap over the sink—a few gurgling drops emerged and ran down the white porcelain to the drain.

Perla lit candles, and made a breakfast of bread and jam. Izreal said a blessing over the food and they ate, aware that this would be their last meal in the house.

The earliest rays of dawn shone through the broad windows not long after they had finished.

"I'll gather the food," Perla said.

"I'll help you wrap it—in the kerchiefs," Stefa said.

"We have two bags apiece—"

"One . . . for me," Aaron said, cutting off his father.

"Except my son . . . who has one," Izreal said. "We don't have a cart, a donkey, or a car, so we must load on our backs what we can carry. Anything heavy must stay."

"The chair from my parents' home?" Perla sniffed.

"No," Izreal replied.

"The silver . . ." she pleaded.

"The menorah, my shochet knives, the silver, and the ration cards are in one suitcase," Izreal said. "The other holds my clothes."

"The pictures . . ."

"Our memories will have to do."

Her father's words reminded Stefa that she hadn't packed the Ringelblum diary she kept in the nightstand drawer. She rushed to her room, located the book, and buried it in her suitcase under her clothes. A debate raged in her head over one other item. Finally, she made up her mind. She opened the dresser drawer, reached for the jar of face cream that had been so carefully concealed there, and placed it in her case.

"The world will get better," she said as she closed the lid. "It must."

A trio of German officials, none of whom Stefa had seen or encountered before, arrived shortly before noon, starting their official visit at the first floor, working their way up the marble stairs to the top. Unlike earlier visits, when shouts and despondent cries had accompanied the Nazis, this inspection was different: a simple knock on the door, a smile from an SS officer, followed by a soft order in Polish asking the Majewskis to go to the street. Then, the men were on their way to Mrs. Rosewicz's.

Izreal asked them why the electricity and water had been turned off.

"Everything has to begin anew for the German families who are moving into this building," one officer said officiously. "We want to make the transition as smooth as possible. I'm sure the living quarters are immaculate, but we need to inspect and *disinfect* it." He stepped forward, his field coat rustling against his legs, and peered into the apartment. "Very good. You're leaving the furniture—of course."

"Of course," her father said. "We can't carry it on our backs."

The man smiled again, his lips slightly parted.

"I'm a mashgiach," Izreal said. "There's no need to disinfect our home."

The white teeth clenched and the jaw tightened. "A kosher home. You understand we have orders that must be obeyed. What is done isn't personal. Every apartment must be cleansed for the new German families." He saluted, clicked his heels, and turned again to the neighbor's apartment.

"Time to gather our things," Izreal said in an uncharacteristically loud voice, as if urging his family on to the formidable task. "The food is ready?"

Perla nodded, but Stefa thought her mother might collapse from the strain. Her face had turned ashen at the sight of the men.

"Can we take the chair?" her mother pleaded again, as she had the night before. "It's all I have to remember them by."

"No," he said. "We have to leave it."

Perla's eyes reddened and she brought her hands to her mouth to stifle the sobs.

"Come, Mother, we haven't time for that," Stefa said. "It's only a few minutes until noon."

Perla tried to compose herself as Aaron, panting, lugged the suitcases to the door. His face grew red from his father's heavy case loaded with silver.

Stefa stuffed her and Perla's coat pockets with the wrapped

food. "Stand still while I put these on you." Her mother obeyed. Stefa then positioned a makeshift rucksack loaded with canned goods on Perla's back. Then, it was her turn to do the same.

"I took the best jewelry," Perla told Stefa, while reaching for one of her suitcases. "I want you to have something after I'm gone."

"Don't be silly," Stefa said. "You should enjoy it now." She patted her mother's shoulder. "You can wear it in our new home." How strange the words "new home" sounded. As much as she wanted to remain optimistic, she doubted whether her mother would have any use for jewelry, other than as a source of needed cash. Her father's bank account had been frozen for nearly a year, allowing the family to use only the zlotys he received from work. He was paid in small bills to avoid Nazi oversight.

They filed into the hall, ready to start the trek down the stairs to the street. Everyone wore two coats and clutched their cases. The only one with a free hand was Perla because Aaron had taken one of his mother's suitcases.

They stood with the door open, looking at the furniture they had to leave behind, silent and ghostly. The dining room table they had taken shelter under when the war started, the green couch that faced the south bank of windows, the chair that Perla wanted so desperately to take, the sideboard that had held their most precious objects—all sat hollow and sad, like objects in a still life.

The neighbor's door creaked open and Mrs. Rosewicz stood stonelike in front of them. Her thin arms clutched a suitcase, dragging her down. It was apparent that she hadn't slept since getting the order to resettle. Her normally tidy gray hair, usually swept back in a bun, streamed down the side of her face in unruly waves; the bright blue woolen cap and scarf she wore did nothing to hide the lines of despair etching her face.

Perla had her foot on the first step when she saw her neighbor. She looked back. "Give me my suitcase, Aaron. Take Mrs. Rosewicz's."

The old woman sighed and her dark gaze rose toward the heavens in relief. Aaron gave his mother the suitcase and took the elderly woman's.

"Take my arm, Mrs. Rosewicz," Aaron said, as they descended the stairs. Izreal led the way, followed by Perla and Stefa.

The woman grasped Aaron's arm as if holding on to a life raft in a tempestuous sea. "Thank you. I don't know what I'll do . . . where I'll go."

"Didn't they give you an address?" Aaron asked.

The old woman shook her head.

Izreal reached the bottom of the stairs. The address boxes had been stripped of the Jewish names, either blotted out or ripped from the metal holders. The replaced mezuzah had been destroyed with orders not to place another, or be charged with a crime punishable by death.

Despite the chill in the air, the fall sun bored into them as they stepped onto Krochmalna. Stefa felt hot and uncomfortable wrapped in her coats, carrying food in her pockets and on her back, and hefting the suitcases. What must her mother be feeling? But there was nothing she could do to make things better. For a few seconds, she resented Hanna for leaving them, imagining that her sister was safe with Lucy and Lawrence, living a life of comfort and security that she could only dream of now that the war had ripped them apart.

They were not alone. The street was filled with Jews wearing white armbands. Others wore no signifying markers. They were Poles, she guessed, whom the Nazis had decided must be relocated to the ghetto as well, perhaps for marrying a Jew. She had seen a stream of Jews flowing toward the walled city before, but nothing like this.

"Father, how are all these people going to fit inside?" she asked.

He shushed her and turned his attention to the armed guards lining the street. For a moment, the crowd stilled, voices dropped, the air silenced except for the wind that rippled down

Krochmalna. Heads turned toward the SS officer who had knocked on their door. He stood on a large shoebox placed in the center of the street.

"Jews and Poles," he shouted, "you're on your way to your new homes within the Jewish Residence District. You will find it as comfortable and welcoming as the homes you have left. We are protecting you against the epidemics that have broken out in the city after the glorious invasion. You will find—if you have not already—that our primary concern is for your health and well-being." He stopped and held up his pistol, barrel pointing toward the sky. "We can welcome you, but you must also welcome your protectors. The police—Poles and Jews—will assist you and guide you to your new homes. So go forward this day, the Sabbath eve if you're a Jew; this Friday, November fifteenth, without fear and with the best hopes for a better life provided by a loving Führer and the generosity of National Socialism."

He surveyed the crowd and then pointed to the guards overseeing the refugees. "Go now, quickly, as fast as you can. We will be watching to make sure you get there safely."

Izreal called them together, including Mrs. Rosewicz, and they meandered down the street like cattle being called to the stall for the evening. The guards, some smiling, some tight-lipped and ominous, mirrored their movements along Krochmalna. Their rifles hung by their sides, not pointed directly at them, but ready to be raised at the slightest provocation. Stefa kept her eyes focused in front of her or to the sky; many of her companions lowered their heads, marching with grim determination in their step.

Looking up, Stefa spotted Janka Danek standing behind the window of her apartment. She kept her head turned, hoping Janka would spot her on the street and that the guards wouldn't notice her behavior. It was impossible to wave or make any gesture that might alert the soldiers.

A ghostly figure behind the window, Janka's pale reflection shifted to one side. Stefa stopped for a moment, lowering her suitcases, and patted the top of her head. Was it enough to draw the woman's attention?

She picked up her cases, caught up with her family, and looked back for a moment toward the apartment. Janka stood with one hand to her mouth and the other pointing toward her. She had been seen! Her heart jumped a bit, knowing that at least one person on the Aryan side of the ghetto knew where they were going—this Polish woman might be of help one day.

The irreversibility of her family's situation weighed on her as much as the suitcases. Empty businesses, many with the star of David painted on the door, stood silent on each side of Krochmalna, a testament that their owners had left the city or were already in the ghetto. Down the street, a brick wall more than three meters high, topped by barbed wire and jagged bits of broken glass that sparkled in the sun like deadly diamonds, encased the previously open thoroughfares of Warsaw.

Mrs. Rosewicz stumbled over a tilted cobblestone and Aaron caught her by the arm. She cried out as if shot, saying, "What am I to do? I'm an old woman. Everything is gone."

Stefa rushed to her side and, alongside Aaron, attempted to console her.

"Hold on," her brother said. "It's only a little farther. We won't let anything happen to you."

"Yes," Stefa said. "We'll take care of you."

The guards herded the crowd left and soon they stood in front of a tall wire gate at Chłodna Street consisting of twelve panels, six on each side. This entrance was guarded by the SS, Wehrmacht soldiers, and the Blue Police. The guards that had accompanied them broke off and left the crowd in control of those who now stood as masters of the ghetto.

"In here," a tall SS man barked, and swept one arm in a wide circle around his body. He had a sharp chin and looked like a flagpole draped in a uniform.

The crowd moved forward like a caterpillar and gathered around the SS officer who stood erect and emotionless.

The gate remained open, but Stefa knew that it would soon

clang shut, sealing them inside the walls. This was the "Jewish Residence District," the air thick and the world shut out. Despite growing up on these streets, walking their sidewalks, shopping countless hours with her mother and Hanna, this new world seemed foreign. She put her suitcases on the bricks and put her arm around Aaron.

"Welcome to your new home," the SS man said without any pretense of warmth. "Some of you have assigned housing, others do not." He stretched his arms, indicating the two different groups of soldiers who awaited his instructions. "Those who have no assignment are to go with the men to my north. All others proceed south."

Mrs. Rosewicz clutched Aaron's arm, a spasm of fear spreading across her face. "Mr. Majewski . . . Izreal," she whispered, "help me. I have no place to go."

Her father grasped the woman and positioned her next to his side. The SS man paid no attention to this small distraction.

"If you have no work, you will find it," the man continued. "Work is necessary. You will need your papers and permits to move about. If you obey instructions and do as you're told—all will be well. Go now. Attention!" He saluted the soldiers who had shifted from a resting position to active duty, as if he had turned on a switch. "Those to the north!"

Gathering their things, about half the group broke away to the soldiers.

"Izreal," Mrs. Rosewicz pleaded, "do something."

"Sir . . . sir . . ." Her father raised his hand and waved at the SS man, who, this time, scowled at the interruption.

"Colonel, to you. What is wrong? Make it quick."

Izreal hesitated for a moment before speaking. "This is our neighbor. She was given no address and can live with us."

The colonel pushed through the crowd and held out his leather-clad arm. "Your assignment."

Izreal patted his pockets. "The paper . . . who has the paper?"

"I do, Papa," Stefa said.

"Give it to the officer," her father ordered.

She had placed it in her coat, keeping it safe since the Germans had given it to her. Fishing with her fingers around the food in her pocket, she finally found the crumpled paper and handed it to the officer. He studied it with disdain for a moment and then flung it back.

"What is your name?" he asked Mrs. Rosewicz, eyes narrowing under the brim of his black cap. "Don't lie to me."

"Rosewicz," she said meekly.

"Your name is not listed." He yanked the woman away from Izreal's side, shoving her through the crowd toward the soldiers.

The group parted as the woman fell to her knees, tearing her stockings and bloodying her knees.

"Get up, filthy Jewish hag!"

"Stop it!" Aaron tightened his fists.

The colonel turned from Mrs. Rosewicz, eyes blazing. "Who said that?"

The officer withdrew the riding crop at his side and stood over her like an enraged brute about to beat a cowering animal. "I will ask once more. Who said that?"

Izreal looked at his son, warning him not to say a word.

Aaron broke away from his father and ran toward the officer. "I did . . . I have her suitcase."

"Bring it here."

Aaron gathered the brown leather case and placed it near the crying woman's feet.

"Now watch what happens when you question an order given by your superiors." He lifted the crop with a vengeful swipe above his head and slashed it across Mrs. Rosewicz's back— once, twice—three, four times.

Stefa turned away, the whoosh of the leather and the cries of the old woman making her sick to her stomach. Aaron stood numbly by Mrs. Rosewicz's side.

"Pick it up, useless Jew," the man ordered. "Pick up your miserable belongings. Soon, they will be ours, anyway."

Aaron helped the woman to her feet, her cries for help turning to muted sobs.

The colonel laid his crop across the case and ordered, "Lift it."

A blur brushed past Stefa and wrapped his arms around her father's chest.

It took a moment for Stefa to realize that the blur was Daniel, attired in his police uniform, standing in front of her, clutching Izreal, whispering in his ear. He was holding her father back, telling him not to interfere, she thought.

"Leave me," the colonel yelled at Aaron. Her brother rushed back to his father.

"Can you help her?" Aaron asked Daniel.

He shook his head. "It would only cause her more pain."

Wincing, Mrs. Rosewicz stooped to pick up her bag, but couldn't hold on to it. The suitcase fell to the ground and popped open, spilling its contents upon the bricks.

"Leave it," the officer said, and pushed her into the arms of one of the waiting soldiers. "We've wasted enough time. Get moving." The soldier grimaced, as if he had touched something filthy, and shoved her away.

Izreal's face reddened and he attempted to wrench himself free from Daniel's grasp. "Who are you? Let me go."

"I'm Daniel Krakowski of the Jewish Ghetto Police."

Izreal's struggle subsided, and he turned to look upon the face of the man whom Stefa had been seeing for more than a year.

"Papa, this is Daniel."

Like many other Jewish policemen, he was dressed in a cinched double-breasted wool coat, dark pants, leather shoes, and military-style cap. The only thing that marked him as a Jew was the white armband he wore on his right sleeve.

"I can do nothing?" Izreal asked. "A man whom the Nazis compliment . . . I can do nothing? A man who ensures the excellence of the food they devour?"

Daniel stepped back, opened his coat, and said in a low voice, "Do you see a weapon, Mr. Majewski? We can do nothing for *now*. But later . . ."

Mrs. Rosewicz disappeared from sight, having been swept

away with the soldiers and the crowd. Only the spilled contents of her luggage, one item being a photograph of her husband, remained on the ground. A Polish policeman casually walked to the case and sifted through it, tossing clothing to the ground, inspecting the few items of jewelry in the case. Stefa wanted to strangle him.

It was time for them to leave the gate. The second group of soldiers moved them south with military precision toward the walled-off portion of Krochmalna. Soon they were on the street, looking for the address given to them by the German officers.

"It must be near here," Izreal said, shielding his eyes against the sun.

"Very close," Daniel said. "I'll take you there. We're all living together."

Stefa couldn't believe what she was hearing. "What?"

"I told you there were benefits to being a policeman," Daniel said.

"You arranged this?" Izreal asked. "How many of us are in this apartment?"

"The four of you and my parents and me—seven in two rooms. We're lucky. Most Jews are living six or seven to a room. Others may join us. I have no control over that, but the Judenrat did grant my request. They know your reputation, Mr. Majewski."

"I'm glad," Aaron said, looking up at Daniel with a bit of joy in his eyes.

Stefa didn't want to admit it, but she was happy, too. Daniel was only a closed door away. She could see him now as often as she liked, and, more important, her parents would get to know him better. If there was a way out of this war, she might be able to marry the man she wanted, rather than one of her parents' choosing.

Daniel pushed through the crowd, withdrew a slip of paper from his coat, and presented it to a soldier. "This is the address for the Majewskis." The man only grunted and pointed his rifle at the building.

A sad, four-story structure that looked as if it had been

neglected for many years stood in front of them. Some of the windows had been broken in the bombing and were covered with wood planks; the stone façade, once white, bled dirty black streaks down its face. The only good thing about the building was that it faced south toward the winter sun.

"This is home," Daniel said and led them up the stone steps.

Home . . . home . . . It was nothing like Stefa had imagined. She would have to make the best of it.

CHAPTER 9

By mid-November, Hanna's doctors were pleased with her recovery.

Their satisfaction didn't mean that she was without pain. Her hospital stay had begun with nearly two weeks of rest while she struggled to move her legs and regain her hearing. By early November, she was out of bed and walking, first with the aid of nurses and then with crutches. She had never broken a bone before, so she found the wooden sticks under her arms uncomfortable and unwieldy. However, the staff had instructed her, to the point of irritation, that movement was the best possible medicine, and despite the rather miserable weather smothering England from time to time, she hobbled about the hospital grounds.

Her recovery was only one of her many problems. First, grief consumed her—the deaths of her aunt and uncle, and Charlie, the King Charles spaniel, occupied her waking thoughts and dreams. Second, she worried about getting word to her parents that her mother's sister had died in the bombing. The sudden lack of money and housing also loomed over her—Lawrence's estate surely was directed to his relatives rather than to her and the Polish family Lucy had deserted.

Betty, one cold, sunny day, visited the hospital and offered Hanna the use of the spare room in her parents' home, assuring her that it was "not an imposition" upon them. "It's the least we can do—you've been through so much," Betty said. Hanna gratefully accepted, welcoming the chance to stay in the quiet garret where she could put her life back together.

"The exercise will do me good," Hanna said about the prospect of climbing stairs. "I have to get back on my feet."

Margaret and Ruth also dropped by for a chat, in addition to Sir Phillip. Hanna was a bit flummoxed by the soldier's unannounced visit. She and the officer didn't talk about much, other than the mundane details of her hospital stay and the general state of the war. As he was getting ready to leave, he grasped her hand and said, "I hope to see you again." His warm gaze touched something in her and she responded with a loving look that normally would have embarrassed her. Everything had changed now—there was no reason to hold anything back. His touch lingered on her fingers.

Still, she was slated to spend at least another few weeks in the hospital until her doctors were satisfied she could go home. One day, in late November, as fog rolled over the Thames, extending its gray tendrils as far south as Croydon, she sat in front of an electric heater in the hospital lobby, crutches at her side, writing a letter on a lap desk. The temperature outside was too warm for snow, but too cold to be comfortable. The chilly air stabbed her legs, making it painful to walk the grounds. Extending them toward the red-hot ribbons of metallic fire was much more pleasant.

A number of thoughts occupied her as she put pen to paper, writing to the only address she had—the apartment she grew up in. She hadn't heard from her parents in so long. Fearing the worst, she wondered if they were alive. How could she tell them what she had been through without incurring the editorial pen of British censors or, worse yet, the prying eyes of Nazis? Her words would have to be chosen carefully, not arousing suspicion, particularly around a pressing choice she felt had to be made.

Since the Croydon bombing, every Nazi air raid had given her the jitters. Most times, the hospital patients made their way painfully to the basement. The lucky ones could walk or limp there on their own. Others were transported on gurneys by an already exhausted staff. The recovery from a single air raid took hours, getting everyone back to their places, even if damage was minimal—as it had been at the hospital.

Her fear of the war, the feeling that she had lost everything she had sought to gain by coming to England, and the dim hope that her parents were somehow alive and needed her help, weighed upon her. One night, she awoke at 3:30 to find the moon's silvery rays settling on the foot of her bed. An anxious jumble of thoughts filtered through her brain as she tried to reclaim sleep; however, nothing eased her mind. Rita Wright, like some military angel, hovered over her like a phantom in the moonlight. The apparition said nothing, but didn't need to. The message she communicated through her tough stance and white, steely face clearly indicated that Hanna only had one choice to make about serving her adopted country.

And, that night, she made it. As soon as she could walk, or pretend to walk with some semblance of normality, she vowed to seek out her angel and accept the offer. She would serve England and do what she could to help her parents, for there was no other choice—only the coward's way out. Doing nothing, she would lose her dignity and peace of mind. She could no longer stay silent after what the Nazis had done to her and her family.

She scratched the pen's nub on a spare piece of paper to get the blue ink flowing and then began:

My Dear Parents:
I hope this letter finds you well.
So much has occurred since I last wrote. Unfortunately, I have bad news. Aunt Lucy and Uncle Lawrence were killed in a bombing raid on Croydon. I'm so sorry that they died. Everyone here mourns the loss. I survived with injuries to my legs, but should make a reasonable recovery.
Beginning in December, I will be living with a friend. I won't give the new address in this letter, but you can write in care of Lucy and Lawrence at the former address and the post will be forwarded.

I know so much has happened in Poland and Warsaw. Uncle Lawrence kept us informed about the war's latest events. I hope everyone is safe and that you are getting along as best you can.

She stopped, placed the pen on the lap desk, and watched the condensing fog collect on the windows, turn to water, and run in ragged trails down the panes. How to finish what she had begun? How could she inspire some hope in her family? She couldn't give Betty's address for fear the Nazis might get hold of the letter. The world had become too dangerous, too murderous to imagine—and she was jumping into the madness. She picked up the pen.

A friend of mine recently said something that stuck with me. She said I should make the world a better place. She told me to be strong and be a War Girl. I'm addressing this letter to you, Mama, but please tell Stefa to stay strong. We are women, but we can all be War Girls together.
I hope to see you as soon as I can. I love you, Papa, Aaron, and Stefa.
Please hold on for your sake and mine.
Your loving daughter,
Hanna

She folded the letter, confident that nothing had been betrayed, and stretched her feet toward the heater. The temperature inside the lobby wasn't getting warmer. She needed to walk, to exercise, to feel the blood coursing through her legs. If she was going to work for Rita, she needed to be in good shape.

After rereading the letter and checking the address on the envelope, she walked unevenly to the front desk. *A War Girl—a woman who stands against the Nazis and fights for freedom.* She dropped the letter off with a receptionist, praying that somehow it would be delivered to her parents after traversing a war-torn continent.

*   *   *

Stefa made up her mind to make the best of it—for what else could she do? She decided to make the one room that she, her brother, mother, and father now called home as comfortable as it could be. If she and Aaron had to search the streets for discarded furniture, so be it.

Climbing the dingy wooden stairs with suitcases in hand, her mother had burst into tears. The corridor smelled dusty and damp, and also of human excrement. The toilet used by every resident in the building sat at the end of the downstairs hall. Only the cool November wind coursing in from the enclosed courtyard at the rear of the building kept the stairs from stinking like a cesspool. Stefa wondered what it must smell like on a sweltering summer day with no breeze. How they would miss the luxury of a private bathroom!

Daniel passed one door on the second floor and opened the one next to it. "I've given you the larger room," he said, "because you have one more family member." He pointed to a connecting door inside on the east wall. "My parents are out. They'll be back shortly, but . . ." He sighed and his jaw clenched. "Perhaps we should take our time getting acquainted—so it doesn't feel so crowded . . . so sudden."

Izreal lowered his suitcases. "That's a good idea." He reached inside his jacket pocket, his hand making a mound inside the fabric. "I have an identification card from the Palais. And a work permit . . . the guards should accept it."

"I'll accompany you to the gate," Daniel offered. "There's one farther south that exits closer to the Viceroy."

Izreal nodded. "Thank you." Her father walked to Perla, who had dropped her cases to the floor and stood silently staring out one of the windows overlooking the street. He patted her shoulders. "It will be fine, Mother."

Perla didn't respond, but kept her gaze fixed on an object only she could see.

"I'll be back after work," Izreal said. "I have permission to be out after dark . . . but things change."

"Don't be surprised if my parents come back," Daniel said to the others. He walked to Stefa. "I'm glad you're here." He and Izreal left, their steps echoing down the wooden stairs.

Aaron sighed and looked around the room. "Well, it isn't the Hotel Bristol, or even the Viceroy."

"Hush," Stefa said and sidled up to her brother. "Don't upset Mother. We all have to live here whether we want to or not."

He arched a brow and turned away, looking for a piece of the room to call his own.

Of course, Aaron was right. The room was stark, uninviting, and smelled faintly of rotting wood. The two windows that looked out upon this walled-in portion of Krochmalna would have been sufficient, even beautiful in their infancy; but now, after months of neglect, their panes were clouded with grime and the spattered earth of war. The once satisfactory patterned wallpaper of silver starbursts inside red diamonds had faded, and, in some spots, peeled from the supporting structure. An old steam radiator, now disconnected, was shoved into a corner, its white paint peeling in rusty icicles. The only source of heat, as far as Stefa could tell, was a rather dilapidated wood stove that was vented through the brick in the west wall. The sunlight did nothing to warm the room. She shivered and rubbed her hands over her wool coat.

There was no furniture in the room: no lovely couch to relax on, no dining table, and no kitchen. The stove's metal top would have to suffice for cooking. There were no embroidered chairs, not even one like the rustic wooden seat that her mother had wanted to salvage from her childhood.

Two stained mattresses of a most unattractive gray lay in the corner by the east wall. They were the beds that the family would have to use: one for Izreal and Aaron, the other for Stefa and her mother. She walked to them, knelt down, and pushed her fingers into the dirty fabric. The odor of unwashed skin rose to her nostrils. Before they could sleep on these filthy things they would have be surface-washed and dried—bedbugs and lice might call them home.

"Come, Aaron, we have work to do," she said, thinking of

all that needed to be done. Scrap wood to collect for the fire—discarded books might work as well—any furniture they could find, and water to draw from an available spigot.

Her brother got up from the dusty wooden floor and nodded. "A lot of work to do. When will things get back to normal?"

Stefa's eyes narrowed, upset that her brother would ask such a provocative question in front of his mother. "Soon. Let's go." She turned to Perla. "Will you be all right?"

Still wrapped in her coats, Perla nodded and sat on one of her suitcases.

"We won't be long," Stefa said.

Once outside, Stefa grabbed Aaron's arm. "Don't ask questions like that! 'When will things get back to normal?'"

"Maybe it's a possibility," Aaron replied, pulling away. "She's taking this hard. If we can't fight, at least we can have hope."

"We're all taking this hard—I don't know when it will get better, but it has to."

"I'll look for furniture and wood . . . the heavy stuff. You get the water."

They turned south, toward the ghetto's southern border of Sienna. "I don't even have a bucket," Stefa said, smacking her palm against her head. "What am I thinking?"

"Don't worry, I'll find one somewhere—even if I have to steal it."

"That's what I'm worried about." She was mad at her brother and also hungry. Maybe Aaron was right—perhaps it was time to question what was normal. She looked at the cold buildings and the few people who trod with their heads down on Krochmalna.

They hurried off because the sun had crossed the zenith, leaving them only a few hours to gather the things they needed before dark.

Yes, she had seen them with her own eyes. Stefa had caught her attention by stopping and patting her head. When Janka stared through the window to the street, she had seen Perla, Aaron, and Izreal as well, framed in the bright sun. Her heart sank, for she knew they were being rounded up and sent to the Jewish Residence District, as Karol had called it. She thought of Polish curses she could fling at the Nazis but hung back, not allowing them to pass her lips. It was the godly and Catholic thing to do.

But the sight of the assembled Jews and Poles had horrified her, and she wondered why she and her husband had been spared from relocation. The only reasonable explanation she could think of was Karol's job at the copper plant. They weren't part of the Nazis' enemies list: members of the Polish Army that the Germans had crushed, the Polish intelligentsia, or anyone connected to a resistance movement. Yet, other Poles, some within her building, had been told to leave and "resettle" in the ghetto. The rumor circulated that nationals of "questionable" heritage were being rounded up. The Nazis had transplanted their obsession with rules and regulations from Berlin to Warsaw, including the theory of race pollution as outlined in the Nuremberg Laws.

When Karol arrived home that evening, only slightly inebriated—she could always tell by his mood and slurred words how drunk he was—he had asked about her day in a pleasant voice that belied some ulterior motive.

"How are you?" he asked, almost gushing over her.

She shook her head at first, refusing to answer, and turned away. But he slunk toward her, wrapping his arms around her waist, his warm, vodka-infused breath rippling over the hairs on the back of her neck.

"Aren't you happy we haven't had to leave our home, leaving everything behind like those wretched Jews? Or impure Poles?"

She knew what he was getting at. *The Jewish Residence District.* He wanted her to admit that she had seen the Majewskis, sad and lugging only what they could carry, leaving their home on a beautiful day as the sun sparkled down upon them. Why were her husband and the world so cruel?

She pried his arms from her waist and walked to the stove.

"Not much for dinner tonight. Some bread and beans. I have to go far to get food now that all the businesses have been shuttered," she said, referring to the Jewish bakeries and meat markets that were now closed.

"Oh, to hell with them," Karol said. "We don't need them anyway. The Commandant has told me that none of *his* workers will starve. I can get as many ration cards as I like, maybe even some meat. He knows you can't find a job—you're not good for much besides cooking." He hurled this insult like it was a casual fact as he walked to the couch. "As long as I'm buddies with him, we're set." Janka could feel his eyes on her back while imagining the whiteness of his once attractive face turned puffy by alcohol.

She lit the stove with a match, and then blew it out. The gray smoke curled over her head.

"Well, did you see them?" Excitement bubbled in Karol's voice.

"Who?"

He slapped his palm on the dining table. "You know damn well, who! Your Jew friends. I heard they were getting rid of them today. Judging from the dark building across the street, our conquerors were successful. Good riddance."

She knew that to resist, challenging him, would only move Karol closer to the simmering violence within him that had grown since the war started. No one could reason with him, and she hadn't the energy to do so. He would only spit in her face for sympathizing with the Majewskis. Any argument that she might piece together would fail. Karol didn't realize that she liked them. She had helped Aaron several times, and in return the family had provided food, which Karol had accepted despite his professed distaste for Jews. But, most important, Janka had admired them as a family held together by love—something she hadn't felt in years. They were *her* friends in her solitary world, not his, and she had no desire to share them. The best she could do was to look out for them. As each day passed, she found herself thinking about them and what she might do to help. There were so many to help, but to *save one* . . . The Majewskis had become her allies.

She told the truth. "Yes, I did see them. They were assembled on the street with others. It was all orderly and precise."

"What else could those Jewish scoundrels do?" he asked. "Hit the guards over the head with their suitcases? They don't have guns."

Janka stifled a laugh. The thought of Stefa smashing her bag against the head of a Wehrmacht soldier popped into her mind. She pushed the image away, chastising herself for thinking it. What did the Bible say? *Turn the other cheek?*

"We'll have a pistol soon," Karol said.

She wheeled from the stove, gooseflesh rising on her arms. "What?"

"I told you . . . I'm on good terms with the Commandant. He wants his people to be armed . . . in case there's trouble."

His words cemented how deeply her husband served the Nazis, and how far they had drifted apart. She wanted no part of violence; in fact, the thought of a gun in the house with a drunken husband made her shiver. Thank God, he didn't have it yet.

She turned back to the stove and stirred the beans that bubbled in the pot. The small piece of pork floating in the brown mixture reminded her that she used to make bacon and stirred eggs for breakfast. Those days were distant memories.

"Supper will be ready soon." Janka looked over her shoulder. Karol was still smiling with satisfaction about his surprise.

A sudden sickness washed over her, nausea rising from her stomach into her windpipe. Sputtering, she clutched her throat and forced the unpleasant feeling down. She breathed deeply, grasped the stove, and forced herself to calm down. She wanted nothing more to do with him.

If he followed his usual routine, Karol would eat, slink off to bed, and leave her alone for the night.

* * *

Dawn rose over Warsaw with icy ferocity, the wind howling down Krochmalna. The morning sun glittered through flurries of white crystals, turning the air a pearly white as a light mixture of sleet and snow fell on the nearly deserted street. Janka had made breakfast for Karol and then stood shivering in front of the stove, undecided about whether to go food shopping or to crawl back into bed to stave off the cold. But going back to bed, she decided, would only depress her and delay the matters that needed to be taken care of. Karol would be angry if she accomplished nothing during the day.

She soaked a washcloth in the trickle of chilly water from the bathroom tap and scrubbed her face vigorously, trying to ease the sting of brisk air on her skin. Hot water was sporadic these days. The same treatment on her exposed arms and legs sent her running to the wardrobe for warm clothes. She clambered into her wool dress and pulled on her warm coat with the lambskin collar, collecting her hat, gloves, and purse. She looked ready for an Arctic expedition.

At the bottom of the stairs, she opened the door and a frigid blast of wind struck her face, nearly lifting her brimmed hat from her head. Krochmalna was deserted, except for a few pedestrians and the almost invisible German guards who had taken concealed positions well away from the icy gusts.

She was surprised to see a boy, or a small man—most of his features were concealed by the scarf wrapped around his face and neck, and by the wool cap with flaps pulled well past his ears. Only his nose and brown eyes were visible. She wouldn't have stopped, but for a moment she thought the lone figure who hovered so close to the door might be Aaron.

He said hello in Polish, and she was surprised to find from his voice that he was a boy. "I'd like to go inside . . . I need to talk to someone." He lifted his arms to his chest and bent over slightly to keep the wind from striking his body. "I've been waiting for the door to open."

Janka stiffened, her guard going up. Why would this child want to see someone in the building?

"Who are you looking for?"

"A woman called Janka. I don't remember her last name."

She gave nothing away, no hint of surprise, no lift of the brows. "Why?"

"I have a message for her."

Turning her back to the wind, her irritation mounted. The boy offered information in precious chunks.

"From whom?"

"She knows him. I need to see her." He sank against the building, his thin frame nearly swallowed by the wide joint between the stone blocks.

She'd had enough. "Do you want me to call for the police . . . or the Germans? Who are you?" After moving closer, she could see that his skin had been reddened by days of cold, his lips blistered, and his brown pupils set in darkened sockets.

"Zeev," he said with some pride. "I'm a friend of Aaron Majewski. I used to go to yeshiva with him."

"You are a Jew?" He wore no armband; no yarmulke was visible under the hat that covered the top and sides of his head.

He nodded, but said nothing.

"Walk with me. I am Janka Danek."

"I'd hoped, Mrs. Danek . . . you seemed like the woman he'd described."

They walked west on Krochmalna, past the boarded-up shops with the star of David painted on the windows along with the slogan, "Only Jews allowed." Those businesses that were open had painted signs above their doors declaring, "No Jews." These were of no use to Janka; in fact, of no use to most Poles because they sold stationery, old clothing, or useless trinkets—items of little interest to a hungry stomach.

"Tell me, Zeev, do you know of a market that's open?"

"A butcher on Wolska, near the train tracks. I think he's bribing the local Germans."

She'd never needed to walk that far west on Wolska, but she knew the tracks. When the wind was coming from the northwest she could hear the rumble of the engines and their whistles through an open window.

"He's Polish, but a fair man . . . at least that's what my parents used to say."

"Come with me . . . I'll buy you something. We can get out of the cold." She hesitated to ask about his parents, suspecting that they had died in the bombing or already been taken away by the Nazis. "So what is the message from Aaron?"

They passed an intersection, striding past a German soldier huddled against the corner of a building. If anything, he looked like a frozen white lump, unhappy in his role as a warden in a city of Poles, warming himself by pacing in circles and smoking a cigarette. He gave them a quick glance and then turned away as they proceeded north to Wolska Street.

"Aaron wants you to know that they are safe at this address." He handed her a piece of paper, which Janka quickly shoved into her pocket. "Any help you might give them would be welcome. They aren't starving because his father works at the Palais." He said the restaurant's name in an oily manner, as if it was distasteful to him. "They still have a bit of high-class about them, but how long will Mr. Majewski be there . . . ?"

She grasped his arm and pulled him toward her. "Tell me. Has something happened?"

He looked up with wide eyes. "You don't know?"

"I saw them being led to the ghetto."

"They're lucky. I've been living on the street. My parents died in the bombings."

Her irritation with the boy ebbed. "I'm sorry. So many died." They turned west again onto Wolska, past the thin shells of bombed-out buildings. The rubble, for the most part, was piled in the craters so the sidewalks and street could be opened. The forced work of the Jews and Poles had been efficient.

The snow swirled around her face and she clutched the lambskin collar, pulling it tightly around her neck. "All this time you've been living on the street?"

"Not all the time. After the bombings, I tried to get to relatives outside of Kraków, but it was too dangerous. The Nazis are everywhere. I've heard the shots . . . heard the screams . . . even ran into the forest with them after me. I held my breath in a freezing river as the dogs passed me.

"I made my way back to Warsaw, but no one could help. I stayed with friends for a while before things got really bad. No one can afford food—no water, no electricity. I've been living by the Vistula with others for a month now. When the wall was being built, Aaron and I found the mortar cracks where we could get through, where the bricks weren't solid. He handed me the note yesterday afternoon."

"Can't the Majewskis take you in?" she asked.

He looked at her with his sad eyes as they walked. "I couldn't ask it, Mrs. Danek. They have their own problems . . . everyone in Warsaw does." He pointed to a small shop farther down the north side of the street. "There it is—Nowak's Market."

It was wedged between two low-slung industrial buildings with tin roofs, and if Janka had not been directed to it, she might have walked past it without ever knowing it was there. The sign marking the store was unobtrusive as well—hand-painted letters on a small board hung over the door.

Five women with shopping bags waited outside. Janka knew that as the day dragged on the line would grow longer. Taking her place, drawing Zeev nearer to the warmth of her body, she considered that luck was with her today. Many people were still in bed because of the early hour and the weather.

They didn't speak while they were waiting; it was too dangerous to talk in front of strangers. Everyone in Warsaw had a story, even small boys. After a half hour of standing, they finally entered the store.

The heated air smelled of raw meat, an odor Janka didn't like, but the warmth that turned the snow on her coat and hat to water felt good. A stout man with black hair stood behind the counter, serving a customer. A younger woman with equally dark hair, pulled back and cascading down her back from a cinched white band, stood unmoving, waiting for customers to approach. She had a hard look in her eyes as if the war had already steeled her soul.

Janka pushed Zeev forward, toward the woman. "I'd like some beef and two loaves of bread."

The woman stared at her and pointed to the glass shelves. "Don't you have eyes?" She shook her head in a derogatory manner. "We only have chicken or pork this morning."

"All right," Janka said, brushing off the woman's foul mood. "Two pork chops and two loaves of bread."

Again, the woman shook her head. "Two chops and one loaf of bread for each customer." She slid the glass door open and reached down to retrieve the meat. "That will be six zlotys, with your ration card."

"Six!" Her husband would be furious if he found out how much she had spent. She would have to lie, or hope that he didn't ask.

"Take it or leave it. You're lucky to get it," the woman proclaimed as she dropped the chops on a piece of brown butcher's paper. "All this will be gone by ten."

Janka looked down at Zeev's hat. He said nothing, but moved against the warmth of her coat. "Do you have any chocolate?"

"No, ten pieces of *krówka*. That's all."

"One, then."

The scarf having dropped below his lips, Zeev arched his head back and smiled, knowing the candy was for him.

"An extra zloty," the woman said.

"For a piece of caramel candy," Zeev said. "That's—"

"Hush," Janka said.

The woman handed her the wrapped meat, bread, and the small piece of candy.

Janka found the money in her purse and paid the woman. Although the cost was high, she felt some small sense of relief, a gesture of good that wrapped her body in its own warmth.

Leaving the counter, they stepped into the biting cold. The sun was higher in the eastern sky, but no warmer. She led Zeev to a building down the street that looked deserted.

"Here," she said, handing him the candy and tearing the bread in half. "I'll tell my husband they would only give me half a loaf."

He wrapped his thin arms around her waist. "Aaron was right—you are an angel." He put the bread in his coat pocket, making sure it was covered by the flap. "Let me show you where you might find him." He clutched her arm and with renewed energy led her down the street.

The wind was at their backs when they reached the place where Zeev said the bricks could be removed so someone small could crawl through. "There between Śliska and Sienna—it's not far from their former home on Krochmalna."

They walked past the gates, keeping their distance from the guards, turning near the south border of the wall.

"I have to go home now," Janka said. "I wish I could do more for you."

"I'll be all right . . . as long as I don't freeze to death. We're burning everything to keep warm." He patted his coat pocket. "This will help, Mrs. Danek . . . I'm keeping it to myself."

"Good for you," she said. "Thank you for delivering the note. I hope to see you again. How old are you?"

"Soon to be fourteen, but old enough to fight."

Their attention was drawn to a Polish woman who skirted close to the bricks, a hundred meters to the east. She looked like any other woman, but her attention to the wall was so obvious that even Janka noticed. She wore white boots and a cloth coat whose dark blue color stood out against the snow.

A German soldier turned the corner after her.

The woman opened her coat, flung a loaf of bread over the wall, and proceeded on.

The soldier stopped, brought his rifle to his shoulder, and fired.

The woman's head snapped violently in a spray of red as the report sounded down the street.

The few pedestrians close by ducked and scurried away.

Janka reached down to clutch Zeev but he was gone. She swung in a circle looking for him, but he had vanished in the sparkling light.

The soldier poked the woman's body with his rifle, blood caking the snow around her head like red frosting. He then moved on as if nothing had happened.

Janka pushed down the horror rising in her chest and hurried home.

Throwing off her coat, she memorized the Majewskis' new address and then burned the note, holding it over the toilet. After its charred bits dropped into the water, she flushed it down. Shivering, she sat on the couch and sobbed. Try as she might, Janka couldn't obliterate the horrific image from her mind of a woman murdered for throwing a loaf of bread over the ghetto wall.

PART 3

CHAPTER 10

March 1941

The imposing façade at 64 Baker Street in London looked as bleak as the weather as Hanna stood in front of its blacked-out windows.

Low clouds and a cold rain had turned the gray stone to rivulets of ebony. She caught her reflection in one of the many dusky windows and wondered why she had made such a fuss at Betty's in order to talk to Rita Wright. The weather had curtailed her efforts. Her hair, which she had curled in the current style, dripped around her neck and shoulders from moisture undeterred by an umbrella. Her coat, from the waist down, was splotched with damp spots; her leather shoes squeaked when she walked. Fortunately, her makeup had escaped unscathed.

Only a few scars, hardly noticeable anymore thanks to the nightly devotional of healing creams, remained from the bombing five months before—along with a slight limp in her right leg. Her hearing had returned to normal except for an occasional popping in her ears. The holiday season had been difficult without her aunt and uncle, and no word from her parents, as others celebrated. Betty and her family had made her as comfortable as possible in their Croydon home. She'd even returned to work at the bookstore a few days a week.

The Nazi bombings had continued unabated, but in a

strange way, they had become part of life. Days and nights were conducted in a strict fashion, the English knowing what to do and how to do it. Panic seemed a rarity now, the hearty Brits resigned to toughing it out no matter how dire the circumstances.

While recovering at Betty's, Hanna had done considerable thinking about a decision to work with the Special Operations Executive. Weeks after her vision in the hospital—which she later chalked up to the medications she was taking—she recognized the folly in accepting a phantom as a sign for her future. Betty's not-so-subtle prodding and a growing anxiety about her family in Poland led to her decision to interview with the SOE—not the spectral visitation from Rita Wright.

She lowered the umbrella spring and shook the canopy, balking a bit before opening the door. Nothing was written in stone, even after she stepped inside, but appearing at 64 Baker Street would mean that joining the SOE was more than an idle fantasy.

A man attired in a brown officer's outfit, gray shirt, and tie tucked neatly inside it, looked up from his typewriter as she entered. A number of workers, male and female, sat at surrounding desks, all intently involved in poring over paperwork. The room smelled of stale cigarette smoke and the bite of pungent mimeograph ink.

"May I help you, ma'am?" the man asked and smiled so thinly that Hanna hardly recognized it as such.

"I have an appointment at two with Rita Wright." She rested the wet umbrella against her leg and unbuttoned her coat.

He looked casually at his watch, lifted the phone, and dialed an extension. "Your name?"

"Hanna . . . Majewski." She had considered saying Richardson, but that phase of her life was over.

"Hanna Majewski is here to see you." He listened intently for a moment, and answered, "Of course," before hanging up the phone.

"She'll see you now," he said, pointing to a dark staircase

near the back of the building. "Second floor, second office to the right of center, at the rear. You can take the lift if you like."

"Thank you, I'll walk." The man returned to his work as Hanna headed for the stairs. When she arrived at the marble steps, worn black by a constant flow of footsteps, she took a deep breath, calming herself. Each step bit into her right leg, more of an annoyance than outright pain. *You just have to let me know you're there, don't you*, she chided her leg.

The dim second floor was lit by a line of solitary bulbs that put out a weak yellow light. Muffled sounds emanated from the row of closed doors: typewriters clattered, muted voices drifted through the hall, chalk scraped across a board.

Second office to the right of center. The door was walnut, smooth, with no ornamentation or sign naming its occupant. Hanna knocked lightly at first, not wishing to disturb if she had the wrong office. Rita's voice called out for her to enter.

The office was as dull as the building itself, tempered by the ashen day. The blackout shade had been pulled up. Only a pale light filtered through the window because the room looked out on another stone building. Rita sat at a large desk. Mahogany armchairs had been placed in front of it. Hanna was surprised to see Sir Phillip Kelley in one of the chairs. He stood when Hanna entered.

Rita remained seated, an understated smile on her face, taking in Hanna from head to toe. "I'm sorry the day is so unpleasant." She tilted her head toward a coat rack near the door. "Hang them there."

Hanna did so, smoothed her dress, and took her seat across from Rita.

"A pleasure to see you again," Phillip said. He was in uniform, sporting the same thin mustache, his inquisitive, pale-blue eyes taking her in as well.

"Welcome to Baker Street," Rita said, withdrawing a cigarette from her gold case. "You've been to London many times, haven't you?"

"This is my first trip since the bombing." She was surprised by the hot anger that blossomed in her neck and face as she remembered that terrible evening. She looked away from Rita for a moment to regain her composure.

"We spoke at the hospital, but I wanted to express my condolences again on your loss," Phillip said. "It's been rough, but I see you're doing better."

Hanna didn't know how to respond. Of course, it had "been rough." No one could truly understand what she had been through—she'd had enough trouble rationalizing why she was alive and her adopted family was dead. She'd even cried for poor Charlie, but nothing could bring them back. All the sympathy in the world couldn't make them reappear. At times, before falling asleep at Betty's, when the world was darker than she had ever known it, she wondered if God was punishing her for leaving her family behind. If that was the case, God was battering everyone by allowing the war to continue.

All she could say was, "Thank you," but the sentiment was half-hearted. She wanted her aunt and uncle alive, the world to return to the way it was before the war started, for her legs to function like they did before the bombing.

As if she could read Hanna's mind, Rita said, "I know what you're thinking. You're right. No amount of grief or tears will bring them back. They are dead because of the Nazis."

"Rita . . ." Phillip scowled after his objection. "Can't we leave them in peace?"

"No time for sentiment." She lit the cigarette she'd been holding, the smoke blossoming upward in a dull cloud. "I hate to say it, but I must. If you are to work with us, death will be your constant companion, and it will seek out the people you know and love. Hitler doesn't shed a tear for those who die. He only cares about himself, or the few he fancies will help him along the way. He inflames with words and passionate speeches and incites others to kill for him. He believes he is blameless while espousing a higher cause."

Phillip nodded. "A maniac with no morals."

Rita turned to the window for a moment, looking at the cold rain dripping down it. "Let's be honest. I've invited you to join the SOE because you can help us, but there's no certainty that we will win this war, or that you will come back alive if you agree to this mission." She returned her intense gaze to Hanna. "Anger, revenge, the willingness to kill if need be, must guide you; otherwise, you should gather your things and walk out the door, never to return."

Phillip clasped his hands, resting his elbows on the chair arms, and brought the tips of his fingers to his chin.

Hanna took a moment to digest what Rita had said, knowing she had been furious at the Nazis, even at her uncle's flimsy Anderson shelter, which wasn't designed to survive a high-explosive bomb strike. Her recovery had muted some of the anger: the medications, the exercises, the hospital therapy, all of them sedating her emotions. The struggle to get on her feet had been more important than grappling with her anger.

The choice was hers now.

Resting the cigarette in the ashtray, Rita straightened in her chair, looking as inscrutable as a porcelain doll.

"I've been angry, but also saddened by the loss of my family," Hanna said. "I'm not sure what's driven me here today— perhaps a sense of duty, my belief that I can make a difference."

"Oh, you can," Rita said, "but a sense of duty or belief isn't enough. Once you make this decision, you can't look back, because you will be too valuable to us. You must want this—more than anything you've ever considered." Rita pointed to Phillip. "My officer friend believes in you—so does your friend Betty."

Hanna looked at Phillip, who studied her with eyes as enigmatic as Rita's. Like the woman across from her, he offered no indication of whether she should accept the post.

"I've already made one decision that I was certain of—and didn't look back. What would I be doing?"

"I need your answer first," Rita said.

One thought filled her mind—the memories and the people who generated them were worth saving—pushing out the remembrances of London and her aunt. She saw her family gathered around the Seder table, enjoying the meal, Stefa and Aaron's smiles, the family observing the High Holidays and birthdays, bristling at her father's inflexibility and her mother's often infuriating devotion to her husband, the feeling that she was smothering while the world raced by. And she remembered that this was life as she knew it, before London. Good or bad, those memories, and the people who had generated them, had brought her to 64 Baker Street today. She only had to muster the courage to serve.

"Yes."

Rita puffed on her cigarette and then stubbed it out. She paused for a moment, and then opened a file on her desk. "You'll be working as our contact with the Polish resistance and reporting on Nazi activities in and around Warsaw. You'll be trained in code, covert operations, radio transmissions, arms, ordinance, and parachuting."

"Parachuting?"

"If you have a safer way of getting into Poland at night, please let us know," Rita said, without the slightest bit of irony.

"I'll be with you during your early training," Phillip said, his face brightening.

Hanna had never been in an airplane, let alone jumped from one. Her insides clenched and she wondered if her legs would be able to stand the strain of a jump. She pictured herself falling through a black sky, the wind smacking her face, the stars and a crescent moon above, the dark ground growing ever closer as she plummeted to earth.

"You'll start in a few weeks—exactly where we haven't decided," Rita said. "Here in London, in Essex, or in Scotland. I'll be in touch." She rose from her chair and extended her hand.

Hanna shook it and turned to gather her coat and umbrella.

Phillip rose from his chair as well. "I'll walk you out."

When they reached the door, Rita said, "One moment, Hanna."

She stopped, her hand on the knob.

"Not a word of this to anyone. Not even Betty—she'll find

out soon enough that you're with us, but she doesn't need to know anything about your activities with the SOE. Once you start, you won't be seeing her anyway."

Hanna nodded. "Of course."

Phillip placed his hand in the small of her back and guided her out the door. When it closed, Hanna stood in the dimly lit hall with the officer. She walked to the stairs and grasped the handrail for the climb down.

"Let me help you," Phillip said, grasping her left arm.

"Please, I can manage."

"She tested you, you understand?" He released her arm, but remained by her side as they descended the stairs.

"What do you mean?"

"Well . . . that bit about parachuting. Many of our agents do it, but not all. Some go by boat and then by train." He smiled. "Many would say that's the end of it, right there, if they were told they had to parachute into occupied territory. Case closed. Jumping out of a plane isn't for everyone. The SOE will decide after your training how to get you into Poland."

"Safely," she said.

He smiled. "Safely."

Hanna stopped at the bottom of the stairs and looked across the crowded office. Cigarette smoke rose from the ashtrays, the metallic ping of typewriter keys against platens reverberated through the room.

"For a moment, I saw myself falling through the air," she said. "But what my parents are going through is so much worse than jumping from a plane. I'll have a parachute to break my fall. They have nothing."

"I'm glad you're onboard, but don't underestimate what you're doing. It will be difficult and dangerous." He grasped her hand in his as if to shake it, but held on instead, threading his fingers through hers. A shadow crossed his youthful face, filling him for a moment with sadness. "I'll see you when you get your orders. I wish we could get together before then, but it's impossible now—against policy."

Hanna studied him. What was he feeling? Melancholy? An attraction that neither of them had yet to define? Betty was right—he cut a dashing figure with his wavy black hair, blue eyes, and neatly trimmed mustache, but there was no reason to expect anything more than a formal, business relationship with Sir Phillip. How could anyone expect romance in a time like this?

"I wish we could get together, too," she said, as they walked across the room.

Phillip helped her on with her coat and held the door open. The rain beat down, puddling around her shoes. She thanked him, said good-bye, and headed for the Tube. She tipped the umbrella backward, letting the cold drops fall onto her face, watching the clouds' dreary tails scud overhead.

Imagine falling through them. Snipers in the woods. Germans on the ground—waiting for me. She shivered and shook her head. There was no turning back now.

The home on Krochmalna took weeks of work to make it habitable. The Majewskis and the Krakowskis were lucky that they lived in two rooms—most had seven or more people in one. Stefa and the others were grateful that Daniel, in his police position, had arranged it.

In the first days after the ghetto was sealed, Stefa and Aaron had collected three wooden chairs and a footstool. They had searched in vain for a couch, finding nothing similar for seating. During the winter, people had burned furniture for fuel and then tossed the charred springs and coils into the street. The Majewskis had managed to save their chairs, although they had come close to burning them. If that had occurred, nothing but mattresses would have been left on the floor.

The suitcases they had brought with them became chests of drawers for their belongings. Stefa and Perla attempted to embellish their stark surroundings by placing dishes and books on a few handmade shelves constructed from empty crates. Aaron found an old oil painting, a dark and dreary Polish forest scene, and hung it on the wall opposite the stove. Its gloomy subject matter provided little warmth, but was better than looking at the faded silver starburst wallpaper.

After a week of cleaning with hard-to-get water and ammonia, which Izreal brought from the restaurant, the mattresses finally were disinfected. While the fabric dried, both families slept on the floor.

Now that the Jews had been "resettled" in the ghetto, Stefa noticed that daily life was somewhat returning to normal—if it could be called that. There were no sanctioned public gatherings, curfew hours were still in effect, but the Nazis didn't crack down on religious observances as long they were held in private. Theatrical companies had begun performing soon after the gates were closed—a review had been held in December at the Eldorado Theater on Dzielna Street with no interference from the occupiers. Politics was discussed at the soup kitchens that had sprung up, and small cultural events, like poetry readings, often were held in such places.

"Normal" consisted of so many Jews crammed into the ghetto that walking down major streets was like weaving through a herd of cattle. "Normal" was women and children selling star of David armbands, cobblers hawking shoes, poor mothers trading the pots and pans they cooked with for food, beggars ripping their coats apart, selling the fabric to buy a small piece of bread. "Normal" was serving thousands of people at the soup kitchen at 40 Leszno Street. Stefa had no idea of the number of Jews in the ghetto, but Izreal had been told by a Nazi official at the Palais that "a half-million of you have been gathered here for respectful treatment. We protect you from disease—and your own worst traits."

All these observations, along with her father's notes, she recorded in her diary for Ringelblum and his Oyneg Shabbos project; however, it didn't include what haunted her dreams. The suffering she wrote about no one would have believed unless they could witness it with their own eyes. In late winter, the weather harsh with bitter winds and blasts of snow, nothing could wipe out the sight of starving children on the street, with no place to go and little to protect them—their skulls and cheekbones pushing against their thin skins. So many were orphans who had been abandoned.

Between their pleas for help and cries for food, the starving released an unearthly wail that singed her ears like heat from a raging fire. Children dressed in tattered rags, huddled in doorways, stretched out in gutters to sleep until death claimed them. The world must have thought the Warsaw Ghetto Jews were cruel. How could you walk past the poor and do nothing? No one could help these waifs because the Jews couldn't help themselves. The moneyed, with their fur coats and fancy shoes, mostly looked the other way, often passing the starving as if they were so much rubbish on the street. The rich Jews gave when they could, or when the mood struck, but there were so many poor and starving it was impossible to help everyone. One never knew when the riches you had might be ripped away. Those descending into poverty could do nothing either.

Stefa volunteered her services at the soup kitchen on Leszno Street. It was one of many formed by individuals and service organizations within the ghetto. At first, the workers had scoured the ruins for pots and pans and food to start the kitchen, only serving those they could. As the numbers grew, a black-market trade blossomed for food and support. Stefa heard that Ringelblum himself had contributed to the cause. She refused to take payment for her shifts because she knew how fortunate she was to have food and a family living under one roof.

When she could, Stefa told emaciated children that they could come to the kitchen for food—she would make sure they were served—but some were so weak they could only moan after hearing her words. When she tried to help them to their feet, they crumpled like rag dolls in her arms. Their bodies smelled of death and were riddled with lice. Often they died during the night and by morning they had vanished like fog in the sun. At other times, the corpses lay on the sidewalk until the burial cart

marked with the star of David arrived to haul them ignomini-
ously to the mass grave at the Jewish Cemetery, northwest of the
ghetto. If you were rich you could buy a plot, but those on the
street couldn't afford a traditional burial.

People had burned everything they could to survive the winter. The trees were gone, chopped to the roots. Stray dogs and
cats, even horses or donkeys that weren't safely stabled, had
been killed and eaten by the starving. The promises of help from
the Nazi General Government rang hollow. Everyone suffered,
everyone paid the price, under the occupation. These details she
recorded in her notebook.

Work permits were as basic as food and water. People who
couldn't find work, or were ill or weak, often disappeared or
died on the streets. One evening, the conversation turned to
Perla and what she might do for work. This was an extra pre-
caution. Izreal already had registered his wife and children under his permit. Daniel broached the subject, feeling that it might
be necessary to ensure Perla's safety.

In March, they gathered in the larger of the two rooms that
Daniel had secured for them in November. With their coats on,
they huddled around the stove because it was the only source
of heat for the apartment. Daniel's parents, Jakub and Wanda,
were welcomed to sit by the stove after a sparse evening meal.
Stefa thought Jakub looked like a man who would be more comfortable teaching at a university than working as a garment cut-
ter at a German-owned shop on Leszno Street. He and his wife
were quiet people. Jakub always seemed to have a book at hand,
either a religious text or an academic study on natural sciences.
He would spend most evenings reading by the fire, wire-rimmed
spectacles perched on his nose, long legs stretched out from his
chair, occasionally ruffling his full head of black hair. His wife,
who worked at another plant in the ghetto, would sit quietly by
his side mending socks or patching trousers and jackets for the
families, like the job she did most of the day on German military uniforms. She had a round face, not unpleasant, but her

dark hair fell from her kerchief, enclosing her features like an ebony picture frame, giving her a severe appearance. She wore no makeup on her colorless face.

"I'll get Perla an application from my shop," Wanda said, putting down her needle and thread for a moment. "I'll bring it tomorrow. You can do something with a needle, Mrs. Majewski?"

Her mother had draped a shawl over her head and shoulders to stave off the cold on her back. Lately, Perla had seemed preoccupied with everything and nothing, as if she was anywhere else but in the room. Many times, Stefa would have to ask her the same question twice before getting an answer. Perla's response to Wanda's question was no different—a meek yes after a second prodding.

"The application might cost you, Mr. Majewski," Jakub said to Izreal, who had a rare night off from the Palais.

"One thousand zlotys, if I'm lucky, Mr. Krakowski," Izreal replied. "Families have paid up to twenty thousand for a work permit. Then they find the business doesn't exist and the Germans have taken the money. Terrible."

"The Nazis are behind that," Daniel said. He sat as close as he could to Stefa without offending her parents. "We should save our money in case we really need it."

"We should hide the funds we have," Izreal said. He threw a precious piece of wood into the stove—part of a large branch he'd found behind the hotel from a tree that had died in the winter.

Such family time was a rarity because of their different lives—even though they were thrown together by Nazi regulations. Izreal had permission to work late at the hotel—still a favorite of those Poles who could afford it, amid their segregation from German officers. Daniel, as a policeman, could be out past curfew if he was working on Judenrat business or with the Blue Police. Those men had the most freedom of the group. The others were bound by work and strict rules.

Stefa looked at Aaron, who had pulled away from the con-

THE WAR GIRLS 187

versation and sat hunched on the mattress in the corner. He was plotting something, she suspected.

Her father noticed as well and called out, "What are you thinking, Aaron?"

They all looked at him.

He raised his head slowly. "Nothing."

The wood sizzled in the fire. "Now I know you're lying," Izreal said. "Your head is always full."

Aaron shook his head. "No. Nothing."

Daniel raised a brow and looked at Stefa.

Izreal fixed his gaze on his son. "Stay away from the ghetto wall and those friends of yours. It's dangerous. You could get killed."

Daniel nodded. "Your father's right."

"What will we do when we're starving?" Aaron asked. "Who will bring us food?"

Izreal bunched his fists and lowered them to his lap. "We're not starving. And we won't."

Perla looked up, the shawl around her neck and head keeping her wan features in shadow. "Life will get better . . . won't it?"

Stefa wanted to reassure her mother that the world would be better in the spring when they could open the windows and enjoy the warm sun. "Yes, Mother, it will."

Aaron chuckled.

Izreal shot him a withering look. "Yes, it will." He turned to Wanda. "Get that application, Mrs. Krakowski. Make sure it's something she can do."

Perla lowered her head, shutting them out once again.

"I've found something, Mr. Majeswki," Daniel said to Izreal. "Everyone in this room should see it." He motioned for Stefa and Izreal to follow him. He got up and led them into the hall.

"Here," he whispered, knocking softly on a panel that covered the end of the corridor near the bend in the stairs.

Stefa put her ear to the wood, listening to the knock. "It's . . . hollow."

Daniel grasped a seam and pulled the wood gently forward. Empty black space appeared behind it. "You'd never guess unless you knew it was here. It covers the wiring that runs down the back of the building . . . but there are beams between the wires, a wooden slat to stand on, and enough space that one person can squeeze into. Mrs. Majewski, Aaron, and my mother could hide easily enough—one at a time, of course."

"Can we hide our money there, too?" Izreal asked.

Daniel peered into the dark cavity. "No—nothing there to keep it from slipping down the wall."

Stefa returned to the room, dismayed that life had come to finding hiding places from the Nazis. She sat next to her mother, wondering if the hole Daniel had discovered would hold her. She had lost weight since the war started, but she had always been shorter and stouter than Hanna and doubted the panel would protect her. She put her hand to her forehead and swiped away a few drops of perspiration. The fire was hot, but in the corner, away from the heat, the cold stabbed into your bones. Why were Daniel and Aaron always thinking ahead, always planning a move to outsmart the Nazis? She simply tried to help people and record the terrible events that were taking place. Perhaps she should be more thoughtful, more aware of what might happen, instead of hoping. For an instant, she pictured herself with a rifle in her hand, pointing it at a German soldier standing on Krochmalna. The thought terrified her. Could she kill a man? Would she have the courage? If it came to saving her family, only one answer would do.

Yes.

That night, as in the past months, the inner door between the two rooms remained open. During the winter it was a necessity—the Krakowskis would freeze in their beds if the door was closed.

Izreal and Aaron slept in the corner bed nearest the window. The only light that fell into the room came from the moon in its shifting cycles. Her brother slept close to the outside wall, covering his head and body with blankets. It was his job to get up in the middle of the night and stoke the fire—if they had anything to burn. A trip to the toilet meant walking down the freezing stairs to the first floor and sitting over the hole that covered the cesspool below. The air was rancid, the wooden plank cold and smoothed by the bottoms of countless people. No one went for relief unless they had to.

Perla and Stefa slept on the other mattress, Stefa next to the inner door that connected the two rooms. When she turned away from the wall, she could make out Daniel's shadowy form in the dim light, for he was sideways in sleep.

One winter night, she had awakened to find his hand near hers. She extended her arm from underneath the blankets and intertwined his icy fingers with hers for just a moment, knowing that such an unorthodox action would upset all their parents.

A blue power, like an electric spark, flowed from his hand into hers. She wondered if he experienced the feeling but, judging from the strength with which he held her hand, he did.

From that night on, they observed this ritual a few minutes each night—coming within reach of each other, but never touching. Every time Stefa participated in this mock holding of hands, the night seemed a little less lonely, a little less ominous.

Perla took the letter in her trembling hands, tears forming a wet sheen over her eyes. "It's from Hanna." Her mother gasped for breath. Somehow it had gotten to them. The Judenrat had taken over mail delivery from the Germans early in the year, making deliveries more reliable.

"Open it," Stefa said, overcome by an odd mixture of anticipation and anxiety. They were alone in the apartment.

"I can't. What if it's bad news?"

"Give it to me—I'll read it to you."

Perla surrendered the letter. Stefa ripped it open, noting that it had been postmarked in Croydon. A lump formed in her throat as she scanned the words quickly before reading them aloud. "Mother . . ." She stopped, handing the letter back, unable to continue, the lump swelling into a rock.

"Oh, God," Perla said, her voice no more than a squeak. She collapsed in a chair near the stove. "My sister . . . my Liora."

Stefa grasped her hands and the letter fell to the floor. "I'm so sorry, Mama." She hadn't known her aunt as well as Hanna did. Lucy was a distant memory, only conjured up occasionally, like the faded image of an old photograph.

Lowering her head, Perla sobbed, the tears running fast down her cheeks.

"But Hanna is all right," Stefa said, trying to cheer her mother. "She survived the bombing." She chastised herself for not knowing that London had been attacked by the Nazis. All this time, she'd imagined her sister living in luxury at Lucy's while they struggled in Poland. How wrong she had been.

Stefa picked up the letter, turned it over and read part of a paragraph.

A friend of mine recently said something that stuck with me. She said I should make the world a better place. She told me to be strong and be a War Girl. Stefa should stay strong, too. We can all be War Girls together.

Sobbing, she stood behind her mother, hoping to comfort her. Her aunt was dead, but Hanna was alive. She would stay strong for the sake of Daniel, her sister, her family, and to honor the memory of her aunt and uncle.

We are women, but we can all be War Girls together.

She wondered what the term meant—War Girls. She said it aloud and her mother looked at her as if she had lost her mind. Could a woman fight the Nazis? Everything seemed impossible in their ghetto prison.

Perhaps a woman on the other side of the wall might be called one as well—a woman who had shown strength and helped her brother.

Janka Danek.

CHAPTER 11

———◆◆◆———

"They don't suffer fools gladly—or anyone else," Karol told Janka one night after a supper that left him somewhat happy and satisfied. Officially, meat wasn't sold now at Nowak's, the market that Zeev had led her to, but Janka always made it a point to get to the store early. The owner and the dark-haired girl behind the counter knew her now and even kept a few choice sausages and other cuts of meat aside because Janka could pay a little more than some of their customers. Karol's close association with his Nazi boss kept the money flowing.

"Who?" she asked, fully aware of whom her husband was speaking. She wiped the supper dishes with a cloth spotted with grease as Karol stretched out on the couch, his head and body turned toward her. He puffed on a cheap cigar and drank from a snifter of even cheaper brandy. The biting stench of smoke and the sharp tang of alcohol filled the room.

"Who?" Karol guffawed in his own slovenly way. "The Nazis. The, poor, pathetic Jews." He drew out the words on his lips. "And the poor, pathetic Poles who don't fall in line."

"Do you want to hear a funny story?" he asked, snuggling against the couch as if it were his lover.

She was in no mood for a funny story. Winter had spread its icy talons over Poland since the "resettlement." Gloomy, depressing days and bleak nights in bed, listening to her husband snore, unsettled her. Everything was a trial. Even with Karol's connections, their apartment sometimes lacked heat, water ran as if controlled by whim, and food shortages were common. How much harder it must be for the Jews confined to the ghetto.

Being alone so much of the time, Janka often thought of the Majewskis, and prayed they had managed to survive. She remembered what Perla had said about saving one person—that it was like saving the world. Those small good deeds she had undertaken, despite the Nazis and her husband, gave her energy and strength through the winter. She missed having conversations with people who demonstrated common decency instead of cunning malevolence. However, the weather and the shooting she'd witnessed had kept her away from the ghetto walls.

She nodded, knowing it was useless to object to her tipsy husband's "funny" story.

"The Commandant told me the surprises are just beginning."

Her stomach churning, Janka wiped the last plate and placed it on top of the others in the cabinet. *I don't want to hear it . . . I don't want to hear it!* She walked to the window and raised the sash a bit, even though the April night was cool. Winter still had Warsaw in its grasp.

"What are you doing?" Karol barked. "It's cold outside."

"The cigar smoke hurts my eyes. Go on with your story." She looked out on the quiet street.

"Well, this past week a Jew policeman named Ginsburg got shot."

Janka pivoted toward him. *Stefa has a boyfriend who's a policeman. What was his name? Am I imagining that?* She clenched her fists, waiting for him to continue.

"The fool asked a couple of Wehrmacht soldiers to return a sack of potatoes they'd taken from a Jew woman." He chuckled. "Can you imagine? They stuck him with their bayonets and then shot him. He got what he deserved."

She stood silent, a marble-like iciness freezing her body.

"Then, a few days later," he continued, "this crazy woman in the ghetto—a Jew, of course—she deserved to die anyway—they got her to dance. She threw her arms and legs in the air like a lunatic, making them laugh, dancing for their enjoyment." He formed a pistol with his right hand, pulled the imaginary trigger, and blew out a puff of air. "Poof. She's gone. They killed her on the spot." He laughed again, this time so hard he clutched his sides. "Don't you think that's funny?" He slid off the couch, his feet touching lightly on the floor, raising his body slowly, with an air of menace.

"No. It's disgusting. You should be ashamed." She stared at the man whom she once had loved, who now in her eyes was no better than the Nazi animals invading the city. If she'd had a place to run to—if there was any justice in the world—she would have walked out the door, never to return.

Swaying, Karol rose from the couch and approached her. "I'd be careful what I think and do." He pointed a finger smudged with cigar ash at her. "I can't have a Jew-loving wife. And, for your sake, you better not be. You'll ruin everything. I'm the one keeping you safe." He came within a hand's length of her, the sweat from his brow glistening in the light, his acidic breath crashing against her face. "Don't forget it!"

His cheeks reddened. "Or you'll be out on the street." He swayed backwards, as if a funny thought had struck him.

Janka feared the sardonic smile that formed on his lips as much as his threats of violence.

"Or better yet . . . I might turn you in for aiding Jews. You might appreciate where your bread is buttered if you spend time in prison." He returned to the couch, rested the cigar in the ashtray, and gulped the last of his brandy. "The guards know how to treat a lady." He rested his head against the fabric, closed his eyes, and seemed to fall into a deep sleep, his body shivering with each breath.

She had seen the shiny Luger his Nazi boss had given him. Karol kept it under his pillow at night and took it to work during the day. But where was it now? A horrific thought raced through her head, one that before the war broke out she could never have imagined. She saw him dead on the couch, a red stain spreading across his blue shirt, a bullet through his heart.

She gasped and brought her hands to her mouth.

His legs shuddered against the cushions.

God forgive me. Please, God, forgive me. She walked to the bedroom, opened the wardrobe door and looked through it from top to bottom, but found no gun.

The morning sun cut through the clouds, warming her shoulders through her coat. For months Janka had avoided the ghetto, fearing that she would witness another shooting or put herself in danger. Karol had warned her to stay away from the wall and she had done so, always wondering if the Majewskis had survived the resettlement.

This morning was different. Emboldened by the light and the warmth that spread over her like a soothing balm, she decided to walk near the wall, avoiding obvious dangers. She'd left the apartment late, going back to bed for a time after fixing breakfast for Karol. A trip to Nowak's was unnecessary. The pantry held enough food for the day.

She walked down Krochmalna, then toward a gate about three hundred meters above the point where the southernmost wall turned east, pausing near the site of the murder for a loaf of bread. Janka half expected to see Zeev scamper toward her, or tug the back of her coat, but only Polish adults, not children, were on the street.

Standing in the mottled shade of an oak tree—its leaves had just begun to emerge—she stretched against its striated bark and drew in a deep breath. She looked at her watch—almost ten. It was glorious to get away from her stuffy apartment, which of late held no good memories, and free herself from her troubles. The wall stood, ominous, across the street. The bricks, some pale like plaster, others red in the spring light, invited her to imagine what life was like in the prison the Nazis had constructed. Were the Majewskis still alive, and did they have enough to eat, were two of the questions she pondered, and, more importantly, could she help them? What could be done?

Janka was about to turn, not wanting to draw any unnecessary attention from the guards, when a man stepped from behind a barbed-wire barricade near the gated entrance. He wore the star of David on his coat sleeve and walked with a determined step toward her. She assumed he was heading for work outside the ghetto.

As he drew closer, she recognized him, a man she had spoken to once before—Izreal Majewski. His unbuttoned coat flowed around his body, displaying the suit he was wearing. A light blue wool scarf draped his neck; a felt hat tipped from his forehead. Janka thought he looked grimmer, the lines around his mouth having deepened, the formerly longish beard trimmed to a shorter length. Had he cut it to lessen attacks from rabid Nazis?

She fiddled with her purse, giving him a moment to pass by. Yes, it was Izreal. The guards had disappeared behind the gate. Janka decided to take a chance.

She called his name as he walked by, knowing the danger of consorting with Jews.

He kept walking, but his gait slowed, and he glanced back for a moment.

She couldn't tell if he recognized her or if he even remembered the evening they had met so many months ago. She recalled that he worked at the Palais. He was headed in that direction.

"I can't talk to you here," he said, without stopping. "It isn't safe."

"Stop when you can," she said. "I'll follow."

They walked for several blocks until they were well past the ghetto. Izreal disappeared in the shadows between two buildings so quickly Janka thought he had dropped from the earth. She peered into the murky light and then tiptoed into a muddy alley.

"Mr. Majewski?" she whispered, allowing her eyes to adjust to the dark. The corridor, filled with the remains of disintegrating wooden crates, ended at a brick wall.

His head popped out, peering from his hiding place.

"Mrs. Danek?" he asked, in an equally soft voice.

"Yes."

"I'm happy to see you. I have a letter for you."

She was bewildered. Why would Izreal have anything for her?

She stepped past him, blending into the darkness as well, her heart thumping in her chest. If they were caught—a Jewish man and a Polish woman in an alley they couldn't escape from—they'd both be imprisoned, possibly executed. Karol would be the first to testify at her trial—if there was one.

"I'm sorry," he said. "This is the only safe place between the ghetto and the hotel I know—I've walked by it a hundred times. Let me be quick." He reached into his coat. "Stefa told me this would happen. I didn't believe her. 'If it doesn't happen, it wasn't meant to be,' she said." He placed the letter in her hand.

In the grim light, Janka could see it was addressed to a woman in Croydon, England.

"Stefa sewed a false pocket in my coat. I've been carrying this letter for a few weeks." He sighed and leaned against the crate that hid them. "It's a copy of a letter to my . . . daughter . . ."

"Yes?" Janka wondered why it was so hard for him to finish his thought.

"My daughter . . . Hanna. She left for London more than a year ago and was injured in a bombing. She wrote in concern for us. Stefa penned a reply and gave it to our postman who is Jewish, but the Nazis still read the mail. It's addressed to my wife's sister who was killed."

No one is safe as long as Hitler is in power. "I'm sorry . . . is Hanna all right?"

"It seems so." He peered around the wood and then put a finger to his lips.

Voices passed the alley and then faded.

When it was quiet again, he said, "I was angry . . . determined never to speak her name . . . but when I read her letter, I cried . . ." His voice constricted. "She needs to know that we're safe for the moment. Stefa put a false return on the envelope. If the Nazis open it, there's nothing to see—no names. It's innocuous. 'We are well . . . hope to see you soon.' Nothing is given away." He buttoned his coat. "It's cold in the shadows."

"We've been in the shadows for too long," she said.

He peered around the crate again. "I must go. I can't be late for work. You are mentioned in the letter—only in the vaguest way. No name is given. Stefa wanted you to know."

A shiver skittered across her back. "Why me?"

"To be a contact for Hanna—if she returns to Warsaw. I told Stefa the idea was insane. She said not to underestimate you."

"Do you think Hanna will come back?"

"I didn't want to upset Stefa . . . but I doubt we'll ever see Hanna again."

Janka nodded and put the letter in her coat pocket.

"Thank you. God be with you." He stepped into the alley, but she clutched his arm.

"Let me go first—it's safer that way. Do you have enough to eat? Is everyone well?"

"I worry about my wife and Aaron, the same as when we met. We are well and have enough food for now. We are lucky. I've tried to remain optimistic, but every day grows darker."

"I want to see your family again. God be with you, as well."

"That's impossible." He gazed at the muddy walkway. "Stefa thinks you might be able to help us . . . in the future. I don't know how. But I hope so." He lifted his head. "Stefa considers you a War Girl—someone who is brave and will fight for what is right."

She was puzzled by his assessment and the nickname, because under Karol's thumb she didn't feel courageous or strong. Could she be brave? Perhaps, if she put her mind to it, and didn't give a damn about her husband. This was another step, taking the name as a compliment.

Janka left him, avoiding the slush created from the melting snow, looking both ways at the end of the alley to make sure no one was within sight. People walked some distance away. Seconds counted. She motioned for him to come forward and his shadowy figure emerged from the darkness.

Janka walked quickly away as Izreal turned in the other direction, resuming his journey to the Palais.

Mud streaked her black shoes—an unfortunate condition she would have to remedy once she got home. A little dirt was fine, but too much mud on her carefully kept footwear would arouse Karol's suspicion.

When she arrived, she cleaned her shoes and placed the unsealed letter on the counter, knowing she had to read it before her husband came home.

My dear sister,

We were sorry to read of your recent misfortune. We are fine, but at a new address. If you visit, we beg you to visit our friend on Krochmalna. Our love goes to you with the hope for a speedy recovery and an end to the war.

Your loving family

That was all it said. Izreal was right—nothing incriminating in the least, but she could read through the lines. *Our friend on Krochmalna.* The words certainly referred to her. Would Hanna be contacting her at some point? Even so, how could she be found on such a large street?

The thought sent a thrill through her—one of excitement or terror? She carried the copied letter to the bathroom, set it on fire, and dropped its burning ashes in the toilet, just as she had done with Zeev's note containing the Majewskis' address.

Almost six long months had passed since the Croydon bombing. Miraculously, the long days and nights of the Blitz, as it had come to be known, appeared to end by May 1941. But, as Hanna knew, Nazi appearances could be deceiving. Most everyone expected the raids to continue.

Her friend Betty, dressed in military uniform for an Auxiliary Territorial Service position they never discussed, saw Hanna off at the train station. Betty always looked smart in her uniform skirt and double-breasted tunic that was cinched above the waist by a wide belt. Hanna was convinced that her friend might be in Special Operations Executive as well.

"Hitler's up to something," her friend said as they waited for the train.

Hanna wore a simple patterned dress like those that most English women would put on during the day. The bombing had reduced her wardrobe significantly; "feminine" pastimes were far from her mind, unlike those of Margaret and Ruth, who still pursued such interests with as much vigor as the war allowed.

Betty pulled a handkerchief and compact from her purse, and, using the mirror, wiped clean a smudge of lipstick above her upper lip. "He's plotting something. Focusing his attention elsewhere, saving his armament for another victim. If I had to guess, I'd say Russia."

"Doesn't he have a nonaggression pact with Stalin?" Hanna asked.

Betty scoffed. "He doesn't give a whit about pacts or agreements. Look what he did after Munich. Chamberlain was a fool." She voiced her opinion a little too loudly and a man on the platform shot her a disapproving look. "Oh, to hell with Hitler. Take care and say hello to that good-looking young officer—*Sir* Phillip Kelley."

"How do you know he'll be in Roydon?" She had revealed that much of her future to Betty. To be honest, she'd thought about Phillip now and then since the interview at 64 Baker Street. Word had come down through a phone call that Hanna was accepted, assigned to an unspecified residence near Roydon, in Essex, about an hour and thirty minutes north of London by train. A comforting thought—if things got too uncomfortable, she could take the rails home from the village and be back in Croydon in two hours.

"I don't, but I suspect he might." Betty leaned over and kissed Hanna's cheek.

"Your handkerchief and compact," Hanna demanded.

Betty laughed and handed her the items. Hanna studied her reflection in the mirror and wiped the outline of Betty's lips from her cheek.

To the south, a bright spot shimmered on the rails. Hanna lifted her suitcase containing all the possessions she could carry: a few dresses, a few pairs of shoes, undergarments, a jar of night cream, a tube of lipstick that she might apply now and then, and a tome on German history she'd found at the bookstore where she worked. The proprietor was sad to see her go and had presented it to her as a parting gift when she expressed her interest. If she was to pass as a German, she needed to know as much about the country as possible.

Betty grasped her hands. "You have a bedroom waiting if you need it . . . but I'm hoping you don't come back. That means you've made it."

Hanna hugged her friend, her nerves jumping a bit as the train screeched to a stop. Wishing Betty good luck, she boarded her third-class carriage for the short ride, and settled in, wondering if anyone else on the train was bound for the same location.

The landscape changed little as the train chugged north, passing through the suburbs of London, with their gray homes and rows of manufacturing plants. Occasionally, a green field rolled by, lit by shafts of an intermittent sun fractured by puffy clouds. She opened her case and brought out the book, hoping to take her mind off the job that awaited her. Was it an assignment or an adventure? According to Rita Wright, it would be a job—a dangerous one that might end her life. She had to think positively or not think at all; otherwise, she would jump off the train at the next stop and head back to Betty's.

She switched trains in London after a brief wait, heading north again. When it passed Cheshunt, the land opened to a wide plain filled with lakes, tilled fields, and rural byways. The train pushed on, taking her farther north of the city than she had ever been.

Hanna, two men, and another woman, all in civilian clothes,

left the train at Roydon Station. Two green sedans awaited them outside the small wooden structure. The driver of one was Sir Phillip Kelley, who smiled and waved vigorously at the women while leaning against the passenger door.

"Hanna! Dolores!"

The woman who had arrived with her waved back. Hanna took a more cautious approach.

"In the car you go," he said. "The gentlemen are getting another lift."

Dolores strode ahead of her, swinging her brown leather suitcase in one hand. She was shorter than Hanna, but powerfully built with strong legs and athletic arms. From what Hanna could see, the woman was attractive enough but displayed a hawklike demeanor, made all the more intense by her pursed mouth and closely set eyes.

"In the back, both of you," Phillip ordered. "This may be the only time I'll be your chauffeur." He held open a rear door for them.

"No, you don't," Dolores said. "Commanding officer or not . . . I'm sitting up front."

"All right," he said, relinquishing his order. "Hanna—in back." He opened the boot and swung the luggage inside.

Hanna slid into the back seat. The sun had heated the interior and the car smelled like warm leather, a pleasing odor she'd never experienced before coming to England. Dolores seated herself gracefully in the passenger seat, while Phillip took his place at the wheel.

"I thought you ladies might relish the chance to get acquainted—in the back seat," he said.

Dolores looked over her shoulder to Hanna. "We'll have plenty of time for that in our quarters."

The seat squeaked as Hanna leaned forward. "We're rooming together?"

"Apparently our contact left you in the dark," Phillip said, as the car's motor sprang to life with a gentle hum. "Dolores will be your roommate through these weeks of training. You may or may not go on together, depending on how well you do." He adjusted the rearview mirror and pulled out on the road, the car with the men following.

Feeling as if she had been ambushed, Hanna watched with some trepidation as the gentle swells of the land, a placid brook of steel blue, the poplars in early leaf, and the tall pines that formed windscreens swept by. Phillip rolled down his window and the warm spring air filled the cabin.

"By the way, after lunch, you'll no longer be Hanna and Dolores," Phillip said. "Answer only to your new names. Be wary of anyone calling you by your birth name. Don't respond."

They had traveled only a short distance when they arrived at an iron gate. A guard stood a short distance back from the entrance, which was flanked by brick piers topped with classical urns. The soldier turned out to be a welcoming companion who waved the sedans through without hesitation. Soon they arrived at the front of the house.

Hanna sat transfixed, staring at the building she was about to enter.

"Welcome to Briggens House," Phillip said as he opened his door. He turned his head and winked at Hanna. "As of now, no one knows you're here."

First, they settled into their quarters, a third-story room overlooking the sloping lawn and terraced gardens on the back of the house. Dolores brushed her way in, taking the bed nearest the window, leaving Hanna to settle near the door. She wondered if this forced "marriage" would last. Dolores seemed to have no manners at all, a fault Hanna's deceased uncle-in-law would have despised.

Barely speaking to one another, they unpacked, and then headed down to the common room for lunch. The staircases were a magnificent dark wood, the sprawling interior walls retaining the forest-green wallpaper that looked as if it had been in place for fifty years. Bucolic landscapes in ornate gold frames dotted the walls.

Hanna spotted Phillip sitting at a table in front of a large window. The room was spacious and filled with light, and had been turned into something resembling a military mess hall since the house had been requisitioned.

Hanna asserted her own authority and quickened her pace in order to secure the seat next to Phillip. He stood and pulled the chair out for her, seemingly pleased that she had chosen the adjoining seat. Dolores's lips puckered as she took the seat opposite him.

"Lunch is over there," he said, pointing to a buffet table near the end of the room set with silver chafing dishes. "Not bad for SOE 'chow,' as the Americans like to say. Sorry I couldn't wait, but I have a meeting in a few minutes." The plate in front of him contained the remains of some kind of ground meat, mashed potatoes, and brown gravy. Despite the rather unsavory appearance, the smell and sight of the food piqued Hanna's hunger.

"I'm starving," Dolores said, rising from the table.

"Before you go," Phillip said, motioning for her to sit down, "there's something we need to discuss."

Dolores, eyes narrowing, took her place.

He pushed back his seat so he could address them both. "You have code names now. You're to use these at all times and answer to no other. A small mistake on this point could end your life. If a man says 'Hanna' in Warsaw and there's the slightest indication of recognition—a glance backward, a turn of the head, a faltering step—the Gestapo will arrest you, torture you until they get what they want, or kill you straight out." He shifted his gaze between them, apparently judging their reaction to such a scenario. Hanna noted the tingle of nerves rising on the back of her neck. In many ways, the four hours that had elapsed between Croydon and Briggens House had thrust her into a world so foreign she felt alone and raw, much like when she'd arrived in London the previous year.

"If you want to back out, now is the time," he continued. "You will be tested." He brushed a finger across his mustache, withdrew a piece of paper from his tunic pocket, and, smiling, reviewed the note in front of him. "You both have husbands now."

"That's comforting," Dolores said.

He looked at Hanna. "Your name is Greta Baur, originally from Munich, working as a typist in Warsaw—Volksdeutsche, an ethnic German not living in Germany. Your husband, Stefan, is never around because he's a private driver who works for the Nazis . . . got it?"

"Greta Baur," Hanna replied. "From Bavaria, Munich to be exact. Husband—Stefan."

"Good." He turned toward Dolores. "You are Maria Zielinski from Warsaw, a seamstress, a butcher's wife. He died in the bombings in 1939. His Polish name is, or was, Borys."

"Oh . . . Boris." She gazed at the table for a moment and then, in perfect Polish, gave a salutation to an imaginary person, relating the street and address where she lived in Warsaw.

Hanna's lips parted in amazement. "You speak Polish?"

"Why do you think I'm here?" Dolores said smugly. "Look around."

She hadn't taken the time to do so; her attention had been focused on Phillip. The tables were filled with men and women, some dressed in uniform, others in civilian clothes, taking a break or working with bowed heads over notebooks. English and Polish drifted through the room, along with a smattering of French.

"We have Poles forging documents, as well as Polish resistance members," Phillip said. "That's about all I can say. You'll see them in the house and on the grounds. If you're still with us when you leave Briggens House, you won't have to worry about your identification papers." He paused for a moment and gazed at Dolores. "Who are you?"

"Maria Zielinski, wife of Borys—my dear, dead butcher."

"Excellent."

"And you?" he asked Hanna.

She panicked for a moment, having let her guard down to take in the room. "Greta . . . um . . . Baur."

Phillip scowled. "You need to be quicker, less tense, and say your name as if you own it. The slightest hesitation will lead to trouble."

"I'm sorry," she said, a flush rising in her cheeks, particularly after her roommate's stellar performance.

"You're on leave this afternoon," he said. "A staff member will show you around the grounds. The Fourth Baron of Aldenham and his family live here under special privilege. That part of the house is off-limits. We start in earnest tomorrow at zero-six-hundred hours. Breakfast is a half hour before that." He rose from his chair and picked up his half-eaten plate of food. "I'm due at a meeting. Enjoy your meal."

The afternoon sun slanted through the window, the light glinting off the silver chafing dishes. Hanna followed Dolores to the table, past the rows of men and women, all of whom looked diligent and absorbed in their work. Did she have the courage to do this job, to face death as cavalierly as these people seemed to do?

She took a plate and watched as Dolores served herself hearty helpings of meat and potatoes. Rationing wasn't in effect here. Her appetite diminished as reality sank in.

Briggens House stood dark, still observing the blackout in case Nazi bombers returned with their destructive fire. The night air flowed into the room through a partially opened window. Slivers of light from a waning moon threaded through the undulating curtains and scattered upon her roommate's sleeping form.

Hanna and Dolores had retired midevening in anticipation of an early start the next morning. Hanna found it hard to sleep, her thoughts filled with family reunions on Warsaw streets, imagined battles with Gestapo agents and Wehrmacht soldiers. Would reality be that cruel? Phillip had hinted that although the danger was real, the stated objective of the SOE agent, particularly a woman, was to gather information. The goal was to blend unobtrusively into Poland in order to accomplish a reconnaissance mission. Sending women into combat, short of defending themselves, was a last resort.

Hanna had just brought a knife to a soldier's throat sometime after midnight, when the door burst open and the gauzy beam of an electric torch shone in her face. A gloved hand covered her mouth, while a pair of hands ripped her from the bed.

"Hanna Majewski?" the rough voice asked. "Nod your head—yes or no."

"Hanna Majewski?" another male questioned, this tone even more threatening.

Dolores shot upright in bed. "What's going on?"

"This doesn't concern you." The form of a pistol appeared in a hand. "Shut up or you'll be next."

Was she dreaming? The voices certainly seemed real. The scattered light from the torch outlined the forms of two men attired in black, their faces covered with hoods revealing only their mouths and eyes.

The man removed his gloved hand from her mouth, still awaiting an answer.

In the shock, in her moment of fear, she almost answered yes, but then her brain fired, reminding her that she wasn't Hanna Majewski any longer. She was Greta Baur. She wasn't in Croyden, she was in Briggens House in the custody of two men.

She shook her head. "My name is Greta Baur."

"Come with us," they said.

They shoved her from the room, dragging her through the darkened hall and down the staircase, nearly lifting her feet off the floor, to a room well away from anywhere she had been in the house. One of the men opened a door, pushed her inside, and told her to take a seat.

The man holding the torch ripped off the cloth mesh covering the light, and in the spreading beam, Hanna saw a straight-backed wooden chair at the end of the room. It was black and ominous, blending in with the nearly invisible walls of the same color.

"What do you want?" she asked, shivering in her nightgown. The floor was cold and damp on her bare feet.

"We ask the questions," another man answered in a slight German accent.

"Who are you?" the man asked.

She sat, staring into the light. "I told you. My name is Greta Baur. I'm German, born in Munich."

A match struck in the darkness, flared, and then faded to an orange glow at the end of a cigarette.

"Would you like a smoke?" The voice was almost kind, appealing to any weakness, any sympathies that might be exchanged between her and the captors.

"I don't smoke," she answered. "German women shouldn't. The Führer says so."

The light bounced and came closer to her face.

"What do you do?"

"I'm a typist."

"For whom?"

The question caught her off guard. She couldn't remember any secretarial company in Warsaw. Her mind clicked; her roommate's name. "I work for Zielinski's on Krochmalna."

"There is no Zielinski's on Krochmalna. Don't lie to me."

"I'm not lying."

"We'll see."

She sat silent, staring into the light, awaiting the next question. A blast of cold air struck her face, followed by an electric shock on her neck and back. Crushed ice slid down her skin—a bucket of the frozen stuff emptied on her. She wriggled in her chair, stunned by the stinging temperature that chilled her back and settled in an arctic mess at the base of her spine.

"We know what you're up to," the man said.

"I'm a typist—I've done nothing. Check my papers, you'll see."

"Not good enough."

Another blast of air hit her, and a second bucket of ice went down her back. She writhed in the chair, but managed to stay seated. "I'm not lying," she gasped. "I'm Greta Baur."

"You work for the Poles, don't you?" The man paused— amplifying the menace—and the silence grew deathly.

"I don't know what you mean. Look at my papers."

The light came closer and then switched off.

Black filled her eyes before a bank of overhead lights blazed on. She squinted in pain, adjusting to the glare. The two men who had taken her from her room took off their masks—army officers recruited for the job.

The man who had asked the questions sat at a small desk at the back of the room. Short with a bald head, he extinguished his cigarette in a glass ashtray and stood up. "That was satisfactory—not bad for a recruit." He threw her a towel. "You're excused . . . say nothing to anyone about this. These exercises are classified. Sorry about the damp . . . but if the Gestapo gets hold of you it will be worse . . . much worse."

"Thank you," she said, not knowing what else to say. She found her way back to the room after navigating the maze of hallways and stairs. When she opened the door, she found Dolores, her mouth agape, sitting on the bed.

"Good God, look at you! I thought you'd been kidnapped, but that didn't make sense."

Hanna looked in the dresser mirror. Her cheeks were flushed from the cold, hair hanging in limp strands, a soaked nightgown clinging to her body.

"What happened?" Dolores asked.

"Can't tell you, Mrs. Zielinski," she said, rubbing the towel over her neck and head. "There are people here who want us dead."

"Wonderful. Just what I signed up for."

"Me too." She collapsed on her bed, realizing her trials were just beginning.

CHAPTER 12

Perla closed the apartment door softly so she wouldn't disturb Wanda Krakowski, who had remained at home because she wasn't feeling well. The stairs creaked under her soft step—that couldn't be helped. On the first floor, she covered her nose with a handkerchief to smother the acidic smell of human waste coming from the toilet. As she opened the door, the bright sun of early June struck her on one of the warmest days in a year. She was happy to be out of the apartment. No one would miss her anyway. Finding her old neighbor had been on Perla's mind ever since Aaron had told her in March that a Mrs. Rosewicz lived at an address on Pawia Street very close to the ghetto prison.

I miss Mrs. Rosewicz. She was such a nice neighbor. No one cares where I am. Aaron was in school—if it could be called that; the classroom meetings weren't as formal as yeshiva. Stefa was at the soup kitchen most of the day. Izreal was at work, as were Daniel and Jakub. Both families had been lucky in that respect, except for her. Wanda had secured an application for Perla, but it had gone nowhere.

"My boss says there aren't enough jobs for the people who need them," Wanda told her. "He'll keep it in the prospective file, though."

This was of little comfort to Perla, although she was the wife of a working husband. Everyone said the work permits provided extra protection from the Nazis and the Judenrat, who took their orders from the Germans. The importance of paperwork couldn't be discounted. Single women in the ghetto were looking for husbands so they'd have the security of marriage papers and an income.

Perla buttoned her sweater despite the heat, relishing the warmth that felt like a hot blanket wrapped around her shoulders. The cold had cut through her all winter, barely allowing her to move a few feet from the stove. When fuel ran short, she would cover herself with all the available blankets and sleep through the day.

Turning north toward Pawia, she passed the orphanage run by Janusz Korczak, also an industrial-looking hospital, and the courthouse. The ghetto was a city within a city, but everything had fallen into disrepair since September of 1939. Latticework shutters covered many vacant businesses. Grime covered the windows. Posters plastered their façades. The sewing machine repair shop sign, white with red lettering, hung at a tilted angle from its pole. The building was in need of a good cleaning and painting, but precious supplies that could alleviate those problems were as scarce as gold. The metal plaque marking a dentist's office had tarnished to a dull purple over the winter. Nothing remained as it was before the Nazis entered Warsaw.

In front of her, two children and their mother stood begging on the deserted steps of a closed bookstore. Books were still sold, but on the street now, along with armbands, blankets, wooden stools, and a few precious loaves of bread.

Perla stopped beyond the begging family, horrified by what she saw.

I should have stayed at home. I can't look . . . I can't stand to see this.

She looked away from the corpses on the street, averting her eyes, pretending they didn't exist. The burial cart was sometimes swift, but other times it lagged behind the accelerating number of deaths. Even policemen like Daniel had to load bodies, limbs limp, thrown on top of one another like worn-out clothing.

But one sight she couldn't look away from—a young man dressed in rags and holding a tin cup had fallen, sprawled like a cross, on the large white stones that made up the sidewalk. Bandages covered his feet and wrists. There was no blood, but his face stared up at her like a skull covered with flesh. Flies with silver wings had begun to flicker in and out of his nose and mouth.

She felt as if her eyes would burst as she watched three children, also dressed in rags, run in circles around the corpse, tickling the fine hair on the fallen boy's head as they played a game of tag.

"Shoo," she yelled. "Have some respect for the dead! Leave him alone!"

She covered her nose again with her handkerchief. The children scattered in front of her angry steps.

As she walked on, tears streaked her face. *It's not fair . . . God, what have we done to deserve this? Have mercy upon us.*

She thought of turning back, but had no wish to abandon Mrs. Rosewicz, and trudged on toward Pawia.

When she arrived at the address Aaron had given her, she found it to be a low stone building of modest construction, whose windows turned out to the street. It seemed as if everyone in the ghetto had congregated here: women in housedresses, barefooted young boys clothed in suspendered jumpers, men and women selling whatever they could. The whole world had gone mad.

She made her way cautiously past the door. *Apt. 14.* That was all she knew. There were no names listed at the entrance. Apartments one through eleven lined the first floor. The air stank of decaying meat and the same fetid odor of human waste that filled the stairwell of her home.

On the second floor, to the left, she found a door marked 14 in black paint. She knocked and no one answered. After a second knock, the door squeaked open.

A young woman no more than fourteen, she judged, peered around its edge. Her plum-colored eyes, set in a thin, white face, studied Perla with suspicion. The girl said nothing through her downturned mouth, only stared with forlorn sadness.

"I'm looking for Mrs. Rosewicz. I was told she lives here."

"The old lady," the girl said. "What do you want with her?"

"We were neighbors. I want to make sure she's all right."

The young woman's thin fingers crept like spider's legs around the doorframe, still enforcing her distance from Perla. "She's almost dead—barely survived the winter. She's got nobody. It would have been better if she'd died."

Perla pushed against the door and the girl fell back as easily as the wind scatters a dead leaf.

The small room was filled with empty boxes and crates, mostly used as beds as far as Perla could tell. Mounds of old clothes and blankets were piled on the floor or thrown over the few functioning pieces of furniture, with hardly space to move.

"Where is she?" Perla stood on a grimy path fashioned between the detritus.

The young woman pointed to a corner near the window. "It's cold over there. That's what nearly killed her."

She moved gingerly forward, passing two skeletal young children sitting on a mound of trash. They stared at her from under a cap and bonnet. Their bodies reminded her of the corpse she had seen on the street, stretched flesh covering bones.

"Have you nothing to eat?" Perla called back.

"Only what the two men bring back. Nine of us live here. There's nothing to spare."

In the dim corner, Perla made out the figure of a woman whose arms and legs reminded her of broomsticks. A dirty gray blanket covered the thin body that rested on yellowed newspaper.

Perla gasped. "Kachna . . . Kachna, what have they done to you? Take my hand."

Mrs. Rosewicz turned her wiry, gray-haired head, the light in her eyes flashing briefly before dimming, her thin fingers crawling over the newsprint.

"Do you recognize me, Kachna? It's me . . . Perla."

"I see . . . I see," the weak voice responded. "They took everything—"

Your life. Your dignity. Yes, they took everything from you—from all of us.

"Oh, God, Kachna . . . I want so much to help you . . ." She fell to her knees and grasped her friend's cold hand, the veins raised like blue tunnels under the flesh. "What can I do?"

"You can't save her," the girl said from across the room. "No one can save us."

Perla dropped the thin fingers and, sobbing, covered her face with her hands. Was there nothing she could do? *Izreal will know what to do.*

"Don't cry, Perla . . . I know you won't forget me. That's what they want. They want us to be forgotten."

"Oh, Kachna, I won't forget you."

"I'm so tired . . . I must sleep." Mrs. Rosewicz pulled the blanket up to her neck and turned her face to the corner.

Perla rose from the floor, her body feeling as if it was filled with lead. She looked at the jumbled clothes next to her friend, and pulling a pair of trousers from the pile, formed the material into a pillow. She lifted Mrs. Rosewicz's head, the back of the neck cold, the flesh light from starvation, and placed the fabric under her. There was nothing more to do; she couldn't bring anything to eat, so little remained in her own house. She would send food over with Aaron . . . but what good would it do? How could she be sure it got to her friend? She couldn't feed nine people—the seven in their apartment barely had enough to eat.

Daniel! He would see that Kachna got something to eat . . . the policeman would protect her.

"Thank you," she said to the young woman as she made her way back to the door. "Take care of her. I'll send food."

"Oh, a rich one," she responded. "Lucky for you . . . but you won't be lucky for long."

The young woman's tone shocked Perla—the finality, the hardened conviction of her words, as if she knew everything in the ghetto would be obliterated and no Jew would be left alive. The girl believed it and it was maddening.

She closed the door, glad to be out of the confining, squalid room.

Pawia Street was as busy as when she'd arrived, but in those few moments with Mrs. Rosewicz something shifted in her mind, her body dazed by a numb sensation like the feeling of a brick in her head. Her feet dragged across the sidewalk.

The girl's right. We won't get out of this alive.

She walked like a corpse toward home, hoping she would see no more bodies on the street.

"*Der Melech iz toyt*," Aaron whispered in Yiddish through the crack in the bricks. The King is dead—the four words he and Zeev had chosen as their code.

The sun had set on the late June evening and the dark was fast approaching, and along with it, the fear that he was out after curfew, risking his life to give two slices of bread to his starving friend. If caught—he didn't want to think about it. His father was at work, but the others, with the possible exception of Daniel, would be in the apartment—the stuffy, boring rooms where nothing happened but sadness and tears. Even Sabbath days were no longer joyful. He found it hard to pray for peace or forgiveness as his father droned on with the ritual—not even at a table—standing with the others in a circle around the flickering candles in the bigger room. The two families preferred to keep to themselves, away from others, not even venturing to ghetto synagogues. However, the isolation, the claustrophobia, was suffocating him. How he longed for the days when he could fling open the balcony doors and walk, as if on air, to the iron railing, no matter the time of year, look across a crowded Krochmalna and imagine the city as his own. He wondered how Mrs. Danek was faring with her crazy husband.

"*Himil iz brukh*," the voice responded. Heaven is blessed— the proper reply.

Aaron surveyed his vantage point from a secluded inside corner of the wall between Mirowski Square and Saski Park, both those locations outside the ghetto's boundaries. Here, a jagged edge, a forty-five-degree angle in the construction allowed him to melt into the shadows. No guarded entrance was nearby. And the foot traffic was light compared to other streets. Zeev had discovered the fault at a joint in the bricks, allowing a small square about a half meter on each side to be taken out and re-placed at will.

The bricks lifted with a scrape and Aaron could make out the scruffy hair that curled in rings around his friend's head, the only signifying feature he recognized in the near darkness. The eyes and face were obscured by shadow.

"Here," Aaron said, taking the bread from his pockets and thrusting it through the hole.

"Thank you, my friend," Zeev said, grabbing the precious food.

"How's the work going?" Aaron asked, referring to a plan to open a larger section of the wall that would allow him to travel to the Aryan side.

"Dangerous," Zeev replied. "I can only work in the dark a few minutes at a time because someone official comes by, the Blue Police or the Nazis. Poles aren't stupid enough to show their faces after sunset."

"Like us."

Zeev chuckled. "How about you?"

Aaron sighed. "We'd be dead if it weren't for my father and sister. He still brings home some food, along with what little he's able to purchase from the restaurant. Stefa rarely gets soup now, not much is left over."

"Count your blessings. You have more than most. I heard people are dying on the street."

"Hundreds a day. My father said people are dying of starvation and typhus, and it will only get worse as the summer heat increases."

"I've seen it," Zeev said, his voice rising and then lowering after catching himself. "It's awful. God damn lice. People go crazy with a rash and shit themselves. I throw myself in the Vistula trying to keep the bugs off."

"I've got to go," Aaron said. "My father isn't home yet, but if he catches me out past curfew, I won't have to worry about the Nazis killing me."

"Meet me in four days—I may have the passage done by then." The dark curls disappeared as the bricks reappeared, a vanishing act as deft as a magician's trick.

Aaron nodded, knowing Zeev couldn't see him. In a way, he envied his friend. He was living outside the ghetto's hell, free to move about if he didn't get branded as a Jew, free to do what he wanted, with no one to stop him—except the Nazis. Living under a bridge wasn't pleasant, scrounging for food wasn't fun, sleeping in the cold was dangerous, always staying ahead of possible arrest was nerve-racking, but Zeev was free to live . . . or die.

He sprinted quickly from the shadows onto Krochmalna, headed for home, passing near the Jewish Police station.

An arm caught him by the shoulder when he was a few houses away from his front door. The hand slid upward, clutching him by the neck, yanking him to a stop.

"What are you doing?"

Aaron recognized the voice and dropped his head in shame, embarrassed that he'd been caught, but grateful that it was Daniel who had captured him. "I was just going home," he answered meekly.

The hand released him. Daniel, attired in his police uniform, stepped to his side. "Are you crazy?" He pointed to Aaron's white shirt. "You're easily seen in light clothing. No armband, after curfew—you're lucky the Nazis haven't nabbed you. Stefa and Perla must be worried sick."

"They know I'm crazy. It's my father who'd let me have it." He walked on. "You're out after dark."

"My shift just ended. Come on, hurry up. I don't want guards to catch us."

They walked quickly west, unobserved, the shadows of the dimly lit buildings serving to hide them. Within moments, they arrived at the front door.

The hall was cooler than the air outside, but humid and still stinking of the toilet. Aaron bolted up the stairs. Daniel followed two steps at a time until they reached the door. He extended his hand and stopped Aaron from opening it.

"What's our story?" Daniel asked. "We need an excuse."

"I was late at school?"

"No. Too flimsy . . . you met me at the station after school so I could show you around. You'd never been inside. Good?"

"Good."

Daniel opened the door and pushed Aaron in. "Look what I found."

Perla, her face grim and unforgiving, sat in a chair near the cold stove. Stefa peered over the book she was reading, her hazel eyes shooting icicles at Aaron. Wanda looked up from her sewing, as well as Jakub from the flyer in his hands. But the figure that made him tremble was his father, who sat across from his mother. Izreal's face had reddened to the point of unleashed anger, the veins in his neck popping out in wrath.

"You're home," Aaron said, as if surprised.

"Never mind about me!" Izreal slapped the stove with his hand. "Where have you been?"

Perla dabbed her eyes with her handkerchief.

"See what you've done . . . you've made your mother sick with worry."

Daniel hooked his arm around Aaron's shoulder. "I'm afraid it's my fault."

Stefa cleared her throat and closed her book. She looked at Daniel as if she didn't believe a word of what he was saying.

"How so?" Izreal asked.

"Aaron met me at the station, and I took him around— showed him what my day is like. He's very inquisitive . . . I think he would make a good policeman."

"He has to be a man first." His father stepped closer, his face burning, until Aaron could smell the soap on his hands, the clean smell that Izreal always had despite his job with food.

"You're fourteen, and you're still a boy in my eyes—not a man," Izreal continued, leaning in toward him. "I know what you're doing when you come home just before curfew. You're not studying or playing or doing anything a normal boy would do. You're scavenging; you're no better than a black-market pirate, a smuggler! The Nazis shoot smugglers. Soon they'll shoot Jews who attempt to leave the ghetto. They don't care if you're a child or an adult. I forbid you to do this! I'll lock you up in this house if I have to."

Aaron broke away from Daniel, pushing him from his side, his own anger bubbling up. "What will we do when the food runs out? Who will slip through the wall to the Aryan side to get supplies? Stefa's kitchen relies on the black market." He bunched his fists and shouted questions into his father's face. "Who will take care of the family when you no longer have a job? Are we to depend upon God? God has declared war against us!"

Izreal swung, smacking his son hard on his left cheek.

Aaron stumbled backwards, but Daniel caught him by the arm, pulling him forward.

"Father!" Stefa rose from the floor, rushing to her brother's side.

Izreal shook his fist at his son. "The Nazis have declared war on God by killing *us*! *We* are the Children of Israel!" Hanging his head, his father walked back to his chair and sat, covering his face with his hands. After a time, he looked up, tears glistening in his eyes. "I'm sorry. You're my only son. I love you with all my heart. I don't want to lose you. Everyone wants you to live, not die . . . I'm doing the best I can." Turning toward his wife, he sobbed and took her hands in his, and then spoke without looking at Aaron. "You're too smart for your own good," he said between strangled breaths. "That is unfortunate in this time, my son."

Aaron rubbed his cheek. His father had never struck him or berated him in front of others. He skulked off to his mattress in the corner, saying nothing. He caught himself sniffling. His body tensed, holding back the tears that needed to pour forth. Anger bloomed inside him, and he felt he would go mad if it wasn't released. He had to do something, anything to save their lives . . . and take revenge upon the Nazis.

He turned toward the window and waited until the lights were out and his father had eased into bed. Aaron grew cold at the sense of the body next to him. Instead, he watched the clouds sweep over the building, revealing a few glittering stars as the night settled in, and imagined himself far away from Warsaw and the ghetto.

Hanna barely recognized that the summer had slipped by. It didn't matter if the heat and humidity made Briggens House feel like a greenhouse, or if the day was coated by pouring rain or dense fog. Training went on without a halt.

A letter had been delivered from Warsaw, forwarded from the Croydon address to Briggens House. The note was slim, but it confirmed that her family was alive, and for that she was grateful. A series of words struck her: *We beg you to visit our friend on Krochmalna.* That was worth remembering. But who?

Neither she nor Dolores spoke much, preferring to keep their conversations polite and perfunctory. Her roommate wore too much makeup, a mistake if she was assigned to Poland, and was too brusque in her manners to make her attractive to anyone—except, perhaps, to an unsuspecting Wehrmacht soldier. Hanna wondered if that was the SOE objective for Dolores—a vamp transformed into a cold, calculating killer of Nazis. She shuddered at the thought.

She even kept her distance from the native Poles, who had arrived in England as an elite corps of forgers and fighters. Rita Wright and Phillip had warned her to keep to herself. She carried on the same exchanges with them as she did with Dolores.

Hanna often asked Phillip how she was doing during training, but only a smile broke out on his boyish face, followed by the words, "Keep up the good work."

She crossed paths with Rita one day in July. The woman passed her in the dim hall, nodding once and saying nothing. When Hanna recognized her and looked back, Rita had vanished, slipping into a room. It was the only time at Briggens House she saw the operative who had recruited her.

Her courses included languages, Morse code, and working with the radio transmitter. It had taken many days for her to get comfortable with this strange way of communicating; and, although she passed her tests, the dots and dashes felt uncomfortable under her fingers. She practiced many nights in her room, tapping out codes on the top of the dresser or on her book of German history. She passed the language portion of her training easily—German, Polish, and Yiddish presented no problems. The instructor had given her passing marks in all three, with an admonition to keep on with her German, particularly the subjunctive case and the conjugated verbs.

Surprisingly, weapons instruction and combat appealed to her more than the classroom training. Perhaps it was a memory of her time spent outdoors in her youth, running or swimming, when she could sneak away from her parents. The hours spent in the company of a Browning pistol at the firing range thrilled her more than sitting at a radio transmitter. Being out of the grand training center, in the open air, was refreshing. Hanna pictured herself in a safe house in the Polish countryside near Warsaw or on Krochmalna where she grew up. Sometimes, as night overtook the long summer evenings and she imagined herself in Poland, the danger of her task came roaring back. This training was necessary to save her life. She might have to kill someday.

She learned technique: never be caught with a weapon if at all possible—a reason for Nazi arrest if ever there was one. Use the flat of your hand, not your knuckles, in a fight. Step close to your oppressor; thrust, don't slash; cut, don't stab. Use whatever is at hand to defend yourself, whether it's a stick or a brick.

One summer day, when the sun bore down upon them, they were taken outside for knife training in the expansive gardens in back of the house. They had practiced on hanging dummies before, but today's setup was different. She and Dolores and the others, attired in their training overalls, were given wooden knives that looked and weighed the same as their real metal counterparts.

"A simple task today," Jack, their trainer, said. Looking more like a barkeep than a fighter, he was a bit of a roly-poly with a heavy mustache that curled over his upper lip. "Slit your opponent's throat. Cut, don't stab. If you make more than one kill— good for you." He pointed to a fresh red smear, a water-based paint that coated the blade. "And don't let yourself get offed. The goal is to keep your neck clean. Use the trees and shrubs as cover." He pointed to the grounds beyond the terraced steps. "All right, split up. Off with you. Good hunting." Proceeding as if taking a casual stroll, he smiled and said, "I'll be observing."

"Well, we're really in it this time," Hanna said to Dolores, thinking about how awful it would feel to slit someone's throat. She thought of her father, who never discussed work at the dinner table. Everyone knew how he handled his first job; for example, slitting a chicken's throat properly so it didn't suffer. Now, he made sure everything was kosher—much like Jack, the trainer.

"Yes, off to the hunt," Dolores said, holding the knife in her outstretched hand.

Hanna thought she was enjoying the exercise a bit too much.

With a snap of Jack's fingers, the group split apart, the trainees heading in separate directions until everyone was alone. Hanna positioned herself behind the trunk of a large beech whose foliage created a spiderweb canopy of twisted branches and profuse green leaves. The gnarled trunk, as wide as two men, was split in two. Drawing in a breath, she squeezed herself into the crotch.

Something popped near her—a foot snapping a branch. Folly, she thought, to jump out and engage in a knife fight. She decided to bide her time, crouch, and when the time was right, strike.

It didn't take long for the moment to present itself.

Hanna had no idea who was approaching. The only thought that crossed her mind was to make herself invisible. Her heart beat furiously and an adrenaline spike sent her nerves tingling. The steps came closer, nearing her hiding spot.

She saw his profile and recognized him as one of the Polish fighters—a strong, athletic man with black hair and dark eyes, who, under normal circumstances, could take her down with no problem. But she had the element of surprise in her favor. He gazed straight ahead, unaware of her position within the tree. A lethal mistake.

He caught a sideways glimpse as he stepped past, but it was too late. She sprang from her hiding place and slashed the wooden knife across his throat. The attack shocked him so much that he staggered back, clutching his neck. The red paint smear was clearly evident when he dropped his knife to the ground.

The man cursed in Polish—words that Hanna knew, but would never have repeated in front of any family member.

From nowhere, Jack bounded under the wide canopy of leaves, a smile breaking out below the bushy mustache. "Excellent, Greta, top-notch job. The element of surprise can be very effective."

The victim sank to his haunches in anguish, spouting a few more Polish curses.

"Tough luck, Alek," he said, offering the man a helping hand. "Save the anger for later. Tomorrow we do it again, in full kit. It won't be so easy to hide." He winked at Hanna.

"How stupid of me," the man complained. "To be had by a woman."

"Buck up, old man, you'll live to fight again," Jack said. "Got to move on. Rendezvous with the group back at the steps."

A sulking Alek wiped the smear from his throat as they walked to the terrace. A few recruits awaited them. Those who had been "killed" were easy to pick out by the paint on their necks. One of them was Dolores, who, despite her rather forlorn look, appeared to be enjoying the company of her male assassin, another member of the Polish fighters. He smiled and laughed, much happier than Hanna's companion.

Jack arrived with the remainder of the group about a half hour later and they sat on the grass and dissected the many techniques of their murders.

The runs and hikes intensified during the summer and Hanna's leg bore the brunt of the exercise. She often returned to Briggens House limping from the effort. Jack was famous for using the words, "Buck up," and many times they were cast in her direction.

The day after she had dispatched Alek, Hanna was done in by Dolores in a gleeful manner when her roommate sprang undetected from bushy undergrowth. The score was now one to one for the women, surprise being the determining factor in both kills. Hanna wondered if her "death" in full uniform might lead to her dismissal from training with a final assignment to "the cooler," where agents who hadn't made the grade were debriefed and sent home.

Nothing happened immediately, and her training continued with drills focusing on messages—dropping them at secret locations in town or rolling them in cigarettes where they could be smoked if necessary. Recall tests sharpened their memories, along with the occasional shouted test of remembered identities. She always remembered her name and the appropriate German phrases.

One night when a full moon cast silky shadows across the lawn, Phillip asked her to take a walk. She gladly agreed, happy for company on the sultry evening, feeling that their time at Briggens House might come to an end soon.

"I've enjoyed my training," Hanna said, as they stepped away from the columned entrance to the house. Phillip stopped at a nearby bench that faced east and motioned for her to sit. They watched the brilliant moon rise, its steady white light glowing above the purple horizon.

"It was too brief," he replied somewhat formally. He turned his gaze from the sky to her. "Tomorrow, everyone will know," he said without any indication of what he meant.

"Know what?" In the fading light, she looked into his youthful face, still sporting a tan from the summer sun. Phillip was hard to get to know despite their close proximity at Briggens House. The days were a blur of training, eating, and sleeping, with little time for socializing. In fact, she could only remember a few meals taken together during the weeks at the estate.

"If you made the cut."

"Have I?"

"I don't know and I couldn't tell you if I did. That's up to the top brass here—Rita has a say, of course." He paused, sliding closer to her. "It's difficult. We're trained to stay apart, to keep our distance, as members of the SOE—for good reason. If you're attached to someone it's impossible to let go—it's unimaginable to know they've been tortured or died at the hands of monsters. I don't want that to happen to you—to us."

She was somewhat flustered by his words. Had he professed an attraction? Hanna stared at the moon. The only thing she could think of was to ask, "Why?"

"Because you're extraordinary." Turning casually to his side, he faced her. "I'm sorry we didn't get to know each other better . . . that we couldn't spend more time together . . . sorry that our jobs are more important than our lives."

Hanna looked at the glorious moon. "I understand how we're supposed to act . . . to keep our feelings in check." She faced him. "What happens now?"

"If you go on, you'll most likely be assigned to a house in Scotland for final training. Dolores might be there, too—but I won't. My assignment keeps me at Briggens House."

She nodded. "I'm sorry . . . we won't see each other again."

He took her hands in his. "Perhaps we will . . . when the war is over . . . if we both make it through."

She sighed. "There are no promises to be kept. People are dying and there's a war to be won. We're both in it." She withdrew from his grasp. "I've often wondered if I made a mistake leaving Warsaw. What drove me to this? Guilt? Hatred of the Nazis? I had to leave my home—I hope you can understand that. Feelings I couldn't control pushed me to England. I couldn't be happy until I'd left everything behind. My aunt knew what I was going through because she made the same choice. Others can never understand. And now I'm going home . . . it seems."

He withdrew a note from his trouser pocket and slipped it into her palm. "Jack gave me this. He said to keep what was written on it an absolute secret at peril to your life."

Hanna looked at the folded piece of white paper—ordinary enough. What was written on it: her next assignment, some secret code that only she was privy to?

Suddenly, the sky went black as a sack was pulled over her head and tied at the back of her neck. The rough fabric scratched her eyelids, forcing them to close, while she spit out the coarse fibers that flew into her mouth.

"Stand aside, Kelley—not your affair. Don't make a move." She recognized Jack's voice, the trainer of combat skills. "But be at the ready for assistance."

"What's going on?" Hanna asked in German, genuinely frightened by the hood over her head. This had to be an exercise . . . or a joke. There were no other plausible explanations. She slipped the note into a pocket in her dress.

"Got her." A voice answered in German as a pair of hands grasped her waist and pushed her into the road in front of the house. Her feet slipped in the gravel. Blinded, she lost her footing before someone pulled her up by the arms.

"Where's the message?" a man demanded in German.

"I don't know what you're talking about." She fought down the urge to retch as the smothering dark closed around her face.

The hood cut off her oxygen; she gulped draughts of air, struggling to breathe.

"I'll ask you once again. Where's the message? We know you're working with the resistance."

"I don't know. I don't have a message."

"Search her."

A strange silence fell and instead of hands roving over her body, she felt nothing. Then a sound, at first faint, drifted through the cloth. It was a motorcar, approaching fast. She was standing in the middle of the road in the dark with a black hood over her face.

"Good God!" Jack's voice burst through in English. "Where's the torch? They won't see us if I don't wave them off!"

"Where's the message?" another man shouted in German.

"To hell with the message," Jack shouted, his trembling voice rising in concern. "Where's the damn torch? I told you to bring one!"

"I don't have it," a man answered.

"Shit! Move out of the way!"

Hanna could tell the car was racing up the drive, accelerating toward her, the wheels spitting out dirt and rock.

"Move!" One last shout from Jack.

She stood rooted to her spot in the road and steeled herself for a hit. It was useless to shift one way or another because she couldn't tell if, or where, the car would swerve. She might accidentally jump into its path—two tons of metal speeding toward her. There would be nothing left of her. The English had succeeded in doing what Nazi bombs had failed to finish.

The car skidded to a stop, throwing stinging rocks and dirt against her legs. Through the haze of the cloth, she saw two stationary headlamps.

Someone ripped off the hood, temporarily blinding her in the glaring light. The lamps went out and her vision gradually returned. A group of men gathered around her.

"Excellent set of nerves," Jack said, stepping in front of her.

He turned toward the door and shouted to a man standing there. "At ease. House doors and windows open again."

Hanna wiped the perspiration from her face and looked toward the bench, where Phillip stood with a bewildered look, eyes wide, mouth open.

"Don't worry—he knew nothing about this," Jack said. "And no one else should either. You can understand why." He patted her on the shoulder as the others dispersed, including the driver of the car, who threw the gearbox into reverse and backed down the road.

"I thought I was going to die," she told Jack.

"You didn't. But, to the point, you didn't reveal what we were looking for . . . and you didn't run . . . a fatal mistake." He grasped her arm and led her toward the bench. "Can't say for sure, but I think you're on your way to Scotland. Bravery can't be bought."

"I don't know that I was brave . . . only so terrified I couldn't move."

"It doesn't matter. You didn't crack."

She collapsed on the bench and Phillip sat again, the moon lording over them.

"I'll say good night," Jack said. "I have a report to write."

After the men had left, Hanna turned to Phillip and shook her head. "You knew nothing about this?"

His eyes were still wide and his voice a bit shaky. "Nothing. I swear it. Jack only told me to give you the message."

She leaned toward him, pulled the paper from her pocket, and opened it. It was blank. "I would have been furious if you'd been in on it."

"I was frightened, too. It was all I could do to keep my distance . . . it happened so fast."

"I guess that's the point. The Nazis will act fast, too." Looking down at her smarting legs and noticing a dark streak of blood running from her shin to her ankle, she smeared the slickness with her hand. "Do we get hazard pay, as well?" She attempted to joke, not knowing how to end the conversation with Phillip.

He gently grasped her neck, pulled her toward him, and kissed her in a way no man had done before.

She treasured the moment—lost in time and filled with sweet emotion. At last, his lips left hers.

"I'll miss you," he said. "Don't forget to write." He stood, offering his hand.

She took it and, rising, said, "That can't happen and you know it, Sir Phillip Kelley, but I'll get a message to you one way or another."

They walked to the door and then went their separate ways. Her legs prickled in pain as she walked up the stairs, but she didn't care. She had passed the final test and was confident that Scotland was her next stop. A little blood on the legs was a small price to pay compared to what the Nazis might inflict.

CHAPTER 13

——◆——

The rumors and stories of death were maddening.

Stefa dealt with the starving who swarmed the soup kitchen in a continuous line, like ants covering a bit of stale bread, and also listened to the tales that filtered into the ghetto. They reduced her to tears and sapped any energy she had. Like everyone in her family, with the possible exception of Aaron, she had so little to give after an exhausting day.

The tragedies seemed endless. Jews slaughtered in the Ukraine by the Einsatzkommando Aktion; any attempt at self-preservation was dealt with ruthlessly. Professors, dissidents, and intellectuals had been rounded up and executed at Białystok, Poland. Jews were murdered in Belorussia, Lithuania, and Romania, and Hitler had attacked the Soviet Union, killing thousands of innocents. The list of atrocities mounted by the day, seemingly by the hour, as people in the soup kitchen whispered and then stumbled away, frightened by their own mortality. The Warsaw Ghetto Jews had little energy or resources to fight for freedom.

Walking to work in the summer took its own emotional toll. Death was everywhere. She was physically sickened by what she saw on the streets—what everyone saw unless they had the capacity to ignore it. And, some did walk by—a few rich men and women, who still had the trappings of money, although fortunes were disappearing rapidly. They walked together, attired in their suits and leather shoes and best dresses with jewels adorning their lapels and fingers. They passed by, hoping to hold on to what little they had left, hoping that they might exchange diamonds for a way out.

What they ignored were the men dressed in rags, huddled against dirty buildings, praying in Hebrew, spouting words in Yiddish and Polish toward the skies, to a God who disregarded their suffering. The heat had caused the beggars to shed their tattered coats, their hats and gloves, the shoes that were nothing more than the remnants of leather straps. They held out their hands but usually received nothing because there was nothing to give. Stefa got used to ignoring them. She had even stopped inviting the children to the kitchen because the facility was overwhelmed.

A boy tottered on crutches, holding out his hand, asking for a piece of bread. She had none to give. A little girl sat half naked on the sidewalk, the skin on her face reduced to an ashen covering, an empty dirty bowl at her side. The child looked up and down, and from side to side, with no tears in her dry eyes, waiting for someone to help. Another boy played a screechy violin tune as other children listened and hoped for a gift of food that might be shared.

These were the people of the ghetto, the people she had to see, or blot from her mind, when she walked from the apartment on Krochmalna to the soup kitchen on Leszno.

Yet, if one looked elsewhere, celebrations and commemorations of Jewish artists and poets still occurred, the theaters still welcomed guests. Life eked out a meager existence. Stefa could close her eyes and imagine that the world hadn't changed that much; she could imagine and hope until her eyes hurt and tears ran down her cheeks, but when she opened them the ghetto still existed. Nothing had changed. Misery still ruled.

She worried that her mother might not be strong enough to survive, that the struggle would wear her down before the war ended. Stefa cried silent tears at night when she reached for Daniel's hand, and not finding it, feared that he might be taken from her as well, that the Nazis would liquidate the Jewish Police and take over the responsibility themselves. In April, Heinz Auerswald, an SS member, had been made commissioner of the ghetto, the "residential district," as his title declared, but conditions had not improved. If anything, they had grown worse. She worried that her father's job might end, thus cutting off their primary source of food, sending her brother into the streets, or even outside the ghetto walls, validating his work as a smuggler.

There were so many things to worry about she couldn't remember the last time she'd gotten a good night's sleep. Daniel's parents, the frail Mrs. Rosewicz, even Janka Danek, who might have left Warsaw, occupied her mind. And what of Hanna? She hoped that the letter she'd composed to her sister had somehow made its way to England.

As the summer dragged on, the lines at the kitchen rose and fell like waves on the Vistula. Hundreds of deaths a day from starvation and typhus might make a small dent in the crowds, only to be followed by a new influx of the half dead the following morning.

One day, Stefa was serving soup when another woman volunteered to take over the duty. "Someone's here to see you," she said and pointed to a man standing near the door. He looked familiar, but Stefa wasn't sure who he was.

She wiped her hands on her apron and stood next to the kitchen door, the suffocating heat pouring out of the tiled enclosure.

He approached her, holding his hat in his hands. "Emanuel Ringelblum. We haven't had the pleasure of meeting."

She was taken aback, meeting a man she knew by reputation only. Attired in a suit, he looked the professorial and important man that her father had described. She brushed her hand through her hair, trying to somehow fashion the unruly strands dampened by the heat into something more presentable. Her stained apron gave her no great comfort either.

"Is there somewhere we can talk privately?" Ringelblum

asked. His thin lips seemed permanently pressed into a smile. Below the arched brows, his eyes were kind and forgiving.

The only other available room, besides the small dining area, was the kitchen itself—a cramped space filled with noisy workers, clanging enamel pots and pans, and tropical heat.

"A deserted building down the street—we can talk in the doorway."

"Fine," he said, and smiled.

"I'll be back in a few minutes," she shouted to her coworker.

Stefa led the way through the crowd, past the line leading to the kitchen, until they found the deserted entrance of what had once been a shoe shop. Production of those goods had been transferred to the ghetto's German plants for military use. Very few could afford a new pair of shoes, anyway. The entrance was set back from the busy sidewalk. They stepped into a small enclosure surrounded by a bank of dusty windows marred by posters and the faded markings identifying it as a Jewish shop. Two years earlier, it would have been bustling with customers— shoes, new and shiny, in the window, the smell of leather drifting coolly out the door.

"How is your family?" he asked, standing stiffly across from her, brushing against nothing, keeping his suit from being coated with dust. "I haven't seen your father in months."

The innocent question brought up emotions buried within her. How was anyone's family these days? Even innocuous social pleasantries were tainted by the Nazis.

"We're holding ourselves together . . . as best we can."

"Is everything in order? Work permits and other documents?" He turned and peered around the doorway. "We must be careful. Two people standing in the entrance of a deserted shop is suspicious."

A tinge of sadness enveloped her. "Yes, except for my mother."

He turned back, a questioning look in his eyes.

"She's not working," Stefa continued. "Of course, she's covered under my father's permit but we're still worried. It would be better if she had work . . . if she could . . ."

"Could?"

"Since we left our apartment—our old home—her health has failed. At times, it's like she's not here, like she's in some other place. We all have to deal with what's going on, but she's having a harder time than the rest of us. I fear we might lose her one day to the Nazis . . . and they will not be forgiving."

He grasped her hand, letting his fingers linger on hers for a moment, and then released them. "I'll see what I can do . . . which may not be enough. We must be prepared for anything." He lowered his gaze and stared at the dirty wooden planks beneath their feet. "I wish I could be more positive . . . sometimes I feel that those who look the other way, those who fail to recognize what we're dealing with, those who believe that the British will rescue us, or that the Nazis will somehow come to their senses, are the happiest." He looked up. "But I can't forget what has happened, how they overtook us, conquered us with their unbending will to deceive and destroy. And we let it happen. Some want weapons, but I have none. The only tools I have are my pen and the pens of others."

Stefa nodded, sensing what he wanted to hear. "I've been writing when I can, mostly at night when the family settles in. I've tried to record what has happened on the street, at the soup kitchen, and at my father's work. I hope it's satisfactory."

His lips pressed together before he spoke. "I'm sure it is . . . they have us . . . we must resist in any way we can. When the time is right—and I hope it never happens—I'll call for your diary and it will be hidden with the others, for another generation to find. I wouldn't have started this project if I believed there was a way out. Another set of eyes will see what happened to the Warsaw Jews. And they *must* believe us—they *will* believe us."

Stefa looked at the crowd that shuffled by, few even noticing them in their shadowy enclave. "I hope we won't be forgotten—no matter what happens."

"A word before we go," he said. "Have you heard the rumors of the Jews of Lvov?"

She shook her head.

"This is why our project is so important." His kind and forgiving eyes darkened. "The Ukrainians, urged on by the Einsatzgruppe, have killed thousands of Jews in our third-largest community. The Nazis don't want anyone to know that they instigated it. A Wehrmacht unit even filmed the riots against our people so they could document how the Ukrainians hated the Jews. The Lvov Ghetto will be annihilated someday and they will blame us—our own people. That's what they hope will happen here."

A violent shiver racked her, and she stood trembling in the shadow, which now seemed cold despite the July heat. "They will kill us, won't they?"

Emanuel didn't answer, only looked at her with his sad eyes.

"I will fight for my family and my life, when the time comes," she said.

"Thanks be to God," he said. "Blessed are You, Lord, our God, King of the Universe, the just Judge."

Putting on his hat, leaving the shop entrance, he walked in the opposite direction from the soup kitchen on Leszno.

Stefa stepped into the sunlight, too, shaken by what she'd heard and convinced that she might not live another two years to see the age of twenty. A hollow numbness swamped her as she walked back to the kitchen, along with a dull awareness that she and Daniel might never be married or have children. Why had God singled out Warsaw for such tortures? Would suicide be better than handing over her life to the Nazis?

She couldn't burden herself with such thoughts—the starving and sick moved in their slow line toward the kitchen.

One Wednesday, the window was open.

The sounds from Krochmalna filtered up, but the life below only served to heighten her loneliness. Everyone was gone: her husband, her son, daughter, and the Krakowskis, including

Daniel, whom she had grown to love because of his kindness to Mrs. Rosewicz.

"Of course, Mrs. Majewski," Daniel had told her when she asked if he would check on the old woman and deliver the food they could spare now and then. "I will do anything in my power for you and your family."

She had been tempted to let him call her Perla, if he wished, but her mind had drifted off to some other thought before she could speak the words. Concentration was difficult these days. It was even hard to focus on mundane laundry duties—her designated job since she wasn't working. At least her hands in a tub of lukewarm water kept her mind occupied.

Perla lifted three pairs of socks from the basin and wrung them out, the gray and tepid water sloshing in the tub. Even Aaron was working now at the Palais, a job coerced by his father upon his son in lieu of school. Izreal had told her how he pleaded with the owner to give Aaron a job clearing tables, washing dishes, and doing odd tasks in the kitchen so he could keep an eye on him. The boss was reluctant at first, saying, "I don't know how long the Nazis will let *you* stay on. They don't care about food that's kosher—only that it's good." Izreal had argued for both their jobs—the Nazis were paying for the "good food"—and his boss finally relented, even providing two uniforms from a former "small employee" that fit Aaron. He wore each for three days of his six-day week.

A donkey's bray and the clatter of wagon wheels drifted in on the summer air. Perla took the socks, leaned out the window, and attached them with wooden clothespins to the rope Izreal had rigged from the sill. It fell almost to the first floor. In the winter, the clothes freeze-dried almost immediately, but in the humid summer they took longer, as the sun crept north leaving the façade in shade.

She dropped the line, the wet socks flopping against the stone. Formerly, she had loved summers in Warsaw, the flowering bushes, the roses, the park begonias, the trees in full leaf, the breeze through the open balcony doors of the old apartment.

But now, the view she looked out on only deepened her sadness. Men and women, moving like sacks of ashes, their clothes hanging from their bodies; emaciated horses and donkeys, orphaned children—those were the sights that turned her stomach and tormented her mind. Few people had died near the apartment, but beggars ventured to the street during the day, and traversed Krochmalna much like the dying, their spirits evaporating in the heat.

"Typhus . . . typhus . . ." Izreal had repeated with solemn finality on many nights. "Watch out for lice and fleas. Stay away from people. Let Daniel go to Mrs. Rosewicz's apartment. It's not safe. Your job is to keep the apartment clean." She heeded his warnings, but felt like he was condemning her to yet another prison. The Nazis had walled them inside the ghetto, and her husband had ordered her not to leave the room. Now, her time was spent looking for insects on bedding, doing laundry, and getting things in order for the Sabbath and holidays.

She returned to the basin, preparing to wash a pair of trousers, when she heard the door open below. The voices that carried up the hall weren't speaking Yiddish or Polish. The shouts were in German.

What do they want? she asked herself as men pounded on the door below. *What are they looking for?*

She panicked, her mind racing, her heart thumping.

"*Was für ein Scheissloch,*" one of them said, and she knew they were referring to the smell that permeated the downstairs hall. "*Öffne die Tür!*" another shouted, while pounding on the wooden frame until it almost cracked. The downstairs neighbor, an older Polish Jew, among others, yelled back. The racket increased until Perla believed there would be nothing left of the door but splinters.

She raced around the room looking for her registration card, but in her confusion found nothing. Izreal, Aaron, and the others carried their papers with them, a requirement in case they were stopped by the Nazis.

They whisper and they don't think I hear, but I do. I know about the murders. I've heard the rumors that we'll be deported to someplace called a "work camp." Are they taking us now? If they find me here, alone, they'll take me away and I'll never see my husband, my Stefa, or my Aaron again. She clamped her hands on her head, trying to think of a solution. *The hall! The hiding place!*

The secret space was her only chance. Izreal and Daniel had shown it to her. She had poked her head into it when she was alone to see if she could manage the wooden panel. The darkness had frightened her—it was like stepping into the blackness of space with nothing around you. She didn't even know if the small beam would support her weight.

The men were in the neighbor's apartment below. She had to act now.

She took off her shoes, placed them by the mattress, and trotted to the door, opening it as softly as she could. The execrable odor of the latrine lingered in the stairwell as she made her way to the panel. The noise below had quieted, causing her to tiptoe the required few steps.

She lifted the panel gently, her hands sweating, fearing that the wood might slip from her damp fingers and strike her toes, or worse yet, fall to the floor with a thud. She managed to keep her grip, and the murky yaw opened before her. The small wooden beam came into view.

Her back to the wall, she leaned the panel against her body and placed one foot on the support. The other foot came next and then a tug with all her might to position the wood in place. A line of gray daylight appeared on the edge below. She took in a deep draught of the fetid air and squeezed herself as tight as she could against the cold wall. With one more tug at a runner on the back of the panel, the seam of light disappeared.

For five minutes—what seemed like hours—she pressed her back against the bricks and the crumbling plaster, barely taking in a breath. Ants crawled on her neck . . . or were they spiders? An itch broke out on her arm, but she could do nothing about it.

Finally, the voices erupted again, along with forceful steps on the stairs. From what she could gather there were two men. Perla didn't know if they were soldiers, Gestapo agents, or members of the SS.

She thought of spring flowers to distract herself from the intruders who had stopped in front of her door. The distraction did little good. They were going to find her, drag her away, and kill her. Her life had come to this—cowering in a torturous hole before being dragged away to her death. Where was Izreal? Where was Daniel? Her feet quivered on the board and a sliver of loose cement dropped into the dark.

The hall grew silent and she sensed the men moving closer to the panel.

The first-floor door opened and closed and she felt the Germans' attention shift from the hall toward her apartment.

They shouted instructions, knocked loudly, and then opened the unlocked door. Thereafter, chairs scraped against the floor and a general commotion arose in the room. The wood stove hinge creaked; things were thrown about.

With the odor of the latrine rising from below, she clawed at the bricks, fighting back the possibility of fainting, hoping not to vomit.

Oh, God, when will this be over? My mother used to sing to me when I was scared. I remember the songs, her voice as smooth as honey, like a balm. She concentrated on the melodies in her head, some happy, some filled with centuries of tragedy.

The men left her apartment, marching past her to the floor above, where they found no one at home. After a few minutes, they retreated down the stairs until their footsteps faded.

Perla waited a short time until she was sure they were gone and then, gasping for air, pushed the panel open. It fell with a thud to the floor, but no one else was around to hear it. She jumped from the beam and replaced the panel, happy to have her feet on the floor again, happy to have escaped whatever the Germans had in mind for the residents of the house.

The apartment was a mess, with cookware and books strewn about, the mattresses turned over, but nothing had been damaged. It could be cleaned up with a little work. Wondering what the men were looking for, she went to the window and peered down. They had disappeared—her neighbor from the first floor was walking back to his apartment.

When he came inside, she called out from the stairwell, "What did they want?"

"Where were you?" he asked. "I knew you were home, but I didn't say anything."

"I hid," she said softly, not wanting to reveal her secret.

Placing his fingers upon the doorknob, he shook his head. "I was the only one home. I'm not sure what they wanted, but if I had to guess, they were looking for stragglers like me who can't work. They wrote down the names and occupations of everyone who lived here."

"Did you tell them?"

He chuckled. "Of course. What choice did I have? You can't lie to the Gestapo." He went into his apartment.

She returned to hers and sat in the chair by the stove, uninterested in continuing her laundry until the fear that bubbled inside her had dissipated.

Perla looked at her hands, turned pink from her washing, and wondered: *What did they want? Stragglers? They will come looking for me before others. The hiding place must remain a secret.*

She sighed, knowing that her life depended on making herself invisible.

Janka pulled on her coat as she sat in the pew, praying for peace and for the Majewskis' safety. An unsettled feeling came over her as she mouthed their names. She had heard nothing about them through Zeev or anyone else; in fact, there had been no word since Izreal had given her Stefa's letter.

She wished she could do more—Catholic Poles and Jews didn't naturally mix. A long history of distrust simmered between them—but Aaron had triggered her warmth. She had done something good for the boy, perhaps saved him, and that small bit of resistance against the Nazis felt like nothing she'd ever experienced. The sense of danger and accomplishment had left her feeling exhilarated. But there was something else as well. In the Majewskis, she saw the family she didn't have, and as Karol had transformed with the Nazi occupation, the Majewskis became the family she couldn't have. She abhorred the thought of children with Karol. She wished she could do more for all those imprisoned—the Nazis made that impossible.

The silver-haired priest heard her confession in the booth at the back of the church, but she was too embarrassed and felt too guilty to admit the sin of wishing her husband dead. The confessional opened almost silently, the latticework slid across the red cloth, revealing the shadowy face of a man, the calm voice filling her ears. Janka dropped her gaze, not wanting to meet his eye in any way. How could anyone ever confess something so terrible—and to a priest she had known for years? *Father, forgive me, for I have sinned.* She made something up on the spot—*not paying enough attention to her husband*—a wife's dereliction of duties. He seemed almost amused, with a stifled laugh, by her admission, but quickly corrected himself and administered a penance of Hail Marys and prayerful absolutions.

After confession, she left the church, and stood on the sidewalk as the fall sun wrestled with the clouds. Intermittent shafts of light struck her body in an almost heavenly way. Another long winter approached—one without adequate food or fuel for Poles, let alone for the Jews imprisoned within the ghetto.

She walked to Nowak's, arriving later than usual, to find the store almost deserted except for the owner and his daughter. The shelves were empty, too. "We may have to close soon," the man told her. "Even we Catholics aren't eating." If the situation was this bad for Polish Catholics, she could only imagine what the Majewskis were going through.

Janka thought of walking past the ghetto, perhaps encountering Zeev or one of the family, but considered the danger, and returned home. As she had seen, the Nazis had no hesitation about shooting anyone who appeared suspicious. She could be arrested for anything, even for being "an observer." If she wanted to get in touch, she'd have to think of another way.

The afternoon dragged by. There was no shopping to be done. She occupied her time by preparing a pot of noodles and canned meat. Karol would be snippy, but if he'd consumed his usual amount of alcohol before arriving home, he'd either burst into a rage because of "another shitty meal," or be drunk enough that he wouldn't care.

He was somewhere in the middle of those extremes when he arrived, shortly before seven. She was used to the smoke and vodka that permeated his clothes, and left him alone while she took refuge in the kitchen. He sat, with a boozy grin on his face, in his usual place at the table, in the chair that looked toward the windows.

"Aren't you eating tonight?" he asked, while she prepared his plate.

"I've already eaten," she said dryly, as she sat across from him. Her chair looked toward the back of the apartment in the direction of the bathroom and bedroom.

He reached across the table, grabbed her arm just below the elbow, and rubbed his fingers roughly up and down her skin.

"Stop it," she said. "You'll bruise my arm."

He flung it away as if it were on fire and scowled at the food in front of him. "Slop." He raised his head and smiled. "Don't worry. We won't have to eat this shit much longer."

"What do you mean?"

He twirled noodles on his fork, ate them, and leaned back in the chair. Some women still might consider him handsome from a cursory glance, she thought, even though his cheeks sagged from too much liquor, and his wavy black hair had lost much of its luster, now pomaded and oily from hours at work. However, on the surface, and beneath the skin, his personality had twisted in a perverse turn, his smile sardonic and often cruel. His thoughts had transformed him from a handsome man to one full of contempt and loathing. Janka understood that often that disdain was directed at her.

"I got a promotion," he said, somewhat proudly. "Now I can use the gun. Things are going to change soon."

He must have seen the horrified look in her eyes. "I'll make money!"

"How?" she asked, quaking inside because she didn't really want to know. Her mind exploded with terrible thoughts.

Karol took another bite of noodles. "Can't say. The boss says I have to keep quiet. Extra money will be coming in."

"You're going to shoot people—Jews!" She was immediately sorry she'd voiced that conjecture.

"Get me a match. I'm out. I need a cigarette to wash down this mess."

Karol treated everything with a blasé attitude. She got up, grabbed the box, and tossed it on the table.

He pounded the pack against his open palm, withdrew one, and lit it. "You have a good imagination—you know what has to be done. Let me tell you a *real* secret, though."

A haughty complacency crossed his face and his lips tightened. "Your Jew friends aren't going to be around much longer. The Nazis plan to resettle them again—somewhere more suitable . . . for work. The ghetto's too crowded . . . too many of them."

"Who told you this?"

He leaned back in his chair, the front legs lifting off the floor. "The boss. Who else? He trusts me." He inhaled and blew a large puff of smoke toward the ceiling. "Do we have any brandy?"

Janka shook her head.

"Vodka?"

"A little."

"Get me the bottle. One more shot before bed."

She did as she was told, but with only one thought on her mind. No one could save the Jews if the Nazis put their plans in motion, but she might be able to warn the Majewskis. It was the least she could do. But how?

Karol poured the vodka, swirling the clear liquid until it

reached the rim of the glass. "Did I mention a shot? They're going to start shooting Jews. Those who go over the wall illegally." He gulped the liquor. "It'll be like hunting ducks."

"Ducks," she said, returning to the stove, looking down at the unappetizing dish still in the pan. *He thinks they're animals to be slaughtered. I've got to warn them.*

She looked over her shoulder at her husband, still eating, still drinking what remained of the vodka, rocking in his chair like a schoolboy.

"They'll have no mercy for Jew lovers, either." He unbuttoned his shirt and stared at her. The holstered pistol was strapped over his shoulder.

The next morning, after Karol left for work, Janka peered into the wardrobe, looking for her best dress. The ones she wore for shopping weren't good enough. They were beginning to fray around the hems and sleeves, and she wouldn't be seen on Krochmalna in any of the three housedresses she wore while cleaning or cooking. On the other hand, her wedding dress, carefully wrapped in brown paper, held a sentimental attachment and hadn't been touched since she was married in it . . . Would it work? The dark blue dress with the white lace collar and matching trim on the sleeves would be dressy enough for the Palais.

She loosened the paper and spread the dress across the bed. Certainly, she could fit into it—she weighed less than she did when she was married. It might swamp her.

Janka held it close to her body and studied her reflection in the beveled mirrors on the wardrobe doors. Buoyed by its possibility, she tried it on. The dress flowed freely around the waist. However, a cinched belt and her coat might give the impression of a woman who had money, a woman who would be comfortable in the Palais.

After dressing, she stood in front of the bathroom mirror and applied a pale lipstick that had begun to harden into brittle chunks in its tube. For years, Karol had deemed makeup an extravagance—such niceties cut into his liquor money. She had given up hope of ever appearing "presentable" when there was no need to impress her husband or anyone else. She brushed her hair, noticing an intrusion of gray at the temples, and felt she had done as much as she could. Putting on her hat and coat, she left the apartment and walked down the stairs.

The walk to the Palais took about thirty minutes. She avoided the ghetto wall, but couldn't help but glance from a distance at the stern, forbidding structure that cut off that portion of the city from the world.

The air was cool, the sun obscured by high clouds that floated over the city like a silk sheet. If she had passed the Viceroy Hotel before, she hadn't given it a second glance, never having been inside. Of course, everything about it was too expensive. Wealthy Jews used to congregate there, along with rich Poles. Karol had no use for anyone with money unless they offered it to him.

A doorman in a black tuxedo and white vest held the large doors open for a family leaving the hotel. Two blond children, accompanied by their Aryan parents, pranced out. A porter followed with luggage neatly packed on a cart. A tall man, thin and straight-stick erect, whom Janka assumed to be the husband of the pair, wore a swastika on the right sleeve of his coat. Was he a member of the German High Command sequestered at the hotel for an official meeting? She would never know. Few people in street clothes wore the insignia in Warsaw.

She walked in after the family left, the doorman welcoming her with a stiff nod. The lobby, despite the cool day, retained some of the summer mugginess. The smell of leather furniture seasoned by years of use, as well as the biting odor of cigar smoke, coursed through the humid air. When she asked about the restaurant, the man at the front desk directed her to the rear of the hotel.

She had planned an early lunch arrival for more privacy. The hotel clock read 10:58, right on time. She had no idea whether

Izreal would be working, but it was a chance she had to take. The most important task was to convey what Karol had told her. Maybe the family could find a way out of the ghetto before it was too late.

A regally attired maître d' greeted her, and when she asked to be seated for lunch, he led her through the mostly empty dining room to a chair situated between two potted palms—exactly what she had hoped. Few people would be around to witness a conversation with Izreal.

He pulled out her chair and she sat, the leather padding feeling luxurious against her body, the glass and metalwork arching over her, the only sound being the muffled footsteps of the wait staff. She felt like a canary in an ornamental cage.

A waiter brought a leather-bound menu with *The Palais* written in gold-leaf script on its cover.

"May I take your order, madame?" he asked, returning after a few minutes.

During that time, Janka had opened her purse and checked to make sure she had enough money to cover the luncheon bill. She had taken zlotys from a kitchen tin, a hidden stash she'd saved over the years from buying groceries.

"Yes, thank you," she said, eyeing the prices. "I'll have the tomato soup aspic to start, followed by the pot roast and roasted potatoes." It was one of the least expensive entrées on the lunch menu.

"Very well. Is there anything else I can do for madame?"

"Yes, is Izreal Majewski in today?"

"The mashgiach?" The waiter's brows scrunched together, perplexed by her question.

Janka had no idea what the word meant, but nodded.

"I'll tell him that you wish to speak to him," he said.

"After dessert."

"Certainly."

After the waiter left, she lauded her civilized performance. So, this was how the rich lived, how they carried on despite the war. The palms, the quiet ambience, the rich expanse of glass and metal felt comforting, as if the world outside were far away; the war, the killings, the deaths were a bad dream.

In a short time, the meal was delivered, along with an ample serving of water in a crystal decanter. She savored each bite, for the experience was truly like nothing she'd ever known. The soup was seasoned with just the right amount of spice, the warm pot roast melted on her tongue, and the potatoes swam in a savory gravy, almost overpowering her taste buds. Dining at the Palais was like being on holiday—and there was nothing to clean up. Rarely had she experienced such luxury.

She was ordering a slice of white cake with strawberry sauce for dessert when a cacophony of voices entered her ears,' like a murder of crows in a snow-covered park in midwinter. She looked to her left and her blood chilled. A group of uniformed Germans, including some in suits, were directed to two tables near the door. The eight men looked around the room, indicated that they were satisfied with the seating, and then directed the waiter to bring them four bottles of Riesling, two for each table. They made themselves comfortable, settling deep into the leather chairs, lighting cigarettes and cigars, and joking in a boisterous manner. Janka recognized some of the German words, but most of their conversation was unintelligible to her.

The waiter returned with her dessert. "Herr Majewski will be out shortly," he told her, putting the emphasis on the word *Herr*. She wondered if he did that for the benefit of the Nazis at the two tables.

She kept her eyes focused on the kitchen doors, now concerned that her meeting with Izreal was a mistake. However, she needed to relay what she'd learned from Karol.

A few minutes later, the doors with the glass portholes swung open and Izreal appeared, walking calmly toward her, ignoring the Nazis near the door. He stopped, stood by her side with his back to the men, shielding her from their eyes.

"My compliments on the meal," she said, forcing the nervousness from her voice. "Everything was perfect."

He stood, looking thinner in his dark suit, unmoved by her words. Finally, he whispered, "You are taking a great risk." He leaned closer and said in a louder voice, "I'm so glad you enjoyed the food, madame."

She smiled and peered around him toward the men. They appeared to be paying no attention, all absorbed in their conversation and wine.

"I will say it quickly—once," she whispered. "I came to warn you. They plan to resettle the Jews. They will shoot anyone who goes over the wall illegally."

"When?"

"I don't know. My husband says it will happen soon. His boss told him. I don't know if anyone in the ghetto knows."

"The Judenrat only knows what *they* order." He tilted his head backward slightly to indicate the men behind him, and again raised his voice. "Try the cake. I'd like to know if it's to your satisfaction."

Janka thrust her fork through the airy slice, brought the dessert to her mouth, and tasted it. "It's delicious. The strawberry sauce is the best I've had in years." She wiped her mouth with a napkin, gazed at the table, and lowered her voice. "You must leave the ghetto."

"That may be impossible."

"Promise you'll try. What about your daughter in London? Can she help?" She took another bite of dessert.

"We haven't heard from her. How can she help?"

"If she comes to Warsaw, give her my address."

He nodded and resumed his normal voice. "Thank you for the compliments, madame. It's good to see you again. I hope you'll favor us soon."

"Of course."

He bowed slightly and walked back to the kitchen.

She was alone again—it seemed as if loneliness and desperation defined her life: waiting at the apartment for her surly husband to return, waiting at Nowaks' for a cut of beef, waiting for the end of a war that now looked as if it would drag on until Hitler had conquered all of his enemies. She thought of her husband and shivered as she watched the Germans drink. She had to be strong—stronger than the men at those tables. No one could give her courage except herself. Perhaps she could be a War Girl, as Izreal had said.

Janka finished her dessert at leisure, unobtrusively watching the Nazis near the door. A few of them now appeared to be tipsy—laughing louder, swaying in their seats—after their share of a bottle of wine.

The waiter presented the bill and she paid it. She got up, buttoned her coat, and headed toward the door. She knew a few basic German phrases. When she passed by the men, she nodded and said, "*Guten Tag.*" Three of them rose and replied with the same greeting. The others only nodded, particularly those clad in field gray, who displayed a subtle smirk on their faces.

Janka walked slowly through the lobby, past the desk, and out the door. When she found herself on the street, looking at the cloudy sky, she was suddenly aware of her fast-beating heart.

In two hours, she'd had the experience of her life—thrilling and adventurous, but also dangerous, precarious. It had sent her adrenaline racing, causing sweat to break out on her arms and neck. She wondered if she could steel her nerves; perhaps she might be called on to do something even more perilous in the future. She had taken a stand, without her husband's knowledge or approval, and the betrayal felt good.

She strode toward home, happy that she had helped the Majewskis.

CHAPTER 14

November 1941

Daniel had cautioned Stefa that her brother might be smuggling despite the dire warnings not to.

"I can't keep an eye on him all day," Daniel told her as he headed out for his rounds. "You need to watch him when he's not working."

Aaron did have a Monday off in mid-November, and Stefa decided to follow him before going to the soup kitchen. Her brother could be sneaky when he put his mind to it. Stefa watched from the window. He told her he was going to the toilet—but had taken his coat with him; after all, it was colder in the latrine than in the apartment. However, after a few minutes, she spotted him slipping out of the building dressed for the cool weather.

"I'm going to work," she told Perla, the only family member left in the apartment. It was a lie, but a necessary one. She kissed her mother, who sat in a chair by the stove, looking lost and kneading her hands next to the heated metal.

Stefa put on her coat and fled the room, spotting her brother a block ahead. Clearly, he was headed in the direction of Mirowski Square, someplace he had no business going. *What is he up to?* If she caught him smuggling, she planned to drag him home by his ear.

She struggled to keep up with him, ducking out of sight when Aaron occasionally looked back. *How could he do such a stupid thing?* He certainly wasn't dumb. Was he really doing this to protect the family?

Maybe she had a false sense of security, a way of glossing over everything that was happening in order to keep her sanity. Typhus was still prevalent, but not nearly the threat it had been in the summer. The cold weather and the public lectures about the disease had helped slow the infection. Her father was still able to get food, although the portions were growing less generous. Daniel anchored them, giving the two families a sense that they were protected while he was in police service.

But fear and death were never far from her mind. The stories she heard at the kitchen chilled her—tales so horrible they were hard to believe, told by the members of Oyneg Shabbos, Ringelblum's writing project, or refugees who had made their way to the ghetto after being forced out of their homes. In the late summer, a Jewish butcher in Lithuania had bitten into the throat of an Einsatzkommando soldier, killing him. In retaliation, the butcher and two thousand Jews had been shot. Members of a Jewish Council in Poland had been executed for cooperating with the resistance. Jews were massacred in every territory that the Nazis invaded—those executions were often conducted by locals who satisfied their bloodlust under the view of German cameras, recorded for history. Resistance members, those in the underground, or anyone who aided the "enemy" signed their own death warrants.

Some stories were so frightening they were told in hushed whispers. Nazis had drowned thirty ghetto children, most of them homeless beggars, in water-filled pits near Okopowa Street. The German authorities had referred to them as a "scourge." In early October, after the first snowfall, seventy children had been found frozen to death on the streets. Stefa didn't doubt the veracity of these horrors—she had seen suffering with her own eyes.

The killings continued unabated until the mind *refused* to

believe. She had noticed that Daniel had become more sullen, sterner not only with her but with his parents, as if to distance himself. The darkness that had always been part of him had grown. Some evenings he slipped out of the apartment, for police business he'd said, but Stefa doubted that was the truth. She believed he was meeting with resistance members.

My brother . . . losing track of one's thoughts was easy under pressure. Aaron weaved in and out of the crowds, past the Jewish Police headquarters, traveling toward the wall that bordered Saski Park. Stefa remembered the time that she and Daniel had talked in the park and how his news of becoming a policeman had upset her. Now, she was grateful. He had been right about the protection the post offered.

Aaron stopped at an angled joint in the wall, his black coat standing out like a dark marble gravestone against the reddish-white brick. He faced the barrier, his back to anyone who might be looking, like he was urinating upon it. She doubted that was the case.

She held back, keeping him in sight, concealing herself in the recessed doorway of a tenement building, also keeping an eye open for Nazis or Blue Police that might be in the area.

To her amazement, a square opened in the wall, and a hand thrust through the empty space. Aaron took a package wrapped in white from his coat and gave it to the disembodied hand. The wall quickly closed and Aaron turned to leave.

He was too late. A member of the Blue Police attired in his navy uniform, flat-brimmed cap, and knee-high leather boots grabbed Aaron as he tried to sprint away. Normally, the Polish Police were at the gates—rarely did they step inside the ghetto, unless they had a good reason.

Stefa gasped as the man swung her little brother around, his baton pointed at Aaron's forehead. A holstered gun hung at his side. She had no choice but to intercede.

As she neared the pair, the Polish policeman towering over her brother exclaimed, "What were you doing? You have no business here. You could have been shot, you little shit."

"I was . . ." Aaron's face contorted as the policeman wrenched her brother's arm behind his back.

"Lying will get you shot," the man said.

Stefa screwed up her courage and stepped up to the man. "Officer, this is my brother."

He turned his head, studying her with cold eyes. "Are you part of this?"

"No. I was following him."

The man released Aaron's arm. "Why?"

"Because he wants to help people—even Poles on the Aryan side—and I suspected he would get into trouble." Stefa hoped her comment about Nationals might elicit some sympathy.

He took off his cap and ruffled his hair. "Well . . . at least you're honest. I don't get a lot of that these days." He shoved Aaron toward her. "What did you slip through the wall?"

"Bread," Aaron said, looking at his feet.

"Bread. Who did you give it to?"

"My friend—who is starving." With determination blazing in his eyes, Aaron stared at the man. His voice didn't crack, and he gave no indication that he was lying.

"I'm going to tell you something, and you'd be wise to listen," the officer said, returning his cap to his head. "You're lucky to be alive because I saw you. I'm here checking Jewish permits. Any German would have shot you on sight. I'm reporting this breach in the wall and it will be repaired. Don't come back—someone will be watching."

Aaron nodded, but Stefa took her brother's gesture as one of condescension rather than contrition.

"Let's go," Stefa said, grabbing Aaron by the arm.

"Wait—not so fast," the policeman said. "There's a penalty of one hundred zlotys or he'll be arrested."

Stefa could hardly believe her ears. The policeman was blackmailing them. She shook her head and shot Aaron a look indicating that *he* had gotten them into this mess. The officer had caught Aaron; there was no escaping the guilt.

"I don't have one hundred zlotys," Stefa said while rummaging through her coat. Indeed, there was nothing in her pockets except lint.

Opening his own, Aaron dug a hand inside, pulled out the money, and handed it to the officer.

"I won't ask how you got that," the policeman said.

"I work."

"It would be best if you left now," the man said, turning his attention to the wall.

Stefa hurried away with her brother. "Are you crazy?" she asked, her anger boiling over, "and look what it cost you." She looked back at the policeman, who was studying the area where the bricks had been dislodged.

"You're crazy for following me," he said in a voice spiked with anger.

"Don't blame me for your stupidity. I'm taking you home before I go to work. You can sit with Mother—she needs us." She clutched his arm, in case he had any idea of bolting away. "Who did you give the bread to?"

"My friend Zeev."

She vaguely remembered Aaron mentioning the name but could not picture the young man.

They were nearing the Jewish Police station when shots rang out, followed by muffled cries. Stefa slowed, keeping her brother in check. He was eager to see what had happened.

To their left, at the base of a blood-spattered wall, lay the bodies of six women and two men. She covered Aaron's eyes with her hand, but he brushed her fingers away and stared at the corpses. One of the women twitched and then lay still, as lifeless as the others sprawled around her. The executioners were members of the Blue Police, like the officer who had caught her brother. A group of German soldiers looked on, photographing the scene, laughing and smiling at the deaths spreading near their booted feet.

As horrible as the sight was, an even greater horror came into view. Daniel was leaning against the station door, the lapels of his coat stained crimson, a bloody handkerchief pressed against his face.

She left Aaron and ran to Daniel, wanting to throw her arms around him. "My God, what happened?"

He struggled to catch his breath, the air rushing in and out of his lungs in smoky bursts in the cold air. "The Nazis tried to get me to shoot them. I told them no, so they beat me up. I'm lucky they didn't shoot me! They forced the Blue Police to kill them."

She lifted the handkerchief. Daniel's right cheek was swollen from a sizeable purple bruise. A cut from the center of his forehead to his left eye gushed red.

"The Polish Police saw what the Nazis did to me," he continued. "After that, they had no trouble killing a few Jews."

Tears rose in her eyes, but she felt more than sadness. An immense rage filled her body. All the stories she'd heard about the slaughter of Jews had been confirmed in a matter of minutes. The ghetto wasn't a place of resettlement or work; it was a prison of death. Now she knew what the Nazis planned for their future. The truth had come to her in blood. She daubed the soaked handkerchief against Daniel's cut. "You must have that bandaged," she said. "Where's Aaron?"

Daniel pointed to the crowd that had now begun to gather.

The Germans shouted: "See what happens when you disobey. This could happen to you. Be a good Jew and stay within the walls." Aaron stood a few feet from the dead, his young mind taking in the carnage.

"Take him home," Daniel said. "I don't want him to see this. I'll tell you more this evening."

She walked to her brother and put her hands on his shoulders. He said nothing as she turned him from the bodies and guided him down the street toward home. Aaron shook under his coat as they walked.

After they'd arrived, he shouted, "I'll kill them," and slammed his fist against the door.

He trembled in front of her and his mother, a terrible mix-ture of rage and sorrow turning his face red with fury. Stefa did nothing to stop his anger because she was filled with her own. Perhaps rage was good for them. They weren't cowards. They would stand against this terror—as long as they could—even if they had to die. Something shifted within her, a lever in her mind that flipped from complacency to action. She felt it in her heart and soul.

The next day, posters went up in the ghetto explaining why the eight had been killed. Daniel told his story that night be-cause he refused to talk about it the evening of the executions. His emotions were too raw. The families gathered around the stove in the large room, warming their bodies against the No-vember chill.

"Why?" his mother asked, looking up from her knitting.

"They left the ghetto without permission," Daniel said, hold-ing a damp cloth to his bruised cheek.

"We're lucky to have food," he said. "The Nazis are starving the ghetto with their rations quota. So many Jews have died, driven to madness by hunger." He touched the bandage on his forehead. The coagulated blood had turned the once white cloth to a rusty brown.

"I fear the restaurant may close soon, even with Nazi sup-port," Izreal said. "They'll be fed elsewhere." He nodded at Daniel. "I honor your courage."

"Don't treat me as a savior," Daniel said. "Many Jewish po-lice avoided me today because I took a stand. They're uncom-fortable because I made a choice they couldn't. I couldn't kill my neighbors. A few congratulated me on my 'war wounds.'"

Daniel spotted Aaron, silent and unmoving, with his knees pulled up to his chest in his usual place in the corner. How he wished that this young man, whom he considered a younger brother, hadn't seen the bodies on display. Stefa had told him how Aaron had been stopped by the Blue Police at the wall and of his anger after seeing the corpses. Daniel wished he could channel Aaron's rage for something other than self-destruction in the face of the Nazis, but he was uncertain what to do.

"One of the men was Yosef Peykus," Daniel said, turning his attention back to the group gathered around the stove. "He had a wife and small child. Twelve days before he was executed, he'd climbed through a hole in the wall to buy bread for his family. They arrested him when he returned. He was so young to go to the grave." He leaned forward, lacing his fingers together as if in prayer.

The silence in the room was interrupted only by the *pop* of burning wood. They were feeding the stove with items they'd found on the street. It didn't matter what—luggage, clothing, wicker baskets, discarded furniture, like the old chair frame they were burning now. Everything was disappearing as heating sources dried up.

"Who were the others?" Jakub asked. His father had grown older since they'd moved into the apartment, his hair grayer, his back stooped like that of a much older man.

"I know of two," Daniel said. "Feyge Margolies—she had two children, one very young. She went to the Aryan side to buy goods, so she could sell them here. She needed food for her children. The other was Dvoyre Rozenberg, a woman who was taking care of her sick mother, as well as her children. She smuggled meat into the ghetto, earning a little money. Dvoyre had spent time in prison already for the same crime. She couldn't let her family die, so she smuggled again." He bowed his head. "The others I didn't know. None of them were over forty."

His mother sighed, while everyone else in the room sat with stunned faces. Stefa nodded, offering her support for his words.

"I was helpless," he said, as tears welled in his eyes. "I watched them die."

"Nazi pigs." The words drifted like a whisper from the corner. Everyone turned to look at Aaron, who was staring out the window into the night.

"Anger will destroy us," Izreal said after a few moments.

"God will destroy us," Aaron said.

Izreal rose, ready to confront his son, but Perla grabbed his arm. "Sit," she ordered. "Leave him alone."

"I pray for us all," Izreal said, taking his seat again.

Daniel looked at Aaron, the young man's back rigid, his arms stiff at his side, fists clenched. Slowly, Aaron raised one hand and brought it to his face.

Daniel was certain that the young man had wiped away a tear.

The secrets of the Special Operations Executive came sharply into focus when Hanna left the relatively open surroundings of Briggens House for an undisclosed location on the Scottish coast. She and Dolores had made the cut, and found themselves on a small transport bus traveling at night through central England, past Manchester, Glasgow, and northward. No official orders were issued. Only six trainees from Briggens, four men and two women, had been crammed into the jouncing vehicle, along with boxes of equipment and supplies.

The driver, a military man, told them he was delivering them to "House A," where they would be spending most of the winter crafting their identities and learning how to "become agents." He preferred that word to "spies." On a refueling stop in Manchester, he told them that they would most likely return here to the Ringway Aerodrome for parachute training, jumping first from a balloon and then from an Armstrong Whitworth Whitley. She had no idea what any of that meant, and, at this point, really didn't want to know; it all sounded so foreign, so military, and devoid of any real connection with humanity, other than war and survival. She'd had enough of war and survival at the moment, and only wanted a good night's sleep.

She looked across the narrow aisle at Dolores, who slept scrunched up in a seat, her head bouncing lightly against the window, her legs stretching over the cargo boxes in front of her. Even covered up to her neck in an army blanket, she still looked put together, Hanna thought. Her lips were the perfect shade of red, the black tresses falling against the glass looked as if they had been coiffed at a beauty salon. Her shoes, extending from underneath the blanket, were of a slightly higher heel than those suited for rough terrain—definitely not for military training.

Their warm breaths had fogged the windows, except for the windscreen. Hanna saw little of the countryside as they traveled, but when the bus veered west toward the coast the landscape blackened. Only a sliver of moon provided any light upon the terrain.

She wished for a moment that Phillip was with her. Their good-bye had been perfunctory, a quick kiss on the cheek, then a longer embrace festooned with promises to see each other when they could, along with the hope that coded messages, one way or another, could find their way to each other despite the Nazis. She'd shed no tears upon parting, and as far as she could tell, Phillip hadn't either, both taking the practice of emotional distance to heart. Hanna believed the English "stiff upper lip" had been in play. Their separation was the way proper relationships were conducted in the SOE.

A short time after midnight, just as she was nodding off, the transport came to a stop on a gravel road. She swiped her hand over the damp glass and found that the bus had parked in front of an imposing stone mansion, nestled in the dark hills that surrounded it.

"Up and out," the driver said.

Dolores stretched her arms, yawned, and drawled a sleepy question. "Are we there?"

"Yes," the man shot back. "Scotland. Get packing. I have to drive back to Manchester tonight, while you make yourselves comfy in bed."

Hanna grabbed her suitcase and purse and, bent over, shuffled her way to the door. Dolores and the men followed, dragging their luggage down the narrow aisle.

A few men in army gear near the transport jumped into action, opening the rear doors to haul out supplies.

The tang of ocean air swept past and somewhere the faint

sound of water lapping against a shore sifted into her ears. The night had overtaken everything, and, thanks to the ongoing blackout, the house and the surrounding terrain appeared as a gray outline under the moon's thin light.

However, she could see that the structure was at least the equal of Briggens in size, possibly even larger. It was constructed like buildings she'd seen in Croydon and London—not in the shape of a cross like a church, but a solid main building centered between tall wings with steep gabled roofs. Rows of windows, like dark eyes, had been cut into the stone. The mansion appeared somewhat Gothic, a bit spooky, in the middle of the night.

Hanna hauled her suitcase past one of the impressive wings toward the entrance the men had pointed out. A woman stood in the door, and, to Hanna's surprise, she recognized the figure of Rita Wright, her face as powdered white as the first night she had met her.

Cigarette in hand, Rita looked as if she had just come from a dinner party in her form-fitting black dress. She stepped from the entrance onto the slate porch and puffed on her smoke. It flamed red in the dark, the haze encircling her head. "Congratulations. Welcome to House A."

The six trainees dutifully followed Rita inside, where she directed them to seats in the great room. Large pine logs, at least a meter in length, crackled in the central fireplace, sending a pleasing woody fragrance throughout the room. Hanna and Dolores took their places on a plush red couch that faced the fire.

Rita paced from the middle of the room to the hearth, flicking her cigarette ash into the blaze upon each circuit. "I'll be talking to each of you individually this evening; then you can find your way to bed for a short nap before we begin at zero-six-hundred. Your rooms are on the second floor of this wing—your names are marked on a doorplate. You each have a separate room. I discourage camaraderie during your stay." She walked to a mahogany table bordering the wall and picked up a folder and pen. "So, let's begin. I'll start with the ladies." Rita walked to the couch, stood in front of Dolores and Hanna, and opened the file.

She focused her gaze on Hanna. "What's your name?"

"Greta Baur," Hanna replied quickly, confident in her answer.

"What do you do?"

"I'm a typist." Again, the correct answer.

"Your background?" Rita blew a puff of smoke over Hanna's head.

"Volksdeutsche."

"Husband's name?"

The question caught her off guard. Phillip had given her the name months ago, but she had used it only a few times at Briggens House. She knew it began with an "S," but the hesitation was killing her, figuratively and perhaps literally in Rita's eyes. Her face burned as a thin film of sweat broke out on her brow.

A few names popped into her frantic mind and she tried the most likely. "Stefan."

Rita's seized upon her like a hawk on a rabbit. "Are you sure? You don't seem certain."

"Yes."

Rita nodded. "Stefan—but the hesitation was clearly evident. Mistake number one." Rita checked a page with gusto. "You'd be dead . . . or on your way to Gestapo Headquarters. Not good."

"I'm sorry. It's late." The moment the words came out of her mouth she knew Rita would pounce.

"No excuse! Do you want to live or die?"

Before Hanna could answer, Rita handed her a set of documents, issued a curt, "You're dismissed," and moved on to Dolores.

Feeling like a fool, she gathered her things and trudged up the stairs into a dimly lit hall. She found her room at the corridor's end and opened the door. Two candles burned on wooden stands pulled out from an old writing desk. The flickering light was weak, but provided enough illumination that she could see the room with ease as her eyes adjusted. The accommodations looked very English and ancient, as if a bedroom from a medieval castle had been transported to House A. She pulled open the heavy curtains that covered the room's one window. As far as she could tell, it faced south, looking toward low hills and an inlet that glittered in the moonlight. A small fireplace on the east wall sat cold and dark. A heavy four-poster bed wrapped in a duvet looked comforting, as the warmth from the transport and the great room evaporated.

Muted steps sent her into the hall. Dolores stood in front of her own room.

"I really made a mess of things," Hanna said. "Not knowing my husband's name. Rita must be furious."

"She'll calm down. Did you see your papers?"

"No. Having a look about the room, that's all."

"Best check," Dolores said with an arch smile. "You may have a new hair color." She stepped inside and closed the door.

A chorus of clocks, scattered throughout the house, struck one. Yawning, Hanna returned to her room and took the packet of documents off the bed. She brought it to the candles and saw her newly manufactured German passport. Even in the dim light, she could see that her hair appeared somewhat lighter in the black-and-white photo, cut shorter, and swept back from her face.

She wondered when that would happen—if Rita hadn't counted her first mistake against her.

The kitchen clock at the Palais read fifteen minutes after six in the evening when Izreal noticed that Aaron was missing.

He tried not to panic, knowing that his fourteen-year-old son could be anywhere in the hotel, but he sensed that his son had left. Since he had witnessed the deaths at the police station, Aaron had stayed away from everyone, barely speaking, acting as if he was no longer a member of the family.

Instead of working himself into a fit, Izreal inspected the eggs for various dishes and the large slab of meat that was roasting in the oven. It bubbled in its pan, discharging blood to a satisfactory degree.

Izreal stared through the porthole glass at the Polish diners seated in groups among the palms, fairly crowded for a Thursday. His son was nowhere to be seen.

"Do you know where Aaron is?" he asked one of the chefs.

The man shook his head, wiping his hands on a towel. "I haven't seen him in a while. He was at the sinks."

"I'll be back in a minute," Izreal said, fearing the worst. He took off his apron, retrieved his coat, and walked slowly to the drawer where the shochet knives were stored. The cooks used them every day, yet he had come to know them as intimately as the beautiful ones he'd saved in the move from the old apartment. His first knives—how they had shone, glinted in the sunlight, when he'd first opened their case. Now they were tucked away at the bottom of his luggage.

He found the *chalaf* he was looking for—an instrument forged of molten steel, polished so highly he could see his reflection and any imperfections that might mar it, an eight-inch blade with a curved handle like a pistol grip. He slipped it from its satin cover for a moment, examining it for any scratches or nicks, running a fingernail across both sides and down its cutting edge. The *chalaf* was perfect. No one in the kitchen seemed aware of what he was doing, so he slipped the sheathed knife inside his coat pocket. He had carried a knife every night after work since the massacre at the Police Station. A *chalaf* would be useless against Nazi firepower, but it gave him a small sense of security—something needed during this bleak time.

To make sure Aaron hadn't escaped his notice, he walked through the airy dining room, passing several wealthy Poles, as well as a group of SS men and Nazi officials who sat in their usual tables near the door. His son wasn't in the hotel lobby either.

Izreal opened the heavy doors and stepped outside, unsure where his son may have headed. The sinking feeling in his stomach suggested Aaron was on the Warsaw side of the wall, smuggling goods. He decided to walk the perimeter of the ghetto, despite the danger of being out at night. The Germans would be looking for suspicious activity. He had no concern about the Polish and Nazi guards at the gate near their apartment. They had come to know him and his odd hours, arriving late from the restaurant. Izreal had even bantered with them about this "corporal" or that "major" who loved the food at the Palais, and how *they* should come for a meal. The guards couldn't afford such an extravagance, but it didn't hurt to sow good feelings that might be useful in the future. But other Nazis and Blue Police were prowling about, soldiers who didn't hesitate to kill or torture anyone, even children. That prospect coursed through his veins like ice.

He walked north, not fast enough to draw attention to himself, but with enough speed that he found himself at the southern ghetto wall in a few minutes. At a bleak corner, he was uncertain which way to turn, but decided east was best. After a turn northward, the route would course toward Saski Park, a likely area to transact smuggling among the barren trees.

He kept to the shadows, skirting past a pair of guards who strolled close to the wall. Absorbed in their conversation, they failed to notice him.

Turning toward the park, Izreal kept a block away from the wall, only glimpsing it when it appeared as a barrier at the end of an intersecting street. He had never seen the ghetto from this perspective and the sight filled him with dread and remorse. The prison they were locked within looked like something from the slums of Victorian London—a setting ripped from a Charles Dickens novel that someone had once described to him: dark buildings outlined against a black backdrop of clouds and stars; flashing pinpoints of yellow light occasionally bursting from the stone façades; gray smoke curling toward the heavens from a few tenement chimneys—not all, for cold was a bitter part of the ghetto's punishment. His family lived not far away in this slum, and he was powerless to change the horrid conditions. Perhaps they could escape, but where would they go? They had no place to hide, no safe retreat.

North of Królewska Street, he spotted something out of the corner of his eye that sent a shiver through his body. At first, he wasn't certain what he was seeing—shadows twisting, like a silent ballet, in a crook in the wall.

A German guard, possibly one from an entrance not far away, stood with a small young man he recognized as his son. There was no mistaking Aaron, as the soldier pointed a rifle at his son's chest.

He wanted to scream—a potentially fatal mistake. Instead, he ran as quietly as he could, the knife inside his coat bumping against his ribs.

He muttered a silent prayer, wondering if killing this man in order to save his son met the conditions of *pikuach nefesh*— preserving the life of his son by defense. Would God forgive him for the sin he was about to commit? Surely, He would understand what he had to do. The thousands of animals he had killed in ritual slaughter flashed before him. He had taken such care when he was a shochet to make sure the knife was blessed, the killing done by a single cut across the throat between the epiglottis and trachea, severing the carotid arteries, the jugular veins, and the surrounding nerves. The prey destined for the table had died silently, bleeding to death over the ritual dirt placed on the ground. There could be no pause in the cut, no stabbing, chopping, or hacking, the *chalaf* expertly drawn in a single slice, the back of the knife visible to the slaughterer.

Aaron turned and dropped to his knees, his hands over his head, the rifle now pointed at the base of his neck.

Izreal couldn't hear what the soldier was saying, but he knew his son was seconds away from death. Apparently, the answers the guard had received were not sufficient to convince him that the young man should be arrested or released. Instead, a single shot to the back of the neck, the Nazis' preferred method of execution, would finish him. Izreal expected to hear the rifle report at any moment.

He withdrew the knife, stepped behind the guard, and looked to see if anyone else might be watching them.

"Is anything wrong?" Izreal asked in German, a phrase he knew from the restaurant.

The soldier started to turn, but Izreal snapped the man's head back, knocking off his cap, exposing the soft flesh underneath the chin.

In one cut, from left to right, quickly and cleanly, he sliced into the throat at the precise depth to ensure the man would die.

The soldier dropped his rifle, collapsing to his knees, his hands clutching his bloody throat. Shock set in. Falling on his side on the walk, the man gurgled as his life drained away.

In the murky light, Izreal could see that the soldier was young, a boy really, no more than eighteen, a few years older than his son. What German family had forfeited their future? Was he from Berlin, Munich, or a small village near the French border? It didn't matter.

His anger burst forth as Aaron cowered next to the wall. "Get dirt," he hissed at his son.

"What?"

"Do as I say, quickly!"

Whatever light was left in the young soldier's eyes faded to black. His legs and arms twitched a few times and then he lay still.

Aaron bolted to his feet, collected a handful of dirt near the wall, and brought it to his father.

Izreal closed his eyes, blessed the man who had perished in front of him, and threw the dirt upon the blood that pooled upon the stones.

He grabbed Aaron by his coat collar and forced him into the shadows.

"Do you know what you've done?" Izreal asked. "I've killed a boy like you! God forgive me."

Aaron stood silent, his body shaking against his father's.

A man stepped into the darkness. He was Polish, dressed in a gray coat and hat, his wan face barely visible.

Izreal stopped, stunned by the sudden appearance, his hand grasping the knife.

The man looked at the soldier's body. "Good," he said, and walked away.

Izreal wiped the bloody knife on the dead grass and put it in his coat. They followed the Polish man as he walked south, before deserting him and turning toward the entrance near their apartment. A terrible thought struck Izreal as he stood looking at the Nazi guards and Blue Police conversing at the wire gate. More than a young soldier might die. What if the Nazis exacted revenge upon the Jews? The dirt would be a clue. So much blood would be on his hands.

Before they crossed the street, Aaron said, "God will forgive you . . . but I don't know if He will forgive me. I was looking for my friend."

"Tell no one about this—not even Daniel."

Izreal told the guards, two of whom he knew, that Aaron had become ill and needed to go home. They waved them through.

When they arrived at the apartment, everyone looked at them strangely, as if they had come back from the dead. Perhaps their white faces revealed their pain.

"Keep him safe," Izreal said to Daniel. "I must go back to work. I won't be home until late."

Aaron said nothing, but slumped in his corner, his face to the wall.

Wondering how he was going to clean the blood from the knife and its sheath without anyone noticing, Izreal left. He was blocks away from the dead soldier, but he knew that once the body was discovered the Nazis would be looking for a killer.

PART 4

CHAPTER 15

January 1942

The winter wind cut through Janka's coat as if she was wearing a thin chemise.

Returning home after an effort to find bread, she opened the door and shivered her way up the stairs, stopping at the door because she heard voices inside the apartment. One of them she recognized—her husband, Karol—but the other she didn't know. The men, two as far as she could tell, had been drinking, for the ring of laughter forged by male egos forced their way through the door.

She felt foolish standing in the hall in her coat, boots, gloves, hat, and scarf—there was no getting around going inside. It was too cold to wander the streets.

Janka opened the door, forcing herself to accept an unexpected guest and what he might require. Would he be demanding supper?

The conversation stopped and Karol stared at her as if she had committed an egregious act of infidelity. The other man, young and good-looking, wearing a natty suit, stood when she entered the room.

After wiping her feet on the small carpet by the door, she placed the two loaves of bread she'd purchased where they couldn't be seen—on the counter deep in the shadows. She took off her coat and draped it over one of the dining table chairs.

"You're finally home," Karol said. "Where have you been?"

"You know," she said tersely, not expecting a reply. The promised food from "the boss" had been slow to come through, making for paltry winter meals. "Looking for bread."

"No matter," he said, waving off her comment and turning back to a glass half filled with liquor. The French brandy that sat on the coffee table looked expensive—not the cheap brand that Karol usually kept around the house.

Her husband pointed to his glass. "This is a gift from Herr Mueller. It's French."

"One of the benefits of the occupation," the man said. "Herbert Mueller, Mrs. Danek." He stepped forward stiffly, offering a slight bow, then kissed her hand.

Her face reddened, not only from the unfamiliarity of such a gesture, but from the fact that so handsome a young man had committed it.

"Your husband seems to have a fondness for good brandy, so I obliged," Herbert said. "There's enough in France to go around . . . and Karol is an important man who remains under our guidance."

"My wife, do you know who Herr Mueller is?" Karol asked, after gulping down a shot of the liquor.

Janka shook her head.

"He's the assistant to Dr. Josef Bühler, the State Secretary of the General Government. He's in Warsaw on business."

"I see."

"Please, sit, Mrs. Danek," Herbert said. "I feel uncomfortable and unable to sit while you're standing."

"I don't want to make you uncomfortable," she said, pulling up another chair.

Herbert returned to the couch. Two pistols, gleaming and polished, sat on the table. The one lying in front of Karol she recognized as his. Apparently, the other was the guest's, although a different make of weapon. An open briefcase holding a sheaf of papers sat at Herbert's feet.

Janka quickly realized that the conversation didn't pertain to her, much like a woman denied entry to a men's smoking lounge. Her nerves tightened, her eyes switching between the two as they bantered and laughed like schoolboys. She wondered if he was also a Gestapo agent, in addition to his duties as the assistant to the State Secretary.

"May I offer you something to eat?" she finally asked.

Herbert shook his head. "Fine French brandy is enough of a meal."

The two men carried on for another hour as she sat listening to snippets of conversation, patiently waiting for Herbert to leave.

"Our boys opened fire on a funeral procession," Herbert recounted with glee, his blue eyes flashing from the bottle to Karol. "They killed two of the pigs and had to drag five others away." His smile dropped, and, as an afterthought, he added, "They kindly give us their furs, coats, and clothes, so our boys on the Eastern Front won't grow cold—such a giving, generous people."

Of course, they were talking about Jews—who else would excite such mirth in a Nazi?

"Fifteen of them shot in the ghetto prison courtyard last month," Herbert continued, as if he was tallying a grocery list rather than recording deaths. ". . . on the first full day of— what's that damned Jew thing in December called? I almost don't want to say the word, it's so repulsive."

"Hanukkah," Karol said with a smile.

"Yes, that's it. Better you than me." They arched their necks in laughter. "But we do take care of them, too . . . a film crew came to record the skilled workers in one of the plants. Our companies in the Fatherland can make use of such labor if they open operations in Warsaw . . . at minimum cost."

Herbert shifted his eyes toward Janka, and beneath their

gleam, and the cruel smile, she observed the truth of his soul—a remorseless killer without a conscience.

She wanted to run from the apartment; instead, a creeping terror riveted her to the chair.

"You National Socialists are too generous," Karol said.

Herbert's face flushed crimson. She didn't know if Karol had struck a nerve or the man had drunk too much. He swayed a bit toward her husband.

"There is a limit to our generosity and that time will come soon. Dr. Büller recently returned from a conference at Wannsee outside Berlin. The Jewish question is about to be answered. The State Secretary made sure that Poland will be the first to answer when it comes to that question." He fingered the papers protruding from his briefcase. "It's all in there."

"Jewish question?" Karol asked.

Herbert patted him on the shoulder. "Don't worry—it doesn't concern you now. Your time will come, and the money will be there. Just be sure to bring your pistol."

Karol picked up his gun and held it in his outstretched hands as if he was about to shoot someone.

Janka flinched and rose from her chair.

Herbert retrieved the other pistol from the table and got up as well. "I've overstayed my welcome." He held out his hand to Karol, who shook it. "Keep the bottle with my compliments." He turned to Janka and bowed again. "It was a pleasure, Mrs. Danek." He gave the Nazi salute, lifted his coat from the arm of the couch, and walked out the door.

Karol, his face sweating from drink, shifted on the couch, and pushed himself up with his hands. The thick lines of his face shone as he approached, accenting the ugliness of his gaze. "You could have been friendlier to Herr Mueller. You acted like an eighty-year-old spinster."

"What was I supposed to do, worship at his feet?" she countered, turning away.

He grabbed her shoulders and spun her around. "Listen to

me! Do I have to beat this into your head? The Nazis will save us! Not the Poles. Not the Catholics. Not God. The National Socialists will rule the world. I'll be on top with them . . . with or without you."

"By killing Jews!" Her shout echoed through the apartment, loud enough that the neighbors probably heard her words.

An incandescent rage filled his eyes. He brought his hand back and swung, striking her hard on the cheek.

She reeled, the hard porcelain of the stove breaking her fall. She clutched her jaw, steadied herself, and stared at the man who had struck her for the first time.

"Fix my supper." He turned and slouched toward the couch.

The brandy stopper popped and the amber liquid once again filled Karol's glass.

Hands trembling, shame and rage boiling, she turned toward the stove, wondering if she should walk out the door or make one final meal for Karol. Where would she go in a war-torn city? She had no refuge within a hundred kilometers, no friends she could rely upon. Stefa and Perla Majewski might sympathize with her situation, but they were in no position to help. The two loaves of bread sat where she had placed them.

Janka decided to cut one of the loaves and dip the slices into the grease from the two remaining sausages in the house. The other loaf she'd present to Izreal tomorrow. The frigid winter covered Warsaw and Jews were starving. If Izreal couldn't use the bread, she was certain he would give it to someone who could.

No tears . . . no tears.

She lit the stove, the circular flame ringing the burner like blue hills, and steeled herself for what was to come. According to Herbert, the Jewish question would be settled—whatever that meant. She had to give Izreal another warning.

As her kitchen knife sliced into the bread, she imagined it was Karol's neck she was cutting into, for gradually, in the time since the war had started, she had come to despise him. If he ever struck her again, she might kill him with his own gun. She hated these thoughts—neither Catholic nor Christian—but the war had changed her.

She was becoming the War Girl that Izreal had described.

The feeling of falling was not as frightening as Hanna had imagined it would be, but the parachute-jump training at House A had begun from an elevated slide ending about two meters above the ground, a relatively small drop. *Drop and roll . . . drop and roll.* Her body had been strapped to a parachute harness that sent her gliding gently earthward in the first go-rounds. However, the instructor had more in mind. He swung Hanna and the others, including Dolores, from the slide into the air and dropped them without warning, causing a few scratches and bruises.

A seemingly endless barrage of rain, wind, light snow, and fog kept them inside for most of the early months of 1942. On sunny days, the trainers conducted target practice and the jumping exercises, alerting the trainees that their high-altitude training at Ringway Aerodrome in Manchester would be much tougher.

On the dreary days, everyone, including Hanna, worked on their identities, crafting a personality so ingrained they became the other person, much like an actress immersing herself in a role. At first, the process was difficult and awkward, but over the weeks, Hanna gradually slipped into the persona of Greta, assuming new mannerisms; indeed, assuming a way of looking at life through a different emotional lens. She perfected her German accent and historical knowledge to the knowing approval of a native speaker.

The transformation wasn't just emotional. Her body had filled out, shedding some of the lithe traits of youth; a stylist cut and lightened her hair—two bottles of dye would be dropped into Poland to maintain her new identity. Her face transformed as well: the eyebrows plucked to a different contour, the lips defined with pencil to a slimmer shape, the face powdered a bit whiter, while keeping the overall use of makeup to a minimum. All these changes were revealed by the mirror in her room one day. She gasped, barely recognizing herself, and wondered whether her family in Warsaw would have the same reaction.

Her interactions with the other trainees were limited, as Rita had suggested. Sitting around the fire in the evening, they would ask questions and talk about themselves, constructing their histories, cementing in their minds the "facts" that would populate their new identities. Hanna would go to bed and do it over again the next day, continuing her relentless studies of code and radio operation.

One evening, after falling asleep on the red couch in front of the fire, Hanna awoke to find Rita sitting in one of the wing chairs on either side of the hearth. She felt the woman's uncomfortable gaze even through sleep, the powdered face and dark brows examining her as if through a magnifying glass. No one else was in the room. The hands of the tall clock in the corner approached midnight. Vases and other glassware reflected the flames. Through a crack in the drawn curtains, silvery drips of fog glistened on the window.

Startled, Hanna shot upright, her back straight against the couch. "I'm sorry. I dozed off."

Rita said nothing at first, alternating her gaze between the fireplace and the object of her attention. Oddly, her hand was free from a lighted cigarette.

"How are you feeling, Greta?" Rita asked after an uncomfortable silence.

Hanna immediately switched to German. "*Sehr gut. Danke.*"

Rita exhaled through pursed lips. "You may speak English, Greta. You do know some English, am I correct?"

"Yes," she replied in a German accent.

"I have something important to talk about, and it concerns someone you know—Hanna Majewski."

She nodded despite the odd tone of the conversation—as

if Hanna didn't exist in the room—and wondered if Rita had come to dismiss her after two months of training at House A, or perhaps lecture her on some aspect of a "poor" performance.

With hands as white as her face, Rita grasped the end of the wingchair's arms. The gesture seemed as cold and calculated a movement as Hanna had ever witnessed from the woman. Whatever was on Rita's mind was of extreme importance.

"Greta . . . there is something you should know about Hanna . . ."

"Yes?" The conversation was so strange in a way, but in other ways it made sense. She was Greta now and the bits of Hanna that she saw here and there were disappearing. It was all for the best if she was to complete her mission.

"It's difficult to talk about . . . Hanna may be upset, but you have to be strong for her." At last, the gold cigarette case came out of a dress pocket and found its home in Rita's lap. "You see, Hanna has a family imprisoned within the ghetto and she may feel that it's necessary—or a priority—to save them—to help them escape.

"They're Jews and they're being terrorized by the Nazis—your people. We know that much . . . but Hanna can't give in to what she sees. It's up to you, Greta, to make sure you fulfill your duties as a radio operator, a messenger, an observer of the Nazi military presence, and not let a family get in the way. You must keep Hanna safe and away from any undue emotional attachment." She took a cigarette from the case, thrusting the end of it into the fire. Leaning back, she inhaled, setting the tip aglow.

"I understand," Hanna said, knowing that her buried self didn't want to hear the words. Greta had to harden her heart to whatever came her way. Duty was paramount . . . family later. She represented England and the Allies, now that America had entered the war. She stood in service to millions of oppressed people, not just the Majewskis of Warsaw. Hanna felt as if a hand had squeezed her heart. "It will be difficult, but I will keep her safe."

"I know you will," Rita said, turning toward the fire, melancholy ringing in her voice. "It's these long days and nights of darkness with no light that destroy the soul. On an evening like this, I'd give anything to be on a tropical island, hiding from the burning sun in the shade of a palm tree, watching the fish play in turquoise waters." She laughed. "It's a dream, isn't it, Greta—getting away from war, that is. It's raging and there's no escaping it, no matter how hard we try."

"Yes, ma'am," she said, fighting a sudden urge to cry. "We'll live to see it end."

Rita threw the remains of her cigarette into the fire and rose from the chair. "I'm off to bed. When the weather breaks, be prepared for training at Ringway with four jumps, one at night. I won't say it's easy, because it isn't. It will take your breath away, but the experience of falling through air might prepare you for what you're about to face. If you can jump from a Dakota, you can face Nazis on their own ground." She touched Hanna gently on the shoulder and walked away.

Hanna sat, staring into the fire for a time, and then lowered her head in prayer. It had been a long time since she had prayed, and she didn't know whether to fall back on the long-held words spoken by her father or recite the Lord's Prayer that she had learned in Croydon.

She gave up after a few minutes because, as hard as she tried, the prayer wouldn't come. Blotting out the memories of her life in Warsaw and the faces of her family was impossible.

Winter dug into Warsaw. There had been so much death on the frosty ground, so many rumors of shootings and reports of killings, including the fifteen who had died in the prison courtyard the previous December. Everyone's nerves were shattered, including Stefa's. When she thought that things couldn't get any worse, they did.

Everyone struggled through the cold months, with little to celebrate, with little joy in their lives. Money was tight—even Izreal's salary was secured for safekeeping behind the hall panel in anticipation that it would be needed at some point.

Stefa passed the corpses buried in the snow on her way to the soup kitchen on Leszno Street. Sometimes they were picked up by the men paid to haul away the bodies on wooden carts, but often they remained buried under the frozen blanket, undisturbed until a hand, an arm wrapped in rags, or a bluish-black frostbitten face appeared in the thaw of sunlight. Everyone who walked the ghetto streets knew what these white mounds of death held and were saddened that they could do nothing but mourn.

Another day of dishing out thin soup awaited her as she crossed the three-story wooden bridge separating the small ghetto, where her family lived, from the large ghetto where the kitchen and Mrs. Rosewicz's apartment were located. The Nazis had constructed the bridge over Chłodna Street and opened it in January. The General Government had decided that the portion of the street inside the ghetto walls was too important to remain closed to Warsaw traffic.

Thousands of Jews, bundled against the cold, crossed it daily going from one location to another, climbing the wooden steps, seeing a view of the ghetto that was reserved for those who lived on the upper floors of tenement buildings, carefully tracing with their eyes the arcs of the electric wires that hung in the air, wishing they could soar that freely. Some had jumped from the bridge and broken their legs only to be shot by the ever-present guards who patrolled the street underneath like stray cats, on the move twenty-four hours a day.

It occurred to Stefa that the bridge over Chłodna Street was an obvious way to escape to the Aryan side—too obvious and too dangerous to ever attempt. She dreamed once of leaping from its wooden railings, but, in her reverie, she sprouted pearly, translucent wings that carried her out of danger, far above the ghetto. In the bleak hardness of a cold February day, with Nazis and Blue Police lurking below, such a dream made no sense.

The bridge had been the talk of the kitchen for several weeks, along with the winter deaths and the dwindling food supplies—even the black market was drying up.

But, this day, when Stefa arrived shortly before her shift, the

kitchen was alive with chatter focused upon one man who sat
at a table near the center of the room. He looked lucky to be
alive. His large eyes, parched lips, and shock of unruly black
hair gave him the appearance of a hunted animal, a man who
had been on the run. His clothes, stained and matted with dirt,
told their own tale of a harrowing escape. Stefa judged him to
be about thirty years of age, but his gaunt face made him appear
older. He smelled as if he hadn't bathed in weeks, but body odor
wasn't uncommon in the kitchen because water and baths were
in short supply.

"I tell you it's true," he shouted at the group of men and
women gathered around him, clutching their soup bowls.

"I don't believe it . . . I *can't* believe it," a wizened old man
with a short gray beard said. "It's an offense against God."

The young man stabbed the end of his spoon on the table.
"Of course, it's an offense against God, you fool. They're killing us."

"Bah!" The old man buttoned his coat, smirked, and walked
away.

The young man pointed his spoon toward the ceiling. "I *will*
write it down, and when you learn what has happened, you will
see I told the truth."

His words pricked Stefa's ears. *Write it down* . . . She went
to the kitchen, took off her coat and gloves, greeted her fellow
workers, and went to the man. He was spooning soup into his
mouth; his face drooped as she approached.

"I overheard you," Stefa said. "Let's sit at the corner table."

The man raised his thick eyebrows. "Will you believe me?
No one does, except a rabbi in Grabów. I told him my story and
since that time he has prayed without ceasing to the Creator of
the World." Carrying his bowl, he got up from his seat and followed her. She asked the two women who were sitting there if
they wouldn't mind exchanging places and, after looking at the
man, they agreed.

"Please, sit." Stefa pulled out a chair for him. "What's your
name?"

"I don't know if I should tell you."

"You can trust me."

"All right. Call me Yakov. I come from Izbica Kujawska, north of Kolo."

"I heard you say 'write it down,'" she said, taking a seat across from him. "Perhaps I can help."

He lifted a spoonful of soup to his mouth. "Will you believe me?"

"I believe the Nazis will do anything. I keep a diary . . . but I know a man who might be interested in what you have to say."

His eyes clouded over. He gazed at the table, as if he were frightened to tell his story. "My family is dead, along with the Jews of my village. They were gassed by the Nazis."

Gassed? Her brain took a moment to process the word, for she had never imagined such a death. Beatings, whippings, shootings . . . she had seen those acts by the Germans, but gassing . . . ? How many Jews could the Nazis kill by this new method? Hundreds, maybe thousands a day. What terrible and tragic efficiency.

"They sent me to Chełmno. Do you know where it is?"

Stefa shook her head. There were so many towns and villages in Poland, each with its distinctive way of life.

"About fifty kilometers north of Łódź." He picked up the bowl, drank the rest of the soup, and then rested the spoon in the bowl. "I was a gravedigger for the Nazis. They forced me to do it." His body shook as if the words stabbed him—doing violence to his soul.

Stefa gently urged him to continue.

"All I see is the SS in their uniforms—they selected fifteen of us and took us down to the castle cellar. The first night they gave us coffee and no food. We cried and prayed, for we feared we would never get out of our prison." He breathed deeply. "The next morning, we were met by fourteen other gravediggers. I hauled out two bodies from the cellar that were thrown into the lorry. Then they drove us to the forest and an SS man ordered us to dig. We were freezing in January, dressed only in our shoes, trousers, and shirts. Then another lorry arrived. That's when I saw what they were doing."

Stefa trembled as well, as she constructed the picture in her mind.

"The lorry's walls were of steel, but, oddly, the floor was a wooden grate covered by mats. Two tubes ran from the cab, generating gas into the back. We stood near the ditch until the doors were opened—they were Gypsies—dead, with their possessions littering the inside. One of the SS men got a whip and screamed at us to get everything out so they could begin again— get more victims. He hit everyone, and if you didn't keep up you were shot.

"We threw them on top of the others in the ditch and two men packed them like canned sardines. A child went in any vacant space. Two hundred bodies to a ditch. Later that day, the SS shot the men who worked with the corpses. This continued for two weeks—Jews, Gypsies, men, women, children—until I escaped by jumping from a transport bus. How I survived, I'll never know." He held up his raw hands. "I lost the skin when I hit the ground. My injuries were minor compared to the others . . ." He stopped, unable to go on.

Stefa could hardly believe the story herself. "You're certain of what happened in the lorries?"

His eyes blazed with an unexpected fire. "Certain? I heard their screams as they died! I saw them tumble from the death-traps—the bodies thrown out of the doors to the ground. The smell of the gas . . . and death. Necklaces ripped from the necks of dead women. I saw the corpses searched, every private part opened in case something was hidden inside. The Nazis want every bit of their blood money."

"I'm sorry," Stefa said. "I believe you, but I can see why people don't." She looked at the sad faces around her, sagging under the weight of hunger, eyes dark with pain. Thin arms and fingers lifting bowls of soup that offered meager sustenance, if that. She sat for a few minutes, digesting what Yakov had said before speaking. "I know a man who will be interested in your story. He might even want you to write it down. Would you do that?"

"Yes," he answered without hesitation. "When I told the rabbi in Grabów, the Jews came and we wept together, we ate, and we prayed. If my story isn't told, there will be no memory, no honor for those who've died. Yes, I will write it—with honor."

"Good," Stefa said. "I don't know where the man who can help you lives—it's better that way for everyone, but I'll have my father contact him. Come to the kitchen any day and I'll let you know his decision."

He rose from his chair. "My name is Szlamek Bajler, but I will write as Yakov Grojanowski to avoid arrest. I want the world to remember."

Stefa watched as he disappeared into the crowd on Leszno Street, wishing she had cautioned him not to repeat his story until he met with Emanuel Ringelblum. Conditions were bad enough without a panic in the ghetto. She picked up the bowl and returned to the kitchen where the others went about their duties—another day in ordinary, but extraordinary, lives. The world was closing fast around them.

She would have to tell her father and Daniel what Yakov had told her. The recollection needed to be told. It was only right that the men knew. She didn't want to upset her fragile mother or Daniel's parents with bad news. There was too much sadness during the long winter months.

Someone packed Hanna's chute at Ringway—someone she would never know.

Under the veil of anonymity, no one could be blamed if something went wrong and Hanna became a "Roman candle," falling to her death through parachute failure or some other unforeseen tragedy with the equipment. The military and the SOE knew the advantage of the procedure. What if someone held a grudge against a jumper? How easy it would be to rig the chute to fail. In the hangar where they were packaged, a large sign read: *A Man's Life Depends on Every Parachute You Pack*. In this case a woman's life depended on a proper job.

She had learned how to roll with a backpack, jumping from a platform about fifteen meters high in the hangar. Everything below looked so small, particularly the men and women on the floor. The operator controlled how fast the jumper fell and the angle of descent. Dolores, who had been fine with the slide, blanched at the hangar tower, but gathered her courage and went through with the exercise.

They practiced dropping through a hole so when the real jump occurred they wouldn't smash into the plane's fast-moving body, knocking themselves out or suffering a serious injury.

On the rare sunny March days, a silver balloon lifted the trainees into the sky a couple of hundred meters. There, as the breeze ebbed and flowed, the instructor adjusted Hanna's harness and hooked the jumping strop, assuring her that falling toward the ground at an immense speed was a "piece of cake."

"Ready! Go!" He almost pushed her to the hole, but the swift exit led to a quick opening of the parachute, her stomach turning over as fast as the wind rushing past her face, the harness flinging her body upward in a firm grip as the air filled the fabric. She found herself floating, as in a dream, the ground rising to meet her, gently, without malice, as she put her previous training sessions into practice. When she hit the ground the roll maneuver was as effortless as jumping off a piece of furniture as a child—accomplished only when Perla had turned her attention away for a few moments.

After a series of jumps, the Polish fighters, Dolores, Hanna, and paratroopers in training were ready to make their last jump—at night in full uniform and pack. For this exercise she needed to fold her chute upon landing, change into a dress, and hide her kit within five minutes. A row of twin-engine Dakotas sat on the field ready for service, but only one was in use this evening.

The sun had set in a blaze of pink behind low western clouds. The gunmetal color of the Dakota's fuselage blended with the darkening horizon. The guttering roar of its engines couldn't be mistaken, leaving no doubt that the exercise was on as planned.

The weather was fine for a jump. Despite welcoming skies, Hanna wished that the exercise could have been postponed. Her nerves, the butterflies in her stomach, had bothered her so much that she'd sworn off supper and even initiated a conversation with Dolores as an antidote for her anxiety.

"How are you feeling?" she asked as they walked in front of a hangar to the idling plane.

Her former roommate looked at her with a calculating smile. "Better than you, it seems. Nerves?"

"I recall that you had some trouble with previous jumps."

"Yes, but I'm over that now. I say a prayer and fall into the blue—right into God's hands."

"Something's got me this evening."

"Perhaps he's over there . . . near the hangar door."

Hanna turned and saw the figure, halfway in the shadows. "Phillip?"

"Yes . . . and I know who he's come to see."

Hanna had never mentioned the "near accident" in front of Briggens House, or the conversation with Phillip on the bench, but she and Dolores had been trained to read emotions. It might not have been obvious to the casual observer, but the woman standing next to her had drawn her own conclusions.

"Go see him," Dolores said. "We've got a few minutes. The plane won't leave without you."

She walked toward Phillip, the pack weighing her down, slowing her step. He moved out to meet her.

Hanna extended her hand in a soldierly welcome. "Good to see you. What are you doing here?"

He smiled and grasped her arms instead. "Can't say . . . but I'm exceedingly happy to see you."

"I'm about to jump—my final one."

"Good luck."

He looked the same except for a new officer's cap he wore over his wavy black hair. Still, the orders to remain aloof, the reticence they'd experienced at Briggens House, tempered her excitement.

"I must be going," she said, backing away, not knowing what else to say.

He captured her, just short of an embrace. "Don't want to touch your pack . . . I'm proud of you. I've been at Ringway for a couple of days, but word came down that the jump was happening this evening. I had to be here . . . to say good-bye."

"Good—"

Phillip pressed his lips firmly against hers. She melted into his kiss, giving up any effort to retreat. She had thought of him many times since leaving Briggens House, always with fondness and the feeling that if peace ruled the world there could have been more between them.

They were somewhat breathless when they broke apart.

"Promise me this. Send messages to code name Romeo. Romeo will be thinking of you in your dangerous homeland and awaiting your return. Take care of yourself."

"You too . . . I'll radio when I can."

A rough voice called out over the roar of the engines. "C'mon, lovey, we 'aven't got all night."

She turned and ran toward the plane.

"Well, that was quite the show of affection," Dolores said, when Hanna caught up with the group. "Lucky girl."

"It's nothing—a slight step out of procedure."

"You seem like you might be flying already. Pull in your wings, Tinkerbell. Save them for the jump."

As she climbed the ramp to the Dakota, she looked over her shoulder. Phillip was still there, urging her on with a wave. Perhaps it wasn't such a bad night for flying after all.

The man who had called out sat across from Hanna, his back plastered against the fuselage and a section of blacked-out window. He stared at her during taxi and takeoff, making her uncomfortable. He had a red mustache, a tumble of like-colored hair sprouting underneath his jump cap, and a two-day growth of auburn beard that appeared like fire on his white skin. Her uncle would have called him "ginger." The insignia on his uniform identified him as a sergeant.

"'Eaded for Poland—like the others?" he shouted when she happened to catch his eye. The plane's body muffled the engines' roar, but he still needed to speak loudly.

Hanna nodded.

"When ya get there," he continued, "keep yer head low. Make certain ya know yer business."

Again, she nodded, not wanting to scream across the Dakota's belly.

"Yer a Jew, aren't ya—like the others?" There was no animosity in his question, but she could tell from his tone that being around Jews was a new experience. Most likely he came from Episcopal London.

"My name is Greta," she shouted back, feeling that he might be testing her.

"Sure . . . sure . . . Kraut as can be, blond 'air 'n all." He nodded. "Yer of better use working for us than dead in a ghetto."

He lowered his gaze and said nothing more as the plane gained altitude, but his words left her unsettled. What did the officers and soldiers know about what was happening in Poland? Was her disguise that easy to see through, or was it because he knew she had to be a Jew? Once again, the reality of the war and her assignment struck her face like a hard slap.

The strop was fixed, the green light given.

When her turn came, she closed her eyes, gripped the harness as if her life depended upon it, and jumped feet-first. The wind smacked her with a force that tore at her face and sucked the air from her lungs.

In scant seconds, the parachute deployed, knocking the queasy sensation of falling from her system. She opened her eyes, the world drifting below her, mostly dark, the fields the color of ashes, the distant hedgerows changed by night from March green to black. Above the horizon, distant stars sparkled and, far off, she spotted the outline of a darkened village.

Her mind jumped ahead to parachuting into Poland in the semidarkness, on a night lit by a half moon. Everything would have to be timed perfectly—her jump, the containers of supplies, including the most precious equipment of all . . . the radio transmitter.

Her legs were fine now—they had been for some time—fully recovered from the blast in Croydon. She thought of her aunt and uncle and wondered if they would be proud of her. She also thought of Phillip. Would he be waiting for her when the war ended? Would they both be alive?

Life had given her too many questions and not enough answers.

The earth was coming to meet her and there was no time for daydreams. She was on her way.

CHAPTER 16

Stefa saw it with her own eyes, the night of April 17, 1942, a Sabbath eve. Her father, mother, brother, and the Krakowskis had celebrated in the apartment, burning a candle, reciting blessings, and eating a meal of thin soup and bread. Their festivities were far removed from those they had observed in the past. Thousands were starving in the ghetto and both families were acutely aware of how blessed they were—for the moment.

The Polish owner of the Palais had been kind and granted Izreal's demand not to work the Sabbath for the past two years, but eventually, like cruel clockwork, the Nazis had changed everything. Stefa knew that the Germans didn't care if the food was kosher—only that it was "excellent." Soon, she thought, the owner would make her father work the Sabbath as well.

As the families prepared for sleep, Izreal spotted a paper edge curling up from Aaron's part of the mattress. Her father pounced on the bed, flipping up the corner, producing an underground newspaper printed by the Jewish resistance.

"Where did you get this?" Izreal asked, on the verge of another tirade against his son. "You'll get us killed." He stumbled off the mattress, struggling to keep his footing, then collapsed in a chair near the stove. Stefa put her arm around her father while Aaron stood defiant, arms crossed, in the center of the room.

The Krakowskis, separated only by the doorway, couldn't help but overhear the commotion.

Daniel, already in his nightshirt, stepped into the room, playing the peacemaker with steady eyes and a calm voice. "They're everywhere, Mr. Majewski—the ghetto is bombarded with them. There are so many calls to resist, but no coordinated effort." He lowered his gaze and Stefa wondered if he was hiding something.

"A man on Twarda Street gave it to me," Aaron said. "*He* believed I'm old enough to fight."

Izreal burst into tears. Perla rushed to comfort him, muttering about his health. Stefa couldn't remember a time when her father had cried in front of her, let alone others. He sobbed, his eyes reddening, his pale cheeks overtaken by a flush of crimson. He was thinner now.

"I don't . . . know what . . . to do." His voice shook. "My family asks me for help . . . you say, 'Father will know what to do . . . Izreal will know what to do.'" He covered his face with his hands and cried out, "I beseech God every day because I don't know how to save us."

Aaron knelt before his father and gently grasped his hands. "That's why we must fight. We have no other choice, Father. That's why I read the papers. That's why I will join the resistance."

Izreal lurched forward. "You must not . . . you can't kill and be saved. Think what we've already done." He lowered his head.

"What have you done?" Perla asked with alarm.

Izreal shook his head. "Nothing . . . nothing."

"German soldiers have been killed near the ghetto wall on the Aryan side," Daniel said. "The rumor is that the Nazis will seek revenge. They may even be putting together a list of targets."

His parents nodded.

"I heard the same rumor at the kitchen," Stefa said. "It's all over the ghetto." She wondered if Daniel knew something she didn't, about her father and Aaron. No one had confessed any killing to her.

Perla sat on the floor next to her husband. "My God . . . I can't take any more. I don't know how to think."

Daniel said, "We have to go on . . . be strong."

"I know a hiding place—like the hall, only bigger," Aaron said to his father. "I'll take you there when it's safe."

Stefa turned to him. "How did you find this sanctuary?"

"I've stopped going to the wall because it's too dangerous . . . so I've been looking. I found it in the corridor connecting the building behind us. It should be a secret only we know."

Daniel nodded. "You must show me, too."

"I will." Aaron kissed his father's hands. "Father, I will protect you. I owe you my life."

In that moment, something unseen but powerful moved like an electric current between Izreal and Aaron, father and son, causing them both to tremble. Stefa saw the moment as clearly and forcefully as anything she had ever witnessed. Everyone stared at Aaron, but no one questioned him.

The thought of Aaron fighting the Nazis terrified her, but also gave her some hope for the future. Perhaps with America in the war, and an armed resistance in the ghetto, all was not lost. Perhaps she and Daniel would have a future together when their captors were defeated.

That was the best she could hope for as they made their way to bed.

The man downstairs screamed as the door splintered.

Stefa sat up on the mattress. Perla, sleeping beside her, did the same, clutching her throat and gasping for air as if awakening from a nightmare. She saw Daniel jump from his bed, pull on his pants under his nightshirt, and throw on his police cap.

A voice pleaded at the bottom of the stairs, exhorting the man in the apartment below to "come quietly . . . bring your documents and a toothbrush . . . you will be relocated . . ."

Aaron bolted toward the door, but Izreal caught him and swung him back to his corner on the mattress.

Daniel poked his head inside the room and put a finger to his lips, admonishing everyone to remain silent. He stepped into the hall and closed the door quickly.

Stefa raced after him, staying inside, listening to the noise below. Izreal crept behind, placing his hands on her shoulders.

A struggle broke out as the neighbor resisted. "Get into the car," a voice ordered in German.

"Shimon? What are you doing here?" Daniel asked.

Someone raced up the stairs. "Is your family here tonight?"

"Yes," Daniel answered.

"Stay here and let the SS go past. Let me handle it. They're only looking for one man."

The building door opened and closed, and more men climbed the stairs.

Stefa didn't understand everything that was said in German, but the men interrogated Daniel, one question after another, as he answered with lightning speed: his name, who lived in the apartments, and one final disturbing question, "Why aren't you participating in the Aktion?"

Shimon's voice broke in. "Because he only knows a little German. You wanted Jews who spoke German."

After some grumbling, the men moved up the stairs to the next apartment. A crash and the splinter of wood echoed through the hall when no one answered. After a moment's silence, footsteps rushed past Daniel and down the stairs.

The door opened slowly and Daniel stepped inside, sweating through his nightshirt, his police cap angled on his head as if someone had tried to knock it off.

"What's going on?" she whispered.

"I don't know," he said, and ran to the window.

Aaron made room for him as he pulled up the sash and peered out, letting the cool air flow into the room. Stefa and Izreal looked over his shoulder.

The Germans forced their neighbor into a sedan. The vehicle slid away from the apartment building and stopped at the western end of the wall on Krochmalna.

"What's happening?" Stefa asked.

"Get back. Don't look." Daniel ducked as a shot rang out.

"Oh, God, give us strength," Perla said, doubling over in bed.

Stefa gasped and sank near her brother. "Why kill him? He was just an old man who helped clean the building."

"To demonstrate their power over us," Daniel said. "They threw him face-first against the wall and shot him in the neck . . . at least it was a quick death. The Nazis were recruiting Jewish police who spoke German this afternoon, but I didn't know what for. They were told to report this evening to Pawiak Prison."

"It's begun, hasn't it," Aaron said, softly. "The killing . . . systematically."

"I won't give in," Daniel said. "They beat me once for not killing and now they're giving the Jewish Police the power to take lives as if it doesn't matter."

"You kept us safe," Izreal said.

"We'll be picking up our neighbors' bodies," Daniel said, sliding off the bed. "I have to sleep," he said, and shuffled back to the adjacent room.

The night was shattered by the sound of gunfire and screams. Stefa tried to sleep, but she couldn't get her neighbor's terrified face out of her mind as he was thrown against the wall, even though she hadn't witnessed his execution. She wished she could hold Daniel's hand.

The next day, Adam Czerniaków, President of the Judenrat, issued a statement that Daniel brought home from the police station. It read that the Aktion had been designed to punish those who did not mind their own business. No such activity would take place again, Czerniaków wrote, if people went about their daily affairs calmly.

Daniel told them that fifty-two men and women—bankers,

printers, janitors, alleged members of the resistance, and even a noted economist—had been targeted for death in one bloody night.

"We are marked for extinction," he said flatly, after taking off his reading glasses. "Every Jew who isn't already half dead knows it."

For the first time, Stefa felt in her bones, perhaps in her soul, that the only way out of the ghetto was on a cart to the Jewish Cemetery.

The seventh, eighth, and ninth of May 1942 were the optimal dates for the drop. If not, they would have to wait another month before the moon phase was favorable. After a week of fog and rain, the black-painted Dakota was ready to fly. Dolores, now known as Maria, Hanna, and two Polish resistance fighters were the scheduled drop for the night—and it would be early morning before they parachuted over Poland. The mission had to take advantage of good flying weather on the continent.

The Royal Air Force captain piloting the craft the first half of the journey told them that the low clouds over Manchester would give way to a tail wind over the North Sea. The aircraft was scheduled to land at a secret base in southern Sweden near Malmö.

"We're going north instead of south?" Dolores asked.

The captain rolled his eyes. "Northeast, to be exact."

"Don't look at me like I'm an idiot," she shot back. "I know there's more than one route for a drop."

"Yes, but the weather to the south isn't favorable," the captain said, making his way up the slanted aisle to the cockpit. "Buckle up and relax—a four-hour flight ahead. Hope you brought a book."

Dolores shook her head. "Of course, we get an RAF comedian." Her hair had been lightened a bit and the usual makeup and lipstick were gone from her face.

In addition to the passengers, cargo containers to be dropped lined the center of the fuselage. Hanna's contained her wireless, clothing, and counterfeit zlotys worth nearly one hundred thousand English pounds. Her forged papers were secured in her uniform.

"Once we get to the base, you change planes for another three-hour trip. You might as well get some sleep." He pointed to Hanna. "You're the last drop—zero three hundred hours."

Three in the morning? Another seven hours before she could parachute out. It seemed like an eternity.

The ignition fired and the Dakota's twin engines sputtered before being throttled to taxiing speed. Soon, the plane was banking toward the east and Hanna settled in, making herself as comfortable as possible in the stripped-down military transport. The aircraft rattled along over England and then hit turbulence over the North Sea as a cold front pushed it forward. She wouldn't have known this, except one of the stolid Poles looked up and said, "Low pressure over water." The rocking, which seemed heightened by the darkness and the blacked-out cabin, lasted about thirty minutes before the plane settled back into a smooth rhythm.

Hanna dozed when she could, but a random bump, a shift in the purr of the reliable engines, jolted her awake occasionally. She never really slept, running the plans for the operation over and over in her head. Every last detail had to work for the mission to succeed: the cargo drop, her jump, changing as quickly as she could out of uniform, hiding the chute and containers, making her way to the safe house where she would be sheltered. She didn't even know where it was—somewhere within fifty kilometers of Warsaw.

The Dakota touched down in Sweden after 23:30 hours, having left about 20:00 from Manchester. The captain saluted everyone as they deplaned. A ground crew scurried around the aircraft, as Hanna and the others walked to another equally dark plane that would fly them to Poland. She scanned the horizon, but couldn't see much except for the flat expanse carved out for an airstrip whose lights had now been extinguished, and the distant line of trees that encircled the airfield. A receding half-moon hung in a black sky filled with stars.

After about a half hour on the ground, they were in the air again, this time flying under the auspices of a spit-and-polish Royal Air Force pilot and two crew members.

One of the officers, an affable man who gave her a warm smile, approached. He knelt in front of her as the plane gently swayed in the air. "You have your identification papers?"

Hanna patted the buttoned-down pocket of her uniform.

"Good. This should go there as well . . . but take a look first."

"Where are you from?" she asked, taking the packet from him.

He smiled again. "London . . . Highgate. You?"

"I lived in Croydon. My aunt and uncle died in the bombings."

"I'm sorry to hear that." He looked as if he wanted to touch her hand, but refrained.

"Highgate's nice, isn't it? My uncle mentioned it—he was a banker. I think he would have liked to have lived there."

He raised his head slightly, taking on a wistful look. "Everything you could wish for. I've a wife and two children. I hope to make it back someday."

"You will," she said, feeling that he would. "Do you know Sir Phillip Kelley?"

He leaned back on his haunches. "That cheeky blighter? Yes, I do . . . but not before I got into the service. He does your kind of work."

She nodded. "Tell him Greta says hello, if you see him." A sharp pain struck her chest—it wasn't sentimental or melancholy, but one of yearning. On this night, more than any other, she missed Phillip's confidence and cheery company.

The officer smiled again. "I'll be sure to tell him . . . you better look at those orders."

She opened the packet and withdrew the folded papers inside.

"Nervous?" he asked.

"Yes . . . I'd be lying if I said I wasn't. I've made all the training jumps, but this is real . . . my parents and my brother and sister are in Warsaw, and I don't know if they're safe." She leaned back against the fuselage. "I shouldn't have said that."

"I won't repeat it."

She unfolded the papers—orders—and read them to herself, condensing them in her mind as she went along.

Leoncin, about forty kilometers northwest of Warsaw. Eryk and Julia Rybak's farm. Drop about a half kilometer from the house in a field lit by a small fire. Execute landing between the fire and trees lining the field. The vegetation gives good cover. Secure cargo before heading to the house. Use woodpile on the south side of the field. Recover later. Eryk, thirty-five; wife, Julia, thirty-two. He is tall with black hair. She a bit smaller, dark hair as well. Catholic. Members of the Polish Resistance. Your quarters in a loft accessible only by ladder that is removed during the day. Secure transmitter there. Communicate weekly. Be prepared. Nazi actions have taken place in surrounding villages and towns since 1939. Ghettos and camps nearby. Eryk takes vegetables to market in Warsaw every few days. He will transport you two to three kilometers outside the city. Walk the rest of the way. Standard orders apply to mission. Memorize and destroy. You know your duty. Godspeed.

The officer eyed her. "Everything up to snuff?"

"Yes." She handed the papers back to the officer. If she got shot on the drop, the Germans would finish Eryk and Julia.

"Now I have to jump."

"That's the easy part," he said, getting up. "I admire you. You've got—"

"—nerves that are shaking like a leaf."

He saluted her and moved on to one of the Polish men.

Hanna closed her eyes and straightened her back against the cool metal. The Dakota's rocking gave her some comfort, like a baby cradled in a crib. In another three hours, she'd be on the ground.

* * *

The two Polish fighters dropped near Płońsk, a city whispered to be a hotbed of resistance activity. The Dakota swooped low, tilting Hanna and Dolores into a precarious angle on their seats before flattening out. The two men disappeared like phantoms from an interrupted dream: in the plane one second and gone the next. Their cargo, loaded with essentials as well as weapons, had been pushed out moments earlier.

"I'm next," Dolores said, as one of the officers worked with her harness and strop. "Cheers, Maria . . . give them hell," he shouted. Her former roommate disappeared over the village of Załuski. Hanna wasn't certain what "Maria's" assignment was, but radio messages would be their only means of communication now.

"Up," the officer ordered, ushering Hanna toward the drop door at the rear of the plane. She looked at her watch. It was shortly after three in the morning.

For the first time since taking off from Sweden, Hanna was able to look out on the night. The Dakota flew smoothly over Poland, above a dark expanse of earth before crossing the black ribbon of a river. Half circles cast by the moon glittered on the water.

"How high are we?" Hanna asked, as the man checked her chute, harness, and strop.

"Two hundred meters, give or take fifty or so," he said. "Enough air to get you on the ground."

There was no reserve chute—never on jumps this low—there wasn't time for it to open if something went wrong. The parachutist would be dead.

"When I get the green light, cargo goes first—no dropping on your head—then you. Should be a matter of minutes."

He smiled and wished her good luck. She nodded, returning her thanks, suddenly aware that her heart was pounding so fast in her temples that she might pass out. Then, memories of her family filled her head. What would they look like now? Were they still alive? In the upcoming weeks she would attempt to contact them while gathering information and aiding the resistance. Was one job more important than the other? She would answer that question when the time came.

The plane made a steep turn and came in flat over the drop zone. So far, everything was going as planned. Hanna stood behind the two containers that were the seeds of her new existence as Greta Baur. The green light attached to the cargo door went on. The officer wasted no time in pushing the containers out.

"God bless you," the man said as Hanna followed seconds later, jumping into the open sky.

The air was colder than she imagined, the force of it slamming against the unprotected parts of her face as it had on previous jumps, but, once again, the familiar jolt of the parachute flung her back and soon she was floating rather than falling over the dark land. The Dakota roared away, but she was unable to see it because the black chute obstructed her vision. The first light of dawn would streak the horizon in about an hour and a half. She had much to do in that time.

She looked down and spotted a flaming dot in a field to the south. The wind was light, allowing her to guide the parachute toward the fire, while using her legs as a steering mechanism. The trees surrounding the field came into view, just as her orders had indicated. To the east, she spotted the roofs of Leoncin. She couldn't believe that after four years of being away, she was so close to home. A thrill born of the excitement of her jump and an unknown future rushed over her.

The earth was coming up fast, and the closer she got to the fire, the more she realized that she would make it to Poland. She drifted over the tree line, across a broad expanse of field, passing to the left of the fire. When her feet hit the ground, she walked the landing, instead of rolling on the earth as she had been trained. The chute deflated like a balloon bereft of air and fell near the fire.

Her senses heightened; her eyes scanning the horizon for anyone who might be lurking near the tree line or in the scattered bushes now in leaf, her ears taking in the crackle of the fire, the rustle of leaves. The air smelled fresh and of dew. Through a break in the vegetation, she spotted the gray outline of a simple farm home sitting on the flat flood plain of the Vistula—it must have been the river the plane flew over, the one that eventually coursed through Warsaw.

She unhooked her gear, gathered her chute, and looked for the containers that had dropped before her. Hanna spotted them: one near the south tree line, the other on the right side of the fire. By the light of what amounted to a campfire—several large logs burning in an earthen circle surrounded by flat, white stones—she folded her chute, retrieved the two containers, and dragged them to the woodpile at the end of the field. Gathering the forged zlotys and her papers, the wireless briefcase, civilian clothing, and the Browning pistol, she changed into a dress and sweater and stashed the containers inside a hollow that had been constructed in the wood pile. She replaced the logs, covering all traces of the drop.

The farmhouse, a stone structure with a rough-shingle roof, sat like a corpse behind the bushes. A strange thought struck her. What if this was the wrong house? No, it couldn't be—everything had happened according to plan. Carrying the pistol, the wireless case, and a bag containing the money and essentials, she screwed up her courage and walked the rocky path that led to the door.

Less than an hour had passed since her jump, but already the east had begun to lighten from black to yellow.

Crossing her arms to conceal the pistol, she knocked on the door, not knowing what to expect.

No electric light shone, no candle or flame flickered past the curtains, but after a second knock a man opened the door, a rifle slung over his shoulder. He looked exactly like the man described in the orders, but darker in spirit than Hanna had imagined, as if the war had tempered him like forged steel. His sooty beard and raven hair contrasted with his pale skin.

Hanna stared for a moment, waiting for him to speak, but he didn't; instead, he revealed the large central room of the farmhouse.

A woman in a dark blue dress sat near reddish coals flickering in the stone fireplace opposite the entrance. She looked toward Hanna with little feeling or enthusiasm, except for the curious play of light in her eyes. Her long black hair streamed across her dress as she turned.

"Come in," the man said in Polish.

"Before I do," Hanna countered, "tell me your name."

"Eryk . . . and what is my wife's name?"

Hanna remembered. "Julia."

"Come in, Greta, and have something to eat before you rest."

"There's too much to do," she responded.

"After you rest and eat. I will take care of the containers and the fire. You can radio this afternoon from the loft."

"Thank you."

He closed the door, placed his rifle against the wall, and sat near his wife. "We have soup and bread. We are lucky . . . not so, the Jews of Warsaw."

"I know." A place had been set for her at the wooden table and she began to eat, a sudden tiredness swimming through her body. "I'd like to rest after I eat."

"Of course," he said. "Your home will be there." He pointed to the ceiling at the west end of the house. A wooden ladder rested near it against the wall.

"When you eat and sleep, our paths will cross. We must be cautious, but we'll help in any way we can."

"Of course." She looked around the room. She had been in a few Polish farmhouses during her life, including her grandparents'. The Rybaks' looked similar. The windows were secured against the cold by sturdy inside shutters. An oak frame bed was positioned against the wall to the side of the fireplace, its foot facing the flames. A table, chairs, and a cushioned couch that looked out of place filled the rest of the room. The crucifix that hung over the bed in most Catholic homes had been replaced by a framed photograph of Hitler, a portrait displaying his Aryan superiority.

Eryk noticed Hanna staring at the photo. "For security," he said. "We only hang it when we need to—like this evening—in case something went wrong." He reached across the bed and turned the picture to the wall.

"Thank you," Hanna said. "He was spoiling my appetite."

"Better get used to it," he said. "The Nazis are everywhere—on the road, at the gates of Warsaw, patrolling the streets, at the ghetto walls. Everywhere you look. There is no escape."

"Greta doesn't want to hear about that now," Julia said. "Let her relax."

"It's almost dawn—time for work," Eryk said. "I'll secure the containers before it gets too light. Do you have everything you need?"

"I think so. Nothing's inside except my uniform and the chute."

Eryk put on his coat and opened the door. A cool breeze wafted through the room; the fireplace coals sputtered.

"When you're ready, I'll show you where you wash up, and then your room," Julia said, rising from her chair. She was a beautiful woman with a pale complexion like her husband's, and she carried herself with elegance, fed by the serenity inborn to some people. Hanna felt calm just being around her.

After Hanna had finished her meal, Julia led her to the inside washbasin, and, after opening a window, pointed to the outhouse behind the farmhouse. Fatigue, akin to sickness, dragged her down as if her arms and legs were weighted. She excused herself to use the outhouse and came back inside.

Julia climbed the ladder and lifted the ceiling panel that opened to the loft. "It's cold in the winter and hot in the summer," she called down. "There are no windows—only vents for fresh air. You can see through the slats. If there was a window the Nazis would be sure to discover it. If you're inside and an unexpected visitor comes, one of us will knock twice on the ceiling. Keep quiet until all is clear."

302   *V. S. Alexander*

"Thank you." As soon as she was in the loft with her bag and the wireless, the darkness closed around her despite the encroaching dawn. The ceiling panel dropped into place and the ladder scraped away. Julia had handed her a candle in a brass holder, telling Hanna to be careful, for the straw bed would make an excellent pyre. She couldn't see into the dark recesses of the attic-like room that ran the length of the house. She slid the wireless under the bed and collapsed on top of the surprisingly firm ticking. Sleep caressed her with its gentle hand.

Late one afternoon, Aaron led Daniel and Stefa down the steps from the apartment, past the latrine, and into the small courtyard behind the building. A wooden panel separated the yard from the building behind it and stopped them from proceeding farther.

"If you were a Nazi, what would you do?" Aaron asked Daniel as they stood.

"Well, first, I'd see if that panel is secured, or if I could get over it," Daniel answered. "Then, I'd look for ways someone might escape."

"Go ahead," Aaron said.

"There's no way out," Stefa said.

Daniel, surveying the area, wandered to the panel. He shook it and then jumped as high as he could, attempting to look over it. He landed on his feet a little out of breath.

"So . . . ?" Aaron asked.

"The panel is secure on both sides. It won't budge and there's nothing beyond it but a brick wall."

"Good—that's what I wanted to hear," Aaron bent down and looked under the slats. "Did you notice anything else?"

Daniel shook his head. "What am I looking for?"

Aaron wriggled his hand under the small opening between the wood and the ground and pulled out a length of rope. "This," he said triumphantly. He tugged on it and the panel swung up, revealing the dead end.

"I'll be damned," Daniel said.

"How did you discover this?" Stefa asked.

"Just snooping . . . always looking out for the family . . . It was months before I spotted it. The Nazis should have the same problem. This courtyard's depressing, isn't it? Not enough light to grow vegetables . . . wet in the summer, frozen in the winter. Fortunately, once you're past the panel no one can see you." He chuckled. "Wait until you see what else I've found."

They ducked under the panel, which was still resting in its horizontal position. Only after they had ventured into the passage did Stefa see the two black pulleys fastened to the opposite sides of the wall, their color so dark that one had to be in front of them to notice.

Aaron grasped the panel and pushed. It swung down, sealing them off like he'd said.

The air smelled dank, thick against the skin. Stefa rubbed a finger over the slick moss that had grown on the walls.

"Down here," Aaron instructed, venturing deeper into the murky recess. Finally, he stopped and pushed against a section of wood that had been painted to look like part of the brickwork. A small door popped open, revealing a hidden space.

"Do you have a torch?" Daniel asked.

Aaron reached into his pocket and withdrew a box of matches. He struck one and the flame lit a space that could easily fit the seven family members if they crowded together. The match went out, plunging them into the murk.

"Come inside," Aaron said.

Daniel clutched Stefa's hand as they ducked and fumbled their way in. Aaron lit another match and pulled the door shut.

"It's our secret," Aaron said. "Other people have hidden exits and secret passages that run between attics, so I knew we had to have something. I discovered it by accident . . . maybe it was used to store valuables or old furniture. I don't think anyone's been in it in years."

"It's cut into the building behind us," Daniel said. "Maybe those residents used it for storage."

The second match went out and total darkness descended upon them. Unable to see even Daniel, who was standing next to her, Stefa shivered in the absolute absence of light.

Her brother lit yet another match. "This board lowers like the lock on an old castle door." He demonstrated how it worked by bracing the wood. "No one will know you're inside, and they can't get in. Sit it out and then escape."

"No one else knows about this?" Daniel asked Aaron.

"No. I've placed a rock in front of the panel the past few months . . . it's never moved."

"I could kiss you, little brother," Daniel said. "You don't know how wonderful this could be for all of us."

"Let's get out of here," Stefa said as the match went out.

Aaron raised the slat and pushed the door open; the muddy light from the courtyard washed over them. Her brother worked in haste, pushing the door back in its place, reopening the wooden panel, closing it, and securing the rope so it wouldn't be seen.

"I still can't believe it." Daniel almost whistled as they walked back to their apartment.

The unexpected happiness that surged through her boyfriend made Stefa nervous. "How wonderful can this hiding place be, apart from hiding us from Germans?" she asked.

Daniel held back as Aaron climbed the stairs. "Trust me."

Myriad thoughts ran through her head, but one more than the others—the resistance. Aaron wasn't the only one who thought ahead. She remembered how Daniel had announced without warning the day they walked in Saski Park that he was going to join the Jewish Ghetto Police in order to help the family. He had been correct in that assumption, but there had also been personal costs associated with his police work.

"I have to trust you?" she asked, somewhat put off by his rebuff.

"Yes."

"All right . . . but I know you're up to something."

He said nothing as they climbed to the apartment. After

Daniel closed the door, Stefa pictured the two families—the Majewskis and the Krakowskis—silently cowering in the hiding place as Nazis rampaged through the building. The image horrified her. She forced it out of her mind, all the while wondering what danger Daniel was bringing into their lives.

CHAPTER 17

May 1942

Stefa heard screams many times after the night of blood in April.

The Nazis continued their systematic rampage against the ghetto, forcing their way into crowded apartments, clubbing residents, sometimes shooting them, throwing their bodies from the windows into the street, where their corpses joined those who had died of starvation.

If she looked the other way, ignoring what was going on around her, she could walk with the others on the troubled streets: men in their double-breasted coats, wearing hats and carrying leather briefcases; women dressed in their fine outerwear, some wearing jewelry and clutching their purses as if nothing could stop their forward motion—not even the naked body of the young woman sprawled across the sidewalk, legs and arms as brittle and thin as rotted sticks.

But Stefa couldn't look the other way, despite the effort by some, especially those who still had money, to make life as "normal" as possible in the ghetto.

She also worried about Daniel. He had refused to go along with the most brutal tactics of the Jewish Police, and was getting a reputation among his fellow officers as a "weakling." He would talk to the old women who needed to be moved from a doorway, or who were obstructing traffic while selling rags, instead of beating them with his baton, pummeling them with his fists, or kicking them. And he didn't take zlotys for favors—he was like anyone else, trying to get along, he told the poor and starving. Other policemen had no objections to unleashing violence upon their own people—in fact, they seemed proud of it. As the fever within the force heated up against Daniel, so did his hatred for his uncaring compatriots and their Nazi overseers. He never spoke to Stefa of his anger, but she could see the bitterness in his steely eyes, the consuming tension that filled his body. Often, during a night of bad dreams, he cried out.

When May arrived, a Nazi crew rolled into the ghetto to film what Daniel described as "propaganda." He didn't know whether it was to show the ghetto in a good or bad light, or any particular way at all for that matter, but Stefa had seen the men on her way to the soup kitchen and stopped to observe them.

Four German soldiers, with two SS men as guards, maneuvered a cart with the biggest camera she had ever seen. They looked for gaunt faces, searching eyes devoid of feeling, hair cropped to keep the lice away. The men filmed them face-on and in profile, so the pure-blooded Germans in Berlin could get a good picture of what a Jew looked like. Was the film supposed to show that the Nazis had mistreated the Jews or that the Jews had mistreated each other? Stefa believed that the propaganda machine would spread the idea that the ghetto Jews had no concern for each other. After all, the images of those Jewish well-dressed ladies and gentlemen politely stepping over the dead would work to the Nazis' advantage in Berlin.

She had seen the carts loaded with bodies that were pushed to a pit on the outskirts of the ghetto. Filmed by the Nazis, a pile of corpses plunged down a wooden slide into a pit, while aged rabbis stood by offering silent prayers for the dead. Other Jews had been conscripted to cover the bodies with a mixture of dirt and lime.

The Germans herded members of the Judenrat into the council building, presumably to film the hard work of the administrators. The ruse of all this was to convey how ordinary Jews lived of their own accord, when they really didn't live at all. Or the crowd scenes, the men and boys in their flat caps, the women in coats and scarves, being shoved and pushed by the Jewish Police to some unknown destination for the benefit of the camera. Was this a training exercise for something more terrible to come?

Daniel told her that the Germans filmed squalor through open doorways, but contrasted that with well-heeled Jews dining, drinking, and having a social evening in a restaurant like the Palais. What would the Nazis in Munich believe—how the poor masses suffered while the rich ignored them to feast on delicacies? Could the stout, ruddy-faced German, who had just lumbered out of a beer hall, really believe he was seeing the truth on film? All of it had been staged for his benefit—the people walking over the Chłodna Street bridge, linking life between the small and large ghetto; the inside of a resplendent apartment, reminding the viewer that not every Jew lived like an animal.

None of it was real.

Several days after the filming started, Stefa was on her way to the soup kitchen when a voice called out in German, "Girl, come here."

Everyone knew to keep their head down and eyes averted when such a command was given. Perhaps, if ignored, the order would vanish in the air, and another unfortunate would be called.

A heavy hand on her shoulder prevented her from moving forward. "Did you hear me, Jew?" came the brutal question.

She winced and turned to see a young Nazi from the film crew, who harbored a vicious smile that spoke of evil despite a full and pleasant face. He grabbed her arm and pushed her forward through the crowd that parted around them. "You'll do. Young and pretty. You're going to be in pictures."

Everyone stared at them—a young woman forced to walk with a German officer usually resulted from an infraction, but there had been no altercation, no breaking of Nazi law.

"What?" She didn't know what to do, what to say.

"You'll be famous in movie houses throughout Germany."

She had no idea where he was taking her, but they strode over the bridge into the large ghetto, and then north toward the prison. Passing that foreboding structure, Stefa began to fear for her life.

Another voice, one she recognized, interrupted their frantic pace. It was Daniel.

"Where are you taking her?" he shouted, reaching for the German's arm.

Stefa turned. "Don't. I'll be all right. Go away." He was attired in his police uniform, looking as official as she had ever seen him. The white star of David armband on his right arm shone in the sun.

"A smart girl," the German said. "And you'd be wise to follow her advice because if you come one step closer, I'll kill you . . . I don't care if you're Jewish Police." He lowered his free hand to his pistol and spat at Daniel's booted feet.

Daniel's face reddened. He was holding back his fury, like a boxer waiting to pummel a foe; however, there was nothing he could do.

"Go," Stefa ordered, her heart beating fast.

Muttering, he turned and walked away.

The officer dragged her along and soon they came to the mikveh, one of the ritual bathhouses that had been closed since the invasion. The bath held too much significance in Jewish life for it to remain open, according to the High Command. Normally, for purity, men bathed there in preparation for the Sabbath and holy days, women after childbirth and menstruation; sometimes cooking utensils were purified by the natural source of waters. For modesty's sake, the sexes always bathed separately under the guidance of a watcher to make sure a proper immersion was carried out. The Nazi punishment for using the mikveh, posted at the site, was ten years in prison or death. Stefa had heard that some operated in secret. Izreal had forbidden the family to go because of the danger.

Near the entrance, four women and five men she didn't know had been rounded up. They were of varying ages, most mildly affected by the starvation so many had endured. These men and women had suffered as well, but had survived three years of Nazi rule with little apparent physical damage.

Stefa had never set foot in this mikveh. It was clear from the guards circling the entrance and the ramp protruding past the door that heavy film equipment had been hauled inside. A pinprick of terror jabbed her. Were the Germans going to film them inside the bath—the men and women together? She looked around, hoping that someone, even Daniel, might come to her rescue.

The officer who had grabbed her was busy with the crew members. The May sun was bright and warm, but she was chilled to the bone by what lurked behind the mikveh door.

"Inside," one of the men ordered.

She looked over her shoulder and spied Daniel skulking among those on the street. His pained expression grew beneath his lowered cap, as if he would kill anyone who crossed him. She didn't doubt that he would, given the chance.

They were ushered inside by the guards at the door. The crew, including the man who had taken her, directed them to two rooms, one for men, the other for women. The glaring light used for filming shattered the darkness. The building had been closed for so long the air was stale and scratchy with dust; however, not far from her, water sloshed and a thin veil of dampness eventually made its way into the room. Stefa wondered if the Germans had just filled the basin. Surely, the water inside was unclean.

"Undress," the officer said.

"What humiliation," an older woman whispered.

"Shut up," the officer shot back, a lengthy whip appearing by his side.

By tradition, nothing was worn in the bath, and Stefa vowed to honor that practice, stripping off her clothing, and the simple necklace and earrings she often wore to the soup kitchen. The women placed their clothes on the wooden benches and stood, waiting, covering their breasts and genitals with their arms and hands under the light's glare. Somewhere, behind the blinding incandescence, a camera whirred.

The hall rustled with movement, and they heard water splashing. The men had stripped, been herded from their room, and filmed immersing themselves in the bath, she reasoned. The women would be next.

The light narrowed in the hall. A man appeared and Stefa turned her head, avoiding the sight of his naked body.

How degrading. If Daniel knew what was going on, he would kill them. Thank God, he wasn't drawn into this. A woman should never see her potential husband like this . . .

The thought almost made her laugh. Humiliation, degradation, Nazi terror upon Nazi terror, and she worried about seeing Daniel naked? It reinforced how deeply tradition and culture had been ingrained in her. This is what her sister had sought to escape. Her father had tried so hard to make the Sabbath holy, to honor the holidays despite the prohibitions and the constant threat of violence that hung over all the families. He had begun to bend toward Daniel, to recognize his worth, and she prayed that Izreal would give his blessing to their marriage. She would gladly take Daniel's hand on that day—no matter how much time they had left.

"*Schnell bewegen. Schnell!*" The officer snapped his fingers and cracked the whip at his side, goading the women, as the men scampered back to their room. Stefa was the last one out and the officer aimed the lash at her. The leather stung the back of her legs.

"Go . . . dip yourselves . . . like you are being baptized." He snickered at his joke.

The older women led the way down the stairs into the basin, the lights and camera focused on them from above. Stefa followed as the others dipped themselves in the water. Her toes ached from the chill, but the water felt good against the sting on her legs. She lowered herself, shivering in the cold, closing her eyes, and dipping beneath the surface. All was quiet under the water, and she almost longed for death to prolong the silence.

They stood for minutes, rubbing their arms and covering themselves as best they could from the intrusive eye of the camera. An SS man snapped his fingers and the guard with the whip slipped away for a moment, but soon returned with the naked men.

"Get in," the German shouted as his whip lashed their backs.

They splashed into the basin, all of them crammed together, looking at the water in order to avoid each other's eyes. The camera rolled again after a change of film.

The crew conferred for a moment before the SS officer called out: "*Fick . . . fick . . .*" He kept repeating the order, but no one moved, frozen to their spots in the mikveh, until the whip rained down upon them. The Nazi took out his pistol and shook it in the air. "Obey, or I'll kill you."

The German order could only mean one thing—an obscenity for copulation. She stood, shaking, looking at the men and women forced into the basin, feeling as if she were floating free from her body.

The SS man fired a shot into the ceiling. A shower of plaster fell upon them. One of the women screamed.

A man with sidelocks sloshed toward her. He gathered her in his arms and whispered, "Don't look at me. Pretend I'm not here. I'm sorry, my sister."

She looked into his brown eyes and then closed her own.

Stefa felt as if she had died when she climbed out of the bath, her body heavy, her breathing shallow and forced. Her dress, shoes, and coat felt like weights upon her limbs. She shivered from the cold, for the Nazis had given them no towels; their clothing soaked up the water.

Why? was the only question that ran through her mind. Was it to show how depraved the Jews were? How they could flout God's laws in a sacred place? Was it filmed for some perverse titillation?

Walking like the dead, her stomach aching, she stepped into the warm sunshine, feeling hollow and dirty. The man had not gotten inside her, she was certain, but had made a good show of it, rubbing against her to save their lives. That much she was sure of.

She had no intention of going to work now. Her only goal was to get home, lie down, and make sure she'd suffered no serious injury.

The last person she wanted to see was Daniel, but she'd walked only a short distance before he bounded toward her.

She was too numb to think. He wanted to gather her in his arms, but she pushed him away.

"What happened?" he asked, concern filling his voice. "You've been in the bathhouse for hours."

"I can't talk about it," she said.

He saw that she was still wet. "Are you hurt?"

"I don't know!"

"Let me take you home."

She stopped in the crowded street, tears filling her eyes. "Leave me alone! I'll walk home by myself." Thrusting her hands in her pockets, she hurried away.

"Stefa!"

She turned. "Go away!" Her anger exploded—no man should touch her now, perhaps ever.

His eyes brimmed with tears. "I love you," he managed to say. "Tonight . . . we can talk."

"No, I want to sleep." She moved ahead—the ghetto that surrounded her seemed far away, the store fronts, the people inside its walls as thin as cardboard cutouts. The warmth on her shoulders struck her as foreign, as if she had never felt the sun before. The legs that carried her might as well have belonged to someone else.

When she arrived home, she trudged up the stairs, finding her mother in her usual place. Perla tried to make conversation, but Stefa cut her off and lay down on the mattress that had been her bed for so many months. She turned her head toward the window, looked at the still-blue sky, and sobbed. Her mother sat quietly in the chair near the stove.

Hanna had broadcast messages several times since landing at the Rybaks' farmhouse. She had undertaken these communications after setting up her hideout. Sometimes, she helped Eryk in the fields so they could converse about nearby German installations, or she took a walk to the nearby Vistula River, the black strip of water she had seen from the Dakota before her jump. From her vantage point on the south bank, she could casually observe troops or any suspicious movement along the roads that ran near the river.

She limited her Morse code transmissions to two minutes because Eryk told her that radio direction finders operated around Warsaw, homing in on the signal. Sometimes it was only a matter of minutes after sending a message that the Nazis appeared. It was also safer to transmit at shift changes when the Germans were distracted and less likely to detect signals.

The wireless briefcase was bulky, but small enough to fit under the bed. The most conspicuous yet important part of the transmission process was positioning the long aerial, which Hanna fitted through the vent slats and down the side of the stone farmhouse. It also required a trip outside to stretch it carefully over the tops of bushes. The aerial could be pulled in quickly if necessary, assuming it didn't get caught in the vegetation. The message pathway to London was complicated because of the distance between London and Warsaw. According to orders, code was transmitted to a series of partisan operatives and SOE agents in Prague, then to Brussels, and finally to London. The chances for errors amid multiple contacts were magnified by this V-shaped arrangement, but the SOE had no other option but to depend on a communications network that, at best, would reach eight hundred kilometers. Interference and weather also hampered the ability to get word out.

Hanna was inside, helping Julia prepare lunch, when Eryk

yelled through the window. "Turn Hitler out—Germans are coming. Get into the loft—then hand me the ladder, quick."

Hanna dropped the beets into the sink and ran to position the ladder. Julia flipped the portrait over and then held the ladder as Hanna pushed open the ceiling panel and propelled herself into the loft. The day was warm and sultry, and the attic hideaway had begun to heat up. She had to lie on the bed without making a sound.

The panel dropped into place and the loft grew dark, except for the bright slashes of light that poured through the slats.

She heard frantic movements below—the opening and closing of the farmhouse door, the rush of feet to the sink, and, finally, quiet. A motorcar purred near the front door and Hanna dared only a quick glance for fear of being spotted. She saw nothing except the bushes at the side of the house and the bottom half of tree trunks lining the fields. The Browning lay under the bed. She picked it up and clutched it to her chest as if it were a holy object, a sacramental weapon she wouldn't hesitate to fire.

A German's voice—in static belligerence—boomed through the farmhouse. Eryk replied in German, as did Julia, and a chorus of *Heil Hitler*s rose to her ears. The Nazis had professed their devotion to the portrait.

From that point on, she could make out little except for shuffling footsteps, as if an inspection were taking place. One of the men mentioned Załuski, the target that Dolores had parachuted into. A few minutes later the car sped away and the house was silent.

Hanna wondered whether Eryk and Julia had been arrested; however, after an excruciating few minutes of shallow breathing, the ladder scraped against the ceiling.

The panel moved and Julia popped her head into the loft. "You can come down. They've crossed the river."

Hanna put the Browning next to the wireless and descended the ladder.

Eryk was sitting on the couch, wiping the sweat from his brow.

Hanna looked at him expectantly.

"That was close," he said. "I hardly had time to get the ladder outside when they drove up."

"What did they want?" she asked. The Germans hadn't driven to the farm for a social call.

"There were four of them—they want you," he answered. "They picked up signals near here and outside Załuski."

Hanna immediately thought of Dolores, but knew her fellow agent was a courier rather than a wireless operator.

Eryk pocketed his handkerchief and got up from the couch. "That was a warning. They're confused at the moment, but if they detect another signal near here, they'll come back . . . and they won't be so kind the second time. They'll take the place apart stone by stone."

"I know what to do," Hanna said. "I'll reposition the transmitter site."

"The Nazis are fast and always on the lookout. I think you need to suspend communications until we can find a way to send messages safely . . . without endangering us all."

Hanna nodded. She had no interest in putting their lives in danger. "Let it cool for a few days. All I've transmitted so far is 'nice weather,' which means I haven't seen anything of note."

"I can drop you in Warsaw tomorrow, while I'm making a delivery."

"I want to go, but I'm terrified of what I'll see."

"Warsaw isn't what it used to be," Julia said. "The destruction is still evident, and, of course, there's the ghetto . . ."

"My father used to work at the Palais. I wonder if he's still employed there."

Eryk smiled. "As long as you have your papers, Greta, you should be able to find out. Be prepared to adhere to a strict schedule."

She looked down at her legs, the scars from the bombing barely visible past the hem of her dress. "I'm ready. Did they search?"

"Just moved a few things around, more out of curiosity than anything else," Eryk said, and then pointed to the picture. "I think Hitler saved our lives—the murdering bastard."

Hanna savored the irony. The portrait of the Führer had so appeased the men that they had little interest in an exhaustive search, thus overlooking a sweating SOE agent in a bed over their heads.

Tossing and turning, Hanna slept little that night because it took hours for the heat to dissipate from the loft. She was anxious and, at the same time, excited about being *home*; however, the word seemed as foreign as the straw bed that now anchored her life. A bad case of nerves set her skin afire as the hours dragged by in seeming slow motion.

She reminded herself that her first duty, as Rita would have defined it, was to the SOE, but she couldn't help but wonder about her parents and siblings—what had been their fate? If she met them now on the street, certainly they would excuse themselves and be on their way, not recognizing the lighter shade of her hair swept back from her face, or her middle-class German clothes. She was a typist and her husband, Stefan, was a driver for the Nazis, whose duties constantly called him away from her side. Even though her identity had been drummed into her, she had to keep reminding herself that the enemy was trained to sniff out traitors and spies.

But if she could walk into Warsaw undetected, the first place she would visit would be her old home on Krochmalna, looking for the anonymous person mentioned in the letter who might help her find her parents. But the city was big and she held little hope for such a miracle. She might have better luck going to the Palais, seeking her father. Would seeing her be too much of a shock, or would he still disown her, as if she were dead?

She turned over and dug her face into the pillow. There were so many questions she couldn't answer.

The pink light of dawn, filtering through the slats, awakened her after a few hours of fitful sleep. The familiar scrape of the ladder against the ceiling jolted her from bed. Feeling dull and lethargic, she pulled on her dress and climbed down.

Her comb and face powder rested by the sink near Julia's cosmetics. After a trip to the outhouse, she returned to find a pot of coffee brewing over the fire.

"A special occasion," Julia said, looking much more chipper than Hanna. "Seeing you this morning, I thought you might need it. It's weak, but better than nothing." She poked at the fireplace coals, sending a flight of orange sparks up the chimney, poured the brew, and handed her a cup. "Coffee is as hard to get these days as gasoline. The Nazis have siphoned everything for themselves and the 'pure' German families that have resettled here, while we Poles get the dregs. Eryk only gets gasoline because the food we sell ends up feeding German troops."

"So, you support the Wehrmacht?" Hanna asked, suspecting there was more to the story than selling vegetables.

Julia ignored her and walked back to the sink.

"I'm sorry," Hanna offered. "A poor question—I didn't mean it literally."

Julia turned, her brown eyes flaring with bitterness. "You of all people should know to choose your words carefully."

Hanna sat on the couch, clutching her cup. "Yes . . . I understand. It's hard to be someone else all the time—and, at the very least, not indulge in sarcasm once in a while. That's why I left Warsaw. My life had become too routine, too predictable, too stuck in . . . Judaism." She took a sip of coffee. "And look what I got—a free trip back."

Julia leaned against the sink. "We sell to people who used to be wholesalers in the market . . . now they're single dealers lorded over by the Nazis. They've taken over everybody's business. Some of what Eryk sells goes to feed German troops, but we can't do anything about that. It also goes to restaurants in the Aryan section of Warsaw."

"Where is Eryk?"

"In the fields . . . loading the truck. The trip is routine—the same every week—but that's what makes it safe. Some of the guards know him."

Hanna sipped her coffee, the taste somewhere between hot water and a regular brew. "How did you get into this dangerous business of sheltering people like me? So many people wouldn't dare."

"We love our country—enough to die for it. Don't you love Poland?"

"More than ever now, but for a time, I didn't."

Sunlight poured through the kitchen window, glinting in yellow shafts on the bushes surrounding the farmhouse and the leafy trees that lined the fields. High white clouds, free from rain, sailed overhead. The weather reminded Hanna of her childhood, when she couldn't wait for spring to end so she could run or swim in the warmer temperatures as she pleased.

"All I wanted, once I came of age, was to leave Warsaw," she continued. "I don't know why I'm telling you this—we're supposed to keep the past to ourselves—but now that I'm here and on my own, it doesn't seem to matter."

Julia walked to the fire, poured a cup of coffee, and took a seat at the opposite end of the couch. "What matters is life . . . and you can tell me anything. In fact, I think it would do you good."

Hanna faced Julia. "I've never talked about this with anyone, not even my sister." She lowered her gaze briefly. "Our traditions . . . our culture . . . stifled me. If I wanted to do something as simple as swim, I had to sneak around—make sure they never found out. My parents looked down upon my activities, particularly my father. My mother always gave in to him. I never was the daughter he wanted. We fought . . . in our way. Of course, that meant I wasn't able to express anything like anger or hatred. I *hated* how they ruled me, and how they were going to see me married to a man I was sure I couldn't love. My sister didn't seem to mind, which was infuriating."

"It must have been hard to leave."

"I cried so many times alone, wanting only to be myself, and

I couldn't." A sadness she hadn't felt in years filled her, as if she was making the decision to leave again. "So, I decided that I would cut everyone off, renounce everything I'd been. Luckily, I had an aunt in London who had been through the same thing. She agreed to take me in." Hanna drew in a breath. "She was killed in the Blitz."

"I'm sorry," Julia said, leaning toward her. "How do you feel now?"

Hanna sighed. "I'm here to do my job, which I'll do, but I can't stop thinking about my family. Those concerns are clouding my thoughts—I have to be careful."

Julia cocked her head.

"I shouldn't have said that. I will fulfill my duties, but I do owe a debt to my parents and to my homeland—they made me what I am."

"We think often . . . about Eryk's brother, who was killed fighting the Germans during the invasion, and his parents, who were killed in the Warsaw bombings."

"I'm sorry," Hanna said, acknowledging a conversation filled with sorrow and little in the way of hope. "We all know what we have to do."

"My husband and I will give as much as we can to the resistance. We understand loss. I know he would be proud to help your family."

The truck bounced in from the field and stopped in front of the farmhouse. Eryk came through the door with all the energy of a young man. "I'm ready for breakfast. Then we'll be off."

Julia clutched Hanna's hand. "It'll be ready in a moment." She rose from the couch and walked to cut bread for toast and jam.

By eight in the morning, the sun was bearing down upon them. Hanna had taken a few moments to look at the baskets of vegetables carefully packed in the truck bed: the green leaves of sorrel, used in soups and for garnishes; the small, whitish bulbs of kohlrabi still attached to their stalks; pungent rhubarb, when cooked with sugar, made treats she remembered as a child; red beetroot, a staple of soups; and green spears of asparagus.

"Does it meet with your satisfaction?" Eryk asked.

"I was wondering whether the soldiers inspect the truck?"

"What do you think?" He took a final look at the produce.

"The guards lean over the bed, give it a quick glance, and send you on your way. You can't hide rifles in vegetable baskets."

"You could . . . but only a fool would do so. Get in."

She climbed into the passenger seat, making one last inspection of her purse before they left. She had taken several hundred in counterfeit zlotys, but left the Browning under the bed. It was too dangerous to carry a weapon.

Eryk started the truck and headed northeast, following the river's course before turning south into a densely wooded area.

Hanna rolled down the window, sticking her head out in the morning air, breathing in the damp scent of the woods, seeing a few alder and beech. The land was scarred by deep cuts where deciduous trees had been ripped from the earth.

"They've been shipped to the Front," Eryk said, over the whoosh of air streaming into the truck.

Hanna pulled her head back inside the cab. "What about hand grenades?"

"What?"

"Could you hide hand grenades in the baskets?"

He chuckled. "Yes . . . but I can tell you haven't been around a real Nazi. They're meticulous. It's a character trait—and will remain so until they're defeated. Don't cross them or underestimate them." He took his eyes off the road for a moment and looked at her with all the seriousness displayed by his wife a few hours before.

"I won't underestimate them."

"I'm not telling you how to conduct your business, but keep your guard up. You won't see much from our farmhouse—maybe a small convoy now and then—but the danger gets thicker coming into Warsaw. I'll be letting you off a few kilometers after we pass Blizne, west of Warsaw. I'll deliver the vegetables and then pick you up. How long will you need?"

Hanna had heard of the village, but never visited. "How long of a walk?"

"From the drop point, an hour, maybe a little more, to the heart of the city."

"Can you keep busy until one?"

He nodded. "I'll talk with my dealers—slowly—and return at one. That gives you about three hours."

They drove east through the village until Hanna could see Warsaw looming larger in her eyes. The city was not the city she remembered. Even from this distance she could see the burnt shells of buildings, or the tops of those that had been leveled in the bombings or left to stand like the remnants of a burned forest.

Eryk pulled the truck onto a secluded side road sheltered by trees.

"Good luck, Greta," he said. "Remember that signpost and this road. Catch a trolley once you get into the city, if you can find one that's running. You'll have more time that way. I'll wait a half hour past one. If you don't show up, you're on your own until we see you at the farm."

She got out of the truck as Eryk backed up. Hanna waved her hand to disperse the exhaust. A wooden sign shaped like an arrow pointed toward Warsaw.

She was going home.

CHAPTER 18

Four guards stood at the ghetto entrance near Krochmalna Street—two Blue Police outside the gate and two German soldiers inside with their green bowl-shaped helmets covering their heads.

Janka stood in the morning sun a good distance from them, judging which of these "authorities" would be the kindest, which of the four might have the most respect for her situation. Of the two combinations in front of her—one on either side of the gate—neither seemed easy. Of the pair to the left, the Polish policeman seemed the thorniest, with thin lips and a dark gaze like a cat on the prowl. His German compatriot on the other side of the fence, a young man with his rifle slung over his right shoulder, offered talk and smiles, puffing on a cigarette and trying to converse with the unyielding Poles. The pair to the right seemed mildly interested in everyone who passed by, but never smiled or even spoke to one another. She decided to try the Polish policeman to the left, hoping that the young German might see her through the gate.

Everything was in place—the letter from Dr. Josef Bühler, the State Secretary of the General Government. Janka had forged it on a piece of stationery left behind by his assistant, Herr Mueller, after one of his drunken meetings with Karol. Mueller waved important documents about, in an effort to impress Karol, sometimes sharing Nazi plans, sometimes not. It was no surprise to Janka that the letterhead had dropped to the floor under the coffee table.

She'd thought everything out: her neatly folded identification papers; the pretense she had come up with to visit the Majewskis. These points had been carefully plotted and planned by Janka. Still, her mouth was dry and she sought to control the urge to flee—danger lurked footsteps away.

It had been months since she'd had any contact with the family. After several more mentions from Herbert Mueller that the "final solution" would be settled soon, she felt another warning was necessary.

Steeling herself, she took several deep breaths, drawing upon her courage. The gate was only ten meters away. It was time to act, rather than draw attention to herself.

As she approached, the policeman turned, holding up his hand for her to stop.

"What do you want?" He spat out the words in Polish, his eyes looking like ebony holes devoid of feeling.

Izreal had called her a War Girl. She screwed up her courage in order to live up to that expectation.

"How dare you speak to me in that tone," she said, charging at his question. The young German swiveled, now paying attention to the minor altercation outside the gate.

The Pole's face dropped as if he had been attacked—and by a woman! Janka could tell he'd never expected such a response.

"I'm here to observe," she continued with force. "You will let me in, unless you wish to disobey Dr. Bühler, the State Secretary of the General Government—I have a signed letter here." She withdrew it from her pocket.

The Pole eyed her coolly, took the stationery, and looked to the German for guidance.

"I'll handle this," the young Nazi said, walking toward the gate. He swung it open and motioned for her to come inside.

Janka snatched the letter from the policeman and entered the ghetto.

The German closed the gate and drew her to one side. The air smelled different inside the wall—it stank of death and disease. A plague had descended upon this crowded prison of Warsaw.

"The letter," the guard said in German, taking it from her. He read it and then asked, "Do you know Dr. Bühler?"

Concentrate, Janka. Give him your best, confident answers in German.

She spoke halting German, but the guard appreciated her effort. "My husband and I know Herbert Mueller, his assistant. Herr Mueller has been to our house several times. The request came from the State Secretary through him."

"Your identification papers and purse for inspection."

"Of course." She opened her purse and presented both to him.

He studied these before saying, "Welcome, Mrs. Danek. There will be no one to escort you. You must return to this gate when you leave."

"I won't be long," she responded, taking back her purse. "I would only do this at the Secretary's insistence. I'm happy to return—out of this stinking mess."

The guard's eyes lit up. "You're lucky. You can leave. My post is here."

"I'm sorry." She turned to leave, but the man stopped her with another question.

"Once again—the purpose of your visit?"

She stepped forward, showing some exasperation at his question and spoke in Polish. The policeman moved closer to the gate so he could hear. "Do you understand Polish?"

"A little."

"It's all clearly written out. I can say nothing more than I'm to judge the attitude of the Jews in the ghetto—to help the Secretary understand how quickly plans can be put into place."

The young German nodded, as if he understood what Janka was hinting at, even though she didn't know herself. "Yes. Plans . . . in the works. Why didn't the State Secretary or Herr Mueller come?"

Janka pinched her nose. "To this place? I'm doing them a

favor. They have no desire to step into this hellhole." She shook her head in disgust. "I'm taking a bath as soon as I get home."

She left him behind, closed her eyes for a second, and exhaled. She felt drained, but she had made it past the gate. Now, she only had to find the Krochmalna apartment whose number she had memorized before she burned Izreal's note.

Janka made sure she was well away from the gate before turning south toward the cut-off length of Krochmalna. Everything seemed so normal at first glance: the tram cars running along the tracks, the rickshaws that carried those who could afford to pay, the crowded streets. But a closer inspection revealed a star of David on the trolley—for Jews only; a pitiful street café set up by a poor woman using a small wooden table to serve her patrons; a boy selling Jewish armbands and ghetto newspapers; the beggar dressed in rags hoping for a handout; the sunken faces of the people who walked the streets in worn-out clothes. Here and there, the exceptions passed by—men and women dressed in better attire.

Soon she was standing in front of the drab apartment building. The crumbling stone steps needed patching. The front door wasn't locked; in fact, it looked as if it had been broken into. The wood around the key plate was newly exposed and white. Those windows not broken or covered over with wood were black with grime. Before the war, no self-respecting Pole would have let a building slip into such a state.

The rancid, execrable smell in the hall nearly knocked her off her feet. She covered her nose with a handkerchief in order to keep from retching. The apartment door to her left hung at a crazy angle from its hinges. She peeked inside. The room was in a state of disarray: the bed tilted against a wall, glass shards and broken dishes strewn across the floor. Clearly, something horrible had happened. Janka hoped that the Majewskis hadn't lived there.

She climbed the stairs to the next landing and knocked on the door despite her sense that no one was at home. Silence could be deceiving, however, during war.

After a second knock, she heard a woman's voice, low and soft. "Who is it?"

"Janka Danek."

The door creaked open and a pair of sunken eyes peered around its edge.

"Stefa?"

The woman stuttered and fell back, letting Janka enter. If anyone had told her how the family was living, she would have found it hard to believe: mattresses on the floor, a tub for washing clothes and dishes, a rickety stove used for cooking and heat, windows smeared with grime overlooking the battered end of Krochmalna, suitcases and clothes littering the floor.

Janka threw her arms around Stefa, crying out in relief, but also in pity for her condition. Her friend had lost considerable weight, her face sunken and pale, cheeks as hollow as bowls. Stefa wore a faded blue dress that was tattered about the hem and sleeves from many hand washings. Her black leather shoes had turned gray and were on the verge of losing their soles.

A young man, who displayed a similar countenance, stood in his Jewish Police uniform, his baton at the ready in his right hand. A hunched old woman cowered in a chair near the stove. She had to be Perla, the most visibly changed. The woman's hair was gray, thinning, and hung in limp strands from her kerchief. Her eyes were as dark as coal.

"It's good to see you," Stefa said. "This is our friend, Mrs. Danek," she said to Daniel, who lowered the only instrument of force he was allowed to carry.

"You caught us by surprise," Daniel said.

Perla looked up with a weak smile. "Sit, my friend."

"I will." Janka sat in the chair opposite Perla.

Stefa and Daniel sat on the mattress, looking at her expectantly. How could she break the news of a "final solution?" The words were mere speculation. However, Herr Mueller's sodden pronouncements and her husband's eager servitude seemed more than enough reason to voice her fears.

At first, they talked of the ordinary questions of life: How did Janka get past the gate? Who was the Jewish policeman living in their rooms? How were they surviving, especially since the lack of food now cut across all social classes? Janka rose and stood in front of Stefa and Daniel. "I don't want to worry your mother," she whispered. "How are your father and brother?"

"We worry," Stefa replied softly. "They still work at the Palais, but hardly any Jews or Poles eat there these days. The restaurant subsists on what the Nazis spend. We think—if there's trouble—it will close."

"I'm sorry," Janka said.

"My parents work in the German factories," Daniel said. "I work for the Jewish Ghetto Police, but I've grown to hate it. There's so much brutality. . . ."

"He refuses to be cruel," Stefa added.

Janka sighed, sat in front of them, and then looked over her shoulder at Perla. The woman sat staring at the ceiling, her body rocking in the stationary chair. "What can be done for her?"

"She loses a little more of herself each day," Stefa said. "We get through to her as much as we can, but often she's far away from us."

"I have disturbing news," Janka said. "Don't panic, but I've heard from an authority within the General Government that action will soon be taken."

"What action? When?" Daniel asked.

"If I knew I would tell you . . . but be prepared . . . as much as you can."

"What have you heard?" Stefa asked.

Janka shook her head. "The Reich is seeking a 'final solution' for the Jews, and Poland will be one of the first nations to witness it."

Stefa's eyes widened. "What does that mean?"

Daniel, his anger rising, spoke too loudly. "I know what it means . . . they want to kill us . . . to wipe us from the earth."

"Quiet," Stefa said. "Mama shouldn't hear such things."

"It could happen anytime," Janka said, looking at Stefa. "Have you heard from your sister?"

"Not in months."

"Please give her my address if she ever returns. Maybe, together, we can help you get out. If I had more friends and resources . . ."

"Don't blame yourself," Stefa said, shaking her head. "You've been good to us. I don't know if I will ever see my sister again. I hope she's happy in London."

"I can't stay any longer, or I may be missed," Janka said, looking at her wristwatch. "God bless you. Please take care." After telling them good-bye, she left the apartment. The Majewskis were alive, but were living like rats. If only she had more to offer. She had neither the money nor the connections to help them. Karol and his Nazi friends were like weights on her body as she struggled to swim in a fetid lake. Her husband was always watching her, even though his judgment usually was impaired by liquor. Sometimes that made him more dangerous than a sober man. He suspected her—accused her—when the drink talked.

The young German was still at the gate, although through an operational rotation, he had moved to the opposite end. She did as ordered and walked toward him.

"May I see your purse again?" He held out his hand.

"Of course," she replied.

"Did you find out what you were looking for?" He took her bag.

"The Jews are ready."

Nodding, he inspected it and then returned it to her. "I think so."

He opened the gate. She walked calmly past the surly Polish policeman and onto the Aryan streets where, despite the overall misery of the occupation, life felt different. Even the small taste of freedom on the other side of the wall allowed her to relax as she walked, to breathe easier.

She passed her apartment and continued on to church, where she offered a prayer: *Change the heart of my husband and help me discover a way to help my friends.* She wasn't sure, as she sat in the cool confines of the nave, that God would grant either request.

Hanna walked a road that had been rutted and scarred by German tanks and troops. The countryside merged with what was left of Warsaw. The once vibrant roar of commerce seemed muted, and in twenty minutes she heard only one lonely train whistle.

Arriving at the outskirts of the city, she passed a few armed sentries. They gave her a glance and one of them whistled at her. To appease him, she smiled and walked on. Not one asked for her papers. Was this entry into Warsaw less traveled and therefore lower on the scale of Nazi scrutiny? Of course, one could never count on such fortunate accidents. The next time, the road might be blocked by a heavily guarded checkpoint. Her SOE trainers had told her it was a good idea to switch routes.

Near a cemetery, she found a working trolley and paid the fare with counterfeit money. She traveled east and then, after transferring, continued north toward Krochmalna.

Despite Julia's warnings and her own sense of what the devastation looked like, nothing prepared her for the view out the tram's grubby window. Entire blocks lay in rubble, after an invasion that had occurred nearly three years before. The odor of burned timbers, the smell of foul petroleum, and the dust from debris lingered in the air. If one block had been obliterated, another nearby had escaped destruction, although not as bright and shiny as she remembered. Everything seemed to be covered in a film of dirt, as if the world were out of focus, fuzzy in the grim sunlight.

Nazi guards populated most street corners—some looking bored, others perhaps annoyed that their duty was playing out in a destroyed city with little or no action. Hanna made mental notes for her report to the SOE. She spotted tanks and other heavy military equipment off the main thoroughfares, but not as much as she had imagined. Poles went about their normal business. Many shops were closed for a reason. Seeing the ugly symbols and slogans for the first time on a Jewish store shocked her—the white paint now faded, the posters peeling from the glass, condemning the owner and those who frequented it. Everyone wandered under the watchful gaze of the guards, the SS, or the stealthy Gestapo. Warsaw, now a subdued city, had been crushed by the Nazis.

To show emotion about what she saw would be a mistake. She knew that no hardened National Socialist would be shaken by the Wehrmacht's destructive force—she should be used to such sights. *Blend into the city, into the life of Warsaw as it is. No one should see me cry.*

The trolley passed near the Palais. Hanna could see it, but she felt frozen, unable to reconcile her duties to the SOE with her concern for her family. Perhaps someone would recognize her. An unexpected reunion might be too much for her father. There was also the possibility that he would recognize her . . . and turn away. She wasn't ready to face the sting of his rejection . . . again.

She got off the tram a few stops later near the southern border of the ghetto. The wall was clearly visible through the trolley's front glass. Her stomach tightened as she walked near it. The wall was imposing, barbed wire and broken glass lining its top. The gates were well protected by Polish Police and Nazi guards. Then she saw the bridge and the snaking line of people going in both directions from one section of the ghetto to the other, the anonymous movement, their slumping postures a palpable sign of pain—as if an endless funeral procession were being held for the amusement of the Nazis.

Her parents, her brother and sister, old Mrs. Rosewicz, were behind that wall, perhaps in the stream of pedestrians on the bridge. She fought a rising sickness in her body.

A burst of cold washed over her, accompanied by a wave of nausea that hit her stomach. She stopped under the shade of a half-blasted oak. Even the trees were gone! The fountains dry. If she could crush the city in her hand, it would crumble to dust in its brittleness.

The glass along the wall's top glittered, as if mocking beauty. Why go on? She had seen everything about this impenetrable fortress she wanted to see. Death resided there while life took refuge on the other side.

She turned toward Krochmalna—again, the sorrow of the closed shops, the mockery of the Aryan side came into focus. The pedestrians flowed, a man dodging the occasional car on the street, a woman skirting a horse cart as it passed by.

Soon, she arrived near the apartment where she grew up. Pretending to have trouble with her shoe, she rested upon the rubble of a nearby tenement. The old building looked the same, but more weather-worn and drab than she remembered. The "friend" she was looking for was a "neighbor"—she had no idea where this person might live. She assumed that this acquaintance was young, probably a woman Stefa knew. Her parents didn't go looking for friends, and Aaron was too young at the time of the invasion to know someone who could help them.

She crossed the street, casually looking up, taking in its façade. The balcony her brother loved was still there. The apartment was too high to look into the windows, but the curtains had been changed—red and far more decorative and expensive than the plain ones her mother had lived with.

Crossing back, she walked to the door. The mezuzah was gone and the names on the address plate were German. Someone named Schiller now lived in her old home.

She looked at her watch. Time was running out. Walking back to the drop point would take the rest of her day.

As she stood there, she noticed a woman on the opposite side of the street approaching from the west. She was nearing middle age, a bit drab, certainly not rich, but not poor either. Their eyes connected briefly, and then the woman looked away, opening a door across the street and disappearing up the stairs.

Anyone could be the friend, Hanna thought. She didn't have time to find out.

*   *   *

Eryk's truck was parked under a tree. Hanna climbed in, her legs on the verge of cramping from the long walk through Warsaw. The engine ignited with a pop, and for several kilometers she said nothing, but only watched as the green woods and fields flew by.

He spoke first, sounding a bit shy. "Anything worth reporting?"

She shook her head. "Nothing out of the ordinary—nothing that intelligence doesn't already know."

The truck rolled on for several more kilometers before he spoke again. "Coded messages don't give you much leeway, but any small detail could be helpful."

"I know."

"Are you all right?"

She turned, studying his bearded profile and the unkempt waves of black hair, thinking that he and Julia were the true heroes of this war, not she. "I don't know what I was expecting. Warsaw is half a city—much of it destroyed, much still standing—but I nearly got sick to my stomach near the ghetto wall, knowing my family is imprisoned behind that ugly barrier."

"You're strong—but you're human," he said with a half smile.

"No, you and Julia are the strong ones. For the first time— today—I doubted my decision to leave my family. As I walked by the ghetto, I felt like a coward for deserting them, leaving them to the wolves." She looked out the window as they turned toward the farm. "How have you managed it . . . the war? The past three years must have been hell."

"It has been hell, but Julia and I decided long ago that we would take a stand the best way we could. We would fight them to the death if we had to. We decided not to have children because we didn't want to bring them into this world . . . and if something happened to us . . . or to the baby . . . well, you can imagine how hard it's been."

"I respect you and Julia," she said.

"I had some time to think while I was waiting for you. In order for us to avoid the firing squad, you can take the old bicycle I have in the barn and pedal up to a deserted house about four kilometers from the farm. The ride is easy . . . fairly flat. I can build two carriers on each side where you can hide the wireless and the battery. I can make false bottoms and we can cover them with vegetables or flowers. Perhaps cheese. You can give it to the Germans in case you get stopped. You can walk the bike through the fields, if you want to avoid the road."

She nodded. It would be less risky than transmitting from the farmhouse. If she got caught at another location, it would only cost her life and not the Rybaks'.

After Eryk stopped the truck in front of the farmhouse, Hanna noticed that the bed was empty except for the vegetable baskets.

Julia was on the couch sipping wine when they came inside. Hanna thought she looked particularly glum, her eyes downcast and both hands grasping the glass stem tightly.

"Would you like something to drink?" Eryk asked. "We have a little white wine and some Polish vodka left. Not much, but enough to drink to our health."

Julia had lit a small fire, although the day was still warm. The room smelled smoky with a touch of dryness.

"Sit," Julia said to her, bringing the glass to her lips. "I have something to tell you. A friend visited this afternoon—you don't need to know his name." Eryk sat beside her.

"Did you know a woman by the name of Maria Zielinski?" Julia asked.

Hanna's body tensed, as she thought of Dolores. "Yes."

"She's dead," Julia said flatly. "The Nazis captured her at an operator's home near Płońsk. She was tortured for two days and then hanged in the square. Our friend doesn't know if she talked."

"Another reason to be cautious," Eryk said, showing no emotion.

Hanna suddenly realized how the Rybaks had dealt with the war—by distancing themselves from it. Another death was just another death—a cruel fact of life under the Third Reich. That kind of personal detachment was exactly what the SOE had been drumming into their agents.

She longed to tell them about Dolores and her flirtatious personality and her love of makeup, and her granite inner strength, but that wasn't necessary or important to the Rybaks. She didn't believe that "Maria" would have broken under torture, but what if the Nazis had managed to force something out of her? The two resistance fighters had parachuted over Płońsk. Why was Maria there rather than at her drop point in the small village to the south? Maybe she had important information that needed to get to the SOE—after all, Maria was a courier. The chill that enveloped her abated somewhat as she considered what to do next. Were the SS or the Gestapo biding their time, waiting to spring a trap, or planning when they would burst through the farmhouse door?

She rose from her chair and looked at Eryk. "I'd like a vodka . . . and please drive me to the abandoned house at sunset. I need to see the new transmitting point."

Eryk nodded and poured the liquor.

Hanna sipped it and looked into the fire, wondering how much the Germans knew about her. With Dolores's death, time had taken on an even greater urgency.

A large raven sat atop a light pole abutting the Aryan side of the wall. Perla wouldn't have noticed, but it was so rare to see any animal these days in or near the ghetto, in the last hours of a dwindling July. Even the stray cats and dogs had disappeared.

The bird sat for a moment in the rain, then shook its body, sloughing the water off its slick black feathers, and launching itself into the air, winging northeast toward the Vistula.

They can't keep this from me. I have a brain. I have eyes.

Tisha b'Av had passed, the annual fast day of mourning and contemplation commemorating the destruction of the First and

Second Temples in Jerusalem. Every day was like a fast now, and other than saying a few prayers, it slipped by her and the rest of the family.

They had tried to keep the news from her, but she could hear, even when they thought she was dozing, even when they thought she wasn't paying attention. Perla had learned to fool them.

Everyone in the ghetto was in a panic, Daniel had whispered to Stefa. The shops were closed. The Jews were running through the streets like chickens trying to escape the butcher's hand. Men and women, girls and boys, had been rounded up and taken to the Umschlagplatz, a square next to the railroad sidings, formerly used for commerce.

She overheard how the Germans had pulled Jews from a trolley and executed them like they were livestock to be slaughtered. People were wailing, tearing their hair out, stuffing what they could in a suitcase before being herded to the Umschlagplatz, where they were held before . . . *before what?*

Their possessions: clothing, books, utensils, jewelry boxes, cake pans, dishes, lamps, even the furniture they thought they could haul on their backs, littered the streets. The Jewish Police were involved, and Daniel had said he wanted nothing to do with what was happening. Policemen had been shot for standing up to the Nazis, but he persisted: He wouldn't beat anyone or lead people to their deaths. He would strip off his uniform before he became like them. Izreal, however, had urged him to not quit his job, but to help—perhaps he could save a few along the way as the horror happened.

But what horror? The place where they were held before . . . before what? None of it made any sense, except the terror, and it sent her brain spinning.

Stefa had gone to the soup kitchen, Izreal and Aaron to the Palais, and Daniel, reluctantly, to work. Perla was in their room alone, looking out the window at the raven and the heavy rain clouds that separated Warsaw from heaven.

"Mother," Izreal had whispered. "I must go to work. If the Germans come, go to the hiding place on the landing."

She nodded, but had already decided that she would never again venture into that terrible place of darkness and rank smells, feeling as if she was going to plummet into the black pit of a latrine. Daniel had whispered to his father of another hiding place discovered by Aaron, but warned him it was dangerous to go there unless absolutely necessary because "secrets" had been stashed there—secrets so deadly that he couldn't talk about them until it was safe for everyone to use. It all seemed so complicated, like a twisted dream. Anyway, Perla wasn't sure she could find her way there, or open the panel that Daniel had told his father about.

A cough, followed by a moan, rose from the neighboring room. Wanda was sick again, so ill that Jakub had stayed home in order to be with his wife. He blamed her illness on a mild case of dysentery, but Perla knew that Wanda had been pale and wan for months, not getting better, missing one or two days of work each week.

The door between the two rooms had been shut for privacy, the mattress that Daniel and his father slept on shoved out of the way. Perla walked to the window and stared at the morning rain falling in large drops, hoping to find something flying through the skies, some sign of a world beyond the ghetto. She looked down at the street and gasped. A green truck with a swastika on it had pulled up in front of the building.

The front door cracked as a booted foot kicked it open. The terrifying trample of feet resounded up the stairs, followed by another boot against their door. Jakub appeared, peering between the rooms, horror etched upon his face.

"*Aussteigen*," the two Nazis shouted, their faces reddened from screaming, their voices unleashing rage. "*Komm mit uns!*"

She stood, rooted to the floor for a moment, until one of the men flung himself at her, pulling her by the hair tucked beneath her kerchief. Two Ukrainians stood at the door, watching the proceedings with rifles poised. They glared at her, showing more hate in their eyes than the Germans, as if they were the occupiers. The other Nazi stalked into the Krakowskis' room and ordered them to leave. Jakub soon came to the door with a pale and shaky Wanda, who wore a nightgown and a coat over her shoulders.

"Let me get some things," Perla said, reaching for her suit-case.

The German brought his rifle butt down upon her hand, splitting the frail skin.

She yelped in pain and looked at her bloody fingers.

"Get a towel, Jewish bitch," he ordered in German. "Only three of you? We need more! Where are the others?"

"They are at work," Jakub said. "Let me show you our work papers . . . I can give you money." He held Wanda close to his side.

"I don't want your filthy money," the Nazi said. "Where you're going, you won't need it."

"Go, now! Hurry!" The other German moved them forward with his rifle.

Perla wrapped a towel around her hand and looked at the apartment, wondering whether she would ever see the room again. The menorah, the silver, and the jewelry were all left behind. Surely, someone would buy the silver if Izreal had to sell it.

Good-bye, my love.

A Ukrainian whacked her on the back with his rifle as she passed.

Wanda struggled to stand as the Nazis shoved her and her husband down the stairs.

The rain pattered down as the guards herded them into the street. Normally, she welcomed the sound of water hitting the cobblestones. Today, the constant splash sounded like a death knell. As they walked over the Chłodna Bridge, Wanda began to sob and Perla comforted her as best she could. They were wet now, shivering in their damp clothes. Wanda called out for her son, hoping that he would hear her cries for help. Perla doubted that Daniel could do anything now that they had been chosen . . . *for what?*

Others joined them as they were driven northward. The

guards stopped on Leszno and Pawia, ripping people from their homes, pushing them into the street, sending them scurrying before their blows, before traveling up Zamenhofa Street. It seemed that the world was crying for mercy as pleas for help rose from the crowd to unresponsive ears. She heard shots and screams, and a guard yelled, "That's what happens when you try to escape." Perla hadn't the strength to flee as she clung to Wanda. A wave of humanity propelled them forward until they eventually arrived at a dingy square sealed off by the ghetto wall, a fence, and the stone buildings that surrounded it.

The odor of a people crushed lingered in the square, tainting everyone with the toxicity of vomit, feces, and the pungent smell of unwashed flesh. A few Jewish policemen stood at the edge of the square watching the crowd, keeping the surge of humanity within the Umschlagplatz. Perla, in turn, watched them, looking for any sign that the officers were taking bribes, or helping Jews to escape. She saw nothing that indicated any help had been offered.

Others had arrived before them—all was silent except for the occasional cry of a child. The mother, fearing death from the guards, hushed the child quickly. Ten rows of Jews, including Poles relegated to the ghetto because of Jewish heritage, sat on the stones in cramped lines of gray, black, and white, under the sodden sky. Perla, Wanda, and Jakub took their places near the front and waited as the Nazis, in their helmets and rain-slickened coats, paced up and down the square.

The silence, the waiting, took its toll, and she could feel her mind slipping away. The towel around her hand had turned red, browning at its edges as the blood congealed. Was this real? Was she really sitting on cold stones in the rain waiting for the unknown? No one could relieve themselves; no one had water unless they opened their mouths to the sky. Where were Izreal— *Father always knows what to do*—and Daniel?

A weak voice several rows behind her called out barely above a gasp. "Perla?" The question came again before a guard turned in their direction.

After he passed, Perla turned her head and saw a wan face she hadn't seen in months. "Kachna?"

Mrs. Rosewicz nodded.

They sat for hours looking at each other, unable to speak. Perla made up her mind that wherever they were going, they would go together.

The rain had let up a little when the sound of a locomotive and the metallic scrape of its wheels pierced the square.

"Up . . . get up," the guards chanted, pointing their rifles toward them.

They rose like corpses coming to life, clutching at their bags, grasping their children's hands as the whips came down upon their backs. Perla pushed into the crowd, leaving Wanda and Jakub so she could reach Mrs. Rosewicz.

"Kachna," she cried out, clutching the old woman, who felt like a skeleton in her hands. Her friend wept upon her shoulder.

The guards pushed them north, to another section of the Umschlagplatz, where wooden boxcars stretched behind a locomotive. Wagons, guarded by the SS, also stood by. These were loaded with old people who were weak or appeared to be sick. Perla didn't know where they were headed, but the men carried machine guns. One of the guards clutched at Mrs. Rosewicz, calling her "not fit for transportation," but relented after he saw the wagons were full. He let her go. The other Nazis screamed for them to get into the boxcars—with or without their suitcases. Some bags fell to the ground, scattering their contents upon the wet earth.

"I have nothing," Mrs. Rosewicz said. "It's time for this to end."

"I won't let you go alone, Kachna," Perla said. "Hold my hand."

Wanda and Jakub had been pushed farther down the tracks. Perla saw them disappear into one of the cars as others helped them up.

Gloved hands pushed them forward until they were at the

door of a boxcar crammed with men, women, and children. Two men reached down and lifted them to the floorboards.

A guard shouted something in German to another and the door slid shut, barely missing Perla's feet. The lock clicked with an ominous finality.

They clutched one another, their shivering bodies adjusting to the overpowering stench of the wet flesh and blood crammed into the car. A woman cried out for God to save them, and another yelled, "Where are they taking us?"

The train rolls along but I see nothing through the slats except for a few buildings that remain in my beloved Warsaw. We are headed somewhere east, across the Vistula and into the countryside.

The air is frightful and I can barely breathe. I wet my dress because I had no place to go. The smell is sickening and we are packed so tightly together, some have already fainted. Poor Mrs. Rosewicz is clinging to me like the last rose of summer on the vine. She is right—it is time for it to end.

I have lost my husband, my son, and two daughters. Perhaps it is better this way. May God bless them with long lives, far away from those who would destroy us. I'm too weak to fight. I will hold Kachna's hand so we can die together, if that's what God commands. Some say we are going to a camp where we will work . . . but what can I do . . . what can Kachna do? We are old women beaten down by our oppressors, good for nothing. I suppose I might find work if I had to, but Kachna?

We've stopped somewhere for a moment, but all I see through the crack is a bare patch of land and a dull sky. Imagine if the sun were out! We'd all be suffocating. A few clamor that this is where we will get off the train, but I see nothing but the rusty row of another set of tracks.

We've started again, creeping along. I wish the door was open so we could breathe the cool air.

*   *   *

The train hissed to a stop a second time, and those still with a voice to speak cried out. Someone asked, "Where are we? Please . . . anyone . . . tell us."

Perla pushed her eye to the crack and peered out. A blue-and-white sign near the tracks pointed in the direction the train was headed.

"There's a signpost," Perla yelled.

"What does it say?" a woman asked.

"It's a town . . . a village . . . I've never heard of."

Perla paused to make sure she had read it correctly.

"Treblinka," she said.

CHAPTER 19

Stefa arrived home from the soup kitchen before seven. The door stood open—an ominous sign.

Her father, head cradled in his hands, sat in the chair near the stove that her mother took most often during the day and always in the evening. Low sobs burst from his mouth.

Aaron, looking to the ashen sky, huddled in the corner near the window. Her brother's back was straight, his arms firmly planted at his side, as if defying the Nazis outside.

Daniel stood in the doorway to his room, dressed in clothes he might wear to synagogue—yarmulke crowning his head. His eyes were red and his hands clutched his prayer book so fiercely they looked like a bird's talons grasping its prey.

She stood for a moment, wondering what to say, knowing that something terrible had happened. "Where are they?" she asked, for her mother and Daniel's parents were always home by this time.

Izreal lifted his head. "Gone."

"No," she said, shaking her head, knowing it was true. "Gone?" She ran to her father and knelt before him, the tears bursting forth.

"I saw guards driving people forward this morning toward the tracks . . . they kept me away," Daniel said quietly. "At the police station, doing paperwork. They knew I would never allow it to happen . . . not while I was alive."

She slumped at her father's feet, wailing, "Gone . . . oh, God . . . why?"

Aaron turned, looking as if he were dead. "You know why."

Izreal put his hand on Stefa's head. "We must be strong . . . for each other."

"We must fight," Aaron said forcefully, countering his father.

Izreal lowered his head. "I can't think of fighting now. I have to believe they are alive—that what the Germans say is true—they've been sent to a work camp."

Daniel hovered over them. "Czerniaków, the head of the Judenrat, is dead . . . cyanide in his office after he found out the Nazis want six thousand people a day for deportation. He left notes. 'They demand me to kill children of my nation with my own hands . . . I have nothing to do but die . . . I can no longer bear all of this.'" His voice dropped. "Czerniaków understood that deportation means death."

Stefa wanted to cry out in a fierce voice to God, for the deliverance of her mother and Daniel's parents, to smite the Nazis, but the rage, the hate, were useless against so formidable an enemy.

"The ghetto will shrink as we're relocated," Daniel said. "They will force us to move—again."

Stefa looked at him. "Can you do nothing as a policeman?"

Daniel sighed. "I resigned today. I told them I wouldn't be coming back. Like Czerniaków, I can no longer bear it. If you can't pay them off—the ghetto police, the Blues, the Nazis—you have no hope of avoiding the Umschlagplatz. And, eventually, the money will run out."

She fought the urge to panic, her first instinct, as another means of escape vanished; instead, she rose from the floor. "What can I do?"

"You can stand by my side—with your father's permission."

"We must escape," Izreal said, his voice agitated. "I'll get us to the Aryan side."

"How?" Stefa asked.

"I'll sell what we have . . . bribe the guards . . . smuggle us out . . ." He looked at Aaron. "Maybe my son has found another escape route."

"You look to me now?" Aaron asked.

"Don't be bitter—not tonight," Daniel said.

"The wall is more secure now than it's ever been," Aaron said, "especially now that the Aktion has started. If we can't escape, we fight."

"Fight? Fight?" Izreal's eyes shone like a crazed man. "God must save us."

"No," Aaron said. "Come to your senses. He will not reach down and lift us up."

Izreal slumped, and he cried again.

Daniel put his hands on Izreal's shoulders. "Aaron is right. God watches over us, but he has no control over the Nazis, or their killing ways. We have to save ourselves."

"What about the woman who lives on Krochmalna?" Izreal asked. "The one I gave the letter to."

"Mrs. Danek?" Stefa responded.

Izreal nodded.

"Her husband is a Jew-hater," Aaron said. "She hid me in the closet so he wouldn't see me. She's no good to us."

"We'll find a way," Daniel said. "Let's pray for our loved ones."

Aaron turned to the window where the light was fading from gray to black. Izreal and Daniel stood together, while Stefa sat in the chair.

After the prayer, Daniel said to Izreal, "Come, I have something to show you. Aaron found it, and we can use it as a hiding place, but now it's dangerous—filled with weapons. I'm part of an organization that will not rest as easy as the police."

They followed Daniel into the hall, Stefa being the last to leave the apartment. Their footsteps on the stairs sounded as hollow as she felt. How would she live without her mother? How would her father manage without his wife? Despite his role as leader of the family, Izreal had always depended on Perla to be there for him, to be the silent strength, and sometimes anchor, sometimes foil, in their relationship. Now she was gone. She imagined the worst for those that had been taken to the Umschlagplatz—her mother would be worked to death—but what if the Nazis couldn't find anything for her to do? Then what? And Perla's health had faded since they'd been forced into the ghetto. For a moment, she thought of Hanna and where she might be—of course, in London, worrying about her family. That was the best Stefa could hope for. At least, her sister was safe.

Daniel led them to the hiding place, raising the panel and opening the door leading to the enclosure.

"Hurry," Daniel said. "The Nazis are everywhere." He pulled a small electric torch from his pocket and shined it into the cavity.

Stefa was amazed yet frightened by what she saw. Four rifles leaned against the wall and many boxes, large and small, filled much of the space. Before, it would have held both families if they had crushed against each other; maybe two adults could fit into it now.

"You knew about this?" Izreal asked Aaron.

"Yes. Daniel and I have joined an organization . . ."

Daniel switched off the torch and closed the door. "I didn't recruit your son—I want you to know that, Mr. Majewski. Aaron found the group on his own. Three Zionist youth movements have come together to form one group. The resistance is mobilizing for our own protection."

"I've heard nothing of these groups," Izreal said.

"Why would you, Father?" Aaron asked. "We serve Nazis at the Palais. The restaurant is your life. It's better that you don't know. Even my friend Zeev has become part of the Polish underground. People are rising up against the Germans."

"My life . . ." Izreal said, somewhat ashamed of his son's assessment.

"What's in there?" Stefa asked.

"No place for a cigarette," Daniel said. "Rifles are hard to get—we have four—pistols, two magazines each plus ammunition, two boxes of grenades, materials for firebombs."

"I'd be afraid to breathe," Stefa said.

Daniel secured the panel, and they scurried through the courtyard and back to the hall. They took their places again in the apartment, Izreal looking dazed as he reflected on what he'd seen.

Stefa sat next to her brother on the mattress, looking at Daniel. Why hadn't he told her about his secret activities? Once again, he had caught her off guard. Perhaps it was for the best, but his secrecy left her anxious and hurt.

"I see why you haven't spoken of this place." Izreal said, as if addressing her thoughts. "But two of them—your parents—could have been saved."

"No," Daniel said, shaking his head. "It's too dangerous—they could have blown themselves to bits. Besides, they wouldn't have found it in time. The Aktion is conducted with lightning speed. If the weapons were discovered, everyone in this building would have been executed. It was better that they didn't know." He stood next to Izreal. "But the battle is just beginning. Czerniaków knew exactly what the Nazis have planned—and now we do as well. He saw no way out."

Izreal sat in Perla's chair near the stove and Daniel kneeled before him.

"I want to call you 'father' because we are together as one family," Daniel said.

Izreal gave Daniel a questioning look.

". . . I'm in love with your daughter. I want to marry her. Not now . . . not this moment . . . but when the time is right. I hope you will accept me as your son."

Izreal turned to Stefa, gazing at her with soft eyes. "Is this your wish—to be the wife of this man?"

She rose from the mattress, walked to Daniel, and put her hand upon his shoulder. "Yes, Father, more than anything I've ever wished for."

"Is there some joy in this time of tragedy?" Izreal asked, and placed his hand on Daniel's head. "My wife is gone, and you wish to be married to my daughter. I can hardly think . . . but we should look forward to the future. We have nothing else. I have no objection . . . but you will keep me informed. No more secrets."

"No more secrets," Daniel said, clutching Stefa's hand.

"Others will disappear tomorrow," Aaron said. "We must have a plan."

"Go to work," Daniel said. "You'll be safer there."

"And at night?" Aaron asked.

"The hiding place if we can get to it," Daniel answered. "We'll have to sit on explosives."

"Or shoot our way out," Aaron said.

Stefa wanted to believe her father—that God was looking out for them—but her day with the Nazi film crew, and the disappearance of her mother and Daniel's parents, had convinced her otherwise. She could lose her faith, she thought, but never her identity. She was a Jew and would remain so until she died.

A surprising sense of freedom washed over Hanna as she pedaled through the countryside to the abandoned farmhouse Eryk had shown her. The rich, red blossoms of the corn poppy, and a rainbow array of wild irises, dotted the fields. The wheat had been harvested in some fields, leaving the furrows muddy and brown after summer rains.

True to his word, Eryk had constructed two carriers for the wireless and its equipment. He had finished the boxes so well they were practically seamless. "A lock or latch won't do," he said. In addition to the potatoes and other vegetables, she carried hunks of cheese in case she had to deal with unexpected Germans.

The air was thick and moist with humidity. She worked up a sweat even though the dirt road to the house was mostly flat. She had varied her transmission schedule in order to avoid detection, traveling mostly before sunrise or around sunset, forging paths on her own, pushing through tall grass, batting away the mosquitoes and flies swarming the woods.

The abandoned house looked sturdy enough from the outside, but the inside was wrecked. Timbers had been ripped down, apparently for firewood, leading to great gaps in the roof. What remained of the wooden cabinets and furniture lay smashed on the floor. Everything that was valuable, in terms of food or other useable commodities, had been taken away. Hanna wondered who had lived here—did they have children, were they Polish Nationalists or Jews? Had they died? Eryk and Julia, if they knew the story, had offered nothing more than that the house was deserted before the Germans arrived.

Transmitting from the new location was easy enough. Once the equipment had been hooked up, the aerial strung through a broken window and flung into the branches of an aging beech tree, she would wire for five minutes and then quickly pack.

She informed the SOE of German troop movements along the road that ran parallel to the Vistula; messaged them about the surprise Nazi visit to the Rybaks and the increased need for caution; ordered a list of supplies needed within two weeks; and, most important, advised them of rumors of a mass resettlement of the Warsaw Jews. She even included a coded nod to "Romeo."

Eryk had not taken her to Warsaw in several weeks. After hearing about the deportations, she decided it was time to contact her father; otherwise, it might be too late.

One morning in August, Eryk loaded the truck with summer produce. They left the farm, traveling the same route to Warsaw they had taken before. After no contact with German guards, Eryk left her a kilometer beyond the first drop point. This time, she carried more money and informed him she would find a room for the night and make her way back to the farmhouse, even if she had to travel by wagon or on foot.

"What are you planning?" Eryk asked with concern in his voice.

"I'll be back in two days." She revealed nothing more.

"Okay. Good luck." The truck sputtered away as she walked on in the morning heat.

When she arrived at the city, she was stopped by a young German who asked for her papers. He looked uncomfortable, sweat dripping down his cheeks from underneath his field cap, the hot wool uniform keeping his face and neck flushed in the heat.

"Your husband's a driver?" he asked in German after inspecting the documents.

"Yes," she replied. "Stefan's very busy—we don't see a lot of each other."

"I would love to be in a sedan, with the air rushing through the compartment."

"I agree," she said, "but there's not enough room for me and the officers he transports." She chuckled. "So, guess who gets to walk? They should give you a summer uniform."

"Those go to Africa." He smiled and wished her a good day.

She avoided the sun when she could, walking in the shade, until she came to the Palais. Her stomach rumbled, and she chided herself for not bringing something to eat while she looked for her father. She had devised a plan to walk near the hotel, keeping an eye on the door until eleven. If she had not spotted her father by then, she would risk going inside.

Shortly after ten, a man rounded the corner, and although he was half a block away, his walk identified him as the man she sought. He looked older, thinner, showing a slight stoop in his posture. He was not the robust man she had left behind.

She caught up with him at the door and asked in Polish, "Excuse me, sir, may I see you a moment?"

He stared at her, somewhat shocked by the sudden intrusion; his eyes widening in elementary recognition and then contracting in a quizzical look, as if he had been wrong.

She touched his arm. "Walk with me. This way, please."

He resisted at first, but then followed a step behind, as if he were a dog lagging on a leash. "Who are you?" he finally asked.

Hanna stopped in front of a store window, the glass echoing their reflections. He was wearing a suit and coat despite the heat, the star of David band firmly attached to his right arm. Her hair was lighter and shorter, her body heavier than when she had left Warsaw. Perhaps he really didn't know who she was.

"I am Greta," she said, looking at the window, "but perhaps you know me by another name."

"Ha . . . Han . . ." His voice dropped.

She nodded. "Yes. Don't look at me . . . walk in front of me so I can talk to you."

He did so, pacing himself as they passed the burned-out stores, others operating as they had before the war.

His voice drifted back to her. "Are you really here? My daughter?"

"You must call me Greta Baur—never any other name. I'm German and have a husband by the name of Stefan who drives for the High Command."

"A husband?"

"It's not important—can you remember my name?"

He nodded and moved onward. When they came to the end of the block, he crossed to the other side of the street, and she followed.

"You left us," he said, a sudden coldness icing his voice. He stopped in front of a dry goods store. "I have one daughter."

She stood a few meters away, speaking only when others on the street had passed by. "No, you have two. I won't let you forget."

"Mother is gone—they've taken her. It's started."

She felt as if someone had punched her in the throat. The cool reserve she'd practiced for more than a year deserted her as she struggled to keep her composure. Rage smoldered in her chest, and she blinked away tears, not daring to bring her hands to her face. "I've got to get you out."

He walked on. "How?"

"Leave that to me. Who is the 'friend' I can contact in the city?"

"Janka Danek. She lives in the building diagonally across from our old apartment on Krochmalna . . . the second floor."

"Janka Danek. Second floor."

"Yes."

They walked until they were opposite the Viceroy.

"I have to work late tonight. It's not safe to be seen with anyone."

"I'm staying overnight and then back to my base."

He turned. "Let's not talk about the past . . . Greta . . . your brother and sister need your help."

"What about you . . . Papa?"

His lips quivered and then he crossed the street. Not looking back, he entered the hotel.

She ran her palms over her stomach, hoping to calm her nerves. At least she knew the name of the woman to contact. Now she could proceed with the next step of the plan.

Janka stood at the window, looking out on the bright summer day, not unlike others that she had lived through before. However, every day the war dragged on, reports of fresh horrors circulated, leaving her emotionally drained and exhausted. Herr Mueller had been right. The Aktion had begun. Every Pole in Warsaw seemed to know about it, but many had differing viewpoints. Some cheered the removal of the Jews from the ghetto—Karol could attest to that. Others, like herself, feared for the Majewskis, for the children, the elderly, and the sick. The people who weren't strong enough for work were among the first to see "resettlement" to the East—but the selection was random as well. Rumors swirled about what was happening to those taken away, including horrible reports that they were being gassed.

Janka could only stand at the window and wonder. Her one trip to the ghetto had shaken her. Then she had drawn on reserves of courage, only to collapse on the bed, crying, when she returned to the safety of her apartment. For weeks afterward, she'd wondered if the Nazis, and Mueller in particular, might catch up to her. The young German guard who had been so obliging at the gate might have thought to turn her in. Fearing for her own safety, and decrying her own cowardice and guilt, she'd kept to herself in the apartment, only venturing out when necessary for food, or water when the taps slowed to a trickle.

Life with Karol had become even more intolerable since her husband had befriended Mueller. She was the forgotten woman in their marriage—National Socialism, ill-gotten money, and alcohol had become Karol's three mistresses.

When she stood in front of the bathroom mirror in the morning, staring at a face that each day seemed to blossom with lines, loose flesh, dark circles under the eyes, and more strands of gray hair, she wondered what it was all for. Why not spend the day in bed and let the world resolve its own terrible problems? Wasn't that how most people survived—ignoring what was going on around them, just living quiet lives, hoping no tragedy would befall them? That's certainly what many of the Jews thought before the Nazis invaded. Hitler was just a crackpot, they reasoned, who would never have any real power. She'd even searched for Karol's gun, hoping that he might have forgotten it at home. The courage to use it on her husband had lessened, the sin of murder weighing upon her; but what of using it upon herself? Would the sin of suicide somehow be less than murder in God's eyes?

Those were the thoughts she pondered every day in front of the window, looking out at the Majewskis' old apartment, deciding whether to spend another day on such a miserable planet.

When the knock came, she had no idea who was on the other side, hearing no steps on the stairs.

Janka walked slowly to it, listening for any movement. After a second knock, she asked in Polish, "Who's there?"

"May I come in?" a woman's voice answered. "I have news of a friend."

"Who are you?"

"Greta Baur . . . but I know the Majewskis," the melancholy words came out.

Janka wondered whether to open the door, but she gathered her courage again. Besides, who but a friend would know the family anyway?

A tall young woman, dressed much like the German women who now walked Warsaw's streets, stood in front of her. The print dress of white bell flowers over a blue background, with quarter-sleeves and a white collar, was fashionable but not showy. The visitor had hair the color of summer wheat, and a tanned face that only added to her attractiveness. Janka thought the woman must have spent a great deal of time outdoors in recent months, while contrasting her own pale complexion and less vigorous figure.

They stood looking at each other for a moment, before the woman asked, "May I come in?"

"Of course," Janka said, smoothing the fabric of her house dress. She wanted to add, *Please don't mind the apartment, I haven't been the best housekeeper lately,* but was it really necessary to apologize to a stranger during a war?

Janka removed one of Karol's shirts from the couch and offered the stranger a seat. "I'd offer you something to drink, but I don't have much. Tea?"

"Actually, I'd love a cup, if you have it."

She shuffled to the stove, wishing her walk wasn't so deliberate . . . and old. Everything sapped her energy. The burner popped from the match. She poured fresh water in the kettle and placed it on the stove. "What can I do for you?" The blue flames licked the gray metal.

"A letter came to me—telling of a friend that I should contact. Janka Danek."

Of course, she thought . . . the letter Stefa sent to her sister. Could it really be? What was her name? "Stefa's sister from London . . . Hanna?"

The visitor nodded. "Yes, but you must call me Greta Baur . . . to call me Hanna would be dangerous for both of us."

Janka could hardly believe that "Greta" was sitting in front of her and felt slightly foolish and unworthy, considering the courage it must have taken for this young woman to get from London to Warsaw. However, the visitor's presence was like a bright light shining through the morose apartment. For the first time in months, Janka felt a budding sense of purpose, of hope.

"What can you tell me?" Janka asked, bringing the tea to her visitor.

"Very little, but I hope you can provide me with information."

They talked for a long time about everything that Janka had experienced since the war began: what she knew of the Majewskis, how she'd rescued Aaron twice from Nazi guards, how the family had been forced out of the apartment, meeting her brother's friend Zeev, how they'd seen the guard kill a woman who tossed bread over the wall, her failing relationship with her husband and his close association with the Nazis including Herr Mueller, and, most distressing, her last visit to the ghetto and the Nazi Aktion.

Hanna thanked her after Janka had finished.

"Tell me what you can about yourself," Janka pleaded.

Hanna told her stories of growing up in Warsaw—of swimming in the Vistula, of shopping on Krochmalna with her mother and sister, of going to synagogue, of the life she'd turned her back on, but concluded with, "I can't tell you about anything since I left."

Janka, who had taken her place on the couch next to Hanna, held the visitor's hands. "We have to help them."

"I know. That's why I'm here. I have a plan, but it will take time."

"I'll do what I can," Janka said.

Before she could say anything more, they were interrupted by a commotion on the stairs. Karol screamed at a neighbor, "Get out of my way." Janka could tell from his slurred speech he was drunk.

"It's my husband," she told Hanna, her nerves firing. There was no time to hide her visitor, as she had done with Aaron. What would Karol think of the strange woman sitting on the sofa?

"Let me talk," Hanna said. "Stay calm. Remember . . . Greta Baur." Her guest patted her black purse, as if she carried something reassuring inside it.

The key slid into the lock and the door opened. Karol stood in the doorway, his head drooping, short gasps coming from his mouth from the climb, a pistol clenched in his right hand.

Janka gasped and clasped her hands over her mouth. Her husband's blue work shirt was open, revealing a white undershirt splattered with blood. Janka looked at her visitor, who seemed unfazed by the sight.

Karol, his black hair ruffled from the usual slick pomade, leaned against the doorframe and stared at them. "Who's this?" He waved the pistol in the air in a haphazard manner. Janka feared it might go off accidentally. "What's she doing here?" he said in an insistent voice verging on anger.

Hanna rose from the couch. "I'm Greta Baur. I was talking to Frau Danek about the residents of this building. My family may be moving in . . . as others are displaced."

"Displaced?" Karol slid around the door like a snake, and slumped against it, slamming it shut.

"I answered after Greta knocked," Janka said, starting toward him. "What in God's name happened, Karol? Are you hurt?"

Karol waved her away. "Leave me alone. I need to sit down." He staggered toward the couch. Hanna lifted her purse, clutching it to her side, allowing Karol to take his place. He aimlessly pointed the pistol in Hanna's direction. "I'm not hurt . . . it's the Jews who are hurting."

"I'd prefer that you put the gun away," Hanna said.

"Who do you think you are?" Karol fumed. "Telling me what to do in my own house . . . if I wasn't so . . ." He tried to rise from the couch, but fell back. "Let me see your papers."

Hanna opened her purse. "You have no reason or any authority to ask for my papers, but because your wife has been so kind . . ." She handed them to Karol.

He slipped the pistol between a cushion and the back of the couch and squinted at the papers.

"Greta Baur . . . why are you here?" Her husband was relaxing a little now that he was settled, and the drink had reassumed its power over his mind.

"My husband, Stefan, is a driver for the High Command. With all the resettlement that's going on, apartments are opening up, even among the Polish. We wish to be in the city. This seems like a nice building."

"We're not moving," Karol said, tossing back the papers.

"So your wife told me. It seems you're in a good position here. I'm happy to know we're all in service to the Reich. Others in this building are not so fortunate."

Janka studied Hanna. She was calm, collected, sure of her story, prepared for this moment in a way that convinced even her.

"You should leave now," Karol said. "I need to sleep."

"I was on my way out when you arrived," Hanna said. "I'm sorry about your accident."

Karol smirked. "It was no accident."

Hanna shook Janka's hand and told her, "I may see you in the future."

"Not if I have anything to say about it," Karol said, stretching out on the couch.

"Good day, Herr Danek."

She was alone again with her husband. "Greta" had given her the shot of courage she needed, but it rapidly dissipated in the liquor-soaked breath and blood-spattered figure of her husband.

Karol rose on his elbows. "God damn Kraut . . . coming in here like she owns the place. Don't speak to her again. Send her away if she comes back."

Janka stood by the stove, clutching its sides, trying to control her temper. "First it was the Jews, and now it's the Germans. Who am I supposed to talk to?"

"Shut up! Pour me a drink."

Janka found the brandy bottle, which was nearly empty. It was easier to accommodate him than fight. She poured what was left into a glass and took it to him, looking down on him with pity.

"What happened?"

He rolled over, reached into his pants pocket, and withdrew a handful of cash—folded zlotys he waved in her face. "This is what happened—what keeps us going."

"I don't want to hear it."

"I'll tell you anyway," he said, his voice laden with sarcasm. "When they round up Jews in the Umschlagplatz, a few of them try to escape. It's like shooting frogs in a lily pond. The Ukrainians and I are pretty good shots. We drag the bodies away." He pointed to the stains on his shirt.

She turned away. "You disgust me."

"Fuck you! I'm keeping you alive. You should get down on your knees."

She wheeled on him. "No! If I had it in my power, I'd kick you out of this house."

He reached for the pistol. "But you don't."

She ran for the door, flung it open, and rushed down the stairs, hearing his bellows until she was safe on the street.

Running to the only refuge she knew—the church—she sat in a pew and cried. No one bothered her and no one asked what was wrong—not even the priest she'd known for years. She thought of confession, but even that made her sick to her stomach. What did she need to confess? She had done nothing wrong, except wish that she could leave her husband and Warsaw behind.

Janka sat for several hours in the quiet church before getting up the courage to return home. When she reached the apartment door, she prayed to God that Karol was either passed out from drink or dead.

CHAPTER 20

September 1942

They made a pact to stay alive, for their own sakes, pinning a slim hope on Hanna rescuing them. Izreal told them she was in Warsaw, working to get them out of the ghetto. Why not cling to that fragile longing in dire times?

Stefa cried while her father stoically reported the short reunion. Daniel and Aaron looked on with incredulity, almost skeptical of the story he told. How proud her mother would have been to know that Hanna had returned! Stefa and Daniel were filled with questions, but her father had tired easily since Perla's disappearance and would talk no more. For him, recalling the meeting with the daughter he'd rejected apparently was like opening a festering wound.

The Nazi horrors continued at a relentless pace. Stefa hadn't the emotional energy or the time to mourn her mother's death properly, which, by mid-September, seemed certain. Work was all they had to keep them safe: she at the soup kitchen; Aaron and her father still clinging to the Nazi-bloated restaurant on the Aryan side, hoping that their jobs would be saved. Her father had been happy to wash dishes and clear tables in his reduced capacity—the Nazis didn't need kosher meals. After Perla had been taken, Izreal told his family he wouldn't disappear, as some had done, because he worked on the Aryan side—the same with his son. He could think of nothing worse than deserting his children. Daniel, since resigning from the ghetto police, behaved like a wanted man, staying out of sight during the day and moving resistance munitions at night, a dangerous job. On those nights, Stefa lay awake waiting for him, praying for his safe return, squeezing the edge of the mattress as if it were Daniel's hand.

In early August, Stefa witnessed an event that brought tears to her eyes, yet filled her with an added determination to stand up to the oppressors in any way she could. On that day, the Nazis, determined to continue their Aktion, forced Janusz Korczak and the two hundred orphans under his care to the Umschlagplatz. She had watched from a secluded doorway as the bearded and bespectacled Korczak, a teacher and the director of the Jewish orphanage, marched the five kilometers to the trains with his children. Korczak comforted his charges, telling them not to be afraid of the journey they were about to take. They lined up four in a row, wearing their best clothes, rucksacks on their backs, the director leading the way, looking ahead, holding the hands of the children who walked next to him. Stefa wanted to cry out, to kill the guards who were sending these innocents to the same fate as her mother's. Such actions were useless, however. With all that she had been through, this sight, more than any other, made her stronger, drawing from her sister's strength, and Daniel and Aaron's growing resistance.

Surprisingly, Emanuel Ringelblum visited her one day at the kitchen. Walking in broad daylight had become dangerous because the Nazis randomly shot people in the street. Even she was stopped by the guards now, presenting her papers and work permit to prove her affiliation with a service agency, even going so far as to flirt with one of the guards, offering him a kiss on the cheek. Out of his sight, she promptly spat and wiped her lips. Only three people worked in the kitchen now, and the soup was nothing more than hot water with a few pieces of potato or a carrot peel thrown in. Their work had slowed because of the deportations. She knew the kitchen would close soon and her security would evaporate.

Ringelblum now looked as melancholy and scruffy as the remaining ghetto residents. His shoes were worn thin, his toes nearly bursting through the distressed leather. His tattered jacket was dotted with abrasions, small tufts of blue fabric protruding from the shoulders and sleeves. His dark eyes looked even darker today.

She had nothing to offer except hot water.

He sank into a chair and shook his head. "I've come to say good-bye, in case we never meet again."

Stefa sat beside him at the worn table that had held countless bowls of soup. "Please don't say that."

"What else am I to say? They're shooting us in the street, marching us to the trains. Did you see what happened to the orphans?"

Stefa nodded.

"That was not a death march . . . it was a wordless, organized protest against murder. Heads held high."

"I wept," Stefa said, "because there was nothing I could do."

"Resistance fighters shot the commander of the Jewish Police. The old traitor lived."

"I know." Daniel had told her, but said nothing about whether he was involved in the planning of the assassination. She was afraid to ask.

"Four thousand eight hundred Jews were deported just a few days ago. Our lives are counted in seconds—not years, months, days, or hours. We've recorded the testimony of a survivor who escaped from Treblinka. We know what the Nazis are doing there." He tapped his fingers on the table. "I hid the first part of my diary in early August. We don't have much longer. Do you have a way out?"

"Possibly, but nothing is certain yet."

"Your father and brother could escape—just disappear on the Aryan side—but problems exist there."

Stefa sighed. "Yes, Poles would turn us in for tribute; there's no safe place to hide. My father has said he won't leave us behind."

He grasped her hand. "He's an honorable man whom God will favor." He paused. "I want your diary to be hidden with the others. Have you been writing?"

She gazed into his eyes, seeing a burst of fire that leapt into them at the mention of words. "I've found it hard to write since my mother disappeared. She must be dead, but I don't want to believe it. When I pick up a pen I cry. My hand trembles and I can't go on."

He squeezed her fingers. "I heard about the film crew . . . what a despicable act in a place of holy sanctuary. It must have been horrible. Try to go on, however. Write with all the courage you can gather. Your words . . . my words . . . must live on. We *must* tell people what really happened to the Jews of Warsaw. If we are alive, I will come for your diary when the time is right . . . I have plans to leave, but not yet."

"I feel like the world has deserted us—that we're alone on an island with no food and water, surrounded by sharks."

"The darkness of the soul can be devastating—the Nazis have unleashed their most cruel weapon upon us. They've taken away our hope . . . our light." He got up from the table. "Please, take care of yourself. Get word to me somehow, or through your father, so I will know where you are, and that you are safe. Go with God, Stefa."

She watched as he left, slouching across the cobblestones, watching the doorways and the rooftops for Germans in hiding. That was how they all lived these days, since the Aktion began.

After he was gone, one of the women in the kitchen put her hand on Stefa's shoulder. "We're closing today," she told her. "At noon . . . we have no food left . . . and few to serve. We've been blessed so far, but now we must take care of ourselves."

Stefa turned and hugged the woman. "I understand." Then they cried, their thin bodies shaking like rattles against each other.

*   *   *

The loft sweltered during the summer, leaving her feeling as if she was sleeping on wet towels. Hanna kept the ceiling panel open on those warm nights. It offered the only cooling relief when a breeze circulated through the farmhouse. She wanted to sleep in the barn, but Eryk and Julia said it was unsafe if the Germans made a surprise inspection.

During those sleepless nights, vivid images plagued her: wading on the banks of the Vistula, her feet mired in mud; visions of her mother and father on the balcony at the old apartment on Krochmalna. When she moved, her feet felt as if they were stuck in concrete. She awoke anxious and tired, unable to reach her parents.

After her encounter with Janka, and the unpleasant experience with Karol, she'd slept in a hotel before returning to the Rybaks the next morning. On the outskirts of the city, a farmer had given her a lift in his horse cart. When the side road turned west toward the farmhouse, she walked the rest of the way as the cart continued on. The wizened Pole, toughened by years in the field, had refused her offer of money. Hanna, in addition to many thanks, had been prepared to offer him real coins and not the counterfeits that had dropped with her.

For several weeks, she continued to monitor Nazi activities around Leoncin, but there was little to report. The real problem was in Warsaw and the ghetto. She couldn't go to the city every day—a swelling German troop presence made it riskier than ever.

The first air drop since her arrival occurred shortly after midnight on September seventeenth, under a partly cloudy sky and a first-quarter moon. She had tended the bonfire for the plane. The drop had gone flawlessly, and she and Eryk had unloaded the containers and then burned them. Another bottle of hair lightener was included, a necessity because her supply was running out. The goods also included more counterfeit zlotys, winter clothing, and a coded message from Rita Wright, congratulating her on a "job well done," and offering condolences on Dolores's death. No mention was made of Hanna's message to "Romeo." Following Rita's instructions, Hanna read the note, dropped it into the fire, and watched it curl in a ball of yellow flame.

Rescuing her family weighed on her mind, as Poland slipped into fall. A workable plan presented a number of difficulties. There was the issue of documents. She couldn't call upon the SOE to forge them for her father, brother, and sister without tipping off the organization that she was working to get them out of Warsaw. Rita would nix that idea and consider it a direct violation of orders. Allied military personnel, pilots and soldiers, if they needed her assistance, were supposed to be her first priority.

There also was the question of what her family would use for pictures. Identification papers without photographs would result in immediate suspicion and, most likely, arrest. A crude picture pasted on the page would be an obvious tip-off. The Polish men from Briggens House were forgers as well as fighters, but to call upon them would breach conduct and might lead to an unsavory report to her boss.

How would she get her family out? What was the safest mode of travel? Where would they go? So many questions needed to be answered. Slowly, she pieced together a plan. Janka's help would be needed. The next time Eryk traveled to Warsaw, she would return to her new friend's apartment—during the day—hopefully, when Karol wasn't home.

Every day, especially after transmissions at the abandoned house, she wondered whether her family was still alive. Sometimes the tension gripped her like a vise and wouldn't let go. When it became too much, she would wander into the surrounding fields, now tinged with brown from the first frost, and think of Phillip. He was with her, holding hands, and kissing her cheek. For a brief time, those intimate thoughts lifted her spirits.

* * *

She convinced Eryk to take her to Warsaw on a cloudy October day, driving as far as they could without arousing suspicion. Attired in her new clothes, she found herself looking more like a well-dressed German than ever before. She arrived at Janka's apartment after passing by clusters of German guards. Offering a brisk *"Guten Tag,"* she walked past the soldiers, who were more interested in her looks than her identification papers.

She had no idea whether Janka was home, but a risky hand, weighted by time and uncertainty, had to be played. She climbed the stairs with vigor and knocked on the door.

Janka offered no resistance. The woman, in her plain dress and soiled shoes, seemed on the verge of giving up on life. Hanna suspected she would have to use all her powers of persuasion to draw her into the scheme, which would require Janka's total commitment. If mistakes were made, everyone would be doomed.

"Is your husband at work?" Hanna asked, and sat at the small table.

Janka studied her with sad eyes, rimmed in red, as if she had been crying that morning.

"What has he done to you?"

"Greta Baur," Janka replied solemnly. "I'm not supposed to see you. Karol will beat me if he finds you here—maybe even kill me." She lifted a cold cup of watery coffee to her lips and took a sip. "I ran from the house after you left and went to the church where we were married. I prayed that my husband was taken by liquor or death. I've never wished a person dead . . . yet I saw him on the couch, lifeless." She lifted a handkerchief from her lap and blew her nose. "He had passed out when I came home. I still feared for my life. I went to bed, and sometime later when he woke up, he came to the bedroom and fell asleep. The next morning, it was if nothing at all had happened. He took a bath, dressed, and went to work, hardly speaking to me . . . but now I know he's capable of murder."

Hanna reached across the table and clutched Janka's thin

wrist. The flesh surrounding it was loose, like that of a much older woman.

"I have a plan," Hanna said, "but I need your help and your unwavering resolve to carry it out."

Janka looked down at the worn and spotted table, but nodded.

"You're putting yourself in extreme danger . . . as am I," Hanna continued. "I'm going against my orders, but I can't let my family die. I've known that from the first time I met my superiors in London, even when I was training for this assignment. I'm still doing my job, and once my family is safe, I'll return to my duties. I've made that decision."

"What do you want me to do?"

"Let me explain. Do you have any more cold coffee?"

"Half a pot on the stove," Janka said. "Let me warm it up." She rose from the table and Hanna studied her. Janka's movements were slow, methodical, as if she'd been drugged; her general condition worried Hanna. She was so unlike Dolores, an agent filled with energy and commitment to the end of her life. Janka turned on the burner and returned to the table.

"Are you all right?" Hanna asked.

Janka exhaled, a sigh born of exhaustion and defeat. "I'm so tired . . . and I see no way out . . . for me or for the Jews. Did you know your sister called me a War Girl?"

Hanna stifled a laugh and pushed back in her chair. "My boss called me that and the name stuck. I think you're a fine example."

It was Janka's turn to laugh. "I feel as if I've failed at life—in my marriage, in my faith, in my ability to help a family who's been kind to me."

"Maybe my plan will lift your spirits."

The coffeepot hissed. Janka turned off the stove and returned with a cup. Hanna blew on the steam and the faint odor of the diluted brew reached her nostrils. Regardless, the drink cheered her under the cloudy sky and the murky confines of the apartment.

"Much of this still needs to be worked out," Hanna continued, "but keep an open mind." She rested her arms on the table and leaned toward Janka. "We have to get my family out. I believe the best way is to bribe a policeman—he has to be Polish—a Nazi guard would be harder to convince and likely to turn me in for a reward."

"What about your sister's boyfriend?"

Hanna stared at her. "What boyfriend?"

"Daniel . . . he's a ghetto policeman . . . at least he was when I met him."

Another possible spanner thrown into the works, she thought, a phrase her uncle had often used. "I didn't know my sister had a boyfriend."

Janka tapped her fingers against the cup. "You're bribing a Polish policeman so we can get them through the gate? When I visited the ghetto, the German guard was softer than the Polish policeman."

"You've been in the ghetto? That's even better. How did you do it?"

They talked for the next hour, Janka explaining how she got into the ghetto, and Hanna revealing the basics of her plan. Janka listened intently, nodding at most points, and offering her own suggestions. As their time ended, they agreed that the scheme was the best they had, but would still require several weeks of planning before it could be carried out.

"We must set a date, and two or three after, in case they don't work out," Hanna said.

"There's so much to do," Janka said, "but it might work." A spark of life flashed in her eyes, along with a faint smile.

"That's what I wanted to see," Hanna said, rising from her chair. "I've taken too much time already and I don't want another unfortunate meeting with your husband."

Janka led Hanna to the door, but then halted, her hand resting on the knob. "I have a question we haven't considered."

"Yes?"

"What about me?"

At first Hanna was unsure of what her companion was getting at, but then it struck her—Janka was right—another point she hadn't thought of. The woman was searching for a specific answer—how to get rid of Karol. "Do you want to leave your husband?"

Her response was immediate. "I don't want to stay here. I want to disappear."

She hugged Janka, anxious for a good soul who had been mistreated and maligned and was now offering her life, at great risk, for a Jewish family. "We will come up with something."

Hanna descended the stairs. *This is why Rita didn't want me to get involved with my family. Now I have four lives in my hands in addition to my own. My mother always said, "Your father will know what to do." Now I have to outsmart Rita, my father, and Janka's husband.*

She stepped into the cool air, glad to be out of the apartment. A short distance down Krochmalna, two German guards stood at an intersection. *Confidence! Confidence and a good plan will carry us through.* Thinking in German, she walked toward the men.

"Be quiet . . . listen," Daniel warned her.

Stefa cocked her head, listening as silence took over the attic. "It's just a dog howling." The temperature outside was near freezing, but it provided blessed relief for the work they were undertaking in the musty space. The wind rattled against the roof.

"Exactly," Daniel said. "How long has it been since you've heard a dog? Listen . . ."

The wretched sound tore at her heart. The call that rose and fell was not of an animal in pain but of one lost to the world, as if it were the only one of its species left on earth—a mournful cry of loss that pierced her body and soul. Then, the sharp but distant sound of a train whistle entered her ears, reminding her of losing her mother, Daniel's parents, and, as they had just found out from a Jewish policeman, Mrs. Rosewicz, who had been taken from Pawia Street.

Daniel bowed his head and looked away, as if fighting off tears. "The dog is dying . . . like we are dying . . . alone." He slumped against the sloping roof line. "I'm sorry. I'm so tired of 'holding up.'"

"Let's finish," she said, trying to soothe him. "It's late."

"This plank has to fit between the two attics so we can connect them, and we have to make sure the Nazis can't see it."

"That's all?" Stefa asked, trying to get him to smile. He turned. Like everyone else in the ghetto, except for the few who kowtowed to the Germans, Daniel had grown thinner, eyes darker, his black hair thicker and bushier than it had ever been. There was little time for grooming these days. She had even left the bottle of face cream at the old ghetto apartment when they'd abandoned it.

After the Germans had eased the deportations for unknown reasons, the family had moved to one large room at the top of a three-story building at the far west end of Miła Street. The previous tenants apparently had met their fates at the Umschlagplatz. Izreal and Aaron still worked and had to show their permits daily. Stefa and Daniel had escaped the two daily trains to Treblinka by outmaneuvering the Germans, keeping one step ahead, concealing themselves successfully with other members of the underground. They lived their lives like moles, keeping to themselves as much as possible, burrowing in to escape detection.

The original 3.4-square-kilometer area of the ghetto had shrunk by more than half as Jews were "resettled" to the East. The Nazis had "encouraged" everyone to move to the new designated areas through strong-arm tactics and brutal murders. That way they could better control the dwindling Jewish population. Daniel had anticipated this and found the new space, cautioning the family to take only what they could carry to their new home so they wouldn't arouse suspicion. With attic access and a semi-covered outdoor crawl space to the building next door, they might evade Nazi raids. At least that was what he hoped.

Daniel handed the oil lamp to Stefa. "The trick is to make it look as if there's nothing strange going on with the building." He opened the lone window and a rush of cold air poured over them. "Shield the lamp." The building faced southwest, but the north wind wrapped around its corner. The unheated attic was as frigid as the night.

Stefa cupped her hands around the globe holding the precious oil. Daniel grabbed a plank and, hoisting it, stretched his body out the window. He positioned the wood toward the house to the east and worked several minutes before coming back inside. His cheeks and nose glowed crimson from the cold.

"Thank God, this building has a cornice and eaves. Otherwise, we couldn't get out of this attic. That's enough for tonight. I'll test it tomorrow."

"Are you sure it's sturdy enough to support us?"

"You have to crawl. You can't stand up. The only one I'm worried about is your father. If you slip over the eave, it's a long fall to the street."

At the mention of her father, Stefa's mood shifted to despair. She had been worried about his recent behavior since Perla had been taken. Everyone knew what was going on at Treblinka. Only those lucky enough to escape, who made their way back to the ghetto because it was the only place they knew, lived to tell about the murders—the gassings that took place within minutes of stepping off the train. Izreal had become quiet as the months dragged on. He spoke little, had no interest in the Sabbath or ceremony, and offered no help or advice to anyone. He dressed for work and then returned home for another day. Stefa was certain that he had lost the will to live.

The new apartment didn't help either. Nearly everything had been stripped from it. Anything left was useless. One fireplace heated the room. Cooking had to be done in pots placed in the fire, if sufficient fuel could be found. They lived on the scraps

Aaron was able to smuggle out of the Palais—and even those were drying up as the Nazis put pressure on the Polish owner to get rid of "his Jews."

Two windows looked out on Miła Street. A fair amount of sun poured through them on cloudless days. Daniel had picked the apartment for its possibilities, however, not for its light or interior design. A small folding ladder, which was attached to a ceiling panel, connected the attic to the main room. Through the attic's single window, one could crawl across the eaves for a short distance and emerge in the attic next door through an unlocked window. If one was fortunate enough to make it down the stairs in that building, a secret bunker, under construction, awaited. Daniel had discovered all this from his connections in the Jewish Fighting Organization, the ŻOB.

As soon as they'd left their previous ghetto apartment, the ŻOB had moved the ammunition from the courtyard hiding place. None of it had ever been used. All of the weapons had been safely transferred to other secured sites, with only one casualty—a brave member who was shot to death by the Germans when he was caught with a cache of pistols.

Stefa hoped that Hanna's promise to her father would be fulfilled, but each day was like an hourglass with the sand tumbling in a cataract toward doom. The deportations had abated, but the random violence and the killings had not. No one was safe.

"Listen . . ." Daniel cautioned again. "Put out the lamp."

Stefa twisted the burner dial and the flame died, plunging the attic into darkness.

Pleas in Polish. Orders shouted in German. Hurried steps. A staccato volley of shots.

Silence, after the screams.

They moved closer to each other, Stefa barely able to breathe because of the panic settling over her like a paralysis.

Daniel motioned her toward the window, opening it slowly with a slight creak.

The steps they had heard on the street were climbing the stairs and soon would be at the apartment. Fortunately, her father and brother were at work. So little was in the room, the Germans might assume that no one lived there. They had been sleeping on the floor, covered only by thin blankets and using rolled-up clothes as pillows. The hearth was cold. They only made a fire before they went to bed to keep from freezing to death.

No one knocked—the Nazis opened the door and stepped inside, their heavy boots echoing through the room.

God, please don't let them look at the ceiling. Stefa prayed, clutching her hands together. Daniel, visible only from the pale light that filtered through the window, looked calm in comparison, his face stern and unshaken by fear. She wondered if he was as jumpy inside as she felt.

The men started and stopped. The Germans had no chest of drawers or wardrobe to rummage through, no tables or chairs to overturn, so the inspection was quiet, without rancor. Perhaps they believed that the few belongings still in the room belonged to those already sent to the Umschlagplatz. Izreal had hidden the family silver, the money from the stairwell hiding place, the menorah, and his knives under a floorboard.

A German officer shouted from the street. The men left the room and descended the stairs. Stefa and Daniel sat for a half hour waiting, listening, for the soldiers to return. They didn't.

When they could at last breathe somewhat easier, Daniel closed the window and crawled in the dark toward the ladder.

"They're gone . . . for now," he said.

"They'll be back," Stefa replied. "How can we go on like this?"

"At least we have an escape plan, along with others like us . . . working to save our lives."

She had met those others on several nights when Daniel had invited her to clandestine meetings. There was Mordechai, who seemed to be in control of the group, a handsome young man with wide-set, inquisitive eyes, sensuous lips, and a head of black hair as rich and thick as Daniel's; a young woman known as Sarenka, with high cheekbones and thin eyelashes over dark eyes, who also seemed to be in command; Moshe, Antek, and others whose names she couldn't remember. The names weren't important. The cause, the desire to live, the will to resist, fueled their zeal.

Sarenka had stated defiantly to the group, "We will not go like sheep to the slaughter." Stefa had cheered her words, but had shivered at the meaning behind them. Everyone wanted to believe there was a way out, that the Allies would come to their rescue, but at the end of 1942 the war had been going on for more than three years with little indication that Hitler would relinquish his quest for power or his plan to exterminate the Jews.

Daniel put his ear to the panel and listened before lowering the ladder. Hearing nothing, he climbed down, leaving it extended in case they had to use it again. Holding on to the lamp, she followed him into the cold darkness. Daniel sought to reassure her that everything would be all right—that they would find their way out of the ghetto that had entrapped them.

She didn't believe him. Even as he spoke, his words sounded false, as if he had made them up to soothe her. When she looked at him in the stark light of day—when she could see into his eyes and truly see into his soul—she saw more than a struggle for survival. The fires of revenge burned deep inside him, equal to the will to live. Daniel sought out fighters who would take revenge as well as save lives.

Footsteps again sounded on the stairs—but the first of these trudged, followed by a lighter step. Stefa recognized them as coming from her father and brother. Daniel lit the lamp as they came to the door.

Izreal stood bathed in the flickering yellow light, Aaron behind him.

Something was wrong and Stefa knew it from his father's pained expression, which, of late, had been placid to the point of madness.

Aaron stepped around him and, sighing, sank to the floor near them. "We've been fired and told never to return to the Palais."

Stefa stared at her brother, knowing full well the consequences of their dismissal: no more scraps; two more bodies to hide from the Nazis.

"After all my years of service, I was told the Germans don't want Jews touching their food," Izreal said, sidling into the room and settling near his blanket.

An idea struck her as she tried to see some good in the situation. "Father, now you and Aaron can walk out of the ghetto to the Aryan side. The Nazis will never know the difference because you won't be missed at the restaurant." She knew the opportunity had been there all along, but her father had returned home each day after work. Stefa had never doubted that her brother would remain because he was eager to fight.

"I would never leave you and Daniel," he said. "I would never desert my family."

"I wouldn't either," Aaron added. "I'm glad you found this place," he said to Daniel. "It's a blessing."

"And a curse," Daniel said. "The Nazis were here tonight. We hid in the attic."

Izreal's breath caught, and he choked back a sob. Stefa scooted next to her father and put her arms around him.

In the past, she would have asked him what to do, what solution he would think of to ease their pain or free them from their predicament. She had never seen him so tired, weak, and defeated.

She had no more tears and could only lean her head against his shoulder and pray that God would provide the answer—either a way out of the ghetto or—no, she didn't want to think about *it*.

She wondered whether they would be following her mother in a final journey to Treblinka.

PART 5

CHAPTER 21

January 1943

Janka was walking on Krochmalna one Sunday morning in mid-month when someone tapped her shoulder. The jab was unexpected and she flinched, pivoting sharply to see who was behind her.

The man behind her stopped, staring, awaiting some sign of recognition. When none came, he moved closer and whispered, "Mrs. Danek . . . it's me . . . Zeev."

She drew back, assessing him in the gray light. Flecks of snow swirled around them like ash in the wind. She'd hoped to hear from Hanna, but had never expected to see the boy she'd bought candy for so long ago.

He was different now, a bit taller and sturdier than she remembered. Even though his body and face were obscured by a heavy jacket and brim cap, he seemed stronger and fitter. His brown eyes sparkled with life. A rosy hue flushed what she could see of his face; a light beard traced his chin and cheeks.

"Walk with me," he said, as if issuing a command. When they had first met, she had requested the same of him.

"I'm on my way to church," she said, "but I will walk with you that far."

"Good," he said, walking near the curb in a slow and deliberate pace like a soldier.

"You're looking well," she said. "Much better than the last time I saw you."

"I'm treated well."

Janka knew they were dancing around each other, he testing her and she wary of him. It had been so long—had his loyalties shifted?

"Treated?" she asked, as they passed empty shops.

"How are you?" he answered, avoiding her question. "Have you seen the Majewskis?"

"Yes, some months ago."

A broad smile spread across his face. "Then you've done better than I. I've seen Aaron from a distance . . . we even waved to each other once, but he was with his father. They've disappeared . . . but I think they're alive."

Janka stopped near the entrance of a clock repair shop and stood across from him. "Can we talk freely?"

Zeev put his hand over his heart. "I'm working with partisans now, sometimes in Warsaw, but mostly in the Parczew Forest. It's a good job in exchange for food and shelter." He paused. "I'm used to shouldering a pistol under my coat—but not today. If the Nazis searched me, I'd be dead. I feel naked without it."

"You have weapons?"

"Rifles, pistols, grenades, firebombs. Whatever we can get. We're supplying weapons to the ghetto, but it's slow and difficult."

"I pray to God the Majewskis are still alive, but so many have been deported."

"To a place called Treblinka. They are taken off the trains and gassed by the thousands."

She closed her eyes and exhaled. Were her friends dead? Maybe that was the reason Hanna hadn't contacted her.

"So, you don't know if they are alive? That's why I wanted to see you." His voice dropped to a whisper, but she could hear him clearly. "The fighters are building tunnels out of the ghetto. A few have even escaped by the sewers. Some have been captured . . . and killed. But the Germans don't like wading through sewers. They prefer to get our friends when they rise to the surface."

"Are there any Polish policeman who might accept a bribe to get people out?"

"Maybe. Why?"

"I can't tell you why because I'm not certain of the plan, but it concerns the Majewskis."

He thought for a moment. "A Pole named Jan—a member of the Blue Police," Zeev said. "I've heard rumors. He commands a steep price, but I can contact him."

Janka extended her hand and Zeev shook it—a gesture that felt like the closing of a deal between them.

"He must be at one of the smaller entrances, not the main gate," Janka said.

Zeev nodded. "I'll find him."

"Leave a note with his name and the price he commands at the church," she continued. "Slip it under the wooden foot of the next to last pew. I'll check every day."

"No." His eyes focused on her, his expression seared by determination.

"No?" she responded, taken aback by his refusal.

"I will on one condition. You must tell me the plan. I want to help them get out."

She knew Zeev would come to her aid. "All right. Look for me on the street—or in church. I'm never far from the apartment. I'll contact you as soon as I know what's going on."

"I'll watch for you. Look for the note soon."

They left the clock shop. Zeev walked toward Janka's apartment, while she continued on to church.

Stefa wondered how anyone outside the ghetto, even those Poles like Janka who lived only a short distance away, could have any sense of what was going on inside their hellish prison.

Winter landed hard upon them, and those Jews who remained lived on the possessions of those who had been displaced during the Aktion, even the few parcels of food left behind. They sold

the clothing, bedding, books, or household items they had con-
fiscated. Words had even been created to describe these activities: *shabreven*, taking the valuables; and *tshukhes*, selling them
to other Jews or people outside the ghetto—an operation taken
at great risk to the seller. It was illegal now to be in the "old"
sections of the ghetto. Jews caught on those streets were shot.

Wooden buildings disappeared almost overnight, for firewood. The Germans didn't care about the destruction. They
knew that self-preservation in the ghetto was a futile exercise.
No one knew how many Jews remained after the previous year's
deportations. Some said fifty thousand; others thought the total
less, perhaps thirty thousand. However, no one could deny that
the ghetto was smaller, the streets emptier than they had ever
been since the Warsaw Jews and those from the country had
been forced into the ghetto in 1940.

Despair ruled this small pocket of life in Warsaw, draining
Stefa and those around her. The wan faces, the gaunt bodies
appeared as ghosts when they walked the streets, mere shadows
of themselves, blending with the dreary sky and drab buildings.
Typhus still raged and people died daily of hunger and cold. For
sport, the Nazis shot those who displeased them, no matter how
small the infraction.

Izreal took the menorah from its hiding place in early December to celebrate Hanukkah, but hid it during the day for fear
it would be destroyed by the Nazis. The candle stubs rescued
from the restaurant were extinguished if any clatter rose on the
street at night. Everyone was in the apartment each evening for
the lighting.

Izreal recited the prayers, but his voice was dull and timid,
unlike the dedications spoken in years past. He faltered on the
words, "Led them safely through all dangers," and sobbed when
he said, "We thank Thee also for the miracles, for the redemp-
tion, for the mighty deeds and saving acts, wrought by Thee,
as well as for the wars Thou didst wage for our fathers in days
of old, at this season." When their father could go no further,
Aaron finished the prayer he and the family had heard so many

times before. Daniel had rescued a half bottle of wine, which everyone shared—that was the extent of the celebration.

One night during the festival, upon Mordechai's orders, Daniel retrieved two Błyskawica submachine guns made from spare parts, as well as clips and three grenades. The weapons were lifted through a rear window using a rope and basket provided by a resistance member. Removing another section of flooring, Daniel stored them next to the stashed silver.

For days and nights, they sat with little to do except wait, listening to the sounds of gunfire that echoed down the street—anxiously expecting the next deportation as the rumors flew. Aaron brought a few potatoes to the apartment, along with flour that Stefa baked into bread. Her brother wouldn't say where he got it. She wondered if it had come from his friend Zeev.

Their waiting ended on the morning of January eighteenth.

They were finishing breakfast when the Germans called everyone to assemble in the courtyard behind the building. The hearth still crackled in the fireplace. They dropped their soup tins and rushed to the attic ladder. Daniel pulled the rope and the steps swung down.

"What about weapons?" Aaron asked.

"No time," Daniel answered. He directed Stefa to the ladder first and then Izreal. Aaron followed, with Daniel the last to ascend. When they were all in the attic, he hoisted the ladder and secured the rope so it was out of sight to anyone below. They huddled near the window in case they had to crawl across the eaves to the building next door. Daniel had tested the planks several times, always making sure the adjoining window was unlocked.

Stefa remained strangely calm—hiding had become routine. She'd prepared herself for such times, much like the practice of going to a bomb shelter. To her surprise, the Nazis raced through the building but didn't stop to examine the apartments. How frustrated they must be, she thought, that people aren't going willingly to their deaths.

From the attic window, they could see the building across the street and the rooftops to the southeast. Protests and screams followed, however, as people were rounded up indiscriminately instead of gathering in the courtyard.

"We can't just sit and watch," Aaron whispered. "This has got to stop."

"It will . . . it will," Daniel cautioned. "Mordechai said the time is near."

Izreal lowered his head as if praying. The thin January light spread across his face.

Stefa studied the circle gathered around the window, as if she was looking at a painting: her brother, fiery, ready to go to battle against the Nazis; Daniel, cautious, waiting for the right moment, like a commander planning an attack; her father, hunched over, still unsure what plan God had in store for the Jews and uncertain whether people should fight, thinking the Creator might look unfavorably upon His children as murderers. What secrets did her father harbor? Aaron had hinted that his father had saved his life, but he hadn't told her the story.

They sat for an hour while the screams and shots echoed throughout the ghetto. Then, a man's voice called out from below. "Daniel . . . are you here?"

It was Mordechai.

Daniel lowered the ladder and they found him, looking ruffled but exhilarated, his wide-set eyes burning with intent, sweat beading on his forehead despite the cold day. "We're going after them. No more sacrifices. The Germans will see their own blood spilled."

Daniel ripped up the floorboards and reached for the two submachine guns and clips, handing one to Aaron. "Load it. Give it to Stefa. Be careful, it doesn't have a safety."

Aaron flinched. "Why Stefa? I should carry it."

"You take two grenades," Daniel ordered. "You can throw farther than she can."

"I'll meet you on the street," Mordechai said. "The Nazis

are conducting a sweep, forcing us to the Umschlagplatz. Watch for them in doorways and deserted buildings." He raced out the door and down the stairs.

Aaron loaded the weapon and reluctantly handed it to Stefa, telling her to keep her finger off the trigger.

"I don't know what to do with this," she said.

"Keep your hands off the trigger until you're ready to fire," Aaron said. "Place it firmly against your shoulder, aim, and pull. It has a bit of a kick, but it won't knock you off your feet if you stand firm. Aim for the heart . . . or the head. That's as much training as you're going to get."

Daniel told Izreal, "Replace the boards. Hide in the attic if you must, but make sure the rope is hidden. If the Nazis come after you, crawl along the eave to the next building." He hugged Izreal and then kissed him on the cheek. "Pray for us."

Aaron took two grenades, placing one in each coat pocket. Daniel and Stefa put on their coats and carried the guns by their sides, partially concealing them with their arms.

"I'll go first," Daniel said. "Stefa behind me. Aaron, keep an eye above and behind us."

As they started for the door Izreal called out, his eyes brimming with tears. "I must say good-bye to my son and daughter. I prayed that this day would never come, but wiser men than I, rabbis in fact, have wondered if God has deserted us. How could we have stopped the slaughter? Another rabbi has said we have a new commandment: 'We must save our own lives.'" He looked at Aaron. "You are right, my son. God will not save us unless we help Him." He hugged his children and then went to work on replacing the floorboards.

Daniel led the way down the stairs.

Soon, they were on Miła Street, headed toward the Umschlagplatz. Stefa kept her hand poised as they hurried along. Both Daniel and Aaron were doing their jobs—Daniel looking ahead to the doorways and down the street; her brother looking for Nazis on the rooftops or approaching from behind.

As Stefa half walked, half ran, down Miła, she felt as if she had left her body, a feeling she'd experienced only a few times before when the family was deep in prayer and her soul, her inner being, had risen from her body and floated into the ether. The buildings rushed past, her feet moving independently from her form. Even though she knew the neighborhood, it appeared before her like the first time, foreign and new in its aspect.

When they reached the intersection of Miła and Zamenhofa, Daniel waved his hand, directing them to a narrow alley between two buildings. About a dozen German soldiers appeared from a side street and ran north on Zamenhofa toward the Umschlagplatz. Daniel hushed them as they crowded into the narrow passageway.

At first, an empty silence covered them. Everyone, except the resistance, was in hiding, keeping as far away from the Nazis as possible. A little more than a minute later, as Daniel was about to move forward, shouting, gunfire, and screams broke out from the direction of the train yard.

Stefa stood behind Daniel and looked over his shoulder, beyond the bricks and stones that gave them protection. More German soldiers ran past them in response to the fighting, unaware of their hiding place.

"It's a massacre," Daniel whispered. The shots rang out in bursts, followed by periods of silence.

"We have to help them," Aaron said, pushing forward.

Daniel held him back. "Do you want to die? We're outnumbered. We'd be walking into a deathtrap."

Aaron pushed Daniel's hands away. "I'll go alone. Give me the gun."

Stefa clutched the weapon against her body. "No. Think of Father . . . losing all his children in one day." She shook her head and looked at her brother, who was so eager to join the fight. What of Aaron's future? He would be the man carrying on the family name. "You must protect Father and keep the Majewskis alive. You alone can do that."

She tried to judge what her brother was thinking—if what

she was telling him made any sense. His face twisted in thought, a mixture of anger, frustration, and remorse.

The gunfire stopped for a moment, but was followed by shouts—all in German.

"We'll fight another day," Daniel said, peering around the stones, then stepping out and leading them back to the apartment.

The adrenaline driving her had lessened a bit and she was more aware of what was around her. They were on Miła, about halfway home, when they heard, "*Halt. Hände hoch.*"

"No," Daniel said, pushing them both into the doorway of an apartment building. The Germans couldn't see them unless they were standing in front of the structure.

A spray of bullets thunked into the wood over their heads, showering plaster dust and splinters on them. A sliver struck the skin below Stefa's right eye, cutting her cheek. She brushed the blood away.

"Kneel down," Daniel told her. "Fire when I do."

She nodded and did as he ordered, pressing the Błyskawica against her shoulder.

Another round of bullets whizzed past them, the surrounding doorway still protecting them. Daniel turned to Aaron. "Lob one to the east."

"Gladly," Aaron said. He took one of the impact grenades, and reaching over them, tossed it high into the air toward the Nazis.

The unsuspecting Germans, more aware of the device hurtling toward them than their enemies, lurched forward as the grenade exploded behind them. Three of them, looking astonished and somewhat frightened, rushed forward, confused that the Jews had such weapons as well as the temerity to fight back.

The shockwave thrust them into Stefa's sight. Before Daniel had a chance to fire, she pulled the trigger and the clip rattled off its deadly volley, striking the three men in the chest. Shivering like puppets, their coats blown apart, they collapsed in the street. One raised his head, trying to get a shot off into the doorway. Daniel finished him with two rounds to the head before he could fire.

Daniel urged Stefa and Aaron into the street, looking at the bodies as they passed. The acrid smoke from the grenade lingered in the air, obscuring their escape from eyes to the east. Running as fast as they could, they arrived at the apartment in a short time.

Izreal sat near the ladder, his head bowed.

The blood from Stefa's cut had stained her cheek and coat.

Her father looked at her with pity and pointed to the window. "I saw what happened . . . after the explosion."

Stefa sank to the floor as Daniel and Aaron concealed the weapons. She was numb and her tongue felt so thick in her mouth she wondered if she could speak. Finally, she said, "I killed three men, Papa."

He looked at her, the pity in his eyes turning to uncertainty. Izreal had seen the deadly actions of his daughter, the burst of gunfire . . . the truth of his daughter's confession.

"I know," he said. "God will judge us as He favors. Now we live as we must."

He rose, came to her, and put his arms around her.

She cried on his shoulder as she had never cried before.

Janka had gone to the church for several weeks after meeting Zeev and finally was rewarded with a slip of paper tucked underneath the foot of the pew. Janka imagined the young resistance fighter, settled upon the kneeler, a Jew doing his best to imitate a Catholic, bowing his head and furtively slipping his hand to the floor. Perhaps he had learned to genuflect and recite the rosary as well.

The note was written in Polish and said only two things: Jan—and a required payment of twenty thousand zlotys for each person leaving the ghetto. The time and date would have to be worked out. The Gęsia Street gate across from the Jewish Cemetery on the northwest side of the ghetto would be the departure point. Janka knew it was nearby. A fast walk down

Okopowa Street would lead the escapees to Krochmalna and her apartment. From there she had no idea what would happen.

One day in February, Janka spotted Hanna keeping pace with her on the other side of the street. The SOE agent crossed it and was soon by her side. They walked together for a time without talking, observing the muted life of a city still in the throes of winter.

Hanna wore a hat and wool coat, her gloved hands protected by a fur muff. Janka wondered if a pistol was concealed inside it. The cold wind ruffled their coats and slashed against their faces, turning their cheeks red. It was uncomfortable outside, but as safe a place as any to talk.

"I was worried that I might not hear from you again," Janka finally said.

"I'm sorry, but I couldn't get away," Hanna replied. "I can't tell you everything—but there are some things you need to know." She paused. "Some reports have come in from the ghetto and they aren't good. Several resistance members were killed in a fight in January. We think the leader, a man named Mordechai, survived. Nazis were killed and, in reprisal, more Jews were deported."

Fidgeting with her collar, Janka drew it close around her neck. "Have you heard from your family?"

"No." Hanna stopped and looked in the window of a dry goods store. Only a few bolts of colored cloth sat on display. She tilted her head toward Janka. "The Germans are amassing troops near Warsaw. I expect the Wehrmacht will deal with the remaining Jews before being transferred to the Eastern Front. Hitler will fight to the last man. The Red Army has defeated the Germans at Stalingrad."

Janka touched Hanna's shoulder. "That's wonderful news."

"Yes, but if they fail, the Nazis will destroy everything they leave behind—including Warsaw."

They moved on from the window, walking to the church. Janka led Hanna to the pew where Zeev had placed the note and lowered the kneeler. "Do as I do," Janka said.

They knelt side by side, looking at the unpretentious altar and the large wooden crucifix that hung over it. Two other women, both older, prayed near the front of the church.

Janka whispered, "I have a contact. He's found a policeman named Jan who can get your family out . . ."

"Yes."

"Twenty thousand zlotys each at the Gésia Street gate. That's a fortune."

Hanna turned, her gaze intent and determined. "The money isn't important. Do you trust this contact?"

"His name is Zeev. He's a friend of your brother and a member of the Polish resistance. He sought me out long ago."

The silver-haired priest entered the nave from a door near the altar. Janka had known him for years from Mass and confession, but wondered if he would find it odd to see her sitting next to a stranger. She couldn't worry about it now—any obvious discomfort or a sudden departure would seem suspicious. He walked by them with folded hands, giving Janka a nod on his way to the narthex.

"Listen carefully," Hanna said. "Two dates: March twentieth, the start of Purim; or April seventeenth, before Passover—shortly after midnight. If the first doesn't work for any reason, we'll try the second. I'll pay for their release and escort them from the gate to your apartment, where they can change into fresh clothes. My partner, Eryk, and I will hide them in the back of his truck and transport them as far south of the city as we can. From there, they'll go on foot until they make contact with Slovakian partisans. I'll return to the farm with Eryk . . . or to Warsaw to get you."

Janka tensed. "Karol will be there . . ."

"Karol will sleep in the arms of a fine bottle of French cognac, which was dropped to me a week ago, along with sleeping powder."

Janka stared at the crucifix. The altar was dark, except for the light from a few candles on either side of it, the carved body of Christ flickering in and out of shadow in the wavering light.

"It sounds dangerous."

"It is, but it has to work." Hanna pressed her hand against Janka's. "It *is* dangerous, but you'll have a weapon."

"I will?"

"Your husband has a gun. Steal it." Hanna paused. "I must contact my family. They have to know the dates and where to go."

"Zeev will do it," Janka said. "And I'm sure he'll help you rescue them from the ghetto. I'll find him." The plan was coming together slowly in her mind; however, Janka hadn't answered the question about what she was to do after the Majewskis were freed. Getting Karol to drink the cognac would be easy, but what if he somehow awoke and found the escapees in the apartment? As much as she hated him and often wished him dead, she could never kill him. When he finally awakened—the next morning—he would know that he'd been drugged—that she had done something terrible. Maybe she could travel the long distance to her parents' home, but being there would be dangerous as well.

The candles brightened, pushing their flames sideways, flickering and sputtering as if a breeze had rushed over them from an open door.

She couldn't stay at home after helping the Majewskis—not with Karol, not with Nazis like Herr Mueller prowling about. What about the church?

Janka stared at the cross and searched for an answer.

"Tell Zeev I'll pay him," Hanna said. "A lot of money." Then she told Janka the sum was counterfeit.

A few days later, Zeev stood on Krochmalna, hoping to learn if Janka had gotten his message. He hadn't found her at the church, so he walked toward the apartment and spotted her coming from the direction of the ghetto.

She smiled as they approached each other, which he thought was odd. Janka had always been so serious, so defeated by life, he wondered what had caused the change.

They met near her apartment, as if they were two friends casually conversing.

"I'm finally doing something good for this world—something I can be proud of," she told him. "I'm glad you're watching out for me. Other people are looking out for me, too." She grasped his hand and shook it.

"You got my message."

"Yes . . . we need to get word to the Majewskis about the plan. I can't risk going back to the ghetto again. Can you do it?"

He scratched the light stubble on his chin, uncertain that he could make such a commitment. "It's dangerous now . . . more so than ever."

A shadow crossed Janka's face. "How much money is your life worth? How much is anyone's life worth?" She rubbed her thumb across the top of her fingers, as if she was smoothing money in her palm. "You'll be paid more money than you've ever seen."

His face brightened.

"There's only one problem—it's counterfeit."

Zeev forced back a laugh that might have doubled him over, had he taken the chance to be so bold. He composed himself. "That's not a problem. I'm happy to do anything that will screw the economy of the General Government."

They stood in the sun, relishing the warmth that touched them. Janka told him the dates and the specifics of the plan. He absorbed it all, strategizing about how he would get into the ghetto and find the Majewskis. He needed money for bribes.

He left Janka and went on his way toward the ghetto—time to get in touch with Jan again, if he could. The best way to get to the policeman was to pass him zlotys.

As he walked away, he found himself smiling as well. *I'm doing something good—something I can be proud of.*

He picked up his step as the ghetto wall came into view.

CHAPTER 22

The family sat in their apartment in the tepid winter light, taking a break from the construction work on the bunker next door. They ate bread coated with a thin layer of currant jelly, and were happy to have salvaged the treat from a woman who escaped the ghetto.

The bunker walls were brick and sometimes covered in what Stefa described as "slime," as if lime, white and viscous and fed by the dampness, was leaching out of the cracks in the cement. The remains of a wooden bookcase that came up to an adult's belly formed a screen between an exterior wall and the toilet that had been rigged to the building's plumbing. One could sit on the seat and see the others in the room—it was best to bow one's head and look away. The cramped world of bunkers, apartments, and boxcars lacked privacy.

Mattresses strewn about, the wooden frames of cots held together with coarse fabric, constituted the beds on which they slept. A small electric plate provided the only surface for cooking and had to be plugged into one of the conduits that provided electricity for the building. Sometimes the current was off, but occasionally it sparked on. A crude stove, vented into the wall, was the other alternative for cooking, but smoke often clouded the room, causing everyone to choke. Someone had brought in a dozen eggs that sat in a bowl near the hot plate.

Abandoned blankets and fabrics that draped the mattresses

and chairs were the only comforts, but even they succumbed to the musty dampness. A resident could find books on a table or look at wrinkled political posters attached to the damp walls. Those items and muted conversation were the extent of entertainment.

Securing the bunker was the task that all four of them, including Izreal, had been working on for a couple of weeks. The denizens emerged by pushing through a wooden floor, after tunneling under similar panels laid in the narrow passageway between the buildings. The descent was damp, dark, and not for the claustrophobic. The sensation felt like slithering into a black cave on your stomach, not knowing where you were going until you either rammed your skull into a wall of compacted earth or touched the boards above your head.

Stefa, while working in the bunker, often thought of how far her family had fallen since they'd left her girlhood home on Krochmalna. But then she chastised herself for even considering such thoughts—she had suffered, her family had suffered, but many had fared far worse. Whole families had been obliterated by the Nazis.

Their suffering now was the worst so far in their years-long incarceration in the ghetto—a tedious slide toward oblivion, mixed into a terrible cocktail of boredom, anxiety, and terror.

When they heard the faint steps on the stairs, no one panicked. No Nazi, no SS member would walk with such a slow and muted pace. A diminutive knock sounded on the door. Daniel opened it.

Emanuel Ringelblum stood there, his beard a bit heavier than when Stefa had seen him last. His clothes, while in better shape than most in the ghetto, reflected the years of use that deadened their luster. Yet, an air of quiet dignity infused his person—a quality that the Nazis couldn't extinguish from his soul.

"May I come in?" he asked, as if it was really necessary. The question was a requirement of his breeding and a testament to his spirit.

Izreal rose from the floor and embraced the man whom he'd

met years ago but had seen infrequently. "Welcome, my friend," he said and invited him in. "We don't have chairs, so you'll have to sit on the floor."

"Thank you, Izreal. Blessings upon you and your family, but I can't stay long. I've come for Stefa's diary."

Stefa wiped the breadcrumbs from her fingers, somewhat surprised that Ringelblum would show up for her book. His pursed lips, clenched fists, and dark eyes told her that something unfortunate was happening.

"The time has come for it to be hidden with others," he continued. "We all know what's happening." He lowered his gaze, as if admitting defeat. "I've made arrangements for my family to leave the ghetto. A couple on the Aryan side has agreed to take us in."

"We may leave as well," Daniel said, "but we can't be sure. In the meantime, we're working on a bunker."

"I admire you," Ringelblum said. "My family—"

"You do what you must," Izreal interjected. "God will help you."

Aaron coughed from his corner near the window and bit into his bread.

"I'll get my book," Stefa said, walking to the floorboards where the rifles were stashed. She lifted them, removed the diary, and handed it to Ringelblum. "Do you know where it will be hidden?"

"Only I and a few others will know, for obvious reasons, but most likely on Nowolipki Street."

Stefa nodded. "We all wish blessings upon your family." She kissed the diary. "And upon this book, that it may live forever and tell the story of the Jews of Warsaw."

He took it from her. "It is an honor. I will hold you in my prayers—"

He was interrupted by a face that peered around the half-opened door.

"My God . . . Zeev!" Aaron jumped up from the floor and rushed to him. They fell into each other's arms, and after a long embrace, Aaron turned to his family with a smile, patting his friend's shoulders. "Everyone, meet Zeev." He could hardly catch his breath as he studied his friend from head to toe. "You look wonderful . . . much better than the rest of us. What have you been doing?"

Zeev stepped back, somewhat apprehensive at first, but Aaron dispelled his friend's fears by introducing him to each person. To Emanuel, Zeev said, "Mr. Ringelblum, it's a pleasure to meet you. I've heard of your work in the ghetto."

"And what of your work?" Ringelblum asked.

"I'm a fighter, now," Zeev said, straightening, holding his head high. "I know the forest and every street in the ghetto. I'm doing something important, too."

Stefa could see that Aaron was holding on to Zeev's words like gold as they came from his mouth. Izreal would have to hold him back from joining Zeev as a fighter.

"Sit," Aaron said. "Tell us."

"I will leave you," Ringelblum said, tucking Stefa's diary under his coat. "I hope that we meet again, released from this bondage."

Izreal hugged the man. "Thank you. To life."

Ringelblum stepped around the door, his shadow disappearing with him. Stefa wondered if she would ever see him again.

"How did you get inside the ghetto?" Aaron asked. "How did you find us?"

Looking around, Zeev took off his cap and placed it on the floor beside him. "It's not so bad here." He tried to smile, but the expression faded from his lips. "But it won't last . . . I live in the forest or in safe houses—the worst is a shed not too far from here, but the family is kind and no friend to the Nazis."

"Like Mrs. Danek," Stefa said.

This time Zeev managed his smile and pulled a roll of zlotys from his coat pocket.

Aaron gasped at the sight of the large wad held together by an elastic band. "I'm not going to ask how you got it."

Zeev put the money on top of his cap. "We should all bless

and pray for Mrs. Danek and a woman named Greta, who is her friend."

Izreal leaned closer. "My daughter."

"Yes, Greta," Zeev said. "I haven't met her yet, but Janka says she's the most intelligent, determined, bravest woman she's ever met. She called her a War Girl. Greta gave Janka the money I used today to get past the gate . . . and it seems all the Ghetto Police know the address of Daniel Krakowski."

Daniel winced.

"Many of the Blue Police take bribes, but one is especially fond of taking money for favors," Zeev continued, running a finger over the zlotys. "The bills are counterfeit, made in England. He can't be angry if he doesn't know he was wronged."

"My sister has a plan?" Stefa asked.

"Yes. That's why I'm here."

They listened intently for the next half hour as the young man outlined the steps: the two dates, one in March, the other in April; their escort out of the ghetto by Zeev and Hanna; the change point at Janka's apartment, the journey out of the city by truck, and the walk to the partisan camp. "Greta is concerned about the March date. You'll be hidden in the back of the truck, covered by a tarp and tree trimmings. If it's below freezing, the food she's packing for you may go bad, the weapons misfire, or the weather be too frigid for the journey. Too many things can go wrong."

Stefa's lips parted in amazement. "She's thought it all out. If anyone can do this . . . Hanna can."

Zeev placed the money back in his pocket, looked at his watch, and put on his cap. "I have to be out of here in a half hour or my contact will be gone. I'm to return here just after midnight on the two days I've mentioned. If I don't come for you—the plan is off."

Aaron helped his friend from the floor. "I envy you. You're fighting our enemies, and you didn't need permission from God." He glanced at his father.

"No . . . but I pray every day for you and for my life." Zeev walked to the door and turned. "I had a dream the other night that I was fighting in the forest. Snow was falling. The woods were quiet except for the crack of gunfire. My friends had died against the snowbanks, their blood running over the frosty white. They were like angels, arms spread like wings, as quiet in death as the snow falling upon the pine branches. The Germans were rushing toward me when a blinding light shone from heaven and enfolded me in its warmth. The bullets bounced off the beam and fell harmlessly to the ground, like black dots on the snow." He paused and touched the brim of his cap. "I think the dream meant that I'm going to live . . . I pray the same for you . . . bless you all." He disappeared down the stairs.

Stunned by his words, Stefa shook at the power of them and wished she'd had such a dream.

Aaron, frowning and dismayed that he couldn't join his friend, returned to his blanket near the window. Maybe someday her brother would fight, Stefa thought, if the damnable war didn't end soon. But she worried more about Daniel. He'd said nothing, only looked down at his folded hands as Zeev described the plan. She would have to find out what he was thinking. In the meantime, their work break had taken far longer than usual. The others would be worried.

"We must go," Stefa said.

Daniel said nothing as he and the others followed her down the stairs.

Hanna tried to imagine what her family was going through, and every day that passed with inaction tormented her. Waiting was like a simmering madness. However, the strategy to save her family wasn't like attending a concert. One didn't buy a ticket and then sit comfortably waiting to be entertained. Like a battle, every detail had to be worked out, every contingency anticipated, every measure, every movement, had to fall into place—even the weather.

The March date was called off. She hadn't shown up at Janka's apartment that day—a signal that the plan was canceled. Snow had fallen for two days along with a frigid wind, the travel too risky for the balding tires on Eryk's truck. Also, Aaron and Daniel might navigate the snowy fields and icy rivers with some ease, but her father and sister would fall behind. The biting cold would expose them to frostbite within minutes.

Looking back on it, she wondered why she had considered the month at all. Any March day was susceptible to changing weather. The answer was easy—she hoped to get her family out sooner than later. Hanna found herself weeping at odd times during the day, and at night before she retired in the Rybaks' loft, feeling the pressure of her commitments. She carried on as best she could. Her trainers had warned her that she might experience such feelings.

Because Eryk had rigged the bicycle to carry equipment, she varied transmissions from the abandoned farmhouse to secluded fields, often sending a message from brambles or in the shelter of fallen trees. The Germans still monitored the broadcasts, so caution couldn't be overestimated. In fact, reports were coming in from other agents that the Wehrmacht was moving toward Warsaw in large numbers, including Ukrainians who had sworn allegiance to the Nazis.

April had shown some promise with sunny days and warmer weather, but, as she remembered from her childhood, those days were often followed by a cold rain, and sometimes snow. The weather forecast for the seventeenth was cloudy with periods of rain overnight. Rain was good. Rain drove everyone indoors except those who had to be out in it. Rain obscured the faces and forms of resisters behind its watery veils.

On that cloudy day, she and Eryk loaded the truck with provisions for the four people who would be making the long trek through Poland to the center of the burgeoning resistance movement in Slovakia. From there, she hoped her family would find their way to England by ship, from Greece to Portugal and then on to England. Hanna also considered the possibility that they might have to travel through Nazi-occupied territory to Spain and then on to Lisbon, or remain with the partisans until they were able to get forged documents and safety assurances before moving on.

She was more nervous than ever. Parachuting into Poland was nothing compared to the gut-wrenching anxiety she felt. She picked at the breakfast Julia had prepared, as a paralyzing fear invaded every pore, clouding her mind and slowing her movements. Eryk attempted to calm her as they loaded the truck. He had constructed a false floorboard that would rise a few scant centimeters over the escapees' faces. With food and weapons concealed in the bed as well, they would have to lie flat with their arms crossed over their chests, rifles beside them, while the tarp, tree trimmings, and a few sacks of seed potatoes concealed them from the Nazis. Eryk drilled a few small holes into the wood for fresh air.

"As long as everyone's quiet and the Germans don't get too nosy, everything should go as planned," he said, picking up the tarp and showing her what kind of inspection the Germans would have to make to discover their illicit cargo. And, if found, they would fire upon the Nazis. There was no other way out.

"Thank you," she said. Eryk had given his full consent to the plan, except for his hesitation on one nagging detail. "Are you certain you're comfortable returning for Janka Danek?"

"If there's another way, it would be better," he answered. "It would mean another trip in and out of the city, and if something goes wrong . . . well, it won't work out well for any of us."

She could tell from his tone that he wasn't eager to hide the Polish woman—that the risk might not be worth it. Hanna ran the details over and over in her mind. Every possible disaster formed in her thoughts while she tried to focus on the calm determination demanded by Rita Wright and her SOE trainers. She wondered how Phillip was—the prospect of seeing him again, of a life beyond the war, took away some of the nerves—but good thoughts were overpowered easily by the bad.

Eryk took a secondary route to Warsaw and the first test came early. They were stopped by guards outside the city.

The Germans waved them down, halting the truck with their

upheld rifles. Because Eryk had made the trip so many times, he knew some guards, but today was different. A group of men he didn't recognize stood in front of them. Hanna steeled herself.

"Get out of the truck," one ordered. He was a gruff man, short, with ruddy cheeks, and obviously proud of his power over others. His coat was open, but the layers of insignia decorating his uniform indicated that he was a senior officer.

Clutching her purse, she disembarked from the vehicle. The truck's body now separated her from Eryk. *Divide and conquer.*

Another German approached her from the front of the truck. "Papers."

She opened her purse, allowing the guard to look inside, and then pulled out her documents. He studied them carefully, eyeing each page, and then handed them back to her. "Your husband is a driver for the Reich?"

She responded in German. "Yes. Stefan. I'm going to meet him."

"Why are you with this man?"

"My husband was off to work early from Leoncin. Herr Rybak, being a good friend of the Reich, offered to take me into the city. With the number of officers around these days, my husband is very busy." Her jaw tightened, but she was pleased that her response sounded realistic and not forced.

"I see." The soldier looked into the cab before joining the senior officer, who was inspecting the truck bed.

"Why do you have these trimmings?" the officer asked, lifting the tarp and inspecting the wood underneath.

"I've been clearing at my farm—I didn't have time to take them out. Greta asked for a lift into the city to meet her husband. Other soldiers know me, but they aren't here today. I grow and deliver food for the troops."

The officer looked at the other soldier and they nodded. "All right. Will you be returning this way?"

"Yes, but not until this evening. It's my day to make rounds and gather orders."

"Go on," the short man said, waving them forward.

They both got into the truck and settled against the seat. As they drove off, Hanna exhaled and watched through the back window as the soldiers faded in the distance.

Eryk turned to her. "See . . . there was nothing to worry about."

She nodded, relieved to be through the checkpoint.

Eryk left her on Krochmalna after confirming their rendez-vous at Janka Danek's apartment thirty minutes after midnight. After making his rounds, he planned to spend the afternoon at a partisan's house in the city, securing the truck behind a gate.

The plan's execution had to be flawless, all her faculties sharpened when the time came. It was dangerous to be out on the street. The Germans were still enforcing a curfew on the Aryan side, although Polish residents could avoid detention if their behavior wasn't suspicious, or they were accompanied by a German resident. If needed, Hanna was playing that card.

The day dragged by. She'd already dropped off the cognac and sleeping powder to Janka, along with the counterfeit zlotys. Janka's instructions were to break out the bottle when Karol got home from work. He'd probably be half-drunk by that time anyway. If Herr Mueller happened to be with him, he would get a drink as well.

She spent the morning wandering the city, breezing by the ghetto to study the Gėsia Street gate, scouting for guards and locations where her family might hide. Hanna rewarded herself with a late lunch in a coffee shop in the German section of War-saw while trying to shake off her nerves. Skies were growing dark from a light rain when she finally ventured out, looking for the candle in Janka's front window that would signal all clear.

Hanna spotted it shortly after nine.

She climbed the steps slowly, listening for any sound that might indicate danger. Hearing nothing suspicious, she knocked on the door.

Janka opened it about a quarter of the way and quickly

dragged her in. Karol lay sprawled across the green couch, his head thrown back in a drugged sleep, arms limp at his side. The cognac bottle, three-quarters gone, sat on the table.

"I did it," Janka whispered. "He drank two glasses— quickly."

"That should put him out until morning," Hanna said. "Where's his pistol?"

"Where he usually keeps it when he's on the couch—between the cushions. I don't want to touch it."

Karol's body blocked the cleft where the weapon rested. Hanna lifted his arm and then dropped it. It fell back as if the man were dead. "You really knocked him out. He'll wake up with a bad headache." Hanna rolled Karol onto his side, reached between the cushions, and found the gun. "I'll take this." She checked to see if it was loaded and then placed it in her purse.

Janka sank into a chair at the kitchen table and clasped her hands.

"Are you all right?" Hanna asked. "Fifteen minutes is all I ask and then we're gone. I'll be out of your life forever—if you wish."

"That's what I'm afraid of." A sudden sadness darkened her face. "These are my last few hours in this apartment. I've decided what I must do."

Hanna sat across from her and watched as her friend tugged nervously at her fingers.

"I'll seek shelter at the church in the morning," Janka said. "If my priest won't take me in, I'll find a hotel . . . I have a little extra money."

Hanna leaned toward her. "After we execute the plan, you can come to the Rybaks' farm with me. It will be dangerous, but there's enough room in the loft for two. You can't stay here. Are there friends or relatives who might take you in?"

Janka shook her head. "No. That would be more dangerous than going to the Rybaks'. Karol would track me down." She looked at her husband, who moaned slightly and shifted his legs. "First, I'll try the church. If that fails, I'll get a message to you . . . somehow."

"Well, we only have to wait two-and-a-half more hours and then pray that all goes well."

"Zeev told me he's been granted permission to accompany your family to the border. He's a generous young man and a true patriot."

A pinprick of alarm stabbed Hanna. She hadn't considered that the resistance fighter would accompany them, but, on balance, his presence would be welcome. Zeev would be added protection for her family, as well as a competent guide. The trick would be to conceal him—most likely under the trimmings and tarp.

Hanna helped Janka gather her things as they kept an eye on her husband. Time slipped away as they worked.

She walked to the window as it neared eleven thirty and gazed out on her old apartment building framed by the black nothingness of destroyed buildings. The rain pattered against the window and fell in white drops through the haze of streetlights.

"It's time," she told Janka. "If we're not back in an hour, something has gone horribly wrong. We'll only have a few minutes at the gate. They'll change here and then we'll leave the city."

"I've pressed one of my dresses for Stefa and prepared some of Karol's shirts and pants for the men."

She kissed Janka on the cheek. "Be brave . . . and thank you." She looked at Karol, his chest rising and falling in his deep slumber. "He's a sad man. He has no idea what he's about to lose."

Janka closed the door as quietly as she had opened it.

Hanna fled into the rainy night, stepping into the shadows as she raced toward the ghetto.

"I told the Germans to smoke two or three cigarettes," the tall Polish policeman told her as rain dripped from his cap. "We have twenty minutes, but I would only count on ten. Do you have the money?"

"Eighty thousand zlotys in five-hundred notes."

"Five hundreds!" the policeman said. "What am I going to do with those large bills?"

"Break them," Hanna replied, looking toward the ghetto building where the unseen German officers smoked out of the rain, and then searching the streets for any sign of her family. "You get nothing if you back out." She lifted the false bottom in her purse, withdrew the bills wrapped in the required amounts, and waved them in his face.

"Where are they?" he asked nervously. "The kid's been in there for a half hour."

She knew he was referring to Zeev. "How much did he pay you?"

"Two thousand, but most of that went to the Germans for unlocking the gate and looking the other way. They'll get more money when they come back. I told them I was letting a rich Pole leave the ghetto."

Hanna nodded. "Not bad wages for one evening." She caught something out of the corner of her eye and a smile broke out on her face as five dark figures approached in the rain. She had to control her feelings. Now was not the time for a tearful home-coming. Her job was to get them out the gate and to the Aryan side as quickly as possible.

The policeman saw them as well and swung open the two connecting gates. In a matter of moments, they were standing in front of her on the Aryan side. She couldn't believe that her father, her brother, her sister, and two men she didn't really know were in front of her. The evening wasn't over, but she had liberated them from the ghetto.

"Go, quickly!" the policeman said.

Stefa hugged Hanna, her sister's face wan in the murky light. "Daniel and I are staying."

"I should, too," Aaron said. "It isn't fair. Zeev, stand up for me."

"There's nothing to talk about," Stefa said. "You must take care of Father, and live to carry on the family name. That's your task."

Aaron hugged Daniel and Stefa. "I will fight—I promise. I'll come back for you."

"Go," Stefa urged them, the rain dripping down her face, hiding her pain.

Hanna grasped her sister. "Why? You have to come . . . they'll kill you . . . I've worked for months to get you out."

"You can't understand what's happened here," Daniel said. "The pain and horror that we've seen—we have to fight—to honor the dead."

"You have to leave, Stefa," Hanna said, choking back tears.

Her sister pulled away. "I'm staying with my husband-to-be. Go with God's blessings."

"Hurry up," the policeman whispered harshly, as Daniel and Stefa slipped back through the gates. He swung them shut.

In seconds, after a brief wave from her sister, the couple disappeared in the darkness.

Hanna handed the man forty thousand zlotys.

"The amount was eighty thousand," he said, lifting a whistle to his mouth and threatening to blow it.

"An extra twenty for your effort and that's all," Hanna said, pushing the additional bills into his hands. "Not a word. The Gestapo would be very interested in what you've been doing."

He pocketed the money and turned toward the gate.

Hanna led them away, shaken by her sister's refusal to leave. Zeev followed as they darted south toward Krochmalna, dipping in and out of the shadows, using them and the damp night as protectors. She had never been so glad to see rain. The drops hid her tears.

The trip to Janka's was much like playing a children's game of hide-and-seek. She observed guards in the same locations she had discovered the day before. The escapees ran through the rubble of destroyed buildings—rough going, but the debris obscured them from German eyes. Zeev soon took the lead, acting as a spotter while Hanna followed behind.

After sprinting across Krochmalna, they arrived at Janka's after midnight. Hanna looked at her watch. Eryk was scheduled to arrive in fifteen minutes; then, the race would be on. Karol sputtered on the couch, his back turned to the room.

Janka provided toasted bread and water. Izreal and Aaron changed into the clothes Janka had laid out and were ready in minutes. The ones for Stefa and Daniel remained on the bed.

"Get us as far as the Pilica River, and I will take them to Ostrava," Zeev told Hanna as they waited at the kitchen table. "It's safer near the water."

In the time they had left, Hanna studied her father and brother and found the sight unsettling. It was as if she was looking at two people who were shadows of their former selves. Both were thin almost beyond recognition. Her father had lost more weight since she had seen him on the street near the Palais. The two men gulped down the food Janka had given them and then sat at the kitchen table with their heads bowed, like disoriented animals freed from a cage.

The brittle hardness that had grown between Hanna and her father over the years remained. She wanted to hug him, but she was unsure if he would accept the gesture or even appreciate it. Her brother had grown into a man—he was a boy not so long ago.

"Thank you for this," Izreal said to Janka, lifting his eyes briefly from the table.

"You're welcome . . . knowing your family has been the only bright spot for me in this war."

"It's time," Hanna said. "We should go downstairs. We'll return for you."

"No." Janka's eyes were filled with fiery determination. "You must do your work and not be bothered by me. I will go to my priest. I'll pray for you and you pray for me."

Hanna knew better than to beg her friend—she had prepared to meet this loss, if necessary. She hugged Janka and left her with her sleeping husband.

Hanna and the men crept down the stairs. She opened the door a bit and saw Eryk sitting in the rain-spotted truck, its motor and lights off. "There's an uncomfortable hiding place in the truck bed," she said to her father and Aaron. "We've packed rucksacks and weapons in there as well."

As soon as she opened the door, Eryk got out and dashed to the back of the truck. He flipped open the wooden panel and helped Izreal, who had stiffened his thin body like a board, maneuver into the hiding place. Her father groaned a bit, as he wriggled on his back. Aaron followed in the same manner.

"What happened to the others?" Eryk asked.

"They're staying," Hanna replied as stoically as she could. "Zeev is going to accompany my father and Aaron."

"I'll stay under the tarp," the young partisan said. "Hand me one of the rifles."

Eryk grabbed one of the weapons lining the compartment and handed it to Zeev. The young fighter brushed aside the tree trimmings and positioned himself with his head near the end of the truck. Eryk sealed the panel, concealing her father and brother. He and Hanna got into the warm cab.

Eryk turned the truck from the curb, switched on the lights, and accelerated west on Krochmalna.

"We'll be lucky to get through this," he said.

"We will." Hanna stared through the windscreen as the rain pelted against it. They passed a few German guards so fast that the men had no time to react. Eryk turned onto several side streets to vary the route before returning to Krochmalna.

Soon they were at the checkpoint where they'd been stopped the previous morning.

"Trouble," Eryk said. "I thought they'd be gone by now."

"You underestimate them."

A wooden barricade blocked the road—an apparatus on four wooden legs that could be easily knocked over by the truck.

"It's better to stop," Eryk said. "They'll be after us if we crash through it."

"Let me handle this," Hanna said, withdrawing Karol's pistol from her purse and placing it by her side.

As they pulled up to the barrier, three soldiers got out of a sedan parked by the side of the road. One of them was the short, ruddy-cheeked officer they had seen before.

The German came to the window. Hanna rolled it down. "*Hallo, Offizier*," she said and smiled at the man.

He remembered them. "You returned, but you're late." He waved the light from his electric torch into the cab. "Out of the truck. We're inspecting *all* of it." He stepped back.

Hanna peered out the window. "*Offizier?*"

"*Ja?*" he asked, returning to her.

She swung the pistol from her side and fired one shot into his head. Blood sprayed as the man fell to the ground. Caught off guard, a second soldier rushed toward her, raising his rifle. She fired first, hitting him twice in the chest. Zeev rose from his position under the tarp and shot a third German in the back of the neck. He fell on his face in the road.

"Now, you've done it," Eryk said. He pounded his fist on the back glass and Zeev ducked under the tarp. He moved the truck slowly forward, edging the barrier out of the way until he could speed off. When they were well away from the roadblock, he said, "We'll have to return by the back roads to the farm. I hope they're all dead."

"They are," Hanna said. She felt no guilt, no remorse, no ache in her gut other than from hunger. She had been trained to kill, and her first murder was easier than she thought, like squashing an annoying insect, ridding herself of vermin, an unpleasant but necessary action.

They sped south about fifty kilometers until they reached a point where the road paralleled the Pilica. The river lay in the distance, an inky sliver cutting through a flat land lined with dead grasses and trees and shrubs dotted with the black specks of budding leaves.

Eryk turned off the truck's lights, pulled into a field, and jumped out of the cab. Zeev had already crawled down from the bed. Eryk unsealed the panel and Izreal and Aaron wriggled out.

"The rucksacks contain about a week's worth of food if you use it wisely," Eryk told them. "You have your weapons. Take the extras as well."

"Father," Hanna said. "I wish we had more time."

Izreal opened his arms and she fell into his embrace. "After the war," he said, "we'll have more time. Where should we meet?"

"In London, I hope. The operatives will get you there."

Aaron kissed her cheek. "It's good to see you again, Hanna. I'll make sure Father's safe, but somehow, somewhere, I'll fight."

"Your time will come," she replied. "Take good care of him." She turned to Zeev. "Contact me when you reach Ostrava. Go through the SOE contact in Prague if you have to . . . and thank you for your help."

He nodded. "I don't need thanks. This is what I do. We should go."

She handed Zeev the extra twenty thousand zlotys and then returned to the truck. She and Eryk watched as the three men struck out across the dark field and disappeared into the dark silhouettes of the trees lining the river.

"God be with them," she whispered to herself, and then, for the first time in many years, she cried about what she had lost in Warsaw.

CHAPTER 23

April 1943

Janka had wrapped herself in warm blankets and slept until dawn. Karol stirred on the couch, but seemed unable to move his head without wincing.

It was time to leave. She gathered her bag, and, unconcerned about the mess she'd left in the bedroom, or the dirty pots still sitting on the stove, she kissed her husband on the forehead and walked out the door. How handsome he had been when they had married—what a monster he had turned into. But she had no desire to kill him, or even hate him anymore. God was calling her to the church. Her life, from now on, would be devoted to some form of service in His name—if the priest would accept her offer.

For the first time in years, she walked Krochmalna with her head high, not caring if she was stopped by German guards. She had her papers and a reason to be out. They wouldn't get the best of her.

I'm going for a walk. My husband knows Herr Mueller. Now, go away.

No one stopped her as the sun rose; her step was confident and assured as she proceeded to the church. Even her knock on the rectory door so early in the morning echoed with life.

The priest she had known for many years answered, slowly

drawing the door open until she could see his face peering around the edge.

"Janka," he said with surprise. "I'm on my way to morning prayers. Is something wrong?"

"May I come in?"

"Of course," he said, opening it to admit her, revealing his black cassock and freshly combed gray hair. He directed her to a seat in the sparse apartment. She sat in a rigid wooden chair in front of a small stone fireplace. The room was somber, lit by a few candles. The shadowy pictures of Saint Sebastian stung by arrows and Saint Michael trampling Satan hung on the walls. A crucifix lay deep in the gloom.

"I've come to ask a favor, Father." She paused, suddenly uncertain of what his response would be. What if he denied her?

"Yes?" He sat across from her by a small table that held a crystal decanter and two brandy glasses.

"I need asylum . . . a home . . ."

"Why? Where is your husband? What is his name . . . Karol? I haven't seen him in church in many years."

"Karol wants to kill me."

The priest uttered, "Never," and leaned toward her. "What a terrible thing to say about your husband. Are you certain? What makes you think so?"

"He hates Jews. He will turn me over to the Nazis if I return home . . . he will kill me or I will die in German hands." She looked down at her trembling fingers. "I helped Jews escape from the ghetto."

He stared at her as if he didn't believe what she was saying. Then his skepticism turned to a frown. She told him about her association with a woman who rescued the Jewish family, and how she had drugged her husband almost to the point of poisoning him. She described Karol's Nazi business associates and how he killed Jews at the Umschlagplatz . . . for money . . . for sport. "Will you help me, Father?" she asked when she'd finished.

He folded his hands and gazed toward the floor. "I must pray on this—"

"I will work for the church . . . I'll do any job."

He rose from his chair and stood in front of her, putting a hand lightly on her shoulder. "Some Catholics aren't concerned about what is happening to the Jews. You must hold this secret deep in your heart and you must be sure of your decision . . . not because you're scared or you have no place to go. There are other places to hide."

She clutched his hand. "Father, it's what I want."

He let go of her hand, returned to his chair, and sat in quiet meditation for a few minutes. "There is a Sister of God named Marejanna Reszko in Ignacόw. I've heard that she has made sacrifices similar to yours in the service of Our Lord. She may take you in—and under her care you might serve as a menial. That is the best I can offer. There is no path for you as a novitiate."

Janka felt her spirit lighten, the room seemingly filled with joy and sunlight. "I understand. Carnal pleasures have stained me. Divorce would be the least of Karol's punishments upon me, but if I can assist the Sisters . . . I would be happy and grateful for the refuge."

"I will pray for you. In the meantime, you must remain hidden here—in the basement there is a room—I will bring food and water. Stay here until I return."

He left by a door that led into the church, leaving her alone to stare at the flickering candles and the mystical paintings that adorned the room.

She put her hands over her mouth and cried as an unexpected release washed over her. She was safe and free, and would never go back to her husband. A new life, perhaps a new name awaited. That she knew, as surely as Christ was her savior.

When she awoke on Sunday morning, Stefa felt as if seeing her sister had been a dream. She and Daniel had sneaked back to the attic under the shields of rain and darkness and taken refuge near the attic window rather than wake those in the bunker.

They had slept apart, as was the custom. As the dawn filtered in she was able to study his face and recall the strength that he, as her future husband, had given her. Today was to be her wedding day. Rabbi Meisel would marry them in the room below the attic and they would be man and wife forever, until death.

When she'd told her father that they were to be married, Izreal raised no objection, holding out his hands to the two of them, offering his blessing. She shed tears upon his fingers and kissed them away.

Daniel had decided weeks before that he was staying in the ghetto. He wanted to fight or die as a Jew, and help those who remained. She had suspected as much when Zeev had told them about Hanna's plan and Daniel had been silent. Although he didn't say it, revenge for his parents' deaths weighed upon him. He'd put no pressure on her to stay, but after the blessing of marriage was offered and accepted, she had no choice. After his proposal, she never would have left him no matter what happened.

Izreal had cried when they announced that they were staying to fight, but her father was too weak, too driven down by the cruel ghetto years, to voice a strong objection. Aaron, on the other hand, had to be convinced, yet again, to leave the ghetto—to protect his father, to continue the family name, to have his own life as a husband and father. She never doubted that her brother would fight the Nazis after her father was saved—if not in the ghetto, then somewhere in the world.

She was sorry that she'd had so few minutes with Hanna, but fate had decided that. Perhaps, after the war was over, they would find each other and talk of marriage and children and even about the missing years after Hanna had left them for England.

The light fell across Daniel's head and she moved closer, stroking his bearded cheek and his hair until he woke with a start.

After the shock wore off, he stretched and smiled at her. "Hello, my wife . . . ready to get married?"

She wanted to kiss him, but instead placed her hand in his. "Yes."

"After we eat, we'll prepare for the wedding."

"There isn't much to do. We'll be wearing the same old clothes." She ran her hands over the spotted blue dress she had worn so often the past year when other garments had aged beyond repair.

"Your father left a little money for us, plus the silver and his knives in case we need to sell them. Would you like to wear a piece of your mother's jewelry?"

"One piece—a silver brooch—of a bird."

"Yes," he said, rising on his elbows. "Wear it. It's the spirit we need as we observe Passover—our flight to freedom."

Tears crowded her eyes, clouding her vision. "I love you . . . I feel so happy, yet so sad . . . I'm ready for a new life with you . . . and willing to face them . . . to fight."

He wiped her tears away with a gentle touch. "Cherish what we have now—nothing more. Let's leave tomorrow for tomorrow."

"All right, let's start the marriage feast," she said, fully aware of the irony of her words.

They lowered the ladder, descending into the room they called their "apartment." A resistance fighter had given them a small kettle of potato soup and unleavened bread.

Stefa heated the food and Daniel blessed the meal. They ate with smiles on their faces, looking forward to their marriage that afternoon.

The wedding she'd imagined was impossible, but despite withholding tears and fighting back the regret burning in her heart for her missing family, she praised God for His blessings and the gift of marriage to her chosen husband.

The sun had broken through the clouds. The day was bright and cheery if one imagined an existence beyond the ghetto, in a nation still enjoying freedom. Though the calendar was past the month of Adar, the promise of spring and new life remained constant, no matter what the Nazis planned. Death couldn't stop the world's turn, the play of seasons, the planting and the harvest. She imagined blackbirds flocking in the new green leaves of Saski Park, turning their pale yellow eyes to the ground for seed.

If she hadn't been imprisoned in the ghetto, the wedding ceremony would have taken a happier turn—days of dancing and singing, embellished with frivolity and games. Ample helpings of wine and food would have been served. Her parents would have already decided their children's fate and important matters such as the dowry; a pension for the bridegroom; and the kesubah, the marriage contract. In earlier times, those items would have been left to the shadchan, the matchmaker, with the parents giving their approval. Such matchmaking was one of the reasons her sister had abandoned the family.

She would have picked out her wedding dress after the comments, suggestions, arguments, and final nods from Perla and Hanna. Daniel's new suit, shoes, and hat would be the envy of the crowd. She would accept his gold ring as a symbol of the lasting circle of their marriage; the symbolic wedding glass would be broken. A chorus of mazel tovs would erupt in the hall. Rice would shower down upon them. Then they would dance and sing with family before consummating their union.

But none of that had happened, and she found herself alone in the attic, staring into the remains of a cracked looking glass while Daniel dressed below. Stefa had washed herself with a cloth dipped in a bucket of cold water, and also had managed to remove some of the stains from her dress. She dried herself at the window. The ghetto was quiet, but the noiseless streets reminded her that such serenity was temporary, a crumbling façade; the terrible rumors circulating promised more death and reprisals from the Germans. The extinction of the ghetto Jews was held in Nazi hands.

Hushed voices rose up from the floor below, followed by a

knock on the ceiling, the signal that it was time for the ceremony to begin.

She lowered the ladder and descended with her back to those in the room. She turned to find Daniel wearing a black vest over a white shirt, a yarmulke covering the crown of his head. Standing beside him was Rabbi Meisel, a thin yet spry man well over sixty. Stefa thought his features somewhat stern, and wondered if he had always been that way, or if the years in the ghetto had hardened him as they had others. His long white beard obscured his neck, finally resting atop his chest. He had risked much to maintain a beard that stirred the Nazis' wrath. A black hat with a rounded top and a fedora-like rim sat atop his head. A man she didn't know, who looked as religious as the rabbi, stood next to Daniel.

Stefa lit a small taper and carried it toward Daniel.

"You found the pin," he said, his eyes fixated on her.

"Yes . . . it's a dove." She tapped the sweeping silver form and smiled at him.

"The time has come," the rabbi said, as he called them forward.

She wished she could float on waves of joy, like most brides. She placed the taper on the floor, letting the flame gutter as the words and prayers began. Her future was in the candle—as brief, as flickering, as temporary as the day before it descended into night. Even the floor on which they stood contained the evidence of lives lost: the menorah, the family silver, the weapons hidden beneath the wood. What had happened to happiness? Could she just for a moment forget what was going on outside the room where they stood?

The rabbi and the man, a teacher in rabbinical studies, created a chuppah for a brief time. "It will have to do," he said, as the pair lifted a white sheet over their heads. It fluttered briefly over them before floating to the floor in a white heap.

The rabbi continued to surprise them with the gift of a gold ring. He presented it to Daniel, who then slipped it on Stefa's finger after she accepted it. A lump rose in her throat as she looked into Daniel's face, the handsome man who had carried her on wings of love through these difficult years. He offered no explanation for how he got the ring, and Stefa knew better than to ask the question. Too many had died, leaving their precious possessions behind.

"Praised be Thou, O Lord our God, King of the Universe, who has created joy and gladness, bridegroom and bride . . . praised be Thou, O Lord, who gladdened the bridegroom and the bride." The rabbi offered seven blessings as they stood with bowed heads.

He placed a handkerchief over Stefa's head. "Circle the bridegroom seven times." She did so, drinking in the love that poured from Daniel as she presented herself to him.

Stefa removed the handkerchief from her head. Daniel put a glass underneath it and crushed it with one well-placed step. He ground the shards into the floor.

"During these dark times, we remember the past tragedies," the rabbi said. "Despite our happiness, we remember those times of sadness, knowing that they don't last forever. Hope and love remain even when we feel God has forsaken us." He lifted his head toward heaven and muttered a short prayer. "And I will betroth thee unto me forever. Yea, I will betroth thee unto me in righteousness and in justice, and in loving kindness and compassion. And I will betroth thee unto me in faithfulness. And thou shalt know the Lord. So says Hosea."

The Rabbi gazed at them and they stood for a moment listening to the quiet of the day. Past the window, the sun brightened and faded as it toyed with the clouds. A spring breeze filled the room and life seemed almost normal, almost livable. She was a married woman.

The teacher produced a half-full bottle of wine. The rabbi shook their hands and wished them mazel tov. Daniel thanked them for their generosity as he and Stefa drank from the same cup. When they'd finished, the two men drank as well and toasted to "a better life."

The rabbi's eyes turned grim, however, when he had finished

his cup. "I'm sorry to bear this news . . . the Ukrainians and the Germans have surrounded the ghetto. The rumors are true. There is no way out. You are lucky, Stefa, that your father and brother were able to escape. Only those who fight can be trusted now. You must pack and come to the bunker for your safety—on your wedding night."

"Yes, Rabbi," Daniel said. "We will do as you say."

The rabbi said a final blessing and the two men left after Daniel paid them a small amount of money.

Daniel walked to the window and slammed his palms against the frame. "The Nazis are coming for us. We knew they would. We have no choice but to fight or die."

Stefa stood behind him and put her hands on his shoulders. "We should gather our things. They could force their way in at any minute."

"Yes," he said, turning to face her, lifting her chin with his finger. "I love you."

"I love you, too."

Daniel's eyes reddened. "I'm sorry." A tear rolled down his cheek.

"For what?" she asked, trying hard to be strong for him.

"That we only have now and not tomorrow."

"It's all right," she said, and kissed him. "We have each other . . . and I will always be your wife."

They worked through the afternoon in the still-holding calm, transporting the weapons and the few remaining items they possessed to the bunker. They changed into dirty clothes for the dirty job, which meant traversing the stairs numerous times and maneuvering the weapons, the silver, and their clothes between the buildings and through the narrow tunnel. When they were finished, the sun was low in the sky and Stefa was covered with grime. She longed for another pail of cold water to bathe in.

Daniel carved out a space in the corner of the bunker. It wasn't much, but since they wouldn't be sleeping together as man and wife, the arrangement didn't concern her. They had no privacy to consummate their marriage. The important point—a square meter of space—was settled. The other occupants had claimed their own: two young men who were ŻOB members, an older man and his fragile wife, and a young woman with long black hair and her six-month-old baby.

As night fell, Daniel and Stefa made one more trip to the apartment to make sure nothing they needed had been left behind.

As they emerged between the buildings, Stefa was struck by the light of a nearly full moon that bathed the street. She looked at the silver rays that fell upon her arms and felt as if she had stepped into the sun or been liberated from the bunker prison. The thought of freedom plunged her into despair. After a few moments, she was sobbing at Daniel's side. He hushed her and they listened to the sounds of people scurrying about, making preparations as their captors waited outside the walls. Everyone was taking advantage of the lull.

They climbed the stairs to their former home, pulled down the ladder leading to the attic, and climbed out on the eaves. The remains of the ghetto spread to the south, a sunless canvas of drab, blocky buildings and lost memories. The souls of the dead had gathered on this night. Stefa felt them clawing at her as she looked into the stars that hung over her in the black sky. The stars would go on for millennia after she was gone, but the thought gave her no comfort.

She clutched Daniel's arm as he tested the board high above the sidewalk that connected the two buildings.

"It's fine," he said. "We can cross if we need to."

"It's hopeless." She swiped at her eyes with her hand. "We'll never have children . . . we shouldn't even try." She faced him, his features glowing in the moon's light. "Why would the woman in the bunker have a child in a time like this? How can she bring a child into this world, knowing . . ."

Daniel settled against the stone. "She was in love? Her husband was taken away? Nothing is normal. We aren't living the way Jews are supposed to live. We've been driven to this." He leaned against her. "When we come out of this, we'll have children . . . many of them . . . so many they'll say that God blessed us above all people. But not now."

"Yes, many children," she said, trying to hide her disappointment.

Something flashed across the sky, too small for a shell, too fast for a plane, probably a grain of sand from the heavens. First red and then white. The tail faded to green as it evaporated in the west. "A flash, like us," she said.

Daniel said nothing, but grasped her hands. Beyond the rooftops, the Germans and the Ukrainians gathered . . . waiting. Daniel and Stefa sat for hours on the eaves, looking out upon the ghetto, as if they had all the time in the world.

At dawn on April nineteenth, 1943, Passover Eve, German troops entered through an abandoned gate on Nalewki Street. Everyone in the bunker was awakened by the pounding on an outside wall. The two fighters and Daniel and Stefa jumped to their feet and grabbed their weapons while the others stayed behind.

They crawled through the tunnel, the two fighters emerging on Miła Street with their pistols and grenades and disappearing to the east. Miła was still deserted and Daniel and Stefa surged into the adjoining building and were soon on the eaves overlooking the street. Gunfire, as well as the roar of tanks and motorcycles, filled their ears.

"It's begun," Daniel said, hooking his hands over the lip of the roof above. He was tall enough to reach it. He pulled himself up and managed to get half his body on it. With strong kicks from his legs, he fishtailed onto the surface.

"Hand me the guns," he said.

Stefa complied and thrust the two Błyskawicas, butt first, up to him. "Grab my hands." He lay flat, reached over the roof with both arms, and pulled her up beside him. They stood cautiously, for the sound of gunfire and explosions had increased, and then took shelter behind a small shed. From their vantage point, they could see most of the ghetto, the Great Synagogue, and the taller buildings of Warsaw.

The Germans shouted orders: "Leave your homes for resettlement." No one ventured into the streets. Everyone knew that obeying that command would lead to death. A short time later, a Waffen-SS man on a motorcycle rolled down the street, as if taking a leisurely spin on his vehicle. He was followed by a small group of soldiers and a tank.

Daniel clutched Stefa's hand. "Now." He handed her the submachine gun she had used before and shimmied to the roof's edge. She followed.

The troops were coming into range. Daniel held a finger to his lips.

Suddenly, an impact grenade lobbed from the roof of another building exploded on the tank. The vehicle swerved and crashed into a streetlamp. The hatch opened amid screams from the crew as the flames seared into the tank.

Daniel nodded.

They opened fire together. The SS man, hit several times in the chest, fell as the motorcycle careened out of control. The surprised troops fired back, but they didn't know where to shoot, randomly aiming at buildings and roofs as they crouched like ducks in a shooting gallery.

Another soldier fell and what was left of the unit ran down the street, leaving the tank and the dead men.

"They're retreating," Daniel said. He kissed Stefa.

A strange feeling, something like euphoria, settled upon her and she rejoiced inwardly at the dead men who lay sprawled below. German blood had been spilled and she was glad. *No more of going like lambs to the slaughter. We will rise up!*

They kept their position as the sun rose higher, but, after a time, the gunfire ended and quiet ruled again. Daniel helped her down from the roof and they descended to the street. "Keep your eyes open," he said, as Stefa stood in the gutter, submachine gun poised at her shoulder. Her husband kicked the dead SS man over, taking his pistol, as well as the rifle from the soldier. Flames licked the inside of the tank, and the threat of an explosion was possible. A horribly burned man, who had tried to escape death, lay stretched over the hatch.

When they got back to the bunker, the old man and woman were celebrating with wine as the young woman tried to hush her baby boy.

"He's going to get us into trouble," the old man said. "The Nazis will hear him."

"Don't worry," Daniel said, taking a glass of his own. "We'll take care of the Germans . . . like we did today."

Daniel and Stefa crawled into their corner, already exhausted from the day. They closed their eyes and fell asleep in each other's arms.

When they awoke, the Seder table, as basic as it was, had been set by the couple. The fighters had returned. A white tablecloth had been spread across boards, supporting two small candles and the glasses holding wine. Somehow one of the fighters had managed to get matzah as well.

The Seder was nothing like those of previous years, when the dishes would have been washed and stacked, the silverware and pots koshered for use. Her father was a stickler for the ritual. Perla would have cleaned the house to perfection, even as she placed bits of bread for Izreal and her children to find—ridding the apartment of forbidden leavened food. The Seder plate would have been meticulously prepared. This year, no shank bone, no bitter herbs, nor the fruit and nut mixture, called charoses, graced the table—only the roasted eggs.

Daniel was given the honor of chanting the kiddush after filling the cup. A bowl of cold water was passed around for the men to wash their hands. After a blessing, the Haggadah reading began. The young woman, with the child on her lap, asked the four questions about the escape from Egypt. The old man told the story of the plagues.

The Seder was cut short by explosions which rocked the street, causing the walls to tremble and dust to fall around them. The Germans had returned. Not so far away, guns fired and more explosions rattled the bunker.

"We're going up," Daniel said, taking a last sip of wine.

"We'll go, too," one of the young fighters said.

They crawled through the tunnel and entered their old apartment. Soon, the four of them were on the roof with their weapons.

The moon shone again on them, as if they were standing in a searchlight, but they couldn't escape its rays. Gunfire exploded and tanks rumbled through the streets. A few blocks away, smoke and flames leapt from a burning building, turning the sky orange and black.

Stefa pointed at something in the distance, faint in the burning light.

"What?" Daniel asked.

"There . . . on Muranowska Street. Two flags."

She cupped her hands around her eyes, dimming the light from the fire. One flag was blue and white, the other red and white.

"My God," one of the fighters said. "The flags of the Zionists and our homeland."

They marveled at the view, so simple, yet so powerful. No Polish flag had hung in Warsaw since the country had capitulated in 1939. It had been nearly four years since she had witnessed such a sight. Her heart swelled with pride as they watched the flags flutter against the buildings. The Germans had been unable to take them down.

Bullets whizzed over their heads, causing them to drop to the roof. They didn't know where the enemy fire came from. They crawled to the edge and sighted their weapons on the street.

"We will tell our children about this," Daniel said to Stefa.

"God, lead us out of Egypt," she said. "Lead us out of this."

They held hands, in the moonlight, as they waited to attack the German troops on Miła Street.

CHAPTER 24

May 1943

*T*wo wolves have been captured, but one escaped.

That was the cryptic message from Prague that indicated that Aaron and Izreal had made it to the Slovak border and that Zeev had made his way back to the forest outside Warsaw. Hanna had cried when she read it, but her tears of joy had been tempered because of concern for her sister.

The "Ghetto Uprising," as it was called, had made contact with anyone inside it impossible. Even traveling to Warsaw was risky. The controls were strict, identification papers scrutinized instead of being glossed over. Eryk decided to not travel until the resistance had collapsed. He held out little hope for its success.

In the meantime, she bicycled around Leoncin, reporting to the SOE on the few things she knew. Stung with guilt by her actions, she reported in code that she had rescued her father and brother from the ghetto and that they were headed to London. She wanted Rita Wright to know that she had taken the matter into her own hands, devised the operation, and completed it successfully. An added incentive for the transmission was the inclusion of Aaron, and the prospect of useful service he might provide to the SOE if he ended up in England. Hanna wasn't sure he would ever end up in London, knowing her brother's propensity to fight, but she was certain that before he did anything he would make sure his father was safe.

News from the ghetto came to her in pieces and it was never good. Eryk and Julia had heard through one of their contacts that a ruthless Nazi, General Jürgen Stroop, had been placed in charge of quashing the uprising. He was razing the ghetto, setting fire to blocks at a time, forcing the remaining Jews and resistance fighters to jump from the burning buildings or be cremated in their hiding places.

By mid-May, the "Jewish problem" seemed well in hand under the direction of Stroop, so she and Eryk ventured into Warsaw. More than anything Hanna wanted to get firsthand news about her sister, and there was only one way to do it.

Eryk borrowed a car from an operative who stayed with Julia while they went into the city. It was safer, he thought, to take a sedan rather than the truck. The checkpoints remained, but "Greta's" identification papers got them into the city with little fuss. Her "husband" Stefan had since become acquainted with high-ranking Nazi officials, including General Stroop—an impressive story, used wisely, that raised eyebrows in a good way.

He left her on Krochmalna while going about his own business with his contacts. First, she went to the church where she and Janka had held their secret meetings. She didn't have to wait long until she met the gray-haired priest who had passed by her months before.

"Excuse me, Father," Hanna said. The priest stopped and looked at her with wary eyes. "I'm looking for Janka Danek. Would you happen to know where she might be?"

"Why?" he asked, quite roughly for a priest. "I have no knowledge of her."

"I thought you might."

He lowered his head as if he was tired of everything in life, including questions about Janka. "Who are you?"

"She helped me."

He raised his head and his lips parted in recognition. "How?"

"Did she tell you of an escape?"

His eyes flashed for a moment. "Walk with me."

He directed her to the front, near the altar, and told her to sit in a pew, as if she had come to him for some spiritual matter. He prayed over her for a time and then whispered, "What escape?"

"From the ghetto."

"Mrs. Danek is with a woman of God in Ignacόw and is safe." He crossed himself. "Go with God." With a nod, he left the sanctuary.

She stepped out of the church and headed toward the ghetto. She passed her childhood home and Janka's former apartment across the street. When she was within sight of the wall, her breath fled. From what she could see over its dividing boundary, the buildings that she had known since her youth stood as charred tombs, crumbling monuments to Nazi destruction. No Allied bombs had fallen on the ghetto—the Nazis had destroyed it. The extent of the destruction, the lingering smell of smoke in the air, struck her with force. Intuition told her that Stefa and Daniel were most likely dead.

Hanna walked to the wall and spoke in her best German to a young soldier who stood near a wire gate.

"Good day," she said.

He returned the greeting in a flat voice.

"Could you tell me what's going on here? I've just come in from Berlin. My husband is a driver for the General Government."

"It's the dirty Jews," he replied, raising his rifle slightly from his shoulder. "They're all dead . . . or should be."

"Oh . . . they got what the Führer said was coming to them." She pressed a finger to her cheek, as if wiping off a smear of makeup. "Did any of them live?"

"Maybe a few. They've been gassed and burned out. Our troops found the command bunker, gassed it, then blew it up."

Her nerves clenched before she replied. "Well, Stroop certainly knows how to do his job. Good day." She walked away, trying not to hurry as she fought back tears. *The damn Nazis really do know how to do their jobs. Sons of bitches.*

The soldier called out after her. "Stroop is finishing the job today. He's blowing up the Great Synagogue."

She turned, a bit of fire lighting her eyes. "Really . . . I must see that."

She left him and made her way to Saski Park, sitting at first on a bench and then walking to the northwest corner, where she could see the ornate dome rising over the scrolls and pediment of the classical façade. Below the supporting columns were great steps flanked by giant sculptural menorahs on either side of the walkway.

Not far away, a crowd of German soldiers gathered, all looking toward the synagogue with eyes raised. From their excited movements, she could tell that the demolition was expected soon, even as deadly fires still glowed in the ghetto.

She hadn't prepared herself for what she was about to see. A voice called out "Heil Hitler" and an explosive crack shattered the air. The building seemed to rise from its foundation before being swallowed in a fiery burst. Smoke plowed toward the sky, while the flames raged and the dust settled to earth.

Sickened, Hanna turned.

The ghetto was finished, but she wasn't. She looked at her watch. Soon, it would be time to meet Eryk for the return trip to the farm. She walked swiftly away from the burning synagogue until she was again on Krochmalna.

She stopped at a deserted shop, out of sight of everyone, and cried for her sister and the man she'd wanted to marry. Her tears were bitter and hard. After she had composed herself, she wondered if Rita would be angry with her for saving her father and brother, or whether she would applaud her initiative. She would find out later. Phillip entered her mind. Perhaps she would see him again on English soil, and they would have many stories to tell.

Looking up at the apartment building where she had lived for so many years, she made a silent vow.

I will live to see the end of this war.

EPILOGUE

Late May 1946

Sir Phillip Kelley had last seen Hanna getting on a plane for her jump into Poland. Somehow, she had drifted back into his life like a phantom, a moving shadow he only recognized after she'd passed by.

He'd thought he'd spotted her at Baker Street and then at one of the administrative offices elsewhere in London. If Hanna had met with Rita Wright, his superior had said nothing about it. That behavior was standard SOE.

Spies, couriers, army personnel, administrators were getting on with their lives, now that the world war had been over for almost a year. Hitler had committed suicide in his Berlin bunker. The nuclear bombs had fallen on Hiroshima and Nagasaki.

By nosing around he was able to find a telephone number for her in Croydon. A man had picked up, someone older, with an accent, who had a bit of trouble understanding him. Eventually, he was able to get through to Hanna and arrange a meeting at the Stag's Horn, the pub where they'd first met.

As he boarded the afternoon train in London, he wondered what Hanna would be like now—whether she would be open to filling in the years since their last meeting. In the brief conversation they'd had on the phone, she'd seemed somewhat reluctant to talk. War had a way of changing people—certainly, it had changed him. He hadn't been injured physically, but the conflict had taken its emotional toll. Men and women he'd trained had been killed or maimed, and he pictured in his mind what they'd gone through—how they'd suffered. He'd met with disabled soldiers, weeping widows, and teary-eyed children. Offering condolences, he often thought he sounded like a recording, spouting SOE lines of sympathy and sorrow to soothe the family's suffering over the loss of their loved ones. The spiel drained him to the point of exhaustion.

He walked from Croydon Station to the pub, in the warm sun, under a silky blue sky; the finest of rare days in England. The Stag's Horn stood solidly on the corner, its slate roof and stones unscathed by the Blitz. His hand shook a bit as he pulled open the door.

She sat in the same booth, in the same spot where he'd sat beside her. Betty Martin and Rita Wright were missing, of course, but everything else appeared to be the same: the fog of cigarette smoke that wafted through the dense air, the intimate booths that had heard so many tales, seen so many laughs and tears.

Hanna saw him, lifted her coffee cup, sipped, and smiled.

He slid into the booth across from her. An uncomfortable silence took hold as she wrapped her fingers around the cup. A gold cigarette case, one similar to Rita's, lay on the table to her right.

"It's been a few years," he said after a time, and offered a faint smile.

She nodded. "Yes."

Her figure was trimmer, her hair darker, more to its original color and pushed back from her face. The manicured nails were painted red. She wore a dark blue dress, accented by a white scarf tied low around her neck. He still found her as attractive as the moment they'd met. Then, duty had gotten in the way of any relationship. Perhaps it still would.

A waitress appeared and Phillip ordered a stout.

"Still in the service, I see," she said, lifting a finger from the cup and directing it toward his uniform.

"Fulfilling my commission," he responded. "I have another year left . . . then, my future is mine." Another silence fell over them as the waitress returned with his beer. He took a sip from the frothy head, which left a filmy coating on his mustache. "Was this a bad idea?"

Hanna smiled and shook her head. "No. I don't talk about the war much. After I got back to England, I didn't want to relive it."

He leaned back against the high wooden back of the booth. "A lot of people feel that way. You can talk to me—if you care to." He directed his gaze to the cigarette case. "Smoking?"

"Sometimes. I thought it would calm my nerves . . . like the occasional drink. The case was a gift from Rita." She paused, her eyes brightening a bit. "I'm working at the bookstore again . . . old Mr. Cheever took me back. The SOE didn't make me rich."

"I thought I saw you at Baker Street, but you disappeared before I could say hello. I wasn't even sure you were there—like a ghost."

"One thing the SOE taught me was to protect myself, and I've done that. I'm sorry I didn't get in touch, but I've spent a lot of time thinking about my role in the war since it ended." She lowered her gaze. "I killed a man—several, in fact. I'm not proud of it, but I did what had to be done." She finished the coffee and placed the cup at the edge of the table.

"I heard about Dolores. You were lucky." He paused. "How's your family?"

"My father lives with me in Croydon. I'm fine with the arrangement for now, but it won't last forever." She sighed. "My father is—what should I say—he's uncomfortable here. He hasn't made friends and he keeps to himself. He doesn't like English weather or its customs. I try to cheer him up, but it doesn't do much good. He misses my mother. He talks about going to Palestine to live with my brother."

"I don't remember his name."

"Aaron. He brought my father here from Greece and went straight to the SOE. He wasn't quite of age, so he lied. I think that's why Rita was so forgiving of me. More than one Majewski went to work for her. He's smart. He learned French quickly and they sent him over. He fought his way out of a Nazi roundup, got wounded in the left arm. He's recovered and resettling Jewish survivors from Polish ghettos."

The waitress brought another cup of coffee for Hanna. She lit a cigarette. "There's more to the story."

"Those left behind?"

"They're dead—and as much as my father and I want to hope for a miracle, it isn't going to happen."

Phillip leaned forward. "I'm sorry."

"I failed in my personal mission, but my sister and her future husband were determined to remain in the ghetto. In the few minutes I saw them, they were much braver than I." Hanna glanced at her watch, ran her hands over the table, and then looked at the other customers filling the pub.

"I met the most extraordinary people," she said, as if a sudden revelation had struck her. "The Polish couple who risked their lives for me. When the Nazis retreated, we left their farmhouse, keeping our distance between the Germans and the Red Army. That's when I killed two more men. There were others just as brave . . . a woman named Janka. A young man, Zeev, who helped my father and brother escape. I hope he survived the war."

Hanna took a last sip of coffee, stubbed out the cigarette, put the case in her purse, and got up from the booth. "I'd like to take a walk on this beautiful day."

Phillip stood beside her. "I've thought about you many times. Do you mind if I come along?"

"I thought about you, too," she said, and touched the side of his face. "A bit of gray in the sideburns, but otherwise the same . . . let's go."

"Good," he said, putting money on the table.

He opened the door for Hanna, and they stepped into the bright sun.

"You can tell me as much or as little as you like," Phillip said, as they turned the corner, Hanna leading him to a place he'd never been.

"Let me show you where my aunt and uncle lived." She stopped and Phillip noticed tears glistening in her eyes.

He grasped her hand.

She didn't resist.

AUTHOR'S NOTE

The War Girls, after its conception, presented several challenges that I had no idea would be part of its writing.

First, the big story of 2020, the coronavirus pandemic and its lingering effects into 2021, ended my in-person research in the countries I'd hoped to visit: namely England and Poland. Normally, as I did for *The Irishman's Daughter* and *The Traitor*, I would have traveled to those locales to breathe the air, eat the food, absorb the culture, and visit the historical sites so important to the novel. Few published books remain error-free. I've found mistakes that would have escaped me had I not taken those trips. Such was my experience with *The Irishman's Daughter*. My first drafts had gotten the topography of Westport, Ireland, wrong despite my online research. Only by visiting that lovely town did I see the errors I'd made. In lieu of travel, I've used reference books and online tools.

Another unfortunate footnote regarding the same topic—the pandemic shuttered resources that were previously open to the public. Because of Covid-19, museums were closed. Officials and educators were impossible to reach. Repeated efforts to contact them went unanswered as the pandemic raged.

The amount of research undertaken for this book outstripped anything I'd done before. Later in this note, I'll cite some of the many sources I used. After delving deeply into Judaic culture and tradition, I felt I'd only scratched the surface of a five-thousand-year-old religion. I'm fortunate to work with talented beta readers and editors who make my job easier on many levels, including fact-checking. I present the idea and write it, but I look to their expertise to help me get it right. In this case, I owe a special debt of gratitude to the copyediting skills of Marsha Zinberg.

The idea for *The War Girls* had been floating around in my head for some time, and it came to fruition with the blessing of the editorial staff at Kensington. I had to wrap up work on *The Sculptress* before beginning the new book, starting my research shortly after 2020 began, working through the pandemic, and then putting words on paper beginning in late September of that year. Despite having a brief plot outline, it wasn't until I'd completed most of the background research that I was able to put together a synopsis.

The novel contained four distinct researchable categories: Judaism, the Blitz, the Warsaw Ghetto, and spying operations, specifically the Special Operations Executive in England. Over the course of five months, in addition to other work, I read nearly two dozen books on these subjects and viewed many hours of video and internet presentations. Nearly every book and video revealed more questions, which, if you have endless time to write a novel, can be a lifelong pursuit in search of the truth. As I've found in doing this for other books, "facts" often vary according to source. In this case, with differing information, I've taken an educated guess, hoping that I chose well.

There is no doubt that World War II contains more stories than can be told. Someone asked me what makes this book different from any other WWII novel—the implication being, why write another book about the same subject? It's a difficult question to answer, but a reasonable explanation lies in character development and a gut feeling that the story *should be* told in the hope that the characters and their insights offer something new to the reader. As writers know, all "plots" have been done, but the individual stories still linger, waiting to be written. For each *Schindler's List*, for every *The Pianist*, there are countless tales waiting to be unearthed, victories and tragedies waiting to be told. If we find that these war stories become trite, or that they no longer have meaning, we lose our humanity. As the war recedes into the past, the world loses its memory of that terrible time. We cannot, and should not, allow that to happen. Only by digging deeper will more stories come out.

The lives of my characters Hanna, Stefa, Janka, Izreal, Perla, Aaron, and Daniel feel real to me, and I've tried my best to do their stories justice. Frightening as it may be, we should also remember that Hitler's rise to power began about one hundred years ago, but the most egregious atrocities committed by his regime burst forth after he assumed power in 1933 and continued for a dozen years until the end of the European war in 1945. Those years are much closer to our lives than a century past.

I must admit that researching the war's terrible events during a pandemic was at times utterly depressing. There were days that I couldn't read another account of the death and destruction witnessed by the survivors—I had to look away for a day and then come back to the reading. One book in particular affected me so deeply that I could only read two short chapters a day—no more than six pages. My research continued by going on to another book or viewing a video.

The atrocities levied upon the Jews during the Nazi regime are beyond the limits of human comprehension and decency. This simple fact cannot be overstressed. Although I've tried in *The War Girls* to portray these horrors, no work of fiction can adequately convey the terror and pain of those who lived during the war years. We, in our media-saturated culture, tend to categorize our feelings or shelve things aside. If we don't like it— we ignore it. If it makes us sad, we find something that makes us happy. It's easy to do. Nothing, however, can or should erase the tragedy of the genocide perpetrated by Hitler. I write these words only to convey to the reader that often—during points in the book—I felt my words inadequate when weighed against the actual event.

The sources I've cited are primarily nonfiction, except for

two novels. I read those works because I felt I could learn from those authors—and I did. I prefer not to read fiction while I'm researching a new book because I want to focus on my own plot points and style.

Here is an abbreviated list of the books I found most useful in my study:

White House in a Gray City, Itzchak Belfer, Yanuka Books, 2017. This account was written by a student of Janusz Korczak, a teacher and pediatrician, who, in August 1942, went to his death at Treblinka with children from his orphanage after he refused to abandon them. The author, taking extraordinary measures to live, survived the war.

Rescued from the Ashes, Leokadia Schmidt, translated from the Polish by Oscar E. Swan, Amsterdam Publishers, 2018. This is the diary of Mrs. Schmidt, who survived the Warsaw Ghetto, along with her husband and infant son. Much of this book focuses on the family's survival tactics, including separation and moving from place to place to avoid capture.

A Cup of Tears: *A Diary of the Warsaw Ghetto*, Abraham Lewin, edited by Antony Polonsky, Basil Blackwell, Ltd., first published in 1988. Lewin was a member of Oyneg Shabbos, a "brotherhood" dedicated to preserving the history of Jews in the Warsaw Ghetto, the name referring to the Jewish custom of celebrating the Sabbath. Lewin's diary was found hidden in a milk can after the war. He was murdered at Treblinka.

Voices from the Warsaw Ghetto, edited with an introduction by David G. Roskies, Yale University Press, 2019. A collection of prose, poems, and artwork from ghetto residents.

The Warsaw Ghetto: A Photographic Record 1941–1944, Joe J. Heydecker, I. B. Tauris & Co. Ltd. London, 1990 edition. Heydecker, a German soldier, assigned in Warsaw as a photo-laboratory technician, risked his life to preserve the photos he had taken. Heydecker's account lays out his own admission of guilt: "I stood there and took photographs instead of doing something," and includes the chilling response of an armed SS guard, when asked what was going on as the deportations were in process. "He turned tactfully to one side so that only I could hear what he said: 'They are to be done away with.'" Heydecker believed that most Germans knew of the killings (concentration and extermination camps, and ghettos), but chose to ignore the truth because they were under Hitler's thumb and could do nothing to stop him.

Memory Unearthed: The Lodz Ghetto Photographs, Henryk Ross, collection of the Art Gallery of Ontario, Yale University Press, 2007.

Blitz: The Story of December 29, 1940, Margaret Gaskin, Harcourt, Inc., 2005.

The Blitz: The British Under Attack, Juliet Gardiner, HarperPress, 2010.

The Wolves at the Door: The True Story of America's Greatest Female Spy, Judith L. Pearson, Lyons Press, 2005. The story of Virginia Hall, an extraordinary director of resistance activities.

Spymistress: The Life of Vera Atkins, the Greatest Female Secret Agent of World War II, William Stevenson, Arcade Publishing, 2007.

Smithsonian World War II Map by Map, DK Publishing, 2019. This book, showing battle sites and combat operations, is crammed with historical information.

Of the fiction, the first is *We Were the Lucky Ones*, Georgia Hunter, Viking, 2017.

The second: *The World That We Knew*, Alice Hoffman, Simon & Schuster, 2020.

Other support came from numerous websites, including Yad Vashem and the United States Holocaust Memorial Museum. The account of Szlamek Bajler, survivor of Chełmno, was loosely based on content from the Holocaust Education & Archive Research Team (HolocaustResearchProject.org) called "Chełmno Diary," as was the description of Hanna's parachute training, found at the British Broadcasting Corporation's website WW2 People's War, "Ringway, Paratrooper Training."

Because of the research limitations mentioned, I took a few

small liberties with the story upon occasion; for example, the location and circumstances behind the execution of eight Jews on November 17, 1941, depicted in the book. Accounts often differ. I've tried my best to piece together the truth in this instance, along with some others.

I must include a brief note on Polish surnames. These vary based on case, plural form, and masculine and feminine forms. It was my belief that using these forms would be confusing to readers of English, so I opted for the standard plural spellings that English publishers would use.

Texts too numerous to mention on Judaic holidays, culture, and traditions were provided from the collection of Bob Pinsky. Bob has been a beta reader from the first novel I wrote. To say that he is vital to my work would be an understatement. He is a voracious reader and when I deliver a manuscript to him, I simultaneously cringe and rejoice. I know he will pick it apart, but his thoughtful points always make my book stronger. He is the kind of reader authors dream of.

As always, I say thank you to my community of writers who give me hope and support; thanks as well to my agent, Evan S. Marshall; my editor at Kensington, John Scognamiglio, and the readers who have supported my six books. I rely upon all of you to keep me at the keyboard. Thank you!

THE WAR GIRLS

ABOUT THIS GUIDE

The suggested questions are included to enhance your group's reading of V. S. Alexander's *The War Girls*!

DISCUSSION QUESTIONS

1. When World War II begins, the Majewski family, like others in Poland, believed that hostilities might be over soon. Without the benefit of history, would you have felt the same?

2. Different characters have varying opinions about the war. Even at his young age, Aaron wants to fight, much to the dismay of his father. Would you have been like Aaron?

3. *The War Girls* is dedicated to Emanuel Ringelblum, who preserved the history of the Warsaw Ghetto. Had you heard of him? How do you feel about the importance of preserving history through the written word?

4. Many Jews in Warsaw tried to preserve their religious and cultural traditions even after the Nazi occupation and eventual imprisonment in the ghetto. How hard would it have been to do so, knowing that such practices were often forbidden under penalties of imprisonment or even death?

5. How would you have survived in the ghetto?

6. Readers often have differing opinions about the part of the book that affected them the most. What was it for you?

7. Hanna and Stefa had different views about their parents. What were they?

8. Could you have gone through the training that Hanna did to save her family?

9. What character in the book was the most heroic for you? The least heroic?

10. What do you think was the eventual fate of Stefa and Daniel?